Jeanne,

May you and yours
achieve greater heights!

Valerie

Greater Heights

VALERIE DAVIS BENTON

WestBow
PRESS
A DIVISION OF THOMAS NELSON

WestBow Press books may be ordered through booksellers or by contacting:

WestBow Press
A Division of Thomas Nelson
1663 Liberty Drive
Bloomington, IN 47403
www.westbowpress.com
1-(866) 928-1240

Because of the dynamic nature of the Internet, any web addresses or links contained in this book may have changed since publication and may no longer be valid. The views expressed in this work are solely those of the author and do not necessarily reflect the views of the publisher, and the publisher hereby disclaims any responsibility for them.

Any people depicted in stock imagery provided by Thinkstock are models, and such images are being used for illustrative purposes only.

Certain stock imagery © Thinkstock.

ISBN: 978-1-4497-1894-7 (sc)
ISBN: 978-1-4497-1893-0 (hc)
ISBN: 978-1-4497-1892-3 (e)

Library of Congress Control Number: 2011930948

Printed in the United States of America

WestBow Press rev. date: 07/19/2011

This book is dedicated to anyone who has ever suffered loss whether you lost your way or lost someone dear to you. My hope is that this book will point you to God, who gives direction, healing, and comfort until the day we reach greater heights.

For what is a man profited, if he shall gain the whole world, and lose his own soul? or what shall a man give in exchange for his soul?

Matthew 16:26, KJV

Chapter 1

It wasn't a dress she would have chosen for herself. Riley Davenport-Westin looked at the gold halter gown, the heavy gold choker and the matching earrings that dangled from her ears. She could not deny that the dress flattered her blonde hair and sapphire blue eyes. The gown draped perfectly over her tall, evenly proportioned figure. There was no question about it. Aside from that, there was nothing she could appreciate about the dress. She cocked her head to one side as she gave one final check in the full-length mirror before seating herself at her vanity to apply her makeup.

Riley's husband, Paine Chandler Westin IV, had the dress sent over the day before from one of New York's exclusive boutiques just for this night's occasion. The package arrived without warning. She opened it to find the dress, jewelry, shoes, and hosiery perfectly matched and each exactly her size.

Packages of this nature were not uncommon to Riley. When she received the first one just a few weeks after their wedding, Riley was not only elated over her new husband's grand gesture, but also surprised that a man would pay so much attention to details about her. She interpreted the gift as a sign that he had quickly grown to know her well. It was the highest compliment any man had ever paid her.

Many packages later, however, she had come to identify the gifts for what they really were - gifts for him, not her. Paine was merely looking out for his self-interests, ensuring that his wife in no way embarrassed him before society. As a Westin and a fourth generation heir to the family fortune, he went to great lengths to protect his family and his good name from disgrace or scandal. So it was necessary that she be dressed appropriately, befitting her role as his wife.

Riley skillfully and lightly brushed copper-colored powder across one cheek, then the other. She looked at the clock on her vanity. Paine insisted that she always arrive at least five minutes early, no matter the occasion. It was a lesson she had learned early in their marriage. She remembered the first time she had run late. She had arrived no more than five minutes after one of his parents' dinner parties at their country estate was scheduled to begin. Riley, a television reporter, had gotten held up at work and did not even stop to freshen up before dinner. Regardless, Paine had found it unacceptable. He accused her of being disrespectful to him and his parents. He severely admonished her for hours after they returned home. Then he packed, left early the next morning for a business trip and did not call her the entire week he was gone. Even after he returned home, he scolded her once more and warned her never to let it happen again. She hadn't.

Since then, Riley had declined engagements for which she even remotely suspected that her punctuality would be a problem. She carefully planned her schedule to allow for social engagements that were particularly important to Paine, those where appearances might weigh heavily. Tonight happened to be one of those occasions. Riley was keenly aware of the consequences of any wrong moves tonight. With each stroke of her mascara brush, Riley was careful to apply her mascara evenly. Paine would thoroughly scrutinize her upon her arrival. The gala was a gathering of business partners, politicians, and dignitaries from throughout New York and abroad. She had come to dread having Paine lean over and whisper in her ear the short list of flaws that he found in her appearance. Even more, she despised the supercilious smile on his face when he withdrew after citing his quick inventory. He seemed to take great pleasure in privately downgrading her. After each critique, she would shrivel inside next to him as he stood tall, smug and proud at having shared his opinion of her polished efforts. In his eyes, she could clearly see her tarnished image.

But her failures, her flaws represented a well-kept secret between them. While secrets draw some people closer, they have the ability to drive other people farther apart. Paine never shared Riley's shortcomings with others in her presence. And to her knowledge, he had never criticized her to others outside of her presence.

No, it was just the opposite. Riley was the only person who was made aware that she failed to measure up to Paine's high standards. In public, he stayed close to her and clung to her, showing off her beauty and notoriety as a popular television reporter like a trophy he'd won. She was paraded around with his many other trophies. He had a successful career as a New York investor and developer, wealth, an Ivy League education, and respected breeding, and a respected position in society. She belonged to him. Her achievements belonged to him. And he never missed an opportunity in the six years of their marriage to remind her. At an early point in their marriage, his initial tenderness and affection had transformed into a tethered attachment between them. She could make few moves or decisions that went untouched by Paine. More often than not, she was prohibited from having the opportunity to use her mind, to make her own choices or to make plans apart from Paine. Whenever Riley mustered the courage to exercise any independence by making a decision or plotting her own course, Paine reduced her to a fragment of herself with a critical look or a stern word of disapproval.

In the past year, Paine had begun skipping the looks and the harsh scoldings. He had moved to grabbing her arm and pulling her to him so that he could draw his face just inches from her, and terrorize her with his firm threats and, sometimes, his yelling. He would draw so close to her that she could feel his breath with every syllable. He would grip her arm tightly, leaving bruises that needed to be covered for weeks. The last time she had angered him, it was over a meal she had served. She liked steamed zucchini. He did not. The fact that she had put it on the table with the rest of the meal threw him into a tirade. He ranted that he was offended because she had shown him no consideration. Why would she deliberately prepare a dish that he had no desire to eat and serve it when he was there, when she should know how just the appearance of it was upsetting to him?

The discussion escalated until Paine stood up, walked to her end of the table, grabbed her face with one hand, scooped up handfuls of hot zucchini with his other hand and shoved them into her mouth.

"You like zucchini enough to disrespect me, then here. *You* eat it. Eat it!" he said.

Riley fought him, slapping his food-filled hand away. As his fingers pinched her face and brought tears to her eyes, she locked her teeth together to block the food and prevent him from choking her. All the while, she looked into the eyes of a raging monster. Where was the man who had promised to love, honor and keep her? The beast that dug its fingers into her cheeks did not at all resemble her husband. His tan face had turned beet red. His steely blue eyes were penetratingly wild. His full, heart-shaped lips were thin and stretched over clenched teeth. The nostrils of his straight nose flared. His otherwise neatly combed hair showed signs of dishevelment as wisps of hair fell forward over his forehead.

After several attempts to force-feed her, Paine released his grip on Riley's cheeks, calmly shook zucchini from his hand, then picked up Riley's linen napkin and methodically wiped his soiled hand clean. After surveying the table one last time, he cast a look of disgust at her. Without a word, he left the room, left the mess, and left her sobbing and distraught over what had just happened.

She sat in a puddle of wilted zucchini and humiliation with absolutely no idea what to do next, except clean up the mess. She was both stunned and too numb to move. She feared facing him again, so she took her time wiping up zucchini from the floor, the chair, the table and her clothes. The humiliation she felt was nearly unbearable. She also had the duty of clearing the table of the uneaten food and cleaning the kitchen because their cook had the night off. Her mind felt numb as she finished the kitchen duty. Before taking her chances with Paine, she washed and cleaned herself in the half-bath off from the kitchen area.

By the time she made her way through the fourteen-room luxury home overlooking Central Park, she found that Paine had packed and slipped out without a good-bye.

That episode had happened several weeks ago. Paine never apologized for his behavior or mentioned that night. Even before then, however, Riley had noticed that his trips out of town had become more frequent. He did not leave an itinerary or a number where he could be reached. And he had warned Riley not to call his cell phone since he might be in the middle of important business or a meeting. She had also noticed that his resentment toward her coincided with his increased travel. She wondered if he had met someone else. Could that be the reason for his anger toward her?

Riley outlined her full lips with a rust-colored lip pencil before filling them in with a dark bronze color. She wanted to ask Paine if he was having an affair, but given his latest outbursts of anger, she feared how he might react. She glanced at the clock. It was time to go. She'd have plenty of time to think about how to approach Paine with her suspicions. In the meantime, she'd watch and wait. But now, she must get to the gala on time. It was important to keep him happy even though she could not have been more miserable or afraid for her own safety.

Chapter 2

Riley scrutinized her makeup one last time in the mirror of her sun visor before turning the key of her teal BMW convertible over to the valet. She scrambled out of the car and took short quick steps up the stairs leading to the multiplex arts center, where the gala was taking place.

While passing a large fountain in front of the building, Riley cast a quick look at the lights reflected in the water. The tranquil sight and the calming flow of the water made Riley long to stop and sit out the event of the season. Riley had come to resent the many command performances that went along with being Mrs. Paine Weston. Too often, Riley felt out of place at social functions of this magnitude since she was not a native New Yorker. She suspected that her Southern upbringing and lingering accent stood out like a wart on her nose in most settings. To many New York socialites, it was offensive. She had run out of ways to conceal it. To keep from embarrassing Paine or his class-conscious family, she had learned to smile, sip a drink and say little, but to listen intently. Every so often, she got lucky and discovered a kindred soul who was also a Southern transplant. At other times, the fact that she was a TV reporter would leak out in conversation and would either immediately open a door to acceptance or shut off any further conversation.

Riley had learned that people either loved or hated and trusted or feared people in her profession. There was seldom any gray area. Those who loved journalists wanted to turn the tables and ask all of the questions because they were curious or enamored with their uncommon lifestyle. Or they had ideas for stories they felt compelled to share. Those who clammed up were the ones who had either been burned by a reporter or who, in Riley's opinion, had much to hide. They feared their secrets might accidentally be discovered in even the most casual conversations, so they took no chances and kept their distance from her. Also included in the group who detested reporters were those who had their own opinions about how journalists should do their job. The latter were the ones from whom Riley steered clear.

When she reached the top of the stairs leading into the building, Riley's stomach felt queasy. She was on time, so she didn't understand the source of her nervousness. Admittedly, she would rather be at home with a John Grisham novel or taking in a movie.

Riley put her hand to her stomach and took slow deep breaths to try to calm her unrest. Instead of disappearing, her uneasiness grew.

The doors of the conference center opened instantly at Riley's arrival. Doormen hired for this occasion were one of the many amenities enjoyed by the rich and famous. Having money or fame or both, she'd quickly learned, meant seldom ever serving yourself. That was a hard lesson for Riley, who had been taught to be independent and to take care of herself. One area where Riley had maintained her independence was driving. Paine was most often chauffeured in a limousine and he encouraged Riley to also take advantage of that privilege.

But she loved to drive and set her own destination. She also loved to be alone in her car. She often felt uncomfortable under the watchful eye of Paine's chauffeur. Since her profession required that she be on call, Paine accepted that she needed her own vehicle. It was one of the few areas in her life where he had relinquished control to her.

Her salary was another. He had asked her to sign a pre-nuptial agreement before they married. As an officer of his family's company and a member of the board of directors, he gave a convincing argument that since he was very tied to the company and his family's investments, he had to protect both. He assured her that she was free to keep her earnings, but that their money would not be co-mingled. Their mutual arrangement still managed to draw ire and criticism from Paine. He minimized her job and called her salary paltry. He often reminded her that as his wife, she could absolve herself of her contract at WTNY Television, Channel 6, abandon her career and pick up her duties in society. His money was more than adequate to meet their needs and provide for a lifestyle deserving of a Westin, he frequently pointed out. Riley soon realized that it represented another area of her life where he was petitioning for control. He wanted her financially under his thumb and in her place as the wife of a Westin man - silently on his arm socially. To become a socialite wife, he threw out such job descriptions as Junior League member, Charity League member, tennis and golf club member, and art museum fund-raising volunteer. Instead of chasing after stories and using her mind, he hinted that she should focus more on her appearance. He felt she should be spending her days at the salon getting facials, manicures, pedicures and regular, more frequent visits to the tanning booth. He reminded her often that he prized beauty in his wife over brains. Leave the brains to him, he'd say.

Riley looked back to when they dated and how expertly he had hidden his controlling characteristics and abusive ways. He had masked them with lavish gifts of jewelry, elaborate bouquets of flowers, imported silks, and romantic dinners at New York's premier restaurants. But the mask quickly came off after their honeymoon - not all at once, but in spurts the first year. Then he stopped hiding his dark side. That's when the light started going out of their marriage. Riley had become more like a possession, which Paine put on display during events much like the one to which she was rushing.

If only her stomach would settle.

Once inside the ballroom, she scanned the room for Paine. At over six feet, three inches, he often stood heads above the crowd. She seldom had difficulty spotting his coiffed, wavy brown hair, and blue eyes. Those were some of the few characteristics that had attracted her to him and that remained unchanged.

While slowly weaving her way through the designer gowns and tuxedos, she paused to acknowledge an occasional "Hello, Riley." But she didn't stop until she located Paine. Otherwise, he might think she was late.

There he was, standing tall, his broad straight shoulders thrown back as he sipped a drink. He was deeply involved in conversation with a stunningly beautiful dark-haired woman - a scene that had become all too familiar to her. With each time, the woman could be a redhead, brunette or blonde like herself. But all were young and beautiful. Women of all ages naturally flocked to Paine. His charm and good looks were what drew her to him, so it was easy to understand why other women were attracted to his magnetic personality. As of late, however, Riley had begun to question his faithfulness to her. She had noticed how his outward attributes appeared to not only invite the attention of other women, but his actions had begun to encourage it. Even in her presence, she recognized that flirtations identical to those he'd used while they had dated were now being employed to draw the attention of other women. He went out of his way to be helpful to them, sometimes at the expense of caring first for Riley. If he offered to get another woman a drink, he often overlooked Riley's empty glass. She would bite her tongue, but each time she wanted to toss the glass and turn her back on him and their marriage for good. She knew better than to challenge him. He had a way of either accusing her of having an overactive imagination or he would twist her suspicions and blame her for not being attractive enough or interesting enough or well-bred enough to hold his attention. If he was having an affair, she was certain that he would somehow fault her for his infidelity.

Riley could feel a knot tighten in her stomach as she braced for another night of humiliation. He would first parade her around the room, showing her off, as though he was her promoter, while he was still fairly sober. But after a few drinks, he would become her prison warden and, before the end of the night, her persecutor. He had never crossed the line of getting out-of-hand publicly and had certainly in no way brought negative attention to himself or his family. It was the subtleties between her and Paine that did the most damage. Riley had learned to suffer in silence, which kept her insides in turmoil. Maybe that explained her sudden case of upset stomach. It was possible that it served as a warning signal to what she had come to expect during such occasions as these.

Riley moved in closer until the group became a threesome.

"Hello," Riley said as warmly as possible to the woman. She edged closer to Paine and reached out and curled her hand around his left arm, which hung free by his side.

"Hello, my dear," Paine said, coolly. "Riley, do you know Sarah Blackstone? She's the new curator at the Croft Arts Gallery. She's spent the day checking out the competition, you might say."

The woman's eyes sparkled and she cast a wry smile at Paine as he spoke of her. Neither escaped Riley.

"No, we haven't met. I had heard, however, that they had found a replacement for Bernard Milford. He was a dear friend of mine. You have some large shoes to fill." Riley paused, but quickly realized that remaining introductions were being left to her.

"I'm Riley Davenport-Westin, Paine's wife. It's very nice to meet you."

"Likewise," the woman said. Then her eyes fixed again on Paine before turning up her glass.

Riley tried to make conversation with the statuesque woman with sleek, chin-length, straight black hair, china doll face, and deep red lips. She looked like she had just stepped off the cover of Vogue magazine in her fitting black gown with plunging neckline, heavy silver and diamond earrings, and choker. Her deep-set dark eyes rested mostly on Paine as she responded to Riley's question: "Are you from New York?"

"Why, yes, I am. I grew up in Manhattan. My father is an investment banker. He and Paine's father are close friends and golfing buddies."

"I see," Riley said. "So I guess you and Paine already knew each other, I mean, before you took this job."

"Yes, we did," she said, matter-of-factly.

Sarah lifted her glass to her lips and looked away. Riley's eyes shifted to Paine, who looked at her and smiled sardonically. His head turned back, where he met Sarah's admiring gaze. They smiled at one another - a smile signifying that they shared a secret all their own. Riley recognized that smile on Paine's face. She knew instantly that this woman was unlike the others.

From that moment, Riley was invisible to the pair. She had faded into the background. It would be a long night. Her stomach tensed again. She swallowed hard as her pride took another blow. She locked her jaw and fought back tears. Her eyes darted back and forth from Paine to the woman to the green marble floor as she attempted to hide her hurt and shame. But hiding really wasn't necessary since no one noticed Riley's changed mood.

For the first time ever, Riley had been shelved in pursuit of another woman. Paine had dispensed with the formalities of escorting her around the room and making introductions. Was Ms. Blackstone the other woman whom Riley suspected of drawing Paine away? Riley mentally debated the possibility since she was new to the museum. But she wasn't a newcomer to New York society.

It was Riley who was the outsider. Paine often reminded her of that point.

As her eyes searched the room for a friendly face, Riley saw few. There were many recognizable faces - faces she'd seen in *The New York Times* and in an array of magazines. But these were somehow linked to Paine. Aside from having interviewed many of them or having been shoulder-to-shoulder with them at New York's social affairs, Riley could call none of them friends.

There was no one in the room in whom she would confide about private matters. Paine was right. She was an outsider.

But even in her hometown, she had felt like she didn't fit in. She had fought so hard while growing up to escape her South Georgia upbringing. She had pored over pages and pages of magazines as a teenager, dreaming of a successful life in New York. To her, that meant the right career, a wealthy husband, designer clothes, and luxurious vehicles. She had studied how to walk and how to talk by watching and mimicking the rich and famous on TV. She had learned all she could about social graces and etiquette because she was confident that one day they would come in handy. She paid close attention in home economics class to the proper way to sit, set a table and make introductions. While many of her classmates thought these lessons a waste of time, Riley not only paid attention, but practiced outside the classroom what she'd learned. She knew the day would come when the correct way to fold a napkin and which fork to use would be necessary to her success and she had intended to be prepared for that day.

Riley worked hard to change her course and climb both the social and professional ladders to achieve the status, prestige, and success she desired. She was also conscious of the fact that she must pay a price for what she wanted. That price was her past, which included her parents.

In order to look forward and move ahead in society, Riley had turned her back on her family and her simple childhood. Her devout Baptist parents had raised her in a home, where simple, Christian values took priority over the world view of fame and fortune. They had lived modestly and frugally, but happily.

Riley loved her parents. But not only was she on the opposite end of the United States from where her parents lived, she was on the opposite side of an age-old religious argument. She'd heard it her whole life from her parents quoting scripture that it was easier for a camel to go through the eye of a needle than for a rich man to get into heaven. And her parents lived their convictions.

Riley had watched her parents give away much of what they'd earned to people with even less than they had. As a teenager, she resented her parents. When she thought of the things their gifts to others could have bought for their family - a bigger house, nicer cars, and fashionable clothes - Riley grew more resentful of their charitable nature with each passing year. She wanted no part of it.

Riley realized early in life that the things she wanted to achieve, she'd have to gain on her own. And once obtained, she wouldn't give them away. She worked hard in school, achieving high marks and getting involved in extra-curricular activities like the annual staff and the Civitan Club. Having top grades earned her a scholarship to the University of Georgia School of Journalism. Participation in outside activities opened doors to society. Her parents and their mid-level income could not have done either for Riley.

In college, she got involved with the university's own television station and made herself as visible on campus and in the community as possible. She interned at WWOQ, Channel 8, an NBC Network affiliate, in Athens. When she graduated, she had a job lined up in Atlanta with WWPO, Channel 3, also an NBC affiliate.

Not only did grades, hard work and drive open doors for Riley, but generally her all-American girl looks and Southern charm got her through the door. People were naturally drawn to her and quickly warmed up to her infectious laugh and pleasing personality.

Recently, Riley had little to laugh about. Paine had managed to squelch and eventually silence any laughter left in her.

While working in Atlanta, where she felt more at home than in her own hometown, her popularity grew and she was quickly moved up the ranks. It didn't take long before she had captured the attention of the network, which offered her a weekend reporter position in New York. Riley's confidence shot up with her popularity ratings. She was realizing her dream. But before she could get comfortable in her weekend slot, she was advanced again to the six o'clock news as a reporter.

That's where Paine first noticed her.

Little did Riley know, Paine had done his homework long before he introduced himself to her at the premier showing of a new artist's work at the Croft Arts Gallery. He was accustomed to getting what he wanted and did what it took to get it. He had studied what it would take to get her attention and to hold it. He had showered her with gifts, theater tickets, and expensive dinners. Paine had been deliberate in his ploys to win her over. He knew she was ambitious and who and what she had left behind. He knew to the date every major event of her life that had preceded his meeting her. It was one of the benefits of keeping a private detective agency on retainer. After all, he had his family and personal fortune to protect. He needed to know if she was naive and ambitious or a cunning gold-digger.

Riley's stomach began to churn as she stood, waiting out the uncomfortable situation. When it didn't pass, she leaned into Paine and whispered to him, "Excuse me, I'm going to the ladies' room." He simply nodded.

She waded through the crowd, flashing smiles at familiar faces as she made her way to the bathroom. Her stomach started doing somersaults and she felt a wave of nausea at the moment she reached the ladies' room. Surprisingly, there wasn't a line as there typically was. In the nick of time, she pushed the door open to a stall.

There she was, elegantly dressed with her head leaning over a toilet.

Riley heard an unfamiliar soft, melodic voice call out, "Are you alright, dear? Can I get someone? Do you need anything?" Riley, analyzing the questions, realized that, other than Paine, there was no one.

Weakly, she called back through the door of the stall, "No, thank you. I'll be alright."

But Riley had little faith in her own statement. At that moment, she felt more alone than ever despite the growing chatter of female voices on the other side of the stall. She could not remember a lower point in her life.

Slowly, Riley stood and leaned back against the door. She heard women laughing on the other side. She wished she could linger there and avoid their stares and their conversation. Instead, she took a deep breath, smoothed the wrinkles in her dress and commenced leaving the stall.

But she regretted the moment she opened the door. Her eyes met Margaret Tarrington's. Mrs. Tarrington, married to one of the wealthiest men in New York and a lifelong friend of her husband's family, stood at the mirror applying lipstick. She made Riley uneasy because she was overly perceptive with a talent for reading all the details of a person's life just by looking into their face. Riley feared what she might see on her face at that moment.

"Well, DAH-ling, how in the world are you?" asked Mrs. Tarrington, who had the tendency to stretch the "As" in most of her words.

"Oh, well, I'm ... uh ... I'm fine," Riley stammered. She felt her confidence waning more.

"Riley, forgive me for SAH-ying so, but you don't at AH-LL seem fine. Is something bothering you?"

Riley turned on the faucet and uncurled one of the white wash cloths from the stack of terry cloth roll-ups displayed perfectly in a brass bowl centerpiece next to the sink.

"No, I, uh, I guess I've caught a virus. I'm not feeling like myself tonight."

"It's no wonder with AH-LL those people you're exposed to every dAY."

Riley, while lightly dabbing her cheeks and lips with the cold, wet cloth, shot a glance at Mrs. Tarrington in disbelief. She raised her eyebrows at Mrs. Tarrington's reference to her job.

"Yes, well, it's a risk I take, I suppose."

Mrs. Tarrington associated with only a selective few. She could be found spending her days with other pampered wives of wealthy men. They filled their days with shopping, decorating, and spouting orders to servants. When boredom struck, they planned parties, had their hair and nails done, or congregated at the country club for a game of bridge, golf, or tennis. Riley, in her eyes, was an oddity because she worked when she didn't have to and mixed with people socially and economically beneath her.

"Huh!" Mrs. Tarrington grunted. "Don't you tire of punching a time clock?"

Riley paused from freshening up her lipstick to respond. "Being a reporter is what I went to school to do. It gives me a meaningful reason to get out of bed every day. And I enjoy it," she said in defense.

"Yes, but don't you worry that some of your stories cast a bAD light on you and Paine, especially in the eyes of some of our elected officials, particularly those on whom Paine relies for his success? I mean, should you really bite the hand that feeds you?"

Riley slammed her purse shut as she felt the walls close in on her and her face flush at Mrs. Tarrington's interrogation. She was beginning to see how others, including her husband and in-laws, viewed her. Before Riley had a chance to respond to her pointed question, Mrs. Tarrington said, "Speaking of Paine, I re-AH-lize that it's none of my business, but I've noticed that he's certainly been spending an exorbitant amount of time with Sa-RAH Blackstone," she said without taking her eyes off her reflection in the mirror. "From the moment she stepped back into the city a year ago, Paine has been at her side. He says he's holding her hand and helping her get reacquainted with New York," she said, pausing slightly. "You know, he pulled strings to get her the job at the museum. She's very lucky to have him as a friend. I'm sure that it's all innocent. As a MAH-tter of fACT, I probably should not have said anything. Just ignore it, De-AR."

Riley supported herself against the counter with her clenched fists braced on the counter top. She glared at Mrs. Tarrington, who casually packed her makeup into her beaded handbag. Completely oblivious to Riley's changed mood, she patted Riley's stiff arm as she moved in closely and whispered, "Forget I said ANYthing. I'm sure it's nothing."

Mrs. Tarrington paused one moment longer to lift a strand of hair from her forehead with her pinky finger and put it back in place. Before departing, she said to Riley, "Call me sometime, De-AR, when you have time away from that little job of yours. We'll do lunch. Take care."

Riley's body shook uncontrollably as she hung her head and breathed deeply to try to release the anger that had risen in her. So Sarah Blackstone was not a newcomer after all. Thanks to Mrs. Tarrington, Riley was now privy to their secret. Apparently, it wasn't a well-kept secret with Mrs. Tarrington knowing it. Everyone would eventually know with her safeguarding the information.

"What do I do now?" she asked herself, now that the secret was out. Why should she stick around and take more verbal and emotional abuse? Why risk the direction Paine's physical abuse was taking? Why stay with a man whose sport was to humiliate her in the privacy of their home, the place where she should feel safe and free to be herself? And as of this evening, it was official that his game had spread to the public arena, as well. She feared at that moment never knowing peace or happiness again. Riley reasoned that if there was another woman taking her place, there was no reason to continue suffering abuse and humiliation.

Riley stood up straight. She looked at her reflection in the mirror, this time not to examine herself for flaws, but to search for strength in the woman looking back at her. It could once be found in her. Riley was sure it was still there if she only looked closely. She threw back her shoulders and focused on the mirror image as more women entered the room. Riley was not distracted. She had other things on her mind. She grabbed her purse, smoothed her hair with her right hand and exhaled one last time to release any lingering anxieties that were weighing her down.

Riley turned and exited the ladies room. She walked briskly through the lobby and back to the crowded ballroom. She wove a short distance through the crowd until she had a clear view of Paine, still focused on Ms. Blackstone. Riley observed as Paine leaned over and appeared to whisper something in the woman's ear. He pulled back and Riley could see from where she stood that Paine's comments had made Ms. Blackstone's Snow-White complexion turn rosy. She could also see his eyes glisten and light up as he looked around the room before turning back toward the woman. Seconds later, Ms. Blackstone took a step forward and craned her neck to whisper something back.

Riley's stomach began to churn again. She had seen enough. She had endured enough. She had given more than enough to this marriage and gotten too little in return in the way of affection, tenderness, and love.

Tears stung her eyes as she watched this woman move in closer, physically and emotionally, to her husband than she had been in years. Her chest tightened. Riley spun around and her eyes locked again with Mrs. Tarrington's. At that instant, Riley found an unexpected friend, who looked upon her with sympathy. Despite their momentary connection, Riley shriveled underneath her mournful gaze. Was Mrs. Tarrington the only friend she had in the room? Mrs. Tarrington lifted her glass slightly toward her before sipping from it. She smiled mockingly at Riley, and then returned to her circle. "No," Riley said to herself. "I was mistaken. She's without a doubt one of them."

Riley found her way through the crowd, left the ballroom and scampered down a set of steps into the lobby. A valet's hand reached toward her, signaling her to fish her keys from her clutch bag. She dashed out the front doors, opened automatically by eager doormen, and headed toward the curb, where her car would be waiting.

The rhythm of her clicking heels on the pavement slowed, but the tidal wave of emotion that she fought back came faster. A stream of tears rolled down her face and she avoided eye contact with the young man who held her car door open. She should have tipped him, but the thought had escaped her while trying to quickly put some distance between her, Paine, and Ms. Blackstone.

The bright lights of New York were blurred through the tears that could no longer be restrained. Riley's future was just as blurry as she pondered what to do next. Do I stay and make the best of an intolerable situation? Do I confront him and try to resolve it? Do I give him an ultimatum? She quickly decided against the latter given Paine's volatile temper. Do I leave? Her thoughts leaned heavily upon the final question.

The idea of leaving brought with it a mixture of peace and terror. No longer having to tiptoe around Paine until she could determine his mood spelled relief for Riley. But would he make it difficult for her to leave? Why should he? she reasoned. He evidently did not love her and had found someone he did. He would most likely be relieved to have Riley out of the way so that he could live happily ever after with his vogue girlfriend and other New York socialites he called friends.

As she continued to drive toward home, Riley wiped tears from her face. She peered into the rearview mirror to check the condition of her makeup. "What a mess," Riley thought, looking at her puffy eyes and tear-stained face.

Riley returned her attention to the traffic and immediately slammed on brakes to stop at a red light that had caught her by surprise. Her car tires squalled as they slid up to the pedestrian walk, stopping just shy of slamming into a vagrant who was crossing the street.

Riley screamed and the man yelled something back at her before pounding his fist on the hood of her car. Mismatched in a brown threadbare jacket with tattered sleeves and polyester gray pants, the unkempt man looked like a giant to Riley. He then stood shaking his fist at her and yelling, but Riley could not discern what he was saying. His wild eyes and flailing arms told her that his sentiments weren't pleasant.

"I'm sorry," she said softly, hoping he could read her lips. "I'm so sorry."

Riley braced for the worst. She feared he might become violent at any moment. She had been warned to avoid the homeless folks who paraded up and down and slept on the sidewalks of New York. Most of them weren't considered mentally stable - or rational.

The unshaven man stopped yelling and dropped his arms by his side. His eyes softened as he stood looking through the windshield at Riley. After a brief time, he nodded at her and then proceeded to the other side of the street, stopping once to glance back at her again.

Riley didn't understand the change in his mood, but she was grateful. Her eyes followed him across the street to the opposite corner. It was then that she noticed the bank on the other side of the street. It occurred to her that if she planned to leave Paine, it might be a good idea to withdraw some money in case Paine decided to make things difficult for her. About that time, a loud horn behind her startled her. She noticed the light had turned green.

Riley drove a couple more blocks and parked in front of her own bank's automatic teller machine. Fortunately, she had just gotten paid and would have some extra money. She withdrew most of her savings, leaving a small amount in her account in case discussions between her and Paine ended amicably.

She drove back home. There she immediately shed her gown and put on her favorite jeans that were threadbare at the knees. Paine hated them. She threw on a white button-down shirt, and then scurried around in her bare feet to pack a couple of bags, enough to last more than a week. She slid into a pair of worn-out loafers and carried a small luggage bag downstairs and loaded it into the trunk of her car. She would pack another suitcase in the event that their separation lasted longer.

Riley decided to drive down to Georgia to see her parents. It had been years since she'd seen them. She had enough vacation saved and the drive would give her time to think without interruptions or distractions.

While packing the second bag, Paine walked into the bedroom. Riley had not heard him come home. "Are you going somewhere?" he asked. Riley swung around at the sound of his voice. When she did, she dropped the neatly folded shirts she had been holding in her hand.

"Paine, you startled me. I didn't hear you come in."

Riley recognized the look of anger on his face. Nervously, she knelt down and picked up the shirts, then threw them into the suitcase without stopping to straighten them.

Paine's stern face created uneasiness in Riley. "I asked you a question: Are you going somewhere?" Riley looked at how much his facial expression had changed from an hour ago when it was lit up with smiles and bright eyes. When she remembered how he had looked with Ms. Blackstone, her own mood darkened.

"Yes, as a matter of fact. I'm leaving you, Paine. It's obvious and has been for some time that you don't love me. I'm not sure you ever did. It's also obvious that you've found someone else." Riley continued to pack her clothes, but all the while she was apprehensive about how Paine would react. With her back turned toward him, she said, "I've had enough, Paine. I can't stay in this marriage any longer."

As she tucked a black sweater into the corner of her luggage, a sharp pain across the back of her head caught her by surprise. Paine had grabbed her blonde mane and was pulling her up on her tiptoes. Riley reached for his hands to try to loosen his grip.

"Let go of me, Paine!" Riley pleaded.

"How dare you threaten to leave! You belong to me. I will *never* let you go," he roared. "And how dare you make accusations about me. Have you forgotten who I am?"

"Paine, please, you're hurting me." She gripped either side of her head trying to ease the pain in her scalp.

"This is just the beginning. I want an explanation for why you left the gala without so much as a good-bye. I thought you understood how important this night was to me and my family," he said, as he tugged harder at Riley's hair. He pulled her off balance and released his grip on her hair as she fell to the floor. Paine commanded, "Get up."

Riley looked up at him as he towered over her. She began to sob, fearful of what would happen when she did stand or if she didn't. "Paine, please don't. I'm sorry. I wasn't feeling well. I told you that. I had to come home."

"Yes, and I see why."

"No, it wasn't like that. I saw you with that woman, and ... ."

Slowly, she raised herself off the floor and stood in front of him, sobbing and wiping tears from her face. Without warning, he drove his fist into her stomach. Riley doubled over in pain.

"A stomach ache, huh? That was it, wasn't it?"

Riley, shuddering and gasping from Paine's attack, nodded her head. "Yes," she whimpered.

"Well, the next time you decide to leave me, you'll remember this day."

Riley did not see the fist driving toward her face until it was too late. It all happened so fast. After regaining consciousness, she spent the remainder of the night curled up in a fetal position on the beige carpet floor of their master bedroom. She was afraid to move, afraid to open her eyes and find that what she remembered happening was more than just a bad dream.

She would wait out the hours until morning shed its light on her nightmare and signaled the start of a new day. Just like when she was a child and out of the darkness crawled indescribable, unidentifiable terrors, she would hope for daylight to come. When it did, it brought clarity, reassurance, and security. Daylight always chased away the darkness. All she had to do was to wait. Riley lay still, listening, waiting, hoping once again.

Chapter 3

Riley looked to the heavens, but was immediately brought back down to earth when a man hurrying to get into the one hundred and ten-story building bumped into her on his way in. She was temporarily knocked off balance, but she quickly regained her footing in the plaza in front of her office building. While going through the motions of her daily routine, she had convinced herself to go to work despite her reservations.

It would be business as usual.

She realized, however, standing at the threshold of her workplace, that that was a lie she had told herself. She pushed her sunglasses tighter on her face to cover the bruise. No, people would stare. Others with curiosity and more courage would ask questions; still others would talk and surmise in secret about how she got it. Her explanation would be flawed. She was certain her co-workers would see through her attempt to cover the truth, especially since she had never been skilled in the art of lying. Something about her facial expressions or tone had always given her away to her parents, so much so that she didn't bother to tell little white lies to her friends. It was awkward to be so transparent. She had learned instead to change the subject, respond with a nervous laugh, or just keep silent. But her conscience remained clear.

No, it would not be business as usual. She looked up toward the top floor and decided against making the climb to the TV studio. Instead, she looked around for new direction. It was at that moment she discovered how ruled her life had been by her day planner. She found herself completely at a loss when coming up with something spontaneous to do. A day at the salon, tennis at the club, and shopping were activities that denoted spontaneity and a life of leisure. Her life was dictated by work and her husband's social obligations. What would she do if she didn't report to her job?

Touching her swollen cheekbone, she was reminded that she had bigger decisions to make than how to spend her day. What was she going to do with the rest of her life? How would she avoid future confrontations with Paine that might leave her broken and battered on their bedroom floor? His outbursts and abuse were escalating. He had threatened not to let her go. He would throw up more barriers or his fist to prevent her from leaving and to exercise his power over her.

Sliding her sunglasses back on the bridge of her nose, she continued to consider her options. She had just parked her car. It would cause them too much trouble to turn around and retrieve it so soon. Besides, even though she felt lost, getting further lost was what she needed most at that moment.

In her occupation, she was too easily recognizable. Riley hoped that she would not bump into anyone who knew her and who would see the beating she had taken the night before. That morning, she deliberately applied a heavier coat of makeup to mask the black and blue traces of Paine's abuse. But Riley was fully aware of what lay underneath the makeup. Riley's heart began to ache again from the memory of Paine's wrath. She could not hold back the tears. She turned around and broke through the crowd of suits pushing to get to work on time. She hung her head and covered her face as much as possible with her hand to hide from co-workers or acquaintances who worked in the same building.

Riley found a clearing and shuffled to the sidewalk. She decided to walk for a distance to clear her head and put things into perspective. She lightly dabbed the tears before they washed away her makeup. When she got the pedestrian signal to walk, she crossed the street and headed down Fulton Street. She glanced back to see the throngs of white-collar workers marching toward their respective a.m. destinations. It was the same scene every day - like ants scurrying in and out of ant hill tunnels, taking little notice of the other ants. She was one of those rare ants weaving off the beaten path. Apparently, no one had seen her or was following her. Relief swept over her.

But as she strode down the sidewalk heading to no particular place, she remembered. She brushed her fingertips lightly across her blistered, bruised cheekbone and triggered more tears.

"What am I going to do?" she wondered.

She reached deep into her black satchel and pulled out a fresh tissue. She tilted her sunglasses slightly with one hand to catch her tears with the tissue in her other hand. Standing on the sidewalk, she felt exposed to the world. She feared being recognized. She needed to move from the light of the morning to a place where she could hide, even temporarily. It was then she looked up and saw the church spire. Even though she had passed the small chapel every day on her walk to the office, she saw it for the first time that morning.

Riley ducked through the opening of the iron fence and followed the winding pathway shaded by trees, up the embankment toward the church doors, which stood ajar. She looked back toward her office building, but her eyes were drawn to the many headstones that marked graves scattered throughout the front lawn of the churchyard.

She had never been inside the church, built of Georgian architecture. She felt a magnetic pull or maybe sheer curiosity drawing her closer to the entrance.

The small parish reminded her of her hometown church - solid, charming, simple, and lacking pretentiousness. But is it the building or the people that form a church's personality? This one seemed to stand with its arms open, waiting to embrace Riley. She couldn't stop herself from climbing the steps leading to the front doors.

She looked through the open doors into the sanctuary of soft, aqua blue, and ivory. How it paled in comparison to the dark, intricate, and formal architecture of the ornate Episcopalian church she and Paine had been attending. They had been going there since they were married and she already felt more at home in this small church that was a stranger to her than at Paine's and his family's church. And like her place in the Westin family, so was her place at the large church - uncomfortable, awkward, and strange.

Riley looked around and saw a man mopping the gray and white tile floor of an aisle on the other side of the church. He looked up from his work, flashed a warm smile, and returned to his mopping.

Riley walked midway down the center aisle and seated herself at the end of one of the wooden pews on the right side. She admired the altar that was tucked inside an alcove and set apart by oval archways and a short kneeling rail. Inside the sacred altar, she could see the communion table draped in ivory and gold. But there was more. She removed her sunglasses to get a clearer view. Behind the table, light from an embankment of windows outlined a statue holding the Ten Commandments and a gold figure of Jesus Christ on the cross.

The increasing sunlight stung her tear-stained eyes. She reached up and again touched her swollen face as she squinted at the face of the Christ. Seeing the Christ figure stirred feelings of shame and humiliation in her. She returned the sunglasses to her face and dropped her head. Where had she gone wrong? What sin had brought this pain and torture into her life? Was it God's will that she continue to endure the escalating dangers associated with her marriage? She'd always been taught that divorce was not an option. Were there exceptions?

She slid off the pew and onto her knees on the kneeling bench before her. She silently began pleading with God to show her a way out.

"God, you know I love my husband. Why does he no longer love me?"

Forgetting about the make-up covering her black and blue marks, she brushed away tears with her fingers. At that moment, she didn't care about appearances or others' opinions. Grief arose from somewhere deep and erupted into heavy, forceful sobs that echoed throughout the still, small sanctuary. But there she felt safe to let go of what she'd been holding onto.

"Am I to stay in a loveless marriage fighting for my dignity and for my life?"

She leaned her head on her arm, which rested on the back of the pew in front of her, muffling more cries with her sleeve. She lifted her eyes toward the silhouette of the crucifix.

"God, I know I don't deserve your help. I'm not as close to you as I should be, but God, I'm scared. I'm so scared. Show me a way out of this nightmare."

As tears dried on her face, she felt an overwhelming, yet unexplainable peace wash over her. Any anxieties that she had when she entered the sanctuary disappeared. Her mind felt calm for the first time in many months. Riley, while unaccustomed to such a feeling, embraced it. She breathed a deep sigh as her frazzled nerves took a vacation from their otherwise restless state.

Riley jumped when she heard a loud thud reverberate from the corner of the sanctuary. She looked back in time to see the man pick up the mop, which had evidently fallen to the floor.

"I'm sorry," he said softly across the room, then immediately returned to his chore.

The noise reminded Riley of a world outside and interrupted the tranquility of the moment. She gathered her bag and walked toward the altar, getting closer to the crucifix with each step. She wanted to see the image in greater detail. One last look revealed a face of sorrow and pain. Another noise from the back corner startled her again and hastened her retreat. She found her way out of the church and stepped onto the sidewalk facing Broadway.

She stopped under the portico to fish her compact from her bag. Glancing at the reflection in the mirror, she made a face of disapproval. "What a mess," she whispered. She applied a fresh coat of foundation, covering up the patches where her makeup had been washed away by her tears. She fluffed her hair with her fingers and exhaled deeply, then dropped the compact back into her handbag. She pushed her sunglasses securely onto her face. Scanning Broadway for activity, stores and lunch possibilities, Riley searched for places and ways to spend the next eight to ten hours. She was too afraid to go home. What if, by chance, Paine was there? He occasionally worked from home. He was the last person she wanted to see.

She looked at her antique silver bracelet watch, one of the few pieces of jewelry she had picked out for herself. Paine hated it. "Too Bohemian," he said, describing it. "I'll buy you a gold Cartier." Despite his objection, Riley could not part with the watch. And she only wore the gold watch on occasions shared with Paine.

It was 8:30 a.m.

Typically, she would be at her desk with her coffee and a stack of newspapers, which she would comb for news ideas for that day. Or she would already be on assignment. Today, she would learn what it was like to be a woman of leisure. Since she began every day with coffee, why should this day be any different? She spotted a coffee shop at the end of the block, north of the chapel. She began walking and mentally mapping out the rest of her day.

She loved to read and one of her favorite pastimes was hanging out in bookstores. It was a luxury, which she had not afforded herself in months, what with hosting occasional dinner parties, responding to social invitations, running errands and meeting hair and nail appointments on the weekends. She'd had little time to do the small things she enjoyed.

Today would be an exception.

Riley dug her cell phone out of her overstuffed shoulder handbag and punched in the numbers to the television station.

"WTNY-Six," the voice on the line said.

"Brigette," said Riley, who recognized the voice of the woman charged with the job of directing most phone calls from the front desk.

"Good mornin', Riley," Brigette said in her usual perky tone. "How are you this morning?"

"Uh," Riley stammered, looking for the words that would least resemble a lie. "I, uh, ... I'm not in good shape today, Brigette. Would you tell Thomas that I won't be in today?"

"Certainly," Brigette said. "I'll be happy to."

"Thank you, Brigette. I'll check in with him later."

Riley snapped the flip phone shut, cutting off Brigette's opportunity to ask any questions. She breathed a sigh of relief as she opened the door to the coffee shop and entered for her morning dose of caffeine.

After making her purchase, Riley walked out onto the sidewalk and looked up and down the street, contemplating her next move.

It felt rather decadent, but now with her caramel macchiato in hand, she wandered down the sidewalk of Broadway without her planner toward two of her favorite bookstores, one of which covered nearly a block and was filled with used books.

Riley strolled down the sidewalk, gazing up at the windows above the storefronts and noticing the businesses stacked one on top of another. Having come from a small town, it had boggled her mind the first time she went to a dentist's office in New York, located just two floors over an office supply store. Where she grew up, the medical community resided in one section of town, apart from most of the retail district and the residential areas. Here, there were no clearly defined lines of separation, except when it came to the price of real estate.

Even so, Riley had instantly fallen in love with New York City. It had so much to offer and so much to boast of. It had something to share with every individual she passed on the street. And to her, it was the epitome of success. The first time she walked through downtown Manhattan as a resident, she thought she had reached the height of her professional, social, and personal goals. She was on top of the world. Initially, window shopping at Macy's, Louis-Betton, Bloomingdale's, Bergdorf-Goodman, and Prada gave her a glimpse into New York, but with her first purchase at Saks Fifth Avenue, she officially felt like a New Yorker.

As she passed a bakery, the smell of freshly-baked breads, bagels, and croissants reminded her that she had not eaten breakfast - something else she often waited to do at her desk while reading the newspaper and checking emails. Multi-tasking. That was the name of the game for highly successful businessmen and women and she was one of the players.

Riley turned around and ducked into the bakery, where she ordered a croissant from a Sicilian baker. A raisin bagel with cream cheese sounded more appetizing, but too messy to eat while trekking through the city. She waited until she got back on the sidewalk to take a bite of the soft croissant. Its buttery taste and flaky texture melted in her mouth.

"Mm," she moaned to herself. For a second, she forgot her troubles, her bruised face, her heartache.

In that temporary, solitary moment, she was in her own world. She was alone, but not lonely. The sounds of blowing horns in various pitches and tones, the screech of brakes and the rush of engines accelerating created a symphony in concert with her thoughts.

Despite traffic, people dodging her on the sidewalk, and the background music of New York City, she was oblivious to her surroundings. Riley continued to have flashbacks of Paine's fist plunging toward her. Never before had a man hit her and she never dreamed that the first punch would come from her husband.

Riley shook off the memory and focused on the store fronts and their enticements to the avid window shopper. One of the things she loved about New York was how much variety the city offered. City blocks seemed short because of the thrill of what might be waiting in the next block. Life was so large in New York, unlike the small town where she grew up. There, she had few choices.

Ironically, she had begun to not only long for the safety of home, but she was also feeling like her life had once again been reduced to only a few options.

She had just finished the last bite of her croissant and tilted her coffee cup up for a last sip when she heard a tremendous explosion and screaming from people on the street behind her. She dropped the cup on the ground, which shook under her feet, and spun around to see smoke billowing from her office building.

Riley took a few steps forward and then froze. "Oh, God," she said. Automatically, she lifted her hands to muffle her own scream as she viewed with others on the sidewalk the horrendous sight. Riley could see blazes of fire near the upper floors, where her office was located. She dug her hand into her satchel and frantically searched for her cell phone. Meanwhile, she looked around and saw stunned expressions on strangers' faces, which gradually became hidden behind a thin veil of confetti that rained down upon them. Riley looked up to see bits of paper falling from the sky, but was almost knocked down by a woman running north on Broadway. The woman's screams drew Riley's attention away from the burning building as she passed by. The air began filling with a grayness that matched the mood of the moment. Riley was trying to piece together in her mind what had just happened. She also stood motionless, fearing for her co-workers trapped just above the damaged floors of the North Tower - Thomas, Brigette, Sean, Peter, Francis, Catherine, Takashi, Salvatore, and Barbara. That was the short list of the people she worked closest with daily. There were many more that she barely knew. She could see their faces, all going about their daily routines in the newsroom, stopping only long enough to smile, nod, or say hello to her as they tracked and televised daily news to a faceless public.

She found her cell phone and began punching in Thomas' phone number. He was a camera man with whom she worked closely. He was one of the tops in his field and would already be on the scene if he was in the office.

"Hi. You've reached the voice mail of Thomas ... ." Riley pressed the "end" button. She paused to remember Barbara's number - another reporter. Again, no live response, only an automated one. Maybe she could reach Brigette at the main desk. Nothing but a busy signal. She tossed the phone back into her handbag. Riley pictured the switchboard lit up with red glowing beads of lights. She envisioned the fast pace of the newsroom and TV studio accelerated by the events affecting them and other building tenants.

Watching clouds of smoke mushroom from the side of the building and the flames increase, she heard a sound, unfamiliar to that area of Manhattan. Out of the corner of her eye, she saw an airplane flying extremely low.

"Oh, God, no," she said in a low voice. "What is happening?" Riley and strangers around her were awestruck at what they were witnessing – another airplane moving closer and heading toward the South Tower.

Sirens rang through the air in increasing volume. As she watched the horrific scene, she thought to herself that emergency workers would not be able to save those in the path of the incoming plane.

Riley shuddered at the explosion created by the impact of the plane colliding with the building. An orange blossom of fire bloomed from the point of collision. Riley was puzzled over the sight of snowflakes falling from the side of the building until she realized it was also bits of paper. She shielded her eyes briefly, but more screams in the distance caused her to look toward the towers in time to see several bodies flying through the gray fog like rag dolls. She saw a man standing on a ledge of a window high above the flames jump and plummet toward his death. She covered her eyes and began wailing at the sight of life ending - either in a flash or in a desperate leap.

She watched the two giant matchsticks flame and produce a billow of smoke that gradually clouded her view of the actual damage created by the second plane. From out of the cloud, she saw a small fireball drop slowly through the air. She followed it with her eyes until she saw arms protrude from the burning ball. She hid her eyes again from the horrendous ringside view of death and destruction.

Through tears, Riley retrieved her cell phone. She tried again to make contact with any of her co-workers, but this time, her call failed. She looked around and saw other people on the sidewalks with their cell phones positioned for use. The airwaves were evidently being barraged with calls. She stuffed the phone back in her satchel and stood watching, crying and trying to digest the horrifying details.

Smoke and the acrid smell of burning metal, which had made its way to Broadway and Chambers Street, irritated Riley's eyes and throat. She began coughing.

Riley felt helpless and more alone than ever. Her whole world was going up in flames. She couldn't call out and if she could, who would she call? Not Paine. He clearly was not her protector. Her family was thousands of miles away and too many years apart to call upon. The only family she felt she had been able to form in New York resided on the 104th floor of the North Tower - her co-workers. She had spent forty-plus hours a week with her family members of various ages, cultures, philosophies, and backgrounds. Some she had grown closer to than others. Some drove her crazy with their work ethics and ideas. Some she knew only in passing. But even with all of their idiosyncrasies, that was her closest family.

Uncontrollable sobs racked her body as she envisioned their panicked faces and each of them fighting for a way out of the burning building. She imagined them trying to find an escape route in total darkness since the electricity was probably knocked out by the explosion.

They had worked as a team for so long and because she decided not to go to work, they were minus one team member, a family member. Sadly, she could no more help them from where she was standing than had she been trapped with them. She felt useless.

She imagined Thomas with his camera perched on his shoulder as he expertly followed the chaos that most likely prevailed in the newsroom. He could even use the light of the camera if the station's generator failed. She knew him; he was a newsman to the very end.

She guessed that Sean and Peter, both anchors and both highly opinionated and headstrong, were probably competing to lead the exodus out of the burning building. Barbara would still be trying to get the story. She would have Pulitzer Prize at the forefront of her mind. She would not take into consideration the dangers to her own life. Riley always thought Barbara had missed her calling as a foreign correspondent.

Riley plucked a tissue out of her handbag and dabbed her tears. She sniffled as she thought of her co-workers, shocked but all still very much alive. She couldn't think of them as ... well, she just refused to think of them any other way.

With her head cocked back, Riley watched through the enlarging cloud of smoke the fire eat more and more of the building. She coughed more frequently as the smoke grew thicker and visibility lessened. More paper snowflakes floated down, some catching on her Ralph Lauren jacket. Riley began brushing them off and waving them away to prevent them from landing on her.

It was then that she felt the earth move under her feet as a fierce crashing sound startled her. She and others watched as the South Tower collapsed, folding like an accordion. One of the tallest buildings in the world was shrinking right before her eyes. Riley watched in horror until she heard screams that broke her spell.

"Run!" voices screamed.

Riley obeyed and found her legs carrying her away from the devastation. Would there be more explosions? Was she heading toward more danger? The sky was falling. The world she knew was ending. She didn't know what to do, but run.

Buildings became covered with soot and the air filled with smoke. Through tears, ashes, and falling debris, it was difficult to see her direction. Despite the obstacles, she kept running, following closely behind many others who were fleeing. But from what? Occasionally, she looked behind her, wondering what was next. What had become of her co-workers? Did they get out alive? She saw a woman ahead of her fall, then struggle to get back up as the panicked crowd raced around her. Riley stopped to help her. The woman scrambled to her knees as Riley bent low to help her. The woman was completely coated in dust and ash. As Riley pulled her to her feet, her eyes focused on the woman's face, which was indistinguishable as human. The coating made her look like a ghost, but the fear in the eyes of the woman was real. Riley then peered around to see other ghosts, all escaping to safety. Riley realized that she, too, must be a ghost, but one wishing to disappear from the chaos in which she found herself. The woman stood, said "Thank you," and immediately joined the throng of racing pedestrians. Riley watched her and the apparitions floating away on the sidewalk. She looked across the street, peering over the many cars and taxis stalled in the street, to the opposite sidewalk. Through the haze, she could barely make out the outlines of similar apparitions gliding north, away from Manhattan. Riley stood frozen, no longer able to recognize downtown New York, which resembled scenes of war-torn areas of other countries that she had seen on TV and in books.

But war doesn't occur in America, she thought, and certainly not in Manhattan. The most devastation that occurred downtown was the results of the day after Thanksgiving sale at Macy's. Of course, there was the occasional murder from a robbery or gang war, but nothing compared to what she was seeing now.

Riley's cough, provoked by the dust and ash, became more frequent. She cut through the stream of passersby and moved toward an entranceway, where she could stop and catch her breath, as well as examine the situation. In the recess of the building, Riley doubled over, coughing and breathing heavily from her flight. She looked up to see more people running by.

After catching her breath, Riley peeked around the corner at the North Tower consumed by black smoke and flames. From where she stood, the South tower was no longer visible. The view of the remainder of it was blocked by other New York structures. She clung to the corner of the wall to keep from being carried away by the rush of people leaving Lower Manhattan.

She covered her mouth and nose with her arm to keep from inhaling more particles. She watched a businessman, his suit disheveled and his hair covered in soot, shuffle through fallen debris along the street. In one hand was his briefcase and in the other, a once-white handkerchief he used as a mask to cover his mouth and nostrils. Riley imagined that he had gotten up, put on his pressed black suit and starched white, button-down shirt. She pictured him grabbing his black leather briefcase filled with reports he'd labored over the previous night, and heading to the office - expecting today to be much like every other day. She wondered if he even made it to his office. Riley saw the strain in his face and also wondered if he worked in either of the towers. In her trips every day to work, she could not recall ever seeing him or running into him. Is it possible that he had worked in the same building or even the same office complex and had gone unnoticed by her? Had she passed him on the street, but been too hurried or too preoccupied to notice him then?

The man trudged past her. She watched him and others, all strangers to her, cut through the haze.

Riley looked once more around the corner toward the torched buildings. Just as she did, she caught one last glimpse of her office building before the North Tower began collapsing. She wept as the giant structure quickly disappeared after folding into a funnel of smoke.

Riley plugged her ears to keep from hearing the crashing sound of the building. She could not, however, stop the ground beneath her feet from quaking. Meanwhile, flashes of her colleagues' faces appeared in her mind, causing her to weep more. Inwardly, she knew that they could not possibly have survived. She cried until she had no more tears left to cry.

She stood against the wall for what seemed like an eternity - drained and numb. Raw with grief, she slunked down and sat cross-legged with her head leaning against the wall. She watched and waited, taking in the sounds from near and far – sirens, people yelling and wailing, and footsteps passing by. Time also passed. Riley looked down at her dust-covered watch. She wiped away ash to see that the day was almost gone. She had sat paralyzed for hours while the world came crashing down around her. It was nightfall.

In spite of her weariness and grief, she forced herself to regain her composure and resolve. "One last look," she thought. Gray clouds had turned black over the site. She became misty-eyed again, but shrugged it off. "I need to find out what's happened," she determined. Riley resumed her place in the procession filing out of Manhattan. She scoured the street frantically for an electronics store, which might have a television broadcasting the news.

Riley zigzagged through the crowd, moving closer to the street so that she could get a better view of the storefronts on either side of the street. On the West side, a small cluster of people had gathered. As she drew closer, Riley could see the cameras and computers displayed in the window. Her heart leapt knowing that the crowd had found some news about today's events. She snaked through the traffic that had come to a halt on the street and she made her way toward the store. She hastened to join them, fearing that she might miss something even though she knew that the networks would milk an event of this magnitude. Television and newspaper reporters would be talking and writing about it for days to come. She reached the packed crowd, but had difficulty seeing the television broadcast.

"What's happening?" she asked.

"Shh!" a man said without glancing her way.

A woman standing next to her removed her hand from over her mouth long enough to say in a low voice, "We're being attacked." Riley could see the panic on her face just before she covered her mouth again.

"What? By whom?" replied Riley, also lowering her voice.

The woman shrugged her shoulders. She again moved her hand away slightly to say, "They don't know. They think it's terrorists."

Riley needed to know more. She squeezed through the crowd, offering an occasional "Pardon me" until she was where she could see the TV anchor and televised re-enactments of what she and other New Yorkers had just witnessed.

"New York fell under attack this morning as two airplanes, used as missiles, collided with the Twin Towers in Manhattan. Thousands of New Yorkers were working in the buildings as the airplanes, commandeered by terrorists thought to be connected with Osama bin Laden, crashed into each of the buildings within the same hour."

Riley watched as an on-the-scene reporter, being showered with particles from the explosion talked about firemen being trapped when the South Tower collapsed.

Around eight o'clock, President George W. Bush, from Barksdale Air Force Base in Louisiana, offered his explanation: "Today, my fellow citizens, our way of life, our very freedom came under attack in a series of deliberate and deadly terrorist attacks."

Riley noticed the creased forehead of the president and wondered what thoughts were breeding behind those creases. What did he know that he wasn't sharing? What had he known that might have prevented today's tragedy? As a journalist, she had learned to be cautious and skeptical of politicians.

"The U.S. will hunt down and punish those who are responsible for these cowardly acts."

Riley, like others in the crowd, was mesmerized by the screen. After watching for a long while, newscasters had begun repeating themselves and identical scenes of the explosions had started reappearing. Regardless, she was hungry for fresh information and coverage, so she hung on for more.

Occasionally, Riley looked away from the TV toward the devastation for a realistic update, then back at the TV screen to relive over and again the traumatic events that were fresh in her memory.

"I should be down there. I should be getting the story," Riley argued to herself.

She shifted her attention to the other people who crowded in front of the seventeen-inch color screen. She detected terror in their eyes, worry in their crinkled foreheads, anger in their flared nostrils and locked jaws. She also heard fear in their voices.

"I can't believe this is happening," one woman said as she wrung her hands. "I just can't believe it."

Two middle-aged Asian women clung to each other and both spoke in their native tongue. Often their words overlapped, giving an outsider the impression that both were talking at the same time and that neither was listening to the other.

"It's like that movie, uh, uh," an older Caucasian man said while trying to snap his memory into gear by snapping his fingers. "'*Towering Inferno*,' that's it!" he said, pointing his finger at those in the crowd.

A young, black man, standing at the edge of the crowd wanted to fight the unseen enemy. He shouted threats of revenge and cited ways he would retaliate if he were in power. His speech had managed to incite a few other young men in the crowd. "That's right," one or more would occasionally chime in. "Yeah!"

An attractive Hispanic woman, meanwhile, tearfully narrated other events to someone on the other end of a cell phone call. Riley, who'd studied only French in school, eavesdropped, but could not translate her words.

If Riley had had a notepad in her hand, all of these observations would have been recorded in illegible notes. But Riley felt paralyzed and completely at a loss to know what to do. She was certain that she was currently without an employer. She had no camera person at her side or a camera on her shoulder and felt relieved that she didn't. Even though it felt like the world was coming to an end, she didn't feel compelled to call Paine or return to their home.

After last night's altercation with Paine, he had not bothered to apologize for his actions, much less check on her condition this morning. Then she remembered the jammed cell phone lines. Maybe he had attempted, but failed. Regardless, she had no desire to seek comfort from him.

Her closest companions right now were these people who formed this motley crowd of viewers - and this televised window on the world. She was in no hurry to leave either.

But soon the acrid smell wafted to where they stood and ash began blowing in their direction, making it unbearable to stay. The effects of the explosion had caught up with them, so the group parted and broke off into different directions.

Riley watched as the group disbanded. Having nowhere to turn, she was the last to depart. Just as she joined the parade of dusty silhouettes fleeing from downtown, she heard a man say, "It was raining bodies! God, how bad is it up there that they would prefer to jump?"

His comment set off a chain reaction of thoughts and emotions in Riley. Simultaneously, it brought her to a dead stop in her tracks. Someone bumped into her when she did, but she barely noticed. Her mind began racing. Deep in her thoughts, Riley had come face-to-face with the stark reality that she, too, was at the jumping-off place. She was at odds with herself because she was both overwhelmed with guilt at having not gone to work and enormously grateful that she had not shown up that day.

But the man's words resonated in the far reaches of her mind as she wandered aimlessly north on Broadway, falling in and out of step with other pedestrians.

Riley reasoned out her precarious situation. Her job was gone. Her marriage was in shambles. No doubt her surrogate family had not survived the explosion. Paine had threatened her if she attempted to leave him, so going to her family in Georgia meant potentially having to deal with him again, but under less agreeable circumstances. She didn't envision that it would be a happy reunion - explosion or no explosion. Given his wrath, that could also mean possible danger for her aging parents - assuming they would welcome her back home. It was bad enough that she'd had little communication with them since moving to New York. They didn't deserve to have her problems dumped on them. "Where do I go from here?" she kept asking herself.

"Raining bodies." The words haunted her. She tried to visualize her co-workers leaping from the tall building to their death. "Do you hasten death when you know it's fast on your heels? Do you take control of your own fate when fires are all around and there's only one exit? Do you stay and burn or do you take the least painful, most accessible and quickest way out?" she wondered.

Riley's throat grew taut. Her airways were constricted because of the dust and smoke. She coughed sporadically. Riley pushed through the crowd and detoured from the path of evacuees, veering toward the nearest wall, portico, or shelter, where she could stop and sit and even hide. Blinded by tears, she tripped and fell, but quickly got to her feet. She wiped away tears that irritated her burning eyes and distorted her vision. Awkwardly, she reached out through the dense air to cling to something. Her hands touched the brick veneer of a building. Upon reaching something solid, something stable, something on which she could lean, Riley folded into a heap on the ground and cried profusely.

In that instant, she knew that she had to make a crucial decision. It had been a long time since before she and Paine were married that she'd held the reins governing her own life. She'd fallen out of practice.

"Should I jump or try to survive the aftermath?"

As the tears dried on her face and she watched the dusty figures pass by, Riley slumped forward. She tucked her legs close to her and wrapped her arms around them. Everything in New York that she cared about - her marriage, her job, her co-workers - was dead. "My life is over. What more do I have to lose?"

She watched apparitions float by. The scene appeared surreal to her.

Riley rested her head on her knees. She saw one of the apparitions stop briefly to adjust her load - a briefcase, jacket, and handbag. Before stepping back in pace with the other evacuees, the apparition caught sight of Riley. Through the dirty coating, Riley recognized the sadness and distress also creating a heavy burden upon the woman. She looked at Riley as though she was made of glass. Her expression remained unchanged. At that, Riley suddenly felt invisible. She straightened up and leaned back against the wall.

"That's it," she thought. "I will die with them."

Chapter 4

A hush fell across the city that never sleeps.

Aside from the occasional sound of sirens roaring through the streets, there was the eerie quiet of a city in mourning.

The city had witnessed the cruel demise of one of its icons.

When moving to New York and landing a job at the television station, Riley was eager to do well and to make a good impression. She immersed herself in the history of New York, trying to soak up all the knowledge she could about the city that she would call home. Among her extensive research was her study of the World Trade Center, particularly the Twin Towers - two buildings born amidst much controversy, criticism, and hype.

She learned that, over time, the towers ingratiated themselves to New Yorkers.

Originally, they were neither solicited nor welcomed by those living and doing business in Downtown New York. But a few movers and shakers envisioned that the twin buildings would anchor Lower Manhattan and serve as the catalyst for the area's revitalization and renewal.

Their creation did not occur overnight. The idea first germinated in the mind of David Rockefeller, the chairman of the Downtown-Lower Manhattan Association, in May 1959. He was joined later by several more city leaders and financiers who helped carry the torch for the towers' development.

She discovered that the short-lived notoriety of the towers rested on being the tallest skyscrapers in Lower Manhattan. Their height exceeded that of other buildings dominating the skyline: The Woolworth Building, built in 1907, the Singer Building in 1908, the Chrysler tower in 1930, and the famous Empire State Building in 1931, the latter by nearly one hundred feet. The World Trade Center with its massive Twin Towers held the title for the tallest building in the world for only two and a half years. Two months after a formal dedication ceremony for the center that was held in April 1973, the Sears Tower came on the scene and swept the title.

Riley had read about the architect commissioned to draft Rockefeller's vision for the World Trade Center.

Minoru Yamasaki, himself afraid of heights, decided after taking a walking tour of Lower Manhattan in search of inspiration for his project that he did not want his intended design to be lost among the other skyscrapers that filled downtown New York. By the same token, his motivation, unlike those who hired him, did not rest on his design being the newest entry to the Guinness Book of World Records. He wanted it to speak for itself.

Yamasaki touted the World Trade Center as a representation of peace.

In his words, "World trade means world peace and consequently the World Trade Center buildings in New York ... had a bigger purpose than just to provide room for tenants. The World Trade Center is a living symbol of man's dedication to world peace ... beyond the compelling need to make this a monument to world peace, the World Trade Center should, because of its importance, become a representation of man's belief in humanity, his need for individual dignity, his beliefs in the cooperation of men, and through cooperation, his ability to find greatness."

While Yamasaki had intended the Twin Towers to symbolize world peace, ironically, Riley and fellow New Yorkers had watched them become targets for a worldwide pre-emptive strike against peace by Muslims, who profess by their very religion to promote peace. The twisted-minded enemies of the United States saw the Towers as targets for venting their hatred for America.

Meanwhile, Riley saw news clips of Americans grieving for the innocent victims who got caught in the line of fire. Hearing the numbers of lost lives and watching the great American symbols of power, success, wealth, and prestige each crumble into rubble and ash uncharacteristically brought many New Yorkers to their knees along with millions of people across the nation. The two towers had stood tall and proud and independent and above most other buildings. Seeing them destroyed had shown Americans how vulnerable they truly were.

This wasn't the way of life in America, she thought as she roamed the streets. America was founded on liberty. Its people had fought for the right to rise every morning, go to their respective jobs, be about the business of keeping the country operating affluently and successfully in exchange for being safe while doing that job. On the average, their concerns fell within the realm of buying an affordable house and vehicle, raising a family, staying ahead of their creditors, and with some foresight, setting aside money for their retirement. Among Americans' concerns were not that unidentified perpetrators might interrupt that system with unanticipated means of warfare. It was just not the American way - that is, until now.

Riley thought back to America's history. Of course, there was Pearl Harbor. Granted, Americans expected its military to face and be prepared for attack at all times, but with the assumption that those attacks would not occur on American soil.

Also, there was the Oklahoma bombing in 1997, resulting in 138 victims. But America failed to see in that tragedy its own vulnerability since the domestic crime was committed by an American.

Tuesday's attack on the World Trade Center, however, was not the first time the center had been the target of a group of terrorists. On Feb. 26, 1993, a rented Ryder truck holding a homemade fertilizer bomb and cyanide gas exploded in the basement parking garage between the Vista Hotel and the North Tower. Six people died and thousands of others were injured as they attempted to evacuate the smoke-filled towers. The bomb was the work of two terrorists, leader Ramzi Yousef and Eyad Ismoil, who were both found guilty in 1997 for the explosion.

Riley had followed with the rest of the world the events surrounding the explosion at the World Trade Center. She recalled reading that one of the witnesses had said that the explosion felt like a plane had hit the towers. Remembering those words now sent a chill through her.

She had also followed the story about the September 1993 federal trial of four individuals responsible for the attack. The trial lasted six months. Two hundred and four witnesses were presented and more than one thousand pieces of evidence were introduced. A jury convicted the four defendants on March 4, 1994, on all thirty-eight counts against them. Nearly three months later, a judge sentenced each of the four defendants to two hundred and forty years in prison and a $250,000 fine.

Rehashing the details of the trial, Riley recounted to herself that Ismoil had been the driver of the rental van parked in the World Trade Center garage. Yousef was a passenger.

Yousef, the mastermind behind the World Trade Center bombing, had been on the run and was captured in 1995. He was found in a guest house for Afghan war veterans financed by Osama bin Laden. Ismoil fled to Jordan, where he also was arrested in 1995. Both Ismoil and Yousef were found guilty of conspiracy two years later. Yousef was sentenced in January 1998. Ismoil was not sentenced until April of that year. He also was handed a prison term and a ten million dollar fine. Investigators, in their search of Yousef's residence in Manila, testified that they turned up a computer used by Yousef that revealed several Middle Eastern pilots were training at American flight schools. One of the terrorists had proposed hijacking a plane to crash into federal buildings.

Thinking back on that testimony as she strolled through the city, Riley shuddered to think that the terrorists' plans had actually been allowed to come to fruition. Why had someone not been able to crush their schemes? Had they not been taken seriously by the powers-that-be? Could this day have been avoided?

Memories of those news reports weighed heavily on her mind as she aimlessly wandered down Broadway. She had stopped a couple of times the night before to rest on a park bench, but her mind was too active from processing the events to sleep. Fire trucks with their sirens roaring startled Riley back to reality, where she came face-to-face with others who were affected by the attacks. In the faces of people congregating on the fringes of the devastation, the expressions said the same: fear, sadness, and disbelief. She occasionally got a glimpse of her reflection in store windows while trekking down the sidewalk - evidence that she was still alive despite how dead she felt inside.

While trying to absorb what was happening around her, she tried to focus on where to go from here. She was torn.

Riley resolved not to return to Paine, to her home, or to her life. She would go into hiding. She tried to rationalize her decision, made mostly because it was her only protection from Paine's abuse; and, partly, because she felt guilty for continuing life as she knew it after her co-workers' lives had been so tragically ended.

As she strolled down the sidewalk, she stopped occasionally to look back at the voluminous, dark cloud that filled the space in the skyline previously inhabited by the towers. Maybe it was the shock talking. Once it wore off, would she regret decisions made in this hour of crisis? Would she look back in days to come and wish that she could rewind and return to the comfortable life she had carved out for herself? If not the shock, was it fatigue clouding her judgment? She had been walking the streets of downtown in fear and panic for more than 24 hours without food or sleep, or a shower.

She watched smoke rise over the site. She stood, frozen in her tracks. If she was going to turn back, now was the time, she thought. Riley began wringing her dusty hands as she looked around, then back at the rising smoke. At that moment, all she could see was the ugliness that remained. Flashbacks of Paine's fist coming toward her face, his hatred for her written on his face. She quivered when recollecting the scene. She turned back around. There in front of her, the sidewalk appeared never-ending. As long as she continued to follow it, it would take her farther and farther away from the tragedy, from the pain, from her travesty of a marriage. "No one would know the difference," she thought. "Shock, fatigue, fate," she reasoned, "whatever the motivation, I don't care. I can't go back to Paine."

She remembered the damage, the debris, and the results of the 1993 bombing. But it all paled in comparison to what she had witnessed the previous day. She didn't need to watch the news to learn that all that had existed on the 104th floor of Tower One was lost. As she pondered her future, it occurred to her that in her despair, Riley had not reported her absence to the office switchboard, but to Brigette. As far as her colleagues knew before the explosion, she was on assignment. But there was no documented recording or voice mail of her absence, only a verbal message left with a secretary and a cameraman – both of whom most likely did not live to talk about it. Riley felt certain that anyone who had noticed that she had not shown up for work had perished in the explosion. So as far as the world knew, Riley had died along with the rest of the WTNY, Channel 6 News team.

"The odds are in my favor," she thought. The tragedy provided her with opportunity, she concluded. But it was, by no means, a hard-and-fast solution. Riley realized that it would be a trade-off - a life of abuse, fear, and humiliation in exchange for one of uncertainty, anonymity, and isolation. The thought that a new life might carry with it less pain and more peace of mind and control made it more appealing and worth taking the risk.

The piercing sound of another emergency vehicle dashing by alarmed Riley. She had been walking and had completely lost track of where she was. She looked around for a street sign or familiar place that would help her regain her bearings. She recognized through the layer of dust that had already settled on the streets and store windows familiar signs of Soho. Across the street, on the corner, Riley saw a blonde woman taping a piece of paper on a mailbox. Riley crossed the street and as she stepped onto the sidewalk, the woman stepped in front of her and shoved a photograph of a man in her face. The young woman, whose face was streaked with mascara, evidently from crying, said, "Have you seen my husband? Have you seen this man?" Riley glanced quickly at the photograph, but did not recognize the man in T-shirt and jeans. Had he been dressed in a suit, maybe he would have been more familiar to her, she thought. But she was relieved that she couldn't identify him since it might give away her own identity. "His name is Peter Cavanaugh," the woman said. "I don't know if he was in the building this morning. I don't know if he was there." Riley kept walking, trying to put some distance between her and the woman who trailed her, insisting that she examine the photo. Riley, not wanting to be recognized, avoided eye contact with her. "Please help me," the woman said, her voice quavering. "You would tell me if you've seen him, wouldn't you?" Riley bobbed her head slightly and then picked up her pace. She escaped the woman's attentions, leaving her to solicit the help of others.

Riley looked toward the ground or at store windows to avoid being seen by anyone who might be looking for her. By her count, however, only one person would be the slightest bit interested in her existence and that was Paine. His interest would be strictly monetary. For that reason, he would not show up personally, except when public display of false sentiment was required. He would have to look the part of the grieving widower. In the meantime, he would send one of his hired detectives or company investigators to track her down. At that moment, she knew that it would be necessary to either begin engaging her plan to go into hiding or abandon it altogether.

"How do people become nonexistent?" she asked herself while winding through a maze of people who were making their way toward Greenwich Village.

Fortunately, she had made a sizable withdrawal from her bank account the night before when her plans were to leave Paine and return home to Georgia. Dead people don't show up for their bank balance, so what little she'd left in the bank would have to remain there. Her withdrawal would not go far. She would need more to survive.

Glancing down at her dust-covered Ralph Lauren jacket, khakis, and soot-covered Cole Hahn loafers, she remembered her packed suitcase stuffed in the trunk of her BMW. The thought of her car destroyed by the explosion gave her only slight pause after all she'd witnessed. She brushed dust from her left sleeve to no avail. She would need more clothes. As she passed more window displays, she silently said good-bye to Gucci, Tommy Hilfiger, and Ralph Lauren. Her budget could no longer support her desire for the finer things in life. Her life would be about survival, simple means and, without kidding herself, an ample amount of struggle. There would not be room in her life for her love for Prada shoes or Louis Vuitton handbags.

Speaking of room, it had not occurred to Riley where she would spend the night, much less live. New York hotel clerks snubbed their noses at cash. Theft and vandalism by hotel guests had made credit cards the only acceptable payment for overnight lodging in the big city. Riley could select from a rainbow of credit cards tucked systematically inside her wallet, but using one would sound the bell of her existence. Not to mention, a hotel room would cost at least two hundred dollars a night. Calculating the math in her head, she deduced that she could not afford to be so frivolous, especially now that she was unemployed and without anyone to rely on but herself. Then there were surveillance cameras she would need to avoid.

She felt at once the magnitude of her decision. She could wander the streets again all night, but she had been in the public eye long enough that Riley knew she risked being identified by someone in passing. Fortunately, her dusty veil helped to mask her appearance and hide her identity for the present time. It did not, however, provide guarantees. She knew she needed to get off the beaten path, but in so doing, she also risked walking headlong into danger.

"So many open-ended questions," she thought. Riley could not remember a time when her life was not moving in a particular direction. Most of her life, she had had goals to steer by. When Paine entered her life, he tried to control much of her personal life, creating a power struggle between them. In her professional life, she managed major projects and set goals and objectives. But this situation was entirely different. She felt like she was in uncharted waters without a compass.

Riley continued to cut through the flow of people, making eye contact with no one. It was getting late and would soon be dark again, but until then, she was vulnerable.

She passed a souvenir shop. There were so many throughout the city - at least one on every block - that Riley had become blind to them. But something in this particular one caught her eye. She spun around and quickly darted into the tiny store that was packed with most any memento or piece of clothing that could be stamped with a New York symbol, logo, or icon. Its inventory could aptly satisfy a New York tourist's desire for cheap tokens to the nation's financial capital. She pushed her way through the narrow aisles, flanked by overstuffed T-shirt racks positioned too closely together. She stopped at a wall of shelves lined with hats and ball caps of varying designs and colors, but all bearing New York insignia.

"That's it," Riley decided. "I need a disguise."

After rummaging through the neatly stacked ball caps, she settled on a black ball cap with small lettering that would not draw attention. She scoured the store, looking for something else that would mask her identity. She thumbed through the clothes racks until she found a black nylon hooded athletic jacket - an item unbefitting the New York image she had created for herself, she thought, as she frowned at the sports item. In Georgia, she would have been right at home in this apparel. She had come full circle, she surmised. She also grabbed a backpack to stuff her leather satchel in. It would be safer than carrying a handbag that could be easily snatched from her arm by someone skilled in the trade of purse-snatching. She made her purchase and then plotted her next step.

After exiting the store, she looked for an inconspicuous place where she could swap out her designer jacket for the new purchases. Around the corner, on Spring Street, she ducked under some scaffolding that had been left by some construction workers. She looked around and saw an Asian woman and her child approaching her. But neither paid her any attention as they scurried down the sidewalk. Riley tucked the bag between her ankles to brace it while she peeled off the blazer, folded it and stuffed it into the gray plastic bag. Then she pulled the black vinyl jacket out of the bag, hurriedly snatched the price tag from the collar and put it on over her starched and now-stained white oxford shirt. She looked up and down the sidewalk to confirm that she was still going unnoticed. She frantically dug around in her satchel for a hair band. She removed her sunglasses and tucked them in her pocket. With both hands, she bunched her blonde mane into a ponytail and wrapped the band around it a couple of times to secure it. The sound of footsteps startled Riley until she saw an elderly man trudging down the sidewalk. He cast his eyes down at the sidewalk and never looked up at Riley even as he walked past her.

"Typical New Yorkers," she whispered, sarcastically. "Don't make eye contact. Don't get involved," she chanted. These were mantras by which most New Yorkers lived and that had been repeatedly drilled into her by Paine. It was an attitude that Riley had found hardest to adopt. In Georgia, people didn't ignore other people they passed on the street or in the grocery aisle. Georgians greeted one another with a smile or at least a nod to acknowledge each other. They didn't treat one another as invisible. Her observation garnered a chuckle. "This is one time I'm glad they don't see me," she muttered.

She leaned over and pulled the ball cap from the plastic bag. She grimaced as she broke the plastic tie holding the price tag to the brim of the cap. Riley stretched the cap over her head and pulled her ponytail through an opening in the back without stopping to adjust the cap to her head. After a few twists, she said to herself, "There! It fits." She pulled a compact from her handbag and was aghast at the sight of her soiled face. "I don't even recognize myself," she thought as she quickly checked her reflection in the mirror. She made a slight adjustment to the brim. It suddenly occurred to her that she should probably change her hairstyle or hair color to further camouflage her identity. She pulled the hood over her blonde ponytail to hide it and inspected herself in the mirror once more. She pulled her sunglasses from her pocket and slid them back on. "For now, this will have to suffice," she resolved. She snapped the compact shut. She stuffed her satchel and the gray bag into the backpack and zipped it up.

Riley breathed a sigh of relief. "My first mission in my new life accomplished without a hitch. If only everything else from here is as easy," she thought.

But this decision would be minor in comparison with other decisions she had to make. The problem she was encountering was how to carve out a new life while remaining anonymous to the world. One misstep would expose her attempt to falsify her death, as well as throw her back into the treacherous life she was fleeing. It would also betray her colleagues, who had actually died.

Every decision from that moment would have to be calculated and carried out slowly and methodically, right down to the smallest detail.

Knots began forming in her stomach and she began wringing her hands again. "Maybe I should turn back. It's not too late. I could just call Paine. Maybe he would be so relieved that I'm alive that he'll change and things will go back to the way they were in the beginning."

Riley passed a store window and caught a glimpse of her reflection. She reached up and touched her swollen cheekbone. She immediately ceased from pressing on the painful black and blue memento of Paine's display of care. A streak of pain that ran across her face instantly reminded her of why she had even considered going into hiding.

"In the beginning ... huh!" she thought. "Eve didn't have to tolerate that kind of affection from Adam!"

Riley, dressed in her Jane Doe attire, stopped and faced her reflection. "In the beginning ... Mm ... This *is* the beginning. It's the beginning of my new life as a new person," she resolved. "One who's made to feel no shame for who she is."

She lowered the ball cap on her forehead. "One who's not afraid to live," she whispered to the reflection. "One who's not afraid to die."

Once more, Riley glanced toward Lower Manhattan at the aftermath. "How Eve must have felt when leaving the garden, knowing she could never return." She settled in her mind her next step. With no one looking on, she stepped over to the edge of the sidewalk, where she found a rain gutter. She plucked out her cell phone and saw that the battery in it had died. She casually dropped it on the ground. With her right foot, she kicked it into the rain gutter to be washed away with the city's debris. She took a deep breath and turned toward the open sidewalk leading to Midtown. "No more looking back."

Chapter 5

U nion Square, like many of New York's parks, was a place where groups or individuals could gather and exercise their freedom of expression or quietly demonstrate on behalf of their respective causes or concerns. In a few short hours, it was transformed into a congregation of mourners all reduced to tears and united by a common cause.

At first glance, the park appeared decorated with lights and candles for a holiday celebration. As Riley got closer to the park, she could make out memorials, created from personal mementos, most likely belonging to the victims, as well as candles, stuffed animals, religious artifacts, and photographs. The paraphernalia was indiscriminately arranged at the base of a fence. Even more noticeable was the eerie silence of those gathering to pay their respects to the dead. It was broken only by outbursts of sobbing from individuals in the crowd and the random echo of sirens reverberating throughout the city. Riley also saw where signs, posters, and fliers displaying victims' photographs had been hung on wrought iron fencing around the park, on light poles and on other fixed objects near the park. Riley read messages inquiring about lost loved ones who worked at the World Trade Center or who were thought to have been in the building at the time of the explosion. She did not recognize the faces on the posted signs.

Riley stood in the shadow of a tree and observed as people deposited flowers, handmade cards, statues of angels, miniature American flags, and other things. Some quietly lit a candle and stood or kneeled with others who had congregated in the square. The glow from the circle of mourners grew brighter as the circle grew wider. Riley trembled in the shade of the tree. She wanted desperately to join the throng. A sinking feeling in the pit of her stomach prompted her to search for a park bench on which to sit and rest. Since journalism called for finding out from as many people involved as possible the answers to who, what, when, where and how, she felt uncomfortable at that moment being on the sidelines. She fidgeted slightly while sitting on the cold park bench fifteen to twenty feet away from the candlelight vigil. She could relate to the grief this particular crowd was experiencing since she was a survivor who had lost associates and people she knew in the devastation. But she chose to remain apart from the group to protect her identity. Riley could neither interview the participants of the vigil or pick up a candle and stand at post. All she could do was maintain her position in the shadow of the tree.

Just when she thought she had cried her last tear, another wave of sadness and distress swept over her as she examined the faces of the mourners. It occurred to her that some of these people had lost husbands, wives, fathers, mothers, sisters, and brothers, and some were mourning the loss of sons and daughters. Riley thought of her own co-workers. She looked intently at the faces for relatives of the people who had been in her office day-in and day-out. Would she even recognize their family members if she saw them? She realized at that moment how little she knew about their personal lives.

She was aware that Brigette had grandchildren because she often shared photographs. Riley, remembering her words, could hear her apologizing, "I know I'm an obnoxious grandmother, but I just can't help myself, so just tolerate it," she would quip. Most everyone did tolerate it because she often treated her co-workers like they were her children, looking after them, occasionally giving unsolicited advice, and offering to be helpful at every opportunity.

Then there was Thomas, who was single and who liked chasing women - all women. He had even hit on her early in her career with the TV station, but Riley had a rule about not mixing her work with her social life. She immediately drew that line in the sand between her and Thomas, who for the most part, kept things on a completely professional basis. Occasionally, however, he would ask Riley if she had a friend or a cousin who would be interested in a single Irish guy who liked to have a good time. When she could not offer a name, he would ask her to reconsider his offer. Riley would simply look at him, as if to say, "You're crossing the line, Thomas." He would become apologetic and say, "Okay, okay. I know, you don't play where you work."

Riley thought about his words. She had clearly done a good job of sticking by that rule as she racked her brain to recall details that spoke more to her co-workers' personalities than their work ethics.

Riley knew that Barbara had a dog, a Sheltie, which she doted on. Living the consummate professional life that left little room for a social life, Barbara seldom shared more with Riley than her dog's latest antics. Riley tried to remember the dog's name, but couldn't. She realized how little she had actually paid attention to Barbara's stories about the one love in her life.

What she knew personally about each of her other co-workers was even less. She slumped down on the park bench, her head bent low.

"How could I have been so self-centered," she thought. "They were the only family aside from Paine that I had here, and I treated them like strangers. I deserve to be alone."

More tears fell. But suddenly her tears were stalled by the riveting voice of a young, black woman, whose song rose above the crowd. A spiritual of some sort, the song was unfamiliar to Riley, but soothing to her.

Riley wiped the tears from her face, leaned her head back on the bench, closed her eyes and listened to the woman's melodious, a cappella voice.

"*There's a higher place, far above the clouds,*
Where there's no more pain or suffering.
There you'll see a great light that chases away the night,
Jesus wipes our tears and removes all fear,
And waits for us to join Him in that higher place."

The power and confidence in the woman's voice and in the lyrics stirred something deep within Riley, something she couldn't identify. It was unlike anything Riley had ever heard. This woman believed what she was singing. She believed in a higher purpose, a higher power. Riley did, too, but not nearly with the same confidence or conviction exemplified in this woman's voice.

"*There Jesus waits; there Jesus waits.*"

She sang to the people who were trying to find meaning in this tragedy. Her lyrics fell in cadence with the cries and sobs that provided somber background music for the soloist. Riley noticed that the woman's face was aglow, probably from the candles, she thought. The mental snapshot of her face, the conviction in the sound of her voice, and the words of the song would be embedded in Riley's memory forever. As Riley watched her more closely, she realized that the woman was not singing to the crowd. "No, her audience is elsewhere," she thought.

Riley wanted to feel as strongly about something as that woman who sang with her eyes closed as though no one else on earth existed. But at that moment, Riley could not imagine ever again having something to sing about. Her decision would cost her any connections she had left. She pulled her jacket tighter around her to shield herself from the cold night air. She stared at the candles and could imagine the warmth of being home in her whirlpool bath with bubbles tickling her chin and scented candles lulling her into a tranquil state. She would end her evening in her bed, tucked under her down comforter, surrounded by her books, Vivaldi softly piped in from the stereo, and a cup of freshly-brewed, hot tea on the night stand.

"Would tonight also be spent on a cold park bench?" she wondered.

The thought of hot tea caused the sinking feeling in the pit of her stomach to roll into nausea. It occurred to Riley that she had not eaten since the previous morning. She had been too distracted by everything that had happened to notice. A dull headache, however, had become all too obvious to her.

She glanced over at the grieving crowd and felt guilty for thinking of food at such a time. But the queasiness in her stomach told her that if she didn't get something to eat soon, it would just be a matter of time before she drew unwanted attention to herself.

Riley carefully and quietly stood up and left the park area, trying not to disrupt the memorial service. She meandered up Broadway in search of food. She soon walked upon a grocery that was still open and that had a deli cafeteria. She looked down at her watch to discover that it was seven o'clock. While scanning the layers of sliced meats and breads behind glass, she wished that she could just skip food altogether, jump into her car, go home, and crawl into bed. Since that was not an option she was allowing herself, she dismissed such thoughts and pressed on in her pursuit of food. She leaned forward and propped her hand on the deli case for support. None of the choices appeared appetizing to her. She walked over to the food bar in the center of the room and grew more nauseated at the smell and sight of the prepared Asian courses in metal warming trays. Riley circled around the food bar to the other side of the store where prepared salads were stored in a refrigerated case. She picked up a plastic container of fruit from the colorful display. On the shelves next to the case was an assortment of crackers and cheese spreads and dips. Riley grabbed a small box of wheat crackers and a container of cheese spread. She looked around for a beverage and settled on a large bottled coffee drink - a luxury she would need to break herself from, she realized. But after what she'd been through, she would indulge herself. She grabbed some plastic eating utensils and napkins from near the food bar.

Riley paid for her food, then found a place at a café table on the sidewalk outside the deli. She broke the seal on the box of crackers and peeled back the lid on the cheese spread. With a plastic knife, she coated one side of the cracker with cheese. Riley carefully took her first bite and slowly chewed, wanting to give her body time to readjust to food. She paused before taking a second bite in case the first turned out to be a mistake. It wasn't.

Riley uncovered the rainbow of fruit and stabbed chunks of pineapple and cantaloupe and red grapes and shoveled them into her mouth. Each sweet bite made her realize how ravenous for food she was and fed her craving for more. After about four mouthfuls of fruit, she ripped the plastic seal from the coffee drink and popped the lid, then turned up the bottle, downing several swallows of the cold drink. After a few more cheese-covered crackers and chunks of fruit, she felt satisfied. Her queasiness was gone.

Riley lightly dabbed her mouth with a napkin. She then sank down in the plastic patio chair and watched people pass in front of her as they came and went in different directions. She muffled a yawn, then another. Her eyelids grew heavy, reminding her that she still faced the question of where she would spend her second night underground. At that moment, she knew she could be content to remain seated outside the deli, comfortably watching others come and go, but that was not a practical solution. She was exhausted from having walked for days. She would need somewhere to shower and to sleep for the night. "How about the YWCA?" she thought, then dismissed the idea. They would require her to sign in and possibly ask for background information. She had already ruled out a hotel downtown. A less reputable hotel in other parts of the city posed physical dangers as well, not to mention a sizable rate for what few amenities one received in exchange.

"It's too much of a gamble," she thought. She had not seen a city transit bus running since the explosion. Most likely, all public transportation had ceased running routes as part of the city's emergency response protocol.

Besides, her simple disguise did not guarantee her anonymity. Her hair color and length had not changed. Her face was slightly distorted and discolored, thanks to Paine. But how long would that confuse people who faithfully watched the news and might recognize her? While they served their purpose now, Riley hoped that the bruises would eventually heal. Nor had she been officially declared dead. Until she was, it would be difficult to convince them that Riley Davenport-Westin no longer existed if someone did spot her in a crowd.

So avoiding taxis, public transportation, hotels, and places where her photograph might be broadcasted on television was in her best interest.

Riley thought of her parents, of home, of things she was sacrificing by going into hiding. At that moment, none of it mattered. Sitting incognito in front of the deli, sipping the last few swallows of the cold drink, her thoughts turned instead to all the lives sacrificed that morning. "And for what?" she wondered. It occurred to her that she would really be dead had she gone to the office as planned - were it not for Paine.

"Paine saved my life," she thought. "What poetic justice."

She snickered at the notion.

"Maybe I'll thank him someday."

A cool breeze caused Riley to shiver. She still had not grown accustomed to the short summers, abbreviated by weather colder than she had experienced in the South. She pulled the jacket tighter around her. She considered putting her other jacket back on and wearing it under the athletic jacket. It might be bulky, but appreciated if temperatures continued to drop. Riley decided to begin walking again to generate some heat and to move closer to a solution about where to spend the night.

Riley walked up Broadway. The crowd was much thinner than usual. Fear, most likely, had driven people indoors. Warnings from city officials probably also kept New Yorkers behind closed doors until the all-clear siren was sounded. Broadway, lined with theaters and nightclubs and four-star restaurants, was typically a hotbed of nightly activity. Riley and Paine had spent their share of evenings at Broadway openings, followed by dinner with other couples. Riley always enjoyed the famous Twenty-One Club because its ambience, with New Yorker cartoons and its forties historic decor, brought home to her the things of New York that had long existed in her dreams. Paine generally turned his nose up at her suggestion to go there, saying it was too trendy - even though it was notably a hangout for the rich and famous.

What would start out as social events generally turned out to be business socials with investors or partners associated with The Westin Company. Riley would find the wives of Paine's business colleagues both bored with the quasi-business meetings, as well as boring. They would talk amongst themselves about who did their hair or nails. Riley's attention gravitated naturally to the men's conversations. She would tune in as attentively as the male participants until Paine cut her off with comments like, "Riley, I'm sure all this talk of mergers and Wall Street must be boring you. Why don't you stick to something you're more comfortable with, like fashion and fund-raising?" Riley's face would burn from the sting of Paine's insults; then shying away from the conversation she would eventually give in and congregate with the wives in the women's restroom. There, however, she would find herself on the sidelines of a game of one-upmanship in which the women would see who could serve up the most and the cruelest complaints about their husbands. It never ceased to make Riley uncomfortable, especially since she viewed complaining about Paine, no matter how imperfect he was, as disrespectful. Had she had a different viewpoint and joined in the game, she's certain that Paine's anger and rage against her would have escalated if he found out. She was convinced that without a doubt he would have retaliated.

The horn of a taxi that screeched to a halt in front of her startled her and reminded her of her situation.

"I'm so tired," Riley whispered under her breath. The lights of the city were blurred and her legs ached from having walked for so long. "I've got to find somewhere to stay," she muttered again under her breath. She stopped at the corner of Broadway and Twenty-eighth Street and looked around. She saw no options for overnight lodging in sight. She closed her eyes and slowly shook her head in disbelief.

"What am I going to do?" she thought to herself. She sighed deeply, then turned completely around again in search of a solution. After turning full circle, however, a police car siren caused her to spin another ninety degrees north. The siren that came up from behind her frightened her, even though it was headed toward Lower Manhattan. It occurred to her that she definitely needed to stay out of sight from any type of law enforcement.

She decided then that it was time to stray off the beaten path. She veered off Broadway onto Twenty-eighth, which was not as heavily lighted as Broadway. Walking down the dimly-lit sidewalk created a pang of fear that seized her stomach. She looked back to ensure that she wasn't being followed.

Riley felt immense uneasiness as she ventured farther from Broadway. She stopped and looked around again before proceeding. She scoured the block for dangers. Riley saw that she was alone on the street. She had stopped about ten feet short of an alley. She approached as quietly as she could so as not to provoke anyone who might be lurking there. Riley's heart began racing with each step toward the dark alley. Upon reaching it, she timidly peered around the corner and scrutinized the long, dark space. All she saw down the empty stretch of alley were trash bins and fire escapes, as well as litter and reflections from small pools of water, probably from poor drainage.

Glancing backwards once more and then in the other direction down Twenty-eighth Street, she looked to see if she was still alone. She was.

"Whew!" she sighed.

Inhaling deeply and turning up her nose at the stench of garbage, she drew in courage to gamble on sleeping in the dark, damp corridor for the night.

Lightly and quietly, she walked toward a shadow cast by a fire escape located in the middle of the alley. It was adequately distanced from any trash bins where the main tenants were probably vermin. The thought of rats as bedfellows sent shivers down her spine. Hopefully, the shadows would conceal her from any other predators. Nesting halfway down the alley would also give her sufficient warning of anyone approaching from either direction, she reasoned.

Riley stepped into the shadow of the metal staircase. She opened her bag and retrieved her blazer. She slid off the athletic jacket, stuffed her arms into the sleeves of the blazer, and then put the jacket back on over the blazer. She pulled the hood snugly over her head and zipped the jacket as reinforcement against the cold night air.

She lightly patted the ground with the soles of her shoes to check for any broken glass, debris, or moving insects and vermin that might be hiding in the darkness. Before sitting on what she anticipated to be cold, moist concrete, she scanned the alley and noticed that it was relatively uncluttered by garbage other than occasional newspaper pages and fliers strewn throughout the alley. She looked up at windowsills, some holding potted plants; others decorated with various forms of pottery. She closed her eyes and held her breath as she squatted down in the corner of darkness and braced for whatever she had overlooked. She was relieved to discover no surprises. Riley sat cross-legged against the brick wall behind the building facing Broadway. In that space, she found cover and isolation. She also came face-to-face with the reality of assuming her new identity. Her life in the shadows had officially begun.

She sat and listened to the sounds of the city. The volume was lower than usual. Familiar sounds of sirens, taxi drivers blowing their horns or squalling their tires in haste to maximize their time and profits, and low chatter of people on the streets could be heard from where she sat. On this particular night, she heard above all the noise the music of a saxophone. She had no idea where or how far away he was, but the eerie sound of the lone saxophonist cut through the night air and calmed her fears. It sounded somewhat like a funeral dirge. At the same time, it had a comforting, quieting effect on her.

As she listened intently, she leaned her head back on the brick wall. She looked for stars in the night sky. Even though many of the lights in Lower Manhattan were out, she still was unable to see them. She had not seen a constellation since leaving her parents' home in Georgia. Stars reminded her of nights at her childhood home spent in the backyard. She recalled the spontaneous flickering of fireflies lighting up around her as she would move back and forth in the backyard swing. Counting stars and identifying constellations had been a pastime she and her father had enjoyed doing together.

"One, two, three," she silently pretended to count stars from her secluded spot under the stairs.

Tears trailed down her face. She pulled her legs to her in a fetal position and wrapped her arms tightly around them.

"Four, five, six," she continued. Before reaching seven, her sorrow became overwhelming. She covered her mouth with her hand to muffle any sobs that might give away her presence in the alley.

The tears eventually subsided. When they did, she looked up once more in search of stars. "Oh, Daddy," she whispered. "I miss you so much. I'm sorry. I'm so sorry."

The saxophone music wafted through the city. Riley heard the sounds of loneliness played out in each note of the song. It touched a deep-seeded emotion. She had felt it for years, lying just under the surface of her neatly held together facade. While sitting in the dark, dingy alley, perception and reality intersected. For the first time ever, she was truly alone.

Across the alley, movement in the shadows caught her attention and made her gasp in horror. She held her breath, waiting to identify the source of the movement. After a few seconds, a mouse scurried past and ran behind a trash bin about ten feet away. Riley deeply exhaled.

Wiping remnants of tears from her face, she snickered to herself and shook her head.

"Well, I'm not entirely alone," she whispered.

Her eyes turned back to the night sky. "One, two, three, ..."

Chapter 6

From the penthouse office view, Paine could look down on the wealthiest sections of New York City. With one hand tucked in the pants pocket of his Armani suit and the other holding a fresh cup of some of the finest imported coffee from Italy, he looked out over the city. But he did not see the view since his mind was preoccupied with national events that were affecting the stock market and, consequently, the company's bottom line.

Development projects in downtown Manhattan ceased the instant planes collided into the World Trade Center. Plans that were on the drawing board for future developments were immediately abandoned by investors. And profit margins began to dwindle with each announcement President Bush made about war on terrorism.

His was a fourth-generation company. While it was a multi-million dollar corporation, the responsibility of keeping the business in the black rested mostly on Paine's shoulders. He'd read the statistics about the poor success rate of third-generation family businesses, and with a fourth-generation company, the odds were even greater against it succeeding. Because the Westin Company had always been such a wealthy company, he had ignored the gloomy predictions. But the last couple of profit-loss statements he'd read were causing him angst.

Then there was the matter of Riley. He had not received word whether she was alive from the explosion, whether she had gotten out or whether she was an unidentified patient in a hospital.

Their last encounter had been an unpleasant one and they had parted badly. That had never caused him remorse before, but the possibility that she might be dead left him with regrets.

It was true that he did not love her. He wasn't sure that he ever did. Her celebrity status had been good for an up-and-coming executive, as well as for the company's image. That is until Riley began reporting on some controversial issues that had hit too close to home with the company. She covered topics, such as zoning issues that impacted downtown residents, but served to benefit developers like him, and city leaders' push for impact fees, which would eat into developers' profits with each permitted development. With each story, Riley became a public relations problem for The Westin Company. Her profession was contradicting her role as wife of the company's CEO and thereby harming important projects necessary to the success of the company.

Also, her professional status did not live up to social standards for an executive's wife. She was too involved politically in the inner workings of New York City Hall. She knew too much and it was becoming more difficult to hide things from her, things related to the company's internal affairs. He had become fearful that she might stumble upon certain information, in the course of doing her job - information that when placed in front of a television camera could do much damage.

In hindsight, maybe he should not have married her, but divorcing her was certainly out of the question. A scandal of any degree would tarnish the Westin name and mar the company's integrity as a family-owned company with a long-standing history in New York City. Moreover, it would be injurious to his relationship with his parents and grandparents, who were still major stockholders in the company. Most of the board of directors was made up of old New York stock with old money and deeply-entrenched, traditional family values. They would frown upon Paine's broken marriage. Paine's future as CEO of the company rested on the success of those relationships.

Not to mention, a divorce would mean subpoenas for financial records and the company's proprietary information. In the hands of his wife, who happened to be a journalist, release of such information would be the downfall of the corporation. He had to make it work.

Secretly, Paine hoped that Riley was dead. It would be his escape clause from the marriage. The considerable amount of death benefit on her life insurance policy would also pay off nicely and help him recoup any personal stock losses he might suffer during what he was predicting would be a financial downturn in the market, as well as repay personal debts he had recently incurred. As morbid as it sounded, the loss of Riley would actually be his gain, he calculated in his mind.

Paine lifted the bone china cup to his lips and sipped the smooth, black coffee.

Her death would also free him to marry Sarah. He thought of his true love, not to mention of Sarah's ties to the Blackstone fortune. With her, however, it would be more than a marriage of convenience and the merging of multi-millions. He and Sarah were of the same breed, New Yorkers born and raised. Their ideals, their outlook, their upbringing were the same. They understood each other, and what was required to be successful and on New York's social register.

Riley never had an appreciation for society or for the family name.

But there was the matter of Sarah's annulment. She had married some Broadway actor in retaliation for Paine dragging his feet when it came to discussions of matrimony. She quickly discovered that it was a mistake when the actor wanted to give up the theater and move to California to audition for film and television while Sarah supported him. Paine, angry that she had not been patient with him and had married someone she didn't love, went off in search of someone to fill her shoes and the void in his own life. If only he'd been as patient as he was before she married the first time. They might be married now. His timing had been inexcusable. Paine was willing to share the majority of blame for them not being together. Regardless, they were meant to be together.

Paine's eyes roamed over the city's skyline. His eyes settled in the direction of where the Twin Towers had stood two days ago. He could see smoke still rising from the site. He promptly dismissed a twinge of guilt that seeped into his thoughts. Replacing those thoughts, the image of Riley in the gold gown she had worn to the gala suddenly appeared in his mind. A slight smile came to Paine's face as he recalled how beautiful she was in the gown he had personally picked for her. One look at Riley when she walked up and he knew he had made the right choice at the boutique. Her captivating beauty made it difficult to remember their incompatibility. Her beauty had drawn him to her in the beginning. Her smile. Her big blue eyes. Her all-American good looks. Even Sarah's sophistication paled alongside Riley. But that night, he refused to be blinded again to what he wanted.

Power. Wealth. Prestige. Paine intended to stick to the ingredients of his formula for success.

If Riley was still alive, he did not know how he would deal with the situation. She would certainly continue to complicate matters for him - personally and professionally.

A buzzer from Paine's desk abruptly interrupted his thoughts. His secretary's voice followed.

"Mr. Westin, I know you asked not to be disturbed, but it's Mr. Weitzmann. He's called five times in the last two hours and says it's urgent that he talk to you."

Panic struck Paine at the sound of the caller's name. Paine had been successful at avoiding Joe Weitzmann for days. He supposed he should take the call.

"Send it through, Pat, but no more after this ... unless, of course, it's related to Riley's disappearance."

"Yes, Mr. Westin. Certainly."

"Nice touch," Paine thought. The role of the grieving husband was new to him, he also thought.

Paine picked up the receiver.

"Joe," Paine said, sounding mournful.

"Paine, I'm so sorry to be calling at a time like this. I heard about Riley. It's all over the news. How distraught you must be."

"Yes, well, I'm ... I'm not giving up hope just yet."

"You must be in absolute agony not knowing whether she's alive. I was really surprised to find you in the office today," Weitzmann said. "If that were Ellen, I'd be half out of my mind."

Paine had not realized the flaw in his act as the grieving spouse. This would require fast thinking. It was time to lay it on thick, he thought.

"You're right, Joe. I am half-crazed with worry, but, well, work helps keep my mind off the situation. Meanwhile, I'm using all my available resources to help locate her and determine whether, ... well, you know ... Joe, I'm afraid I can't talk about this now. I really need to go."

"Paine, I'm sorry, but I wanted to talk to you about another matter."

"Well, I really need to keep this phone line clear in case someone calls with news about Riley. You understand. Later, Joe."

"Off the hook," Paine thought as he abruptly ended the conversation.

Paine was quite familiar with the matter to which Joe Weitzmann was referring, and he had no intention of talking with him about it. Paine would forego the conversation about P.W. Developments with Joe as long as possible.

"The longer I can keep him and other naive investors like him in the dark, the more I can benefit from their generous investment," he thought as he returned to his view of Manhattan. "What they don't know can't hurt me. But it will buy me time."

Paine took another sip of his imported coffee, which had grown lukewarm. He looked again toward the thin stream of smoke rising out of Lower Manhattan.

A cynical smile crossed his face.

"Time and money," he thought. "My two greatest allies."

Lifting his cup toward the explosion site, Paine said smugly, "Here's to you, Riley, wherever you are," then turned up the cup and drank the last sip.

Chapter 7

Riley looked up toward the skyline. There it was again, like a giant pencil pointing up at the sky. It was the fifth, maybe the sixth, time over the past three days she had come to this same spot and saw the same view. Each time, the view lost more and more of its appeal.

After three days of roaming the streets of Midtown New York, the Empire State Building looked like one more tall building. It had come to serve only as a landmark to help her keep her bearings and not stray too far north or south. It ceased having any more value to her after witnessing first-hand what could happen to a building with the right amount of explosives targeted at just the right pressure points.

She looked up at the skyline and, for a second, thought how she had displaced her faith by believing in buildings and what they represented. "How foolish," she thought while gazing skyward to the pencil point top of the skyscraper.

As she contemplated her new direction, another tickle rose in Riley's throat. She swallowed to fight off another coughing spell. She noticed that they were coming more frequently. Sleeping in the alley at night and breathing in the dusty air that resulted from the explosion by day was bringing on a cold. Not to mention, she was weary from continuously roaming the streets and looking for somewhere to settle.

Riley was no closer to a solution about overnight lodging.

She had successfully ducked into a bus station restroom without drawing attention to herself and dyed her hair red and kept it in a ponytail, which significantly changed her appearance. Keeping her anonymity was of utmost importance since Paine's family knew so many people in New York. Even though her face had most likely appeared in the households of many New Yorkers and residents of New York suburbs, she was close to so few people in the city, none of whom she could actually trust, and none she could call upon to hide her or keep her secret. The Westins were a powerful and influential family. Her television notoriety would not weigh heavier against Paine's family name. For now, the streets of New York were her safest and best option.

After surviving two sleepless nights outside, she was beginning to think of the streets as her new home.

Riley's cough returned and continued until she felt like she would choke. A shiver ran over her. She shook it off. "No," she thought. "I can't afford to get sick now." At that moment, seeking a doctor was out of the question.

Another chill caused her to pull her jacket tighter around her. She felt a slight fall breeze sweep past her and she shivered once more. She looked around for a diner or café, where she could buy some soup or hot tea. That was always her mother's remedy for cold or flu.

"Oh, I wish you were here now, Mom," Riley mumbled under her breath.

Riley's thoughts drifted to her parents' home, to her own bedroom, painted lavender and filled with white French provincial furniture. She could recall a day when she had fought fever for several days. She had lost track of the days as she drifted in and out of unconsciousness and a deep sleep state, where her dreams had been so vivid to her that she had been unable to distinguish between them and reality. When the fever broke and she was exhausted from fighting its effects, she awoke to see her mother's warm smile. "That was real," she thought, as Riley moved slowly down the sidewalk in search of a place to rest and recuperate.

Now, while scanning the building signs, she began questioning whether she was experiencing a bad dream or if this was indeed her reality. How many more days would be spent wandering around downtown New York? The days and events had begun to run together. At what point would she awaken to see her mother's smiling face and be reassured that her nightmare was over? Would she ever see her mother again? Another chill.

She spied some patio tables, indicating there was a deli or cafeteria ahead. She went inside, keeping her head bent low so store cameras would not pick up her facial image. She had covered enough crime stories to know the cameras do not lie.

The deli had among its Asian dishes, only a few American selections. Riley spotted a broth. She stirred the soup with the ladle to see what rose to the top. Green onion, mushrooms and small bits of beef swam around in the mixture. Riley could feel the steam rising from the warming trays and breathed in the blended smells that wafted from the banquet of food. Being near the warmer comforted Riley, but it did not make her chills subside.

Riley nervously scooped soup into a Styrofoam cup. She fumbled with the plastic lid as she hurried to seal in the heat. She looked around for hot tea. She found Earl Grey tea bags and hot water. She grabbed a Styrofoam cup and brewed her own. She ripped the tea bag from its outer covering and dunked it several times in the hot water. She grabbed some packets of sugar substitute and ripped the corner off two packets at once before pouring their contents into the steaming water - an art form developed by professionals on the run. Again, she immediately sealed the cup, trapping the heat inside. On the way to the checkout counter, she noticed some cough and cold medicines and aspirin. She grabbed familiar brands of each and moved toward the counter. While she was reaching out with money in hand, Riley noticed her wedding ring still on her hand - a detail she had overlooked. Panic struck as she realized that the piece of jewelry specifically designed for Riley by a prominent New York jeweler served as an identifier of her existence. On the street, however, it was also a red flag to anyone who might be more interested in her valuable assets than her existence. She discreetly pulled her sleeve down over her hand to cover the emerald-cut platinum ring worth over half a million dollars.

After paying for the food and medicine, she took a seat at one of the tables outside.

Her hands worked underneath the table to remove the wedding ring. Riley had not had it off since Paine placed it on her finger on their wedding day, so it was not easily removed. After sliding it off, she tucked it deep in her pants pocket to keep it close to her. She held her left hand up to view its nakedness without the ring. It gave her an odd feeling. Another chill fell over her, reminding her that she needed to eat before her food grew cold.

She slurped the soup from the spoon, trying to get as much down before the chilly air cooled it. "It's not Mom's," she thought. "But it'll do in a pinch."

The hot liquid warmed her insides while the chilly air continued to create shivers over her body. She finally turned the cup up and drank the remainder of hot broth in hopes of combating the fever rising within her.

Riley looked up from her empty soup cup to make sure she was not being watched. She appeared to be invisible to all who passed by. It was currently to her advantage that all seemed preoccupied and oblivious to her. People walked by, their heads and eyes forward, as though no one else existed. No "hello" to the person they met in passing. No acknowledgment that anyone else was alive. No human touch.

While it was important to her to go unnoticed at this point and time, how Riley longed at that moment for human touch - the touch of her mother's caring hands feeding her soup, her father's bear hugs - and, yes, even Paine's tender touch.

In the beginning, when their relationship was new and young, Paine treated her like one of his treasured possessions. He handled her delicately. She could not remember at what point he changed from being gentle to abrasive, mainly because the change did not occur overnight. It was a gradual metamorphosis. And even on those early occasions when he was brutal, he would sometimes apologize and return to his kind and gentle manner. Little did he know, each outburst from him brought about change in her. Maybe he had sensed her change of heart because over the past year he had stopped showing remorse for his coarse behavior or fits of rage.

If only they could turn back the clock to the beginning, she would run back to him now, announcing her survival. If she knew that Tuesday's events and news of her possible death had changed his heart toward her, that he was suddenly remorseful for his actions, she would drop the masquerade and find her way back into his arms. But without such guarantees, she was fully aware of the greater risk she would be taking by returning to him after three days. With no word, no apparent sign of injury and no reasonable explanation of her whereabouts, he would undoubtedly take her absence as a sign of betrayal. The punishment for returning would be greater than the penalty for forfeiting her life with him and missing out on his most tender moments.

Riley realized that the memory of those moments would have to suffice. After much thought, she was reminded that her decision had been the right one. She might never have gotten as ideal an opportunity to leave Paine as the one presented by current affairs. Riley thought of the irony of it, that attacks on the World Trade Center - a most cowardly and horrendous act of terrorism by foreigners on innocent bystanders - had gained her an opportunity for freedom from personal attacks by someone she had known and trusted. Fortunately, she survived both attacks.

"I'm a survivor," she whispered. "I'm a survivor," she reiterated, without conviction.

She shivered again and she felt a wave of fatigue come over her feverish body.

Riley popped open the bottle of aspirin and extracted two tablets. She picked up her cup of tea, placed the tablets on her tongue and quickly washed them down with the liquid that was now lukewarm to her tongue. She swallowed the last of it before it grew cold. She noticed the sun going down. She wrapped her jacket tighter around her, picked up her backpack and looked left, then right, trying to decide which direction to take. She decided to head back to the alley that was fast becoming her own private bedroom. Aside from rats and roaches, it had been quiet, unfrequented and uninhabited by anyone else at night - at least to her knowledge.

Walking an unsuspecting distance behind her - at least twenty paces back - D. Roy Manley kept one eye on Riley to avoid being spotted by her and one eye out for cops. D. Roy had been at the right place at the right time, he thought, when he noticed Riley cautiously duck into the alley the night before. He watched her bunk down underneath the stairwell. He later followed her and saw her when she pulled money out of a leather wallet hidden inside the backpack she strapped over her shoulder.

"Classy," D. Roy thought when he saw the way she walked, moved, and interacted with the salesclerk at the deli. "Was she lost or was she hiding?" he wondered.

It was rare for a woman of her manner and outward appearance to be pitched out in the street. He had lived in New York all his life. "A woman like that," he thought when he first saw her, "usually has friends. Unless they're crazy, they rarely see this side of city life."

D. Roy, while curious about the woman's circumstances, was more interested in the contents of her wallet.

D. Roy had not only been on the streets, but he'd also been in and out of jail for petty theft. His first offense was shoplifting a pair of sneakers from Macy's when he was ten. Billy Romanoski, an older kid from the neighborhood, dared him. He was scared to death, but Billy had been his role model and the only male presence in his life.

In one fell swoop, he stole the sneakers, launched his career as a petty thief and broke his single mother's heart. His life was never the same, and Billy Romanoski became a name of the past. After recruiting D. Roy as a new disciple to the dark side, Billy moved on to his next victim.

D. Roy kept his distance while trailing the redhead. So far, she appeared to be easy prey. He had noticed, too, that she appeared to be sick.

"This could turn out to be an easier job than I thought," D. Roy surmised as he saw and heard her coughing from where he was more than ten feet behind her.

Assuming that she was heading back toward the alley, D. Roy decided he would follow her as far as the corner and then hang around, waiting until the early hours of the morning to strike. He saw her stop at a newsstand, where she picked up a newspaper. He stopped, too, at a store window, pretending to admire the electronics in the store. With one eye on her, he watched her rifle through her knapsack for money to pay the vendor. The trick would be to get her backpack as quickly, quietly, and smoothly as possible. He had seen her stuff the backpack under her head, using it for a pillow. If she did that tonight, it would be difficult to swipe it without incident.

D. Roy pulled his sock cap tighter onto his head, then scratched his scraggly goatee. He ran through a variety of scenarios, plotting his next job. He was getting low on cash. "With luck, this will be a cinch," he thought.

D. Roy saw the woman round the corner leading to the alley. He walked up to the streetlight at the corner and saw that she was halfway down the street. He watched her walk farther until she came to a stop near the alley.

She began turning around. At that point, he casually walked a few steps away from the lamp post moving out of her view. He paused for a few minutes, allowing her time to sneak out of sight.

D. Roy walked back over to the light post and stood with his back to the alley. Slowly, he turned his head to the side, using his peripheral vision to check on the woman's position. She had ducked out of sight.

"Now, I wait," D. Roy murmured.

He leaned on the lamp post and watched the sun begin its descent behind the skyline. He looked at his watch. Almost 7:30 p.m. "It's going to be a long night," he thought, "but well worth the wait."

Chapter 8

Riley sat and read the newspaper until her vision became blurred and her head began swimming. Even at her worst hour, she was hungry for information, wanting to know the latest on the attacks.

She read about the terrorists who had plotted and been successful in their attempts to destroy the Twin Towers and to handicap the Pentagon. She also read that another plane had been hijacked with intentions to destroy either Camp David, the United States Capitol, or the White House, but that some brave passengers foiled their plans.

Riley saw photos of the search and rescue attempts to find more survivors and to identify the dead by retrieving body parts from the wreckage. Tears splattered onto the newspaper page. She trembled this time as much from weeping as from continuous chills. She neatly folded the newspaper and tucked it into her bag. She zipped the bag and turned it on its side.

Riley's eyelids grew heavy and her head light. She curled up in a fetal position, resting her head on the makeshift pillow. Riley wrapped her coat and her Ralph Lauren jacket worn underneath her outer wear, tighter around her to try to find warmth and stop the chills.

Riley drifted off to sleep. It was not a sound sleep as she wrestled with fever. Every so often her eyelids popped open to watch for predators of any species. But keeping watch became increasingly difficult the more the medicine took effect. Soon, her eyelids allowed in only a sliver of light before they stopped opening at all.

D. Roy lurked at the end of the building. He had been secretly watching and waiting for Riley to fall asleep. He had not counted on the medicine he had seen her consume. His job suddenly got easier, he thought, when he saw her take a second swallow.

D. Roy leaned against the building with his foot propped against the wall. He looked back and forth, casing his surroundings for anyone who might deter him. He peeked around the corner again and saw that the woman appeared sound asleep.

He pulled out a cigarette and lit it, trying to steady his nerves before moving forward with his plan. He took a few more drags on the cigarette before stamping it out on the ground with the toe of his shoe. He looked back and forth again for anyone approaching. He saw no one. He peered around the corner one more time before moving in for his spoils.

"Still out cold," he thought when he looked at the woman. He tiptoed toward her. D. Roy's breath caught after the crunch of glass underneath his shoe created an unexpected noise. When he saw no reaction from the sleeping woman, he proceeded toward her.

D. Roy got close enough to touch her. He crouched down beside the woman. He looked into her face to ensure that she was sleeping and not feigning sleep. Much to his surprise, D. Roy was mesmerized by the angelic face of the woman. He had been watching her from afar for days, and her beauty had not escaped him. But he had no idea just how beautiful until, up close and personal, he could see her face dimly lit by moonlight.

"Wow," his mouth formed the word. He exhaled, trying to regain his composure and his nerve to carry out his plot to make her his next victim.

"What a shame," he thought. "What's a babe like you doing sleeping with the rats?" He scratched his chin. "What are you hiding from?"

Riley whimpered and clung tighter to her jacket.

At that, D. Roy jumped up and prepared to flee if she opened her eyes. He waited. After a few minutes, he exhaled with relief and crouched down again to move in for the steal.

D. Roy examined the woman's face again. Pangs of guilt had never before been an occupational hazard. But at that moment, while staring into this beautiful woman's face, a fierce battle went on in his conscience. D. Roy glanced at his watch, realizing that he had also never lingered this long in thought over whether to carry out a job.

"What's the hold up, D. Roy?" a voice inside him said. "You'll probably never see this woman again. Besides," he reasoned, "it's a sure thing."

The woman, other than appearing to be shivering in the cold, had moved only once since he'd approached her.

"Okay," he thought. "Here goes."

He stood up straight, positioned himself to grab the bag, then run. He took a few deep breaths, mustering courage.

With one swift movement, D. Roy grabbed one corner of the bag and snatched it out from under the woman's head. The woman immediately awoke and to his dismay, latched onto her possessions despite her groggy state. D. Roy, in his tug-of-war for the bag, found himself eye-to-eye with the woman who had moments before taken his breath away. Now, she was clearly his enemy and he would have to gain control. He could see in her eyes days of work, time, and energy lost. He would have to start all over with a new victim. He needed this score. His funds were too low to lose any more time. Also, this woman would be able to identify him if he allowed her any more face time.

D. Roy pulled on the bag. Had he realized before grabbing the bag from her that she had curled her hand around one of the straps, he would have attempted the job later or on the street. She now gripped the strap with both her hands and held tight with all her might.

"Let go, lady," D. Roy muttered. "Just let go!"

Riley said nothing, but tightened her hold on the straps as she fought for all that she owned in the world against a silhouette. In her semi-conscious state, she wasn't certain whether the figure was real or whether she was imagining it.

Suddenly, the tension on the strap was released and Riley was relieved that she had won the battle. But then, a fist flew at her face and knocked her backwards against the brick wall behind her. As she attempted to protect her face from additional hits, she lost her hold on the bag.

Through her tears and blurred vision, she could clearly see that the man was gone and had taken her backpack and in it, her money.

She reached up, touching her swollen cheek.

"This is what I left Paine for, to escape this kind of treatment," she thought. "At least this time, it was from a stranger."

Meanwhile, D. Roy ran down the alley without looking back. He rounded the corner and ran face first into a two-by-four swinging in his direction. D. Roy fell backward, landing prostrate on the alley pavement and was out cold, never knowing what hit him.

Riley was sitting up in a fetal position when she heard a plop on the ground next to her. Fearing the man's return, she scrambled to get away. She crawled backwards on her feet and hands, but found herself cornered under the stairwell.

Then she saw him.

Riley rubbed her eyes. Had her eyes been playing tricks on her? Standing before her was not the young man with whom she had just wrestled for her backpack. Even in her groggy state, she had noticed his small build, his thin face.

The dark shadow of a giant who stood towering over her was not the same man who had just robbed her and plunged his fist into her face. She could make out the outline of a beard and wild hair. The other man was wearing some sort of cap.

Riley broke out in another cold sweat.

"Please, don't hurt me," she said. "Please?"

Riley sobbed. Tears rolled down and stung her hot cheeks. One side of her face burned from the blow to her face; both sides burned from fever.

Riley shrank when the giant took a step toward her. He paused, then with his foot, nudged something on the ground closer to her. Riley saw the backpack for the first time. She watched his reaction while she slowly reached for it. When it appeared safe, she grabbed it and held it tightly to her chest.

Riley furrowed her brow as she looked up at the man who resembled images she'd seen on television of Big Foot sightings. Maybe it was the cough medicine causing her eyes to distort his image. Riley drew into a ball with the backpack tucked securely against her. She shivered from the fever, from the cold, and now from the fear of what was about to happen. She didn't understand why this burly man had dropped her backpack next to her. Had the other man emptied it of its contents before dropping it in the alley?

"Come with me," a low, deep, stern voice said through the darkness.

Riley swallowed hard and fought back more tears at the suggestion.

"What?" she said, her voice quavering.

"Come with me," the voice repeated.

"Where?"

"Come with me."

Riley slowly arose from her ground-level position. All she could see was a large silhouette of a man or beast, she didn't know. With her back against the wall, Riley contemplated her next move. Do I bolt? Or do I follow the giant?

"Why should I?"

"Because when he wakes up, he may be back for what he came for."

Riley's eyes widened. The two men were not together, she surmised.

"What happened?"

"Lady, do you want to stand around and play twenty questions until he returns or do you want to get out of here?"

Riley's cheekbone throbbed. She reached up and lightly pressed it to relieve the pain. But the reminder of the other man's last visit convinced her that Big Foot was right. She couldn't risk waiting around for his return. She would have to find another place to roost.

"Okay," she said. "Okay."

The man turned and shuffled down the alley. Riley followed reluctantly at a slow pace. She kept distance between them and stood prepared to part company at any time.

Riley looked back occasionally, watching for the younger man's reappearance and watching her new home fade into the shadows.

"Let that be a lesson to you," Riley thought to herself. "Nothing is permanent. Tuesday should have taught you that."

Riley thought about the robbery and how close she came to worse treatment. "Thank you, Lord," she whispered, offering a quick prayer. After being led back onto the street and into the night lights, Riley opened the backpack and fished out her wallet, which appeared to be intact, still containing money and credit cards and, "Oh, no! Identification!" Riley realized. She frantically pulled her license, press pass, bank card, and credit cards - anything that revealed who she was - from her wallet and slid them into her back pocket for safekeeping. She then stuffed the wallet back into the backpack and zipped it closed. It had not occurred to her how close she had come to being discovered alive. Her mind was racing, plotting ways to dispose of her ID and any other incriminating evidence to her mortality. She needed to discard them before she experienced another close call.

"Next time, I may not be so fortunate to have a knight in shining armor, such as he is, come to my rescue," she thought as she cast her eyes upon the gruff, hunched man steering her course. She watched the creature in front of her amble forward on the sidewalk.

"Where are we going?" she wondered as she trailed behind him.

She wanted to ask him, but she feared antagonizing him. It also occurred to her that he may have cracked open her wallet and learned who she was. Until she knew for certain, it might be in her best interest to stay as close to him as she comfortably could.

Riley wandered in the shadow of Big Foot. Each step she took drained her further of any energy she had left after the tug-of-war for her belongings. If her tired, feverish body were a car, it would be running on fumes, she thought. How she longed for her car at that moment.

How nice it would be to have valet service deliver her special order BMW to the curb. She would get behind the wheel, drive to the nearest four-star hotel, charge the room to her American Express and sleep off everything that had occurred over the past three days.

"I would wake up tomorrow and all of this would have been a nightmare," she thought.

Riley's cheekbone throbbed with pain. Her chills continued. Her legs were like jello as she followed Big Foot. Riley lightly shook her head to clear her mind of cobwebs. She felt dizzy. She narrowed her eyes to avoid the bright lights of the city. Occasionally, she would blink hard to relieve her irritated eyes. But when she did, she felt her body begin to sway off balance.

The farther they walked, the darker the streets appeared. Riley thought maybe fatigue was blurring her sense of judgment and perception. But when they reached an intersection, she could see that they were about to cross

Twenty-ninth Street. She had not realized in her foggy state what a short distance they had walked. They had made their way to Ninth Avenue, which was only about three blocks from where she had been camping at night. It seemed much farther.

Riley looked around and noticed, much to her surprise, that the streets and sidewalks had become deserted. Panic set in and her heart began racing. She swallowed a lump that had formed in her throat.

"Wh-where are we going?"

Silence.

"I said, 'Where are we going?'" she said, raising her voice to be heard.

"You'll see," he said without turning and facing Riley.

Riley wrinkled her brow and continued to scope out her surroundings. She folded her arms over her chest at the sight of building facades splattered with graffiti. It was obvious with the amount of debris on the street that Public Works did not frequent this area of town for trash pick-up. The deeper they ventured into the dark area of town, the more it became clear that the city had also been sparing with street lamps. Riley heard a crunch underneath her feet and looked down to see that she had stepped into a pile of shattered glass. She looked up and saw where the glass cover of the street light above her now lay in shards under her feet. Another chill ran down her body and she crossed her arms tighter over her chest.

Meanwhile, she watched closely for any strange or sudden movements from out of the shadows. Her eyes returned to her guide, who evidently knew his way through this section of town. The more she watched Big Foot, the more she realized that he wasn't as large as he had initially appeared to her. His shoulders slumped as though he had been beaten down by his circumstances. She could see long, slender fingers protruding from under his oversized jacket. She could also see shirt tails with multiple conflicting patterns peeking out from underneath his jacket. Apparently, he was wearing layers of clothing, inflating his actual size. Riley also noticed that her guide walked with a slight limp. She wondered how long he had been wandering the streets of New York on a bad leg. Despite the limp, he walked with determination, as one on a mission and not easily discouraged by obstacles in his path.

Riley dragged along behind him, but secretly longed to stop and rest. As if reading her mind, the man turned to her and said, "Just a little ways now." His words infused energy into her, encouraging her to go the distance.

The spotlight of the moon cast low light on her surroundings, enough to capture some detail on this particular section of the city.

The moonlight danced through some sort of a gate or fence from somewhere above them. It created a lattice-work image against what appeared to be a brick wall to her right. On the brick wall were images, graffiti in white lettering. On her left, Riley could make out a chain-link fence. After a few more steps, she could hear the roar of traffic overhead.

"A turnpike," she surmised.

It sounded to Riley like she had stepped into a hollow drum. An echo from the vibrations above was haunting, especially in areas where it was pitch black.

In the moon's glow, Riley squinted to read spray-painted messages on dull, white block walls. She finally recognized it as graffiti, as well. Riley could also make out sliding warehouse doors and boarded windows. More self-expression, but larger and more defined, spread from the end of one brick building to the other and was broken up in the middle by advertisements of assorted theaters or musicals that hung on a boarded window.

Riley trudged along behind the man while trying not to miss any details of her journey.

Ahead, she noticed scaffolding outside the entrance of another warehouse. Whether it was vacant was unclear to her, but flattened Chiquita banana cardboard cartons, newspapers, and empty drink bottles lay at the foot of the entrance steps. There was no sign of a company name, only more artistic messages scrolled haphazardly on the walls of the building.

Riley walked cautiously since only every other step she took seemed to be lighted by the moon's glow. She turned to look behind her and could see the definition of the turnpike against the city lights. She turned back toward her guide and gasped at being caught off guard at bodies splayed out in the corner of the next building entrance. A sliding door with large, yellow, black, and white bold lettering provided the backdrop to the bodies stretched out on flattened cardboard boxes. A small cardboard box turned on its side served as camouflage for one body, also covered with a thin blanket.

Riley held her breath, hoping that she would not disturb them or rile them if they could be roused. Riley became squeamish at the thought that they might not. She lightly and quietly skipped a few steps to catch up with her leader.

The path became darker and the night air colder. Riley shuddered, reminded of the fever that ran hot inside her. She felt her head swimming.

"How much farther?" she wondered. Riley wanted to ask, but she was afraid to say anything. She didn't dare awaken the wrong person asleep in the nooks and crannies near the buildings. But everything in her cried out for rest.

With the roar of traffic on the turnpike behind her, all Riley could hear ahead was the shuffle of Big Foot's flat-soled shoes on the pavement. His limp created a unique rhythm in his step, she noticed.

Then she saw him round the corner and drop out of sight.

Riley's chin dropped, her brow furrowed and her heart skipped a beat as panic set in.

"He's leaving me," she murmured to herself. "Wait," she said louder, but not too loud so as to alarm the vagrants.

Riley ran to the corner and looked to the left in time to see Big Foot duck through a door.

"Wait!" she cried out.

Her cries did nothing to deter the man. He fell out of sight.

Riley ran up to the door, where she stopped cold. She looked to the right, then to the left. There was no one visible to her on the dark, secluded street. She stood battling with herself whether to follow him inside. She looked on the door and the building for some description of the location. Nothing.

Suddenly, a woman's voice broke through her anxiety.

"It's not the Ritz, Darlin', but it's a bit warmer in here than where you're standing."

Riley's eyes widened with amazement. She had not expected to find warmth on the other side of the warehouse door, much less find it in the form of a woman's voice.

From where Riley stood, she could make out little detail in the woman's face, whether it could be trusted. She stood undecided.

"Not to rush you or anything, Darlin', but did I also mention that it's probably safer in here?"

Riley, despite being unable to clearly make out the features of the woman at the doorway, felt drawn to her. Her voice reminded her of her mother's comforting, melodic voice. Her mother could put her at ease with just a hello. From there, every word that followed made her feel at home - no matter how far away she'd been or how long she'd been gone.

Riley bit her lip as she took one last look in either direction. While there were no immediate threats, she had grown tired of being on the streets with no roof over her head. She decided to take a chance on what was behind the door.

She put one foot forward and the door swung open wide, allowing her to enter. Riley offered up a quick prayer, then braced for what was waiting for her on the other side.

Chapter 9

Riley awoke, startled by her unfamiliar surroundings. She propped herself on her elbows on the cot on which she was lying. It squeaked when she moved. She saw rows of empty, neatly made-up cots. Hers was the only one with a body in it. The dormitory setting was sparsely furnished with a few chairs and chests of drawers. The dull, gray walls were bare, except for a wooden cross and a picture of Jesus hanging next to a door, and a mirror over one of the chests. The picture of Jesus, his piercing eyes staring back at her, reminded her of the crucifix at the small chapel, and gave her the same unexplainable sense of peace and assurance that she was in a safe place. Riley looked around the room. There were no windows.

A strong, stale odor of mildew brought a wrinkle of disapproval to Riley's nose and queasiness to her stomach. She sat up and planted her bare feet on the carpeted floor.

"Where are my shoes?" she wondered. She looked under the cot, but found nothing.

"My backpack?"

Riley panicked.

A woman's voice broke through Riley's anxieties.

"Well, you are alive. I must say, I'm very glad. Coroners don't like to come to this section of the city. It can be hours, even days, before they pick up a body here."

Riley frowned at the thought of rigor mortis. Envisioning it taking over her own body made her more nauseated.

"I wasn't sure you were going to make it," said the African-American woman, who had a multi-colored scarf tied around her head. "You've been asleep since Friday."

"What's today?" Riley asked.

"Sunday."

A puzzled look settled on Riley's face. What had she missed? What had happened to throw her into such a deep sleep?

"Where am I? And where are my things?" she asked.

"You, my dear, are at Faith House, a homeless shelter for women. I hope that you will find the accommodations suitable to your needs," the woman said, all the while smiling.

But Riley detected sarcasm in the woman's sentiments.

"As for your possessions, they are safely tucked away in your very own locker for protection."

Still Riley's mind was not at ease.

The woman leaned against the door frame and crossed her arms over her chest.

"I removed your shoes," the woman continued. "I did peek inside your bag to make sure that you were not bringing a weapon or drugs or alcohol into my fine, upstanding establishment. We do, after all, have a reputation to uphold. Aside from that, your possessions are just as they were the night you entered and collapsed on the posture-pedic mattress on which you spent your first two nights.

"Now I know she's being facetious," Riley thought as she looked down at the thin mattress resting on a metal frame.

"How are you feeling?"

Riley, who was still trying to fit the missing pieces of her life together, wasn't sure how to respond. The last she remembered, she was feverish and following a giant through New York City. She last recalled feeling weak, dizzy, and confused about her whereabouts and her direction. She had also been fearful of the giant's intentions. Before Riley responded, the woman walked over to where Riley sat, reached out and pressed the palm of her hand to Riley's forehead, as naturally as her mother had done so often when she was younger.

"Fever's gone, it seems."

Riley stared blankly at the woman, whose round face was nowhere to be found in her memory. Her voice, however, was soothing. But her dark eyes and broad smile were making a good first impression on Riley.

"Are you hungry?"

Riley grimaced, remembering her nausea. She pressed her fingers against her forehead to keep her throbbing head from swimming.

"After all, it's been days since you've eaten," the woman continued.

As much as the thought of food sickened her at that moment, Riley knew that was probably what she needed most.

Again, without giving Riley an opportunity to answer, the woman said, "I'll be right back with some soup." Before exiting the room, she looked back and said wryly, "Oh, did I mention that your stay occasionally includes room service?"

Riley looked quizzically, trying to analyze the woman's sense of humor.

"A woman's homeless shelter," Riley registered in her mind. "How apropos. I certainly qualify."

Humming could be heard from the direction of the open door the woman had exited. It grew louder as the woman reappeared carrying a tray laden with bowl, glass, and silverware. The smell of soup made hunger pangs come alive in Riley. The woman set the tray on one of the chests and pulled a folding table from a closet in the corner of the room. After standing the table in front of Riley, she placed the tray on it.

"I apologize that it's straight from a can. Kitchen's closed for a few more hours."

Riley shook her head, as if to waive the apology. Then she reservedly reached for a spoon on the tray, fighting her desire to snatch up the bowl, turn it up and gulp the hot mixture. Riley placed the spoon in the broth, but before she could measure out her first spoonful, the woman said, "My name is Nadine Franklin. What's your name, Darlin'?"

Riley looked into the mixture and froze. Hoping that a name would be spelled out by the alphabet soup in front of her, she panicked. She knew it would eventually come to this, but in her frame of mind, she wasn't prepared to face it, however inevitable. An "E" floated to the top of the steaming broth. Suddenly, it dawned on her.

"Eve," Riley blurted out. Realizing that her tone may have seemed overly enthusiastic, she calmly repeated her new name. "Eve."

"Well, Eve, do you have a last name?"

Riley could feel her face redden. She hadn't thought that far ahead. She cast her eyes back toward the steaming broth and scooped her first spoonful into her mouth and nodded at the woman as she swallowed. Meanwhile, her mind raced to settle on an imaginary last name. She looked back at the soup. "That's it," she thought. Once again, the bowl of soup served as inspiration to her.

"Campbell," Riley said.

"Eve Campbell."

Riley shot a half-smile at the woman - partly to connect with the woman and partly out of pride in having been so clever under pressure.

"Well, Eve Campbell, I have a practice of blessing my food before I eat it, so do you mind if I welcome you to Faith House by saying a blessing with you over your first meal here?"

Riley's eyes narrowed at the woman's suggestion. The last time she had said a blessing was when she lived in her parents' house. She had abandoned that practice when she left home. She was surprised to discover someone in New York who upheld that tradition.

"No. I mean, no, I don't mind."

The woman had bowed her head and launched into a prayer before Riley remembered that she was supposed to bow her head, too. She listened intently to the woman's blessing, which was unlike any she had heard her parents recite. Riley noticed that the woman talked to God as though she directly had his ear. It was unlike anything Riley had ever heard.

"And, Father, I pray that Eve will come to feel like this is her home, to see these humble furnishings and modest accommodations as equal to any found in the finest mansions this earth has to offer. Father, she is obviously without a home, but you and I know that home is where you are. So I pray that if she does not truly know you and your Son, that you will introduce yourself to her and help her come to know you the way I know you."

Riley's eyes filled with tears. She didn't know why. She'd known God. Her parents had seen to her religious training starting at a young age. She had also prayed to him the day of the explosion. He was that invisible being whose name her parents often spoke of in their conversations. The preacher spoke of Jesus in his long, dull sermons. Jesus' picture was posted on the walls of the church and in her parents' house. She had been unable to escape his piercing eyes. And more recently, those eyes had brought comfort to her troubled heart. Of course, she knew him.

"So why was this woman's prayer having this effect on her?" Riley pondered.

"Now, Lord, would you bless Eve's food, just as you did the rich, abundant food prepared in the garden for Eve, the mother of all mankind? Would you give this Eve who sits before me strength and healing? And would you open her eyes and point her to the right direction in life? And, Lord, I pray that today will be a day of new beginnings for Eve. Thank you, Lord, for hearing our prayer. Amen."

Riley picked up her napkin and dried her tears and wiped her nose.

"Now, now, child. Eat up before it gets cold," Nadine said. "We'll talk later. We have much to talk about."

Riley's eyes got bigger at the implication that Nadine might want more information about her. She peeled open a pack of saltine crackers and shoved one whole cracker into her mouth.

Riley began plotting an escape and looking for a way out of the building when a young woman appeared.

The curly, brown-haired woman, who Riley guessed to be in her twenties, plopped down and sat cross-legged in the middle of one of the cots across from her.

"Nadine hates it when we sit on our beds after we've already made 'em up. But I don't care. It's America. I sit where I want," the young woman said, followed by a pout.

At that, she peeled the clear wrapping off an orange sucker and stuck it into her mouth.

"So you finally woke up. We thought you weren't going to make it."

Riley arched one eyebrow at the coldness of the comment. She glared at the young woman, whose bluntness rubbed Riley like emotional sandpaper. She locked her jaw to keep from speaking her mind.

"I'm glad you did," the young woman said.

The tenderness of the young woman's sentiment immediately caused Riley's face to soften and her defenses to fall.

"I'm Deidra. What's your name?"

Riley opened her mouth to introduce herself, but caught the words before they gave her away.

"Uh, Eve ... Eve Campbell."

She swallowed hard at the near mistake. She thought of the amount of practice that would probably be required before her new name rolled off her tongue as naturally as her real name. Deidra apparently did not suspect a thing because she continued the conversation without skipping a beat.

"You'll like it here at Faith House. I've been at a lot of shelters, but Nadine's is the bomb."

Riley shuddered at the reference to a bomb. Although Deidra had meant the term for good, it triggered memories that came rushing back to her. Only days ago, an explosion had destroyed the TV station where she worked, killed her co-workers, and leveled the World Trade Towers. The reminder quickened her heart and she picked up where the pain had left off. On cue, her eyes overflowed with tears and she began to sob all over again.

Deidra's eyebrows drew together at the sight of Riley's tears.

"What's wrong? Are you hurting? You want me to get Nadine?"

Riley shook her head as she dabbed the flow of tears from her face.

Deidra, frantic over Riley's sudden outburst, asked, "Are you in pain?"

When Riley did not respond, Deidra jumped off the cot and dashed through the door, yelling for Nadine. Seconds later, she returned with Nadine close on her heels.

Nadine did not stop to ask questions. She sat next to Riley on the cot, wrapped her heavy arms around Riley like a blanket and pulled her head to her chest. Deidra stood looking on, concern weighing on her face. Nadine motioned to her to leave them alone. Much to Deidra's dislike, she heeded Nadine's requests and marched out of the room, huffing and puffing with each step.

"This is America, you know," she muttered under her breath as she left the room.

Riley poured out more tears while Nadine rocked her and stroked her hair.

"Now, now, child. Everything is going to be alright. You're in good hands now. Nothing will harm you. You're safe."

Riley felt the tidal wave of emotion, which had been pent up for almost a week, rack her body. There was no stopping the force of it. She would have to ride out the storm. Her only comfort was in feeling at that moment in the arms of this kind stranger that she wasn't alone in the storm.

Chapter 10

Riley closed the door and locked it.

She walked over to the mirror and gazed at the image looking back. The woman peering at her showed signs of fatigue and wear, despite the sleep marathon she had just completed. After experiencing three days of uninterrupted sleep, she could not understand why she should have dark circles under her eyes. Her puffy eyes were the result of tears she had shed since awakening. Riley buried her face in her hands, then uncovered her face to see that nothing had changed. She could explain the bruised, drawn face before her. She had skipped quite a few meals, starting days before her Rip Van Winkle episode.

She looked around the bathroom at the antiquated plumbing, peeling yellow and pink floral wallpaper, and scuffed, dingy checkered linoleum. There was a frayed, rectangular brown rug covering a small patch of flooring. The shower curtain was clear but for the mildew that made it less transparent. It was held to a rusted metal shower rod by fewer shower rings than needed, causing it to sag in the middle.

Riley had stacked some clothes, which Nadine had given her, in the dull metal chair in the corner. She had not had the opportunity to look them over before Nadine shoved them into her arms. It was her way of saying she would not take "No" for an answer. Riley unfolded the clothes to see what Nadine had picked out for her. "From the gift closet," Nadine had said as she gave them to Riley. "Judging from your size, they should fit."

Riley held up a pair of jeans, a khaki-colored denim, button-down shirt, and a white, short-sleeved T-shirt. Riley raised one eyebrow. She looked at the tag on the jeans. A discount store brand. While holding them up to examine them, she cocked her head to one side. "I guess I can make these work - at least until I can get to a store to shop for myself."

Riley let the clothes drop back into the chair, then pushed aside the shower curtain. She twisted the shower knob and put her fingers under the spray to test the temperature. She scowled at the rust spots and dinginess of the bathtub. But she would not let them discourage her, she resolved. It was the first shower she'd had since Tuesday. She positioned the soap and shampoo Nadine had given her so they would be at her fingertips. She peeled off her clothes, which she'd been wearing all week, then laid them neatly across the back of the chair.

She climbed into the bathtub and let the hot spray wash over her, head to toe. Riley sighed.

The warmth of the shower, the way the perfumed soap slid over her skin, the feel of the water hitting and massaging her tight body made her feel alive again. She felt lighter as the layer of dirt and grime accumulated from life on the street was scrubbed away.

She appreciated her accommodations, however meager and temporary. Even though the cot she had slept on squeaked and was not the most comfortable, it was not the floor or pavement. The bowl of hot soup and crackers that fed her hunger gave her strength and served its purpose. And the clothes Nadine had picked out for her were indeed a gift. They don't make a fashion statement, but they're clean and in good condition.

"This is just a temporary arrangement," she kept telling herself. "It's just temporary."

Riley rubbed the shampoo into her wet, straight hair. Almost a week without luxuries and comforts she was accustomed to having had opened her eyes to how fortunate she had been all her life. That, coupled with witnessing the loss of life earlier that week, had given Riley a new perspective on life.

She closed her eyes as she rinsed the suds from her hair. In her mind's eye, she could see her luxury bathroom at home. She could see the green marble tile walls and floors. She could see her Jacuzzi bathtub decked with candles and bath crystals. She could see her vanity topped with expensive perfumes and a brass tray that held her strategically arranged tubes and compacts of make-up and bottles of lotion. She could also see her closet packed with designer wear and shoes that had taken her years to accumulate.

The thought of being reduced to living in a shelter and wearing other people's cast-offs resembled nothing of the life she had built. Even though Riley was thankful for Nadine's help, she couldn't curb her desire for more. She would have to figure a way out and soon.

Riley was discovering that there was much that she needed to learn about starting over with a new identity. If she was going to work her way out of the shelter, she would need the essential paperwork that employers required: Social Security card and photo identification. Fake ones would be risky to obtain.

She dried her skin with the towel that had frayed edges.

Her mind was racing.

Besides what her next step would be once she exited the bathroom, Riley needed to know what was going on outside the shelter. She had no idea what the national headlines had been since Thursday. Her need to know made her anxious. She quickly slid on the clothes, combed her damp red hair, washed her face and brushed her teeth with a new toothbrush and brand new tube of toothpaste that Nadine had also given her. She also transferred her wedding ring and her ID (license, press pass and charge cards) to the pockets of her secondhand pants. She looked in the mirror at her face stripped clean of makeup. It would be easier for her to go incognito without it.

Riley lingered over her reflection in the foggy mirror.

"I feel like a new person," she said to the image. Riley chuckled at her comment. "That's good because you're not the same person you were yesterday," she whispered. "Eve Campbell. Eve Campbell. Hi, I'm Eve Campbell."

Riley repeated the name, trying it on with her secondhand clothes. The name, unless she left town, would most likely become permanent, she realized in that moment. Whether it was being used by another person in New York, she had no idea. She would have to do some research to ensure that she had not complicated matters for herself.

Riley pondered her new name. How much of Riley Davenport-Westin would bleed through her new persona? Would she be able to completely bury a life that she had lived and deliberately shaped for more than thirty years? What kind of woman is Eve Campbell? What are her interests? What is her history?

Riley realized at that point that people would ask questions. Other women in the shelter would be curious about who she was and from where she came. It's the female nature, she thought. She would need to keep her distance to protect her new life from their scrutiny.

Riley felt the urgency to leave the shelter before she was found out. The journalist in her, meanwhile, was not only screaming to know what was going on in the world, but to be able to research her options.

Riley gathered her belongings before beginning her quest. One last glance in the mirror seemed to give Riley the confidence she needed. She threw back her shoulders and exhaled.

"Your life may be dead, but you're not," she whispered to the woman in the mirror. "It's time to start living again. Exit Riley Davenport-Westin. Enter Eve Campbell."

Chapter 11

"Do you have a newspaper?" Riley asked Nadine.

"Sure, Darlin'. Didn't I tell you? Our daily room service includes a newspaper at your door."

Riley furrowed her brow. This woman's sense of humor was beginning to annoy her.

Nadine handed her the Sunday edition of *The New York Times*. Before Riley could begin to digest the headlines, Nadine said, "It's a war zone out there. It's like Pearl Harbor."

Riley looked up from the newspaper, trying to understand her meaning.

"Has something else happened since Tuesday?"

"No, thank God. That devastation alone will haunt us for years to come. But for now, it's sending a scare throughout the country. The city is in complete unrest."

Nadine paused and turned her back toward Riley to get a knife from a drawer across the room. When she returned to the counter, she said, "Where were you when it happened?"

Riley blushed at the question, the first of many to come, she suspected. Her reaction did not go unnoticed by Nadine.

"On the street," Riley said.

"Yes, so I guess you saw the panic, the fear."

Riley went back to reading the newspaper, pretending not to hear Nadine's comment.

Nadine watched the intensity with which Riley devoured the news. The fact that she was interested and that she appeared to know what she was reading reflected that she was an educated woman. She noticed her perfectly cut hair; her nails that were in disrepair, but that showed signs of having had regular manicures; her trim body. She also detected the shadow of bruising around her eye.

Nadine had also inspected her clothes - all brand names. This woman was accustomed to the comforts of a life afforded in other parts of the city. While she had wanted to open her wallet to know more, she had made it her policy to never know more than the women of the shelter were prepared to tell her. Most of them, those who grew to trust her, eventually came around. Nadine would wait until they felt secure with her to tell her their stories, why they ended up homeless, and what were their lost dreams. Others who never reached that level of trust moved on, away from the shelter never to be heard from again. Still others returned from time to time needing a hideout from their problems or from people they would never be able to trust.

Nadine, while preparing supper, occasionally watched Riley turn the pages of the newspaper. She watched her intently peruse each page, her narrowed eyes scanning each word. So many women had come through the shelter over the twenty years she had been shelter manager. While the woman's features looked familiar to Nadine, she realized that she was different. She was unlike the drug addicts and young prostitutes, who were seeking a temporary safe haven from perils that existed for them on the street. She was not like the young single or divorced mothers, who were between abusive relationships. She was not like the rebellious young women tossed out by their parents, who could no longer tolerate their disobedience and disrespect.

Nadine watched Riley neatly fold the paper as she had probably done every day of her adult life.

"No, she's different. But she's also desperate," Nadine surmised. The woman seated before her had not been living on the street for very long. She suspected that whoever or whatever caused the bruising on her face had driven her to seek a new address, one unknown to anyone who would be asking.

Riley returned the newspaper to Nadine. "Thank you."

"Even her manners were impeccable," Nadine thought as she smiled at the gracious newcomer.

Meanwhile, Riley's thoughts ran over the events of the last few days.

According to the newspaper, hundreds of law enforcement officers and firefighters were missing. She read that members of the city's fire department buried one of their own on Friday. The chaplain of the city's fire department was the first to be carried away from the explosion site.

Riley recalled the chaplain from various stories either she or other reporters had done regarding the fire department. Recalling his gentle face, Riley experienced momentary sadness over the loss of the chaplain, someone else who had been only an acquaintance to her.

Also, on Friday, the President had declared a National Day of Prayer and Remembrance Service at the National Cathedral in Washington, D.C. Riley shook her head at the thought of having slept right through it. How long had she done that very thing in her everyday life - sleeping through relationships and taking them so often for granted?

Riley read that the search and rescue for bodies and body parts among the debris continued around the clock. Images of her co-workers' faces flashed through her mind and she shuddered to think of their corpses dismembered and scattered among the ashes and debris.

The New York Stock Exchange was closed, she had read. The business and financial world would take a hit from Tuesday's explosion, as well. News was certainly grim, she thought. She looked around the room in search of a television. She didn't remember seeing one since she'd arrived, so she broke down and asked, "Do you have a TV?"

"Yeah, one in disrepair," Nadine said. "But I can't justify spending money on fixing a TV when we're so in need of more important things, like food and electricity."

Her response brought a mixed blessing to Riley. She was somewhat disappointed since she was eager for more information. But she was also aware that her face might be splashed across the screen or her name mentioned among the missing from the terrorist attack. Having the television on the blink came as a relief to her for the first time in her life.

"So, they do fit."

"What?" Riley said, her thoughts interrupted by Nadine.

"Your clothes, they fit."

Riley looked down at her outfit.

"Oh, yeah. Thanks."

"I'm usually a pretty good judge of people," said Nadine. "It comes from years of sizing up the women who come and go through this house."

Riley started squirming in the chair. She blurted out a nervous chuckle. "How long have you been here?"

"Oh, too long, I think," Nadine said as she chopped vegetables on a wooden cutting board. "I quit at least once every day, sometimes twice. But no one takes me seriously.

"So, Eve, what can you tell me about yourself and your plans? How long do you plan to stay at Faith House?"

Riley was caught off guard first at hearing her new name used in context and second at Nadine's pointed questions. As a reporter in her former life, she was accustomed to being the one who asked questions. Being on the receiving end of an interrogation made her uncomfortable. Besides, she had given little thought to her plans, except to find her way out of the shelter and into a sheltered existence outside of New York. "A fresh start," Riley thought to herself. "A do-over." But she wasn't ready to share those plans with a stranger, no matter how generous and kind she had been.

"There's not much to tell," Riley said.

Suddenly feeling weak, Riley slid onto a barstool on the other side of the counter where Nadine was working.

"So how many tenants do you have here?" she said, evading the cross-examination.

"About fifteen, including you ... it fluctuates daily." Nadine noticed the ease with which she had bypassed her questions. It came as no surprise, however, since most of the women who entered Faith House avoided being put under a microscope. They had deep, dark secrets. And most of them avoided any attempts made to shed light on them. But Eve, particularly, intrigued her. In spite of her curiosity, she would wait for Eve to disclose bits and pieces of her life at her own pace. She would build her trust in the meantime.

Riley watched Nadine's skillful, repetitive motion with the knife. The way she sliced carrots, cucumbers and tomatoes brought back memories of her own mother's skillfulness in her yellow- and green-trimmed kitchen. The smell of meat cooking in the oven made her homesick. She swallowed back the lump in her throat, then asked, "Can I help?"

Nadine arched her eyebrows. She'd seldom had a tenant offer to help in all the years she'd been resident manager. She understood why since they were generally immature or self-involved in their assorted problems. The women who crossed the threshold of Faith House were generally at a point in their lives where they needed to be served and shown love. With time, they had responsibilities assigned to them, but few seldom volunteered for the mundane tasks required to operate the shelter.

"Sure, grab a knife over there," she said, pointing to a drain holding silverware. "My help called in sick today, so I could use an extra hand," she said, facetiously. "Thank you."

"What's for dinner?" Riley asked.

"Baked chicken, rice and tossed salad. It's not much, but it's been a lean month."

"It sounds wonderful to me ... really good."

"I'm afraid that Tuesday's event is going to put us all on a diet for some time."

A crease formed across Riley's forehead.

"What do you mean?"

"Donations go down whenever a national crisis or catastrophe occurs. Everybody wants to pitch in and help. Their patriotic and philanthropic spirits kick in. The problem is, they tend to split whatever amount they're already giving or throw all their weight toward the new cause. They seldom give above and beyond. When that happens, we draw the short straw."

"Oh, yeah," Riley said, recalling her awareness of the problem. She recalled at Christmastime a couple of years before a story that dealt with donations in the aftermath of Tropical Storm Alberto. The storm had hit Florida in 1994, resulting in nearly five hundred million dollars in damages. The Salvation Army and several large national charities with offices in New York had reported that their donations were down and their budgets continued to shrink because New Yorkers had shifted their giving to help storm victims. Many nonprofit organizations suffered from the ripple effect created by several years of declining resources.

"What will you do?" Riley said.

"Cut back on expenses, beg churches and benefactors to dig deeper into their pockets … and pray."

Riley couldn't help but notice that even in the face of potential hardship, Nadine's smile did not fade. It was another quality that reminded Riley of her mother - a quality she missed.

Riley had whittled the skin from a carrot and began to slice it. But she noticed the speed and accuracy with which Nadine worked. Riley recognized her own inadequacy in the kitchen. She felt compelled to increase her own speed, but when she attempted to speed up, she fumbled all the more to the point of dropping the carrot several times. She felt her face reddening.

"I don't seem to be much help to you. I'm not very good at this, I'm afraid," said Riley.

"Oh, you don't worry about that, Darlin'. The fact that you were willing speaks volumes. You'll get the hang of it. Trust me, I did."

Riley looked over at the black woman who exuded confidence and assurance. She couldn't imagine her seated in her chair, struggling to peel and slice vegetables. She appeared to Riley to have always been at home in her role.

"You give me the impression that you cut your teeth in the kitchen," Riley said while slicing the last half-inch piece of carrot.

"Do I? Years of practice, that's all. I haven't always known my way around a kitchen. As a matter of fact, I hated cooking."

Riley's look of surprise made Nadine laugh out loud.

"What happened to change your attitude about it?"

"Life, Darlin'."

Riley couldn't help but notice the rapid change in Nadine's expression. She had evidently struck a chord with Nadine with her question.

Nadine's broad smile suddenly disappeared. Her face became hard and her eyes glistened as though tears might come at any moment.

"Listen, you don't have to talk about it if you don't want to," Riley said.

"I was a successful businesswoman," Nadine proceeded without giving a thought to Riley's comment. "And I was married to a successful businessman, or so I thought."

Nadine sliced the cucumber she held with her left hand with more force and deliberation.

"I didn't know that he also had a gambling problem that would eventually lead to a drinking and drug problem," said Nadine. "Those three things don't co-exist successfully in a marriage. He became an angry, bitter, and desperate man. He often took his anger out on me. It began as verbal abuse and escalated into physical abuse."

Nadine's story and the tears that streamed down her plump cheeks aroused unexpected emotion in Riley. She, too, was moved to tears.

"One day, the abuse became so bad that he pulled out a gun and turned it on me. As I looked down the barrel of the pistol, I thought I would see Jesus that day. I told him that if taking my life would end his torment, then go ahead and shoot me. I told him that putting a bullet in me would only put me closer to meeting my maker. He did not pull the trigger."

Riley thought of the terror Nadine must have endured. Nadine's account of her abusive husband resurrected memories of Paine's episodes of rage and abuse. Nadine's story, however, made her realize how much farther he could have gone in his abuse had she not left when she did.

"I wish he had pulled the trigger."

Riley scrunched her face in astonishment over Nadine's confession. "Why?"

"Because if he had killed me, I knew where I was going."

Riley furrowed her brow - partly because she didn't understand that kind of love and sacrifice and partly because she felt deprived of not having Nadine's assurance of an afterlife.

"You see, instead of shooting me, he turned the gun on himself."

Riley's chin dropped at the unexpected ending to Nadine's story.

"That image of the last look on his face haunts me day and night."

Riley, still stunned, watched Nadine wipe tears from her face with a bottom corner of her apron.

"At first, I blamed myself for his death. Every day I asked what I could have done to prevent his suicide. Then losing everything we owned to pay off mounting debts somehow numbed the pain. At least I wouldn't be living in comfort without my husband."

Riley brushed tears from her own cheeks.

"How could you feel like that after the way he treated you?" she asked.

"You don't stop loving someone just because they have a problem. 'Til death do us part."

Riley suffered a twinge of guilt. "Was I too hasty in leaving Paine?" she wondered.

"The last straw was when I quit my job a week after his death. Looking into the face of death puts everything into perspective. I walked out of my corner office on Wall Street, packed up my silk suits and designer wear and hand-delivered them to this shelter. The manager, who had just resigned, gave me a tour. I not only fell in love with the place, but I talked her into giving me her job. I've been here ever since."

Riley ripped a paper towel from a nearby dispenser and dabbed her eyes. "Have you ever regretted leaving it all behind?"

"Every day. But only for a second. And especially those days when the plumbing fails, or one of the women needs money that I don't have so they can start over clean, or zoning hits us with an ordinance violation, and I'm fresh out of solutions."

Then out of nowhere, Nadine's broad smile reappeared and created an uncommon aura about her.

"But when I stop to think of all of the women's lives who have been turned around or saved because Faith House provided safety, refuge, a fresh start, and a new perspective, I am reminded that my loss was actually my gain. My decision was more profitable than any I ever made while working on Wall Street."

Riley tried to reason how Nadine's philosophical equation could possibly put her on the credit side of life.

"Boy, I haven't told that story in a long time. That was exhausting!" Nadine said. "Do you often have this effect on people?"

Riley did not hear the question. Her mind was sifting through the things Nadine had just told her about herself. Her story made her doubt her own decision to leave Paine. He had never pulled a gun on her. Maybe she should have stuck it out. But what if he had pointed a gun at her? Riley knew her limits, or at least she thought she did. Then again, she had never expected to stay with a man who had treated her with verbal and mental abuse. When it became physical, Paine had clearly crossed a line that Riley subconsciously had drawn in the sand. She had no desire to stick around to see just how much worse it could get for her.

She and Nadine obviously did not share common viewpoints on this matter. Riley suspected that because of their differing points of view, it was probably time to move on. Where or how, she didn't know, but definitely soon.

"There, salad's done, thanks to your assistance," Nadine said.

"I didn't do anything, really."

"Nonsense," said Nadine, flashing a smile at Riley. "Now, Eve, let's talk about you."

Riley immediately felt the heat of Nadine turning the spotlight on her. Being interrogated was the last thing she wanted.

"Uh, you know, I was wondering if I could get my backpack from you?"

"Sure, Darlin'. As a matter of fact, come with me. I'll show you where your locker is."

Riley followed Nadine, who ambled down a hallway into a back room off from the sleeping quarters. Nadine pushed open a door that led into a locker room that resembled the one used by Riley's high school gym class. Nadine walked over slowly, counting the numbers on the locker doors.

"Here it is, One-seventeen."

But then Riley saw Nadine's jaw drop and her cheerfulness transformed into anger.

"What? Oh, no!" Nadine shouted.

"What is it?"

Nadine stood mute, her nostrils flaring. She opened the locker and saw that the backpack was not as she had left it. It appeared to have been opened and ransacked. It was a familiar scene, but no less infuriating. She didn't have to question anyone to determine the culprit. She recognized the handiwork. The mode of operation was always the same. But this would be the last time.

"She has pushed me too far," Nadine said sharply.

"Who?" said Riley, still trying to fill in the blanks.

"Vivi!" Nadine's voice echoed through the shelter.

Riley stood wide-eyed and in suspense, waiting for answers.

Chapter 12

"What am I supposed to do now? That was all the money I had. How could you let this happen?"

Riley ranted and spouted questions at Nadine's back as Nadine marched down the hall to the dormitory in search of Vivi Garcia.

Nadine had been aware of Vivi's drug problem for some time. She had tried to give Vivi the benefit of the doubt since Vivi insisted over and again that she was clean. But when things started disappearing from around the shelter and money went missing from her office, Nadine could no longer deny that Vivi had a problem. So far, Vivi's thievery had just affected her. But lately, it had begun to directly impact the residents.

Nadine had a soft spot for Vivi because of her problems. She often reminded Nadine of her late husband. Vivi represented a second chance for Nadine to help someone who refused to help themselves. Vivi was much like Nadine's husband in that she was also stubborn about admitting her need for and accepting help. Nadine thought that if she failed Vivi, she would be failing her husband all over again.

"What are you going to do about this?" said Riley, who continued to pursue Nadine, following her from room to room.

Nadine ignored the barrage of questions, but charged down the hallway toward the dormitory, where Vivi hung out. When she got to the door of the sleeping quarters, she stopped and propped her hands on her hips. There was Vivi, stretched face down on her cot with her head buried under her pillow.

"Vivi Garcia!" Nadine roared.

Vivi peeked out from under the pillow upon hearing her name called. But her sluggish response indicated that she was not alarmed at Nadine's anger.

"What's all the fuss about? Can't you see I'm trying to get some sleep?" Vivi's speech was slurred.

The young Hispanic woman ducked her head back under the pillow, showing her lack of concern.

"She's already spent the money," Nadine said to herself.

"Vivi, get up! We've got to talk."

Vivi rose up on her elbows. "What have we got to talk about? I've already done my chores. Besides, it's Sunday!"

Vivi noticed for the first time that they were not alone.

"Who's she? One of your new converts?"

Vivi fell back down face first into the pillow. All Nadine could see was a mound of brunette tresses.

"Vivi, get up now! You've got two minutes to meet me in my office. If you're not there, then you're out of here."

"Okay, okay! I might as well get up since you won't let me sleep."

Nadine turned and ambled toward her office, leaving Riley behind. Riley stood at the doorway and glared at the woman, who had robbed her of her money, her way out of the shelter, and of her future. She clenched her jaw and flared her nostrils as her piercing eyes were locked on the woman, still stretched across the cot. She watched her slowly roll over, swing her feet around, and plant them on the floor. Vivi rested her head in her hands as she mustered energy to stand. When she looked up, her eyes met Riley's angry stare.

"What are you looking at?"

Without hesitation, Riley snapped back, "I'm looking at the person who stole my last chance. I want my money back, do you hear?"

A firm voice came from the direction of Nadine's office.

"Eve."

Riley did not recognize her new name at that point. Her thoughts were consumed by anger.

"Eve!"

Nadine's booming voice startled her, bringing her back to her senses. Riley turned her attention to Nadine, who stood at the doorway of her office.

"I'll take care of this," Nadine said, her tone softened again. "Why don't you be a dear and check on the chicken in the oven. We'll be eating soon."

Food was Riley's last concern. She wanted her money and she wanted to get out of there.

She shot one last disapproving look at Vivi, whose nonchalance over the matter only further enraged Riley.

"Eve, please," Nadine said.

"Sure!" Riley said.

She slowly pivoted toward the kitchen and trudged down the hall. Anger swelled up inside her and became so overwhelming that she thought she would implode. She replayed the events of the previous thirty minutes in her mind as she did what Nadine asked and gave a cursory look at the chicken baking in the oven. She slammed the oven door shut, then snatched the oven mitt off her hand and threw it across the counter.

Riley paced back and forth in the middle of the room as she waited for Nadine to return with her money. She stopped for a glass of water. She leaned back against the counter to sip the water and cool her anger. She fumed knowing that her future was being determined by what was being said in Nadine's office while she was left to stand guard over baked chicken.

"What if she doesn't have the money? What if she's spent it?" Riley reasoned silently. "What is my recourse? I can't go to the police. I don't have money to obtain a lawyer and small claims court is out of the question."

"I cannot believe this!" she said aloud, before slamming the glass down on the floor. Riley buried her head in her hands to catch the rush of tears to follow. She collapsed on the floor under the weight of her dilemma. She felt her world crashing down around her. With her money gone, she had no options. She had not planned for poverty, even after having escaped almost being robbed earlier in the week.

"Oh, God, what am I going to do? What am I going to do? I can't do this."

"Can't do what?"

Riley jumped up from her sprawled position on the floor and turned her back to Deidra while she composed herself. She had no idea that Deidra had returned. Riley was both startled by Diedra's question and irritated to find that she wasn't alone.

"And who started World War III?" Deidra continued with her questions, pretending to ignore the condition in which she found the new girl. "I heard the crash at the other end of the center," she said.

Riley was embarrassed once again for Deidra to see her in an emotional state.

Deidra cocked her head to try to get a better look at Riley's face. Deidra could see that she was still upset. She wondered what was causing her so much distress, but held back from prying.

"Should I go get Nadine again? She's better at this sort of thing than I am."

"No, no, please don't. She'll be along shortly, I'm sure," said Riley. "Besides, I'm fine," she said, wishing she could believe her own words.

Deidra saw a glimmer from shards of glass on the floor. She walked over to the pantry and reached for a broom and dust pan. She began sweeping up the broken glass.

'I'm sorry," Riley said. "I can get that."

"No problem. Nadine says I don't do enough around here to help, anyway, so you can be a witness to my productivity."

After sweeping up the glass, Deidra jumped up and sat on the counter, with her legs dangling off the side.

"Nadine hates it when I sit on the kitchen counter." Deidra snickered. "But, she's not here, so it's our secret."

Riley cast a sideways glance at the young woman, who was reveling in her deception.

"There seems to be a lot of things going on behind the scenes in this place," Riley thought.

"Where is she? I'm getting hungry," said Deidra, inquiring about Nadine.

"She's in a meeting."

"A meeting? Are the board members here? The auditors? Was it a surprise visit? Nadine usually lets us know when they're coming so we can scatter."

Riley wrinkled her brow at Deidra's rapid-fire questions.

"She keeps you hidden away from visitors?"

"No! No, that's not it." Deidra giggled at the suggestion. "We just don't care anything about being inspected by a bunch of suits. What could they possibly know about what we go through? Nothing, I can tell you.

"Sure, we've probably got a place to stay because they occasionally open their fat checkbooks. But when they come around, you can just feel 'em looking down their noses at you. We'd rather avoid that."

Deidra snatched up a raw carrot and bit off an end. She quickly chewed and swallowed, eager to finish her thought.

"They sit in their corner offices and look down on people like us as though we were ants in their path to be trampled. Then at the end of the day, they go to their penthouses or suburban homes, where they tell their children happily-ever-after stories. The difference is, when they tell their children those stories, they're more likely to come true."

Deidra nibbled another bite off the carrot.

Riley had noticed an innocence about Deidra from the moment she pounced on the cot in the dormitory. But there was a cynical side to her nature. Riley perceived that possibly she had been dealt some hard blows.

"When we tell our children those stories," Deidra continued, "they're a little less believable. What right do they have to come down here every few months and pass judgment on us? None, I can tell you."

Riley detected the bitterness in Deidra's tone. But Deidra's reference to "our children" piqued her curiosity.

"You have children?" Riley posed.

"Yeah, one. I have a daughter."

Riley's eyes widened at the thought of this young girl having a girl of her own.

"How old are you?"

"18."

"How old is your daughter?"

"She's two."

"Where's her father?"

"Dead. He was killed in a gang brawl over drug money."

"When?"

"Before my baby was born."

"Oh," said Riley, who was trying to comprehend how someone so young could have met with so much tragedy so early in life. Deidra was both a mother and a widow at age fifteen, Riley calculated. Riley could not imagine at that moment dealing with either at such a young age.

"What did you do? Do you have family?"

Her curiosity overcame her desire to maintain her distance.

"No. My parents are dead. The gang I was a member of was my family until it cost B.Z. his life. When I found out I was pregnant, I knew I couldn't risk endangering my daughter's life, so I ditched that scene."

"Where did you go?"

"From shelter to shelter. I thought I had run through them all, until a year ago when I stumbled onto the doorstep of Faith House. I was sick. Nadine took me in, nursed me back to health. She gave me a safe place to live, and helped me get on my feet."

"Where is your baby now?"

"With my grandmother ... she's raising her until I can get on my feet. She didn't approve of B.Z., so I left home years ago. I didn't handle things so good after Mom and Dad died." She shrugged her shoulders and turned up one side of her mouth in regret. "What can I say?"

"What's your little girl's name?"

"Zoe."

Riley caught the warm smile that automatically crossed Deidra's face when pronouncing her daughter's name.

"I always like the 'Zee' in her father's name. His name was actually Bobby Zane Cassitty, but I didn't want a girl named 'Zane,' so I improvised."

Riley thought it admirable that Deidra had wanted her daughter to carry on her father's name. She had once dreamed of having children of her own. She had assumed there would be a Paine Chandler Westin V. She had imagined they would call him "Chandler" to prevent confusion with his father's and grandfathers' names.

Deidra chomped on the carrot while staring at Riley. She couldn't help but notice red splotches on Riley's face - lingering signs that she'd been crying.

"You know, when I first came here, all I did was cry, too."

Riley said nothing. She just looked back at the young woman, taking in her youthfulness and sizing up the vast gap in their ages and attitudes. Riley's attention slowly went to Deidra's apparel: Her bleached, frayed jeans, her black T-shirt with the words, "Delightfully tacky, yet unrefined," across her chest, and her soiled Nikes.

"Nadine has so many rules. I guess you've figured that out by now. She's really strict. And, of course, when she explained that her rules were to help us, not harm us, it was a really difficult pill to swallow.

"I really give her grief about her many 'Thou shalt nots.'" Deidra chuckled to herself. "She's really cool about it, though. Anybody else would have kicked me out by now. Not Nadine.

"After a week here, I started feeling like I was in a jail cell. I was resistant and frustrated and not a happy camper. Then one day, Nadine sat me down and we had a heart-to-heart talk.

"Well, actually, she talked and I listened," said Deidra, smiling as she recalled the conversation. "That day, she became the mother I didn't have. She also reminded me that I was a mother and that Zoe is looking to me for boundaries. Since I had been a gang member, I understood boundaries. She said that what we must be cautious of are things outside those boundaries because they often lead to trouble. Within our territory is safety in numbers and protection. There, family members support and encourage each other and have each others' backs. And that rules aren't the enemy, but are what we use to set the boundaries that protect us against the enemy.

"Without rules, she said, there would be no way of distinguishing good from bad, or dangerous ground from home turf. She made me understand that mine and Zoe's freedom to live without always looking over our shoulders or being frightened for our lives would come from living within the rules," Deidra said. "Anyway, I finally came to realize how much she really cares about us."

Riley listened intently to Deidra. She thought of her own life, how she had always followed the rules. She had believed that following a set of standards would lead to happiness and prosperity and few problems. But here she was, listening to the story of a young woman whose life had started on the wrong road and who was explaining to her the facts of life, according to Nadine.

Riley thought at that moment how she had stayed on the beaten path, but had lost everything in the course of following rules. Thinking about what doing the right thing had cost her, she became angry all over again. She began pacing and wondering what was taking Nadine so long to recover her money.

Without warning, Deidra, who heard familiar footsteps, jumped off the counter and nonchalantly leaned against it. About that time, Nadine rounded the corner. Riley stopped pacing and perked up at her reappearance.

"Well?" Riley said.

"Deidra, would you mind giving Eve and me a few minutes alone, please?"

"When are we going to eat? I'm starving," Deidra demanded.

"In about thirty minutes. Wait fifteen minutes and start rounding everyone up, will you?"

"Sure," Deidra said. "Oh, by the way, I swept the kitchen floor," she said, winking at Riley as she walked past her.

"Thank you," said Nadine, who gave no thought to Deidra's admission. Her eyes were locked on Riley, who glared back at her.

When she was confident that Deidra was out of ear shot, she pointed to the table and chairs in the dining hall nearby. "Let's have a seat, Eve. It's been a long day and I need to take a load off."

Riley's heart was beating out of her chest. She had the feeling that Nadine was stalling, so she emotionally prepared for bad news.

"Whew," said Nadine, once seated.

Nadine cupped her forehead in her left hand. Unbeknownst to Riley, Nadine was offering up a silent prayer before starting her conversation.

Riley's eyes narrowed as she looked quizzically at the woman, and wondered why she continued stalling. Riley's patience had run thin and she opened her mouth to speak when Nadine lifted her head. She looked directly into Riley's eyes and said, "Eve, I'm sorry, Darlin'. This is partly my fault."

"I don't understand. Your fault?"

"Yes. I've known for some time that Vivi has a problem, but I've tried to help her. Unfortunately, I went about it the wrong way. I thought I was helping by turning my head, trusting her, and ignoring the truth."

"What kind of problem?"

"Drugs. She came to Faith House straight from a drug rehabilitation program mandated by the state. She's been straight for nearly a year, but it seems that one of her junkie friends saw her at work one day. Her friend was kind enough to show her what she had been missing. Misery loves company, you know."

Nadine hung her head and massaged her temple, wanting both her headache and the problem to go away.

"What about my money?"

Nadine paused to cast another plea up to God for help before she lifted her head to answer.

"Well?" Riley pressed.

Nadine fought against the inevitable. She didn't want to be the one to tell her that Vivi had blown her money on drugs, but she had no choice. Nadine raised her head and said, "It's gone, Eve. It's all gone."

Nadine's voice quavered when delivering the bad news.

Riley tightened her jaw and bobbed her head up and down, allowing the bad news to sink in. Overcome by anger, she was unsure how to react. She fought back the tears that filled her eyes.

"Great! Just great! What am I supposed to do now? That money was all the security I had. Now what? Can you tell me that?"

Nadine was suddenly overcome with confidence. She sat up straight and threw back her shoulders. She looked squarely at Eve and found courage to answer her questions with firmness and compassion.

"Eve, I'm sorry that you think that because your money is gone, that your life is over. While it may look like Faith House is a dead-end for you, I beg to differ.

"First of all, it's no accident that you appeared on my doorstep in the dead of night," Nadine said. "We were a safe haven for you that night and we will continue to be a safe haven for you for as long as you are a resident here.

"Vivi is checking back into rehab, so whatever belongings she did not take from you and, Heaven forbid, anyone else, should be safe while she's in treatment," she continued. "She gets one more chance here to correct her life. One more slip-up and she's out for good. She's aware of that. Next time, I promise not to be so lenient on her. In the meantime, I suggest that if you have any other valuables, that you allow me to lock them up in our safe."

Riley wiped away tears as fast as they rolled down her cheeks. Nadine wasn't telling her exactly what she wanted to hear.

"Now, as for your question, 'What are you supposed to do?' I can make only one suggestion. I cannot repay your money in one lump sum. I'm neither insured for this, nor do I have that kind of money accessible to me. Also, it's not fair for me to ask you to do what I'm about to ask. But my guess, Eve, is that your name isn't really Eve," Nadine said.

Riley's head dropped. She could not make eye contact with this woman, who had blurted out what she thought had been a safe-guarded secret. Her beet red face gave her away. She braced for Nadine's next comment.

"I would also venture to say that you are running from something or someone. Since you were living on the street, you most likely have not managed to acquire false IDs with your new identity, so you probably don't have a job, either."

Riley waited for the hammer to come down, deciding her fate. She mustered courage to look directly at Nadine, who would determine her future with her next few words. Would she call the police? Did she know more than she was sharing? Riley held her breath in anticipation.

"So I have a proposition for you. You need a paying job and I need an assistant shelter manager. As you can already see, there is a lot of work to be done here. I can't do it all alone. The job comes with room and board and free meals. The hours are long and hard, but rewarding. I will pay you a bi-weekly salary. If you want to leave after you've recouped your losses, I'll give you a reference to take to your next employer.

"What do you say?"

Riley was stunned at the offer. She could no longer keep her tears at bay. She had expected Nadine to eject her from Faith House penniless, jobless, and exposed to the authorities for the fraud she was. Instead, she had shown her mercy - her, a stranger - without first knowing her real name or her history.

"I don't understand. You don't know anything about me. Why would you gamble on someone like me, someone you don't know?"

Nadine chuckled at Riley's question.

"Darlin', weren't you paying attention earlier to my story? My husband … God rest his soul … gambled on the world and lost his soul. I want to win souls. So I gamble on life, hurting women, and God's will."

Nadine paused, then reached out and took Riley's hand and held it gently in hers. The gesture caused Riley to break down sobbing, her anger dissolving with each tear she shed.

"Eve, you're different from other women who've come here. I recognized it immediately. I prayed for someone who would help take some of the burden of responsibility for this place off me."

Riley said between sniffles, "But you seem to have everything under control here. And Deidra says you're like a mother to the women. What do I know about that? I'm not a mother. What makes you think I'm the answer to anyone's prayer?"

"I have no children, either, Darlin'. But that's not what qualifies you to mentor other women," Nadine said. "I see the necessary qualities it takes in you. Trust me, you've got what it takes."

Then Riley noticed an unexplainable glow fall upon Nadine's smiling face.

"I know that you're the answer to my prayer because I've had peace from the moment I laid eyes on you on Friday. And I won't always have things under control, Eve."

Riley sensed there was underlying meaning to her statement.

"Why won't you?"

"Well, I'll let you in on my secret now that I've apparently guessed yours."

Riley sheepishly looked away to hide her embarrassment.

"But I must ask that you not share it with anyone," Nadine said, sternly.

Riley immediately looked back at Nadine and nodded in agreement to Nadine's request.

"I'm sick, Eve … Cancer."

Riley's jaw dropped. Again, she thought, this news was not what she expected to hear.

"I have no idea how much longer I'll be able to serve as resident manager. But I've told God that I want to leave Faith House in good hands when the time comes for me to leave."

Astonishment gripped Riley, who stared into the face of a dying woman.

In just a few hours, Nadine had soft-pedaled her way into Riley's heart and in a split second, announced that Riley should not get attached to her. Only days earlier, Riley had experienced the loss of people with whom she had spent many more days and hours. None of them, however, had connected with her so quickly or as deeply in such a short amount of time as the woman seated across from her whose face gave off an indescribable light.

Riley searched her facial features, but detected no signs of fear, only a peace with which Riley could not relate. In that face, Riley found her answer. She wanted that look, that expression, that secret that Nadine wasn't revealing. If it could be discovered at Faith House, Riley wanted the opportunity to find it. So far, she had seen little evidence of it outside the walls of the shelter.

In all of her years of pursuing a career, she had run across individuals who possessed that same expression, that same glow. Brigette's face immediately sprang to mind. It had intrigued her and even mystified her. But it had never captivated her as it did this moment. Nadine's expression held a familiarity that she could not quite recall.

"So, Eve, what do you say? Will you grant a dying woman's last request?"

Riley's face drew up in shock.

"Oh, I'm just kidding. Where's your sense of humor? I may be dying, but I'm not dead. Until then, I hope there's always room for laughs, Darlin'. Lighten up!"

Nadine cackled at her own sense of humor. Riley fought hard to keep a smile from creeping onto her own face. But Nadine's laughter was infectious.

"Ooh, Darlin', life is short, so short. Seriously, though, will you be my assistant here at Faith House? Or are you going to send me back to my knees praying that God will send me your understudy?"

Nadine tilted her head slightly and arched her eyebrows, as though begging Riley to say "Yes."

Before Riley could say anything, they heard Deidra singing her way down the hall. A curly mop of hair popped around the corner. "I hope everything's copacetic now with you two because the rest of us are starving," Deidra said. "We've been patient long enough. Like it or not, we're starting without you," said the energetic woman as she bounced into the kitchen and proceeded to pull plates from a cabinet shelf.

Behind was a line of women following her into the kitchen. Riley saw for the first time the women, who combined to make up Faith House. How many of them had come to the shelter because they were victims of physical abuse or even sexual abuse? Riley's eyes scanned the many women, some who nodded at her, some who flashed her a welcoming smile. Some avoided eye contact with her. Others, like her, had secrets and feared opening themselves up to this newcomer. Riley wondered which ones were far from their real homes either because they were cast out or were running away. Which ones, she wondered, had lost loved ones and were orphans in the world.

Suddenly, Riley felt a connection with not just Nadine, but the residents, too. Had she found a home? Time would tell.

"Yeah, Deidra, everything's copacetic," Riley spoke up, directing her comments toward Nadine. Nadine nodded and gave a knowing smile, indicating that she understood Riley's meaning. "By the way," Riley said to Deidra, "I hope you don't snore. I'd hate to have to move your cot into the dining hall every night."

Riley glanced sideways at Nadine, who was smiling at her new assistant. Nadine formed the words, "Thank you," with her mouth. Riley smiled broadly at her new boss.

"My cot? I was here first," Deidra said, joining in the friendly banter. "By the way, are you two going to help or just sit there watching us work?" Deidra blurted out.

Riley and Nadine exchanged looks of amusement at Deidra's energy and willfulness. They simultaneously shook their heads, then arose together to pitch in with the work left to be done.

Chapter 13

A month of cleanup at Ground Zero turned up rings, watches, a set of keys, credit cards, driver's licenses, and body parts - all identifiers of loss of life.

But nothing that had been excavated by search and rescue at the explosion site offered proof to Paine that Riley was among those killed.

Paine was anxious to move forward on Riley's death claim. The more he dodged Joe Weitzmann's calls, the more eager Paine was to get his hands on the money that would put an end to his annoying phone calls. Paine knew time was running out. It was becoming increasingly urgent that he replace the money he had borrowed before Joe discovered it missing. He only hoped that Joe had not become suspicious, but was pacified by his explanation for refusing his calls, that he was grieving the loss of Riley.

Paine would milk the excuse for as long as possible. He had come to believe that 9/11 had put the whole world on hold. The timing of the surprise attacks on America and subsequent mailings of anthrax-tainted envelopes and packages by terrorists to select media and to Capitol Hill were working to Paine's advantage. As long as they served as a diversion for the rest of the world, they would buy him time.

Paine had been negotiating with banks and other private investors for months to try and recover Joe's one million dollars, plus money paid in by other investors. Joe had contributed the lion's share of capital made to Paine's newest company, P.W. Developments. But since throwing his cash into the fledgling company, Joe insisted on weekly, sometimes daily reports of the company's activities. Paine was not only uncomfortable with Joe's desire to micro-manage the company, but also with the control Joe exerted as a result of his monetary participation. Paine was finding it more and more difficult to stay several steps ahead of him.

Joe had retired after forty years in the banking industry. He had rapidly risen to the top of one of the city's major financial institutions partly for two reasons: his conservation philosophy on managing the bank's reserves and stringent credit standards required for borrowers. He managed the bank's money as he would his own: wisely, frugally, and closely. Because of his attitude toward his personal finances, he and his wife lived modestly, not buying into the superficial expectations set by New York's elite. They hobnobbed with the city's Who's Who, but did not get lost in the crowd by keeping up with the Joneses. Their charitable donations generally put them at the top of the lists of leading philanthropists of their favorite charities. Otherwise, there was little in their appearance and frugal lifestyles that caused Joe and Ethel Weitzmann to stand out in the crowd in other New York settings. Someone usually had to point out, much to one's dismay, that Joe was the president of one of America's largest banks. He wore humility as comfortably as the bargain basement suits on his back.

Because of his humble posture, Paine had underestimated his keen sense and sharp attentiveness to business matters. Paine had always suspected Joe to be easy-going, possibly a pushover, but best of all, generous with his money.

Since he had been unable to take out another loan with the bank or to restructure the debt, he was on borrowed time waiting for the outcome of Riley's death statement. He didn't know how much longer he'd be able to stall. Joe was getting antsy for details.

Paine paced back and forth in his office. He felt like a caged lion in the penthouse office suite, where he had spent the night. He had gone over the numbers late into the night in search of some way to temporarily siphon the funds from the payroll and pension account within the new company. The most he was able to find, however, was one hundred thousand dollars from an untapped, high-rate line-of-credit from a foreign venture-capital lender. He knew absconding with employees' pension funds would violate federal law and lead to even stiffer charges - a risk he would be willing to take. He had not realized how strapped his company was. He had sworn his financial vice president to secrecy, assuring him that it would soon be resolved.

But if light didn't break soon, Paine would be responsible for the gloomy downfall of the new company and of Westin Company, founded and operated successfully by several generations before him. "How could I have been so irresponsible?" he thought. He stopped behind his desk and fiddled with a pencil, trying to muster enthusiasm for the work splayed out on his desk.

"It was just a few temporary loans to help window-dress the company's financial ratings," he reasoned. Paine sat down, dropped the pencil and ran his fingers through his already tousled hair.

Then his mind ran to the five hundred thousand dollar proceeds of one company loan that he had pocketed for his own personal use in a Cayman bank debit account. The loan never hit the company's books. He used the money to show Sarah a good time without flagging Riley's attention to unexplained expenditures from their personal bank account. It had paid for trips for two to Italy, Vegas and a Mediterranean cruise. He had become known as a good tipper with the jet charter services. Although he had every intention of returning the funds to the company, time passed and it grew easier to ignore the debt.

Paine wrung his hands together, anxious for news. But he wasn't hoping for the kind of news that so many families in New York were wanting to hear - that their loved one working in the World Trade Center had survived the devastation.

Paine had in his mind already buried the memories he'd shared with Riley. He had killed any hope of hearing that Riley was alive. As a matter of fact, he had also killed off Riley in his heart. He wished her dead and longed for proof positive of her demise to surface so that his problems could be laid to rest.

"Buzz. Buzz."

Paine jumped at the sound. He had never gotten accustomed to the annoying intercom system that linked him to his secretary.

"Good morning, Mr. Westin. You have a phone call."

Paine rolled his eyes. It had been a long night and he was in no mood for interruptions.

"Hold all my calls, Pat. I don't want to be disturbed."

"Mr. Westin, he says he's an insurance claims representative calling regarding your wife's death claim."

Paine perked up and knocked over his pencil holder while trying to grab the phone.

"Pat, I'll take this call, but no more," he said, excitedly. Recognizing his excited state, Paine deliberately slowed his breathing. He swallowed hard before engaging himself as the grief-stricken widower he pretended to be.

"This is Paine Westin. How can I help you?"

The deep male voice on the other end identified himself as Martin Beasley, a claims representative with the life insurance company that carried Riley's life insurance policy.

"Mr. Westin, I'm calling, actually, to help you. Do you suppose that I could meet with you?"

"How soon, uh, I mean, when?" Paine said, trying not to let his eagerness get the best of him.

"I can meet with you tomorrow, if that's convenient."

Paine pretended to look at his calendar.

"Well, I have a busy schedule, but I suppose I could meet with you tomorrow morning. How about 10 a.m. in my office?"

"That time is good for me," Mr. Beasley said.

Paine hung up, a smugness illuminating his face. He leaned back in his chair with his hands folded behind his head.

"Riley, may you rest in peace. Thanks to you, I'm going to have peace at last - and a healthy bottom line."

Paine smiled broadly at the thought of the ten million dollar life insurance proceeds that would soon be his and the debts that would be zeroed out. Then his only charge, if his financial activities were discovered, would be commingling of company funds with personal funds, a much lesser charge than embezzlement.

"Yes, indeed, and we'll all live happily ever after."

Paine laughed out loud, as he spun around in his executive chair. At that moment, he felt once again like he was on top of the world.

Chapter 14

Paine had given Pat specific instructions to clear his calendar that morning. He didn't want anything to interfere with his meeting with Mr. Beasley.

The previous afternoon had been quiet. Joe had apparently given up and stopped calling. He had not on the day before had to refuse any of his phone calls. But he had experienced a restless night. He had tossed and turned throughout the night, trying to settle the issue of how the death claim should be distributed. It was tempting to take the money and buy a yacht so that he and Sarah could sail off into the horizon. But that was not the way he envisioned either spending or making his next million. He wasn't ready to join Joe Weitzmann among the ranks of the retired. But if he didn't turn things around soon, he would be in the unemployment line or behind prison bars. He had plans for Westin Company. As of late, it had begun waning in profits. Paine admitted only to himself that his head had not been in the game. Juggling the women in his life had distracted him from concerns that cried out for his attention at the office. His board had also begun to pressure Paine to turn things around. He sensed that his board members were losing confidence in him.

Paine had established P.W. Developments with legitimate intentions to develop a fifty-acre parcel in upstate new York. The farmland would be transformed into an upscale, multi-use residential and commercial development, a gated community for the rich and famous. But lately he had found more use for P.W. Developments as a dummy company from which to siphon funds from private investors for his use. At the beginning, it had been so easy. It had been a tricky balancing act. But lately, the scales had been tipping since Westin's profits were steadily declining and his nerves were wearing thin.

Alas, his struggles would soon be over.

Paine had arrived early at the office to peruse both companies' accounts to determine how much and how quickly money needed to be allocated to pay back what he owed. As soon as he had the insurance benefits in hand, he wanted them immediately distributed to the outstanding loans and to the payroll and pension accounts at P.W. Developments.

When he heard Pat stirring at her desk, he instructed her to have tea and coffee brought in when his ten o'clock appointment arrived.

Paine mentally readied for Mr. Beasley, who he intended to treat like royalty. He wanted their meeting to come off without a hitch. It could mean the difference between Paine's success or failure. Paine looked at his Rolex and saw that he still had an hour before their meeting. He got up from his leather chair and walked over to the floor-to-ceiling wall of glass that opened his office to a panoramic view of the city's skyline. Standing at the window that abutted the sky restored Paine's confidence in himself as the president of the company. He crossed his arms over his chest and looked over the hundreds of businesses that together made this section of New York the thriving, competitive financial center it was. He was reminded that his company had historically hit bumps in the road, but had continued to rise to the top. It would again, he reassured himself as he scoured the rooftops below.

He had followed in the footsteps of successful Westins that had come before him. He wondered if any of them had strayed outside the bounds of the law to achieve their goals or satisfy their desires. He wondered what his father would think of his unscrupulous money transactions. Would he understand that he had done it for love? Then he thought of his father's strict, moral code of conduct.

"No, he most likely would not condone my financial dealings," Paine reasoned. "But would he at least forgive me?"

Soon, it would not be an issue, he resolved to himself.

Paine exhaled, releasing the days and weeks of tension that had built up inside him. He looked out over the city and envisioned his future with Sarah at his side. He would finally have it all - the loves of his life: wealth, position, success, and the woman of his dreams. Fate was, undoubtedly, shining upon him.

"Buzz. Buzz."

Paine's face instantly became like a chiseled stone at the sound of his secretary intruding upon his reflective moment. He walked over to his desk.

"Pat, I gave you specific instructions. What could possibly be more important?"

"Mr. Westin, you have two visitors ... urgent visitors."

Paine shook his head in disbelief. The last thing he had told her was, "No visitors." He bit his tongue, trying to choose his words carefully in spite of the anger he felt at having to deal with his secretary's incompetence.

"Do our visitors have names?" he asked, sarcastically.

"Yes. Mitch McConnell and Carlos Himinez."

"I don't know either Mr. McConnell or Mr. Himinez," said Paine, losing his patience.

A moment of silence made him think he had made his point, but then he heard his secretary break through the intercom again. Her voice was nervous and hesitant as she briefed her boss on his surprise callers.

"Mr. Westin, they say they're with the FBI."

Paine, whose legs became like jello and his face ashen, was struck silent. He slumped down into his chair and squeezed the arm rests to try to stop the room from spinning. His mouth went dry and his pulse began racing.

"Mr. Westin? Shall I show them in?"

Paine tried to focus on her question, but that one introduction sent his world spiraling out of control.

"Uh, yes, of course."

He heard his voice mutter something, but could not recall either Pat's or his exchange. He could hear nothing for the echo in his ears that reverberated that dreaded acronym: FBI. One second he had dreamed of his future. The next second threw him into a nightmare. He glanced once more at the open sky outside his window before rising to let the two agents into his office.

Chapter 15

The sound of a knock on Riley's bedroom door broke her concentration. She arose from her bed, where she had been enthralled in a Madison Ranew mystery novel.

She opened the door to find Nadine on the other side. But one look at Nadine and she knew instantly that something was amiss.

"Eve, there's someone here to see you. He says he's your husband."

No sooner had the words left Nadine's lips than Paine was switching places with Nadine. Terror loomed as large as the figure standing in front of her.

"Hello, Riley," her debonair husband said. A smug look of satisfaction shone on his face.

Riley couldn't help but notice how his Armani suit, his perfectly coiffed hair, stiff with gel, immaculately manicured nails, and shiny leather shoes looked out of place at Faith House.

"It's good to see you again. I thought I'd lost you forever."

Riley's chin dropped. She stood speechless at the sight of him. Foremost, she feared his reaction at finding her at the shelter. She anticipated one of his fists plunging toward her face or her mid-section, as history might repeat itself.

"It's time to go home," he said with a sardonic smile that transformed into a wicked laugh.

"No," said Riley, shaking her head and backing away from him.

His laughter grew and filled the room with such volume that she shrank back from him. The security she had come to know at Faith House disappeared and was replaced by terror as she watched him throw back his head and heard the loud echo of his terrifying laughter.

"No!" Riley yelled, trying to be heard over his boisterous laugh. "No! I won't! No!" she screamed.

Riley stepped backwards to get away from Paine, who closed in on her, until she felt her back pressed against the wall of her tiny bedroom.

"No!" she continued to scream – her only defense against the man whom she knew to be a threat. Then from somewhere in the background, she heard the gentle, familiar voice of a woman calling her.

"Eve … Eve!"

Between her own screams and Paine's laughter, she heard the comforting voice.

"Eve, it's okay. Eve!"

Riley recognized the voice as Nadine's. But her friend was nowhere in sight. Even though she could not be seen, her voice transcended Riley's perilous situation. The more Nadine called to her, the more Paine's laughter subsided and greater the distance between them became. As a result, she cried out less and less until all she could hear was Nadine's tender consolation, saying, "Eve, it's over. It's all over, Darlin'."

Riley opened her eyes upon feeling the physical touch of Nadine's arms around her.

"Where is he?"

"Who? Who, Eve?"

Riley stretched to look around the room and around the door frame to the hallway to see if Paine was lurking outside the room. It took a while before she was convinced that Nadine was right, that it was over, and that Paine was not there. It was just her and Nadine in her little room at Faith House. She sat up in the bed, rubbed her eyes, and ran her hand across her face to help bring clarity to her vision and her sensory perception.

"See … it was just a nightmare," said Nadine, seated beside her on the bed.

Riley looked again past Nadine's full figure to inspect the room for assurance that they were alone. When she was certain that they were, she gazed through sleepy eyes at Nadine, whose raised eyebrows indicated that she wanted details as to the nature of Riley's bad dream. Riley did not respond. Despite her silence, Nadine stared back, still wanting. Instead of satisfying Nadine's curiosity, Riley reached out and surprised Nadine with a tight, lingering hug. When she finally released Nadine, she simply said, "Thank you … I'm sorry if I woke you."

"No, actually, I was trying to wake you. You overslept. It's time to get moving. We've got to get ready for tomorrow's guests, remember?"

Riley rubbed sleep from her eyes again, trying also to clear the fog from her head.

"Oh, yeah, I remember," Riley said, followed by an eye roll. "I'm getting up."

Nadine stood from her place at Riley's side and before ducking out of her room, turned back and said, "If you need to talk about what upset you, I'm free to talk anytime. You know that, don't you?"

Riley nodded affirmatively and then covered her face again with her hands as she recovered from her nightmare. She could still vividly see Paine standing at her door and hear his menacing laughter.

"What if it had been real?" she asked herself. "What if he actually did show up at my door? What would I do?"

She withered under the terrifying thought and slunk down under the sheets. She stared up at the ceiling. She closed her eyes, but quickly opened them for fear that she might return to that place where Paine waited for her in her dreams. The very thought of being face-to-face with him – even in her sleep – motivated her to begin stirring and move into her day. She flung back the covers and climbed out of bed and thrust herself into action.

But the nightmare had left an imprint on her mind. Memories of Paine, her marriage and her comfortable, luxurious life with him crept into her daily routine, causing her remorse and discontent throughout the day. While bent over the dingy tile floor of one of the shelter bathrooms with a scrub brush in hand, she visualized each of the rooms in the Park Avenue home she had left behind. Oak-paneled walls, Persian rugs, crystal chandeliers, mosaic tiles, and clean, freshly painted walls adorned with brass-trimmed mirrors, sconces, and brocade wall-hangings had enhanced the thirty-five million dollar residence. Imported, antique furnishings and accessories added to their comfort, all coming together to create a showcase of grandeur and elegance that was often the envy of their guests.

Paine had instructed Riley to spare no expense when decorating their new home the first year of their marriage. He also requested that their home reflect impeccable taste and the style and traditions of the Westin family. To her credit, Riley had assembled the décor with close assistance from one of New York's notable interior designers – a woman who also had decorated the stately homes of Paine's parents and other members of the Westin family. Without the woman's expertise the result would not have been a sophisticated and distinguished New York home, but a fraction of what Paine had expected. Riley realized that she lacked the skills. She did not grow up surrounded by the finery Paine was accustomed to having. She was certain her idea of decorating would have reflected her meager upbringing. Interior design was one elective she had inadvertently overlooked in college. With the professional interior designer's touch, the result was that Paine felt very much at home. Looking back, Riley realized that she could not say that, but at least it was nicer than her current address.

Riley pressed down harder on the scrub brush while trying to remove a stubborn stain on the permanently marred and tattered tile floor. She grew angrier that she had fallen so far from where she had worked all her life to be. Scrubbing floors was one of the many vocations in life from which she had fled. She felt at that moment that she had sunk to her lowest point.

"Had life with Paine really been so bad? Bad enough to leave everything she had always dreamed of? Other women have endured a lot more in exchange for security," she reasoned. The one-sided argument in her head fueled anger inside her that she had carefully sealed away.

After months at the shelter, she was surprised at how she had adapted to her new way of living, which included helping with assigned chores like scrubbing floors, washing dishes, cooking, washing linens, and cleaning bathrooms, among other mundane tasks. She had grown accustomed to the sound of dripping faucets, to light fixtures with blown light bulbs, tattered and soiled furnishings, and broken or cracked mirrors. With each passing day, she had begun to pay less attention to the faded, cracked and peeling wallpaper, the dull, smudged walls in much need of fresh paint, and ceilings with peeling paint. The lime-stained faucets and rusted plumbing and corroded bathtubs and shower stalls bothered her less than they did when she first arrived – at least, not until today. Today, it all bothered her – immensely.

The memory of Paine was tied to all other memories, including those of her beautiful, clean, comfortable, and posh home overlooking Central Park. Thoughts of him prodded thoughts of her exquisite walk-in closets that were more like rooms unto themselves and that were filled with designer clothes, accessories, and lingerie – nothing secondhand.

The more she thought of the luxuries she had walked away from, the harder she scrubbed and the tighter she clenched her jaw. The anger raged inside until she could no longer contain it. She slammed the scrub brush against the wall and curled up cross-legged on the tile floor island, surrounded by soapy water, and sobbed as she longed for her "paradise lost."

Seconds later, Riley heard someone knock on the door of the bathroom. She muffled her sobs so that no one could hear. Another few seconds passed and Riley heard pounding at the door.

"Are you okay?" a woman's voice could be heard saying.

Riley quieted herself long enough to yell, "I'm fine!" To discourage any further attention, she reached up and turned on the faucet so that running water would drown out the sounds of her crying. After shedding her last tear, she wiped her face dry, then scooped up the scrub brush and picked up where she left off – not just in her chores, but also in her reminiscing.

Flashbacks of her past cropped up relentlessly as she moved from chore to chore, room to room.

Later, while washing dishes, she noticed where her wedding ring once rested comfortably. She had gone so long without it that she rarely missed it anymore. Today, however, she missed everything about her former lifestyle. She missed the beautiful jewelry Paine had bought for her, sometimes as surprises and other times to complete an ensemble he had picked out for her for a special occasion. She missed her wardrobe that had expanded since she married to include exclusive designer wear. She missed shopping for top brand shoes that were attractive and stylish, not necessarily functional – and handbags to match.

As she washed a glass, the shimmer from the watery reflection reminded her of the glitter and glamour of attending performances and gala events at ballet companies, opera houses, Broadway theater companies and museums. She missed dressing up for such events in elegant gowns. These days, dressing up involved donning the same pair of khakis and white button-down shirt she had bought with her first paycheck from Faith House. The ensemble had long lost its appeal and had come to feel more like a uniform. She had a scanty wardrobe, made up of a few items she had pulled from the shelter clothes closet of castoffs – two pairs of jeans, one ink-stained pair of khakis, three T-shirts, two button-down shirts, one navy pullover sweater, and one brown corduroy coat. The clothes she had worn to the shelter were tossed with the garbage. The putrid scent and the dust they had absorbed while she lived on the street had ruined them. She had been able to keep her sunglasses, her jewelry, which was safely locked away in a nearby bus station locker along with the items of identification and her satchel. When she itemized the possessions her life had been reduced to, she again clenched her jaw to sustain the anger and resentment simmering just below the surface.

Her mind drifted to the last time she was dressed in finery. She saw herself in the gold gown and choker she wore when her marriage unraveled. It was the same night she confronted Paine. It was the night before her world changed and came crashing down around her.

Riley slowly ran the dish cloth across a chipped plate and watched soapy bubbles slide down the plate and back into the dishwater.

She remembered how perfect she looked in the dress Paine had handpicked for her. It also occurred to her how unhappy and miserable she was the entire time she wore it. She never even got the opportunity to enjoy it.

It was becoming clear to her as she washed away dried, crusty food from an aluminum pot that that was the case with most of the beautiful clothes she had accumulated over the course of her marriage. Gradually, truth began to sink in. Riley recalled how the beautiful house they shared never felt like a home. It was filled with expensive furnishings, but was missing love, laughter, warmth, and peacefulness – things that had filled her childhood home. It suddenly dawned on her that their house had been more like a cold, impersonal, exquisite museum.

Riley slumped down on the edge of the sink counter. She hung her head and closed her eyes in shame.

"How could I have been so blind?" she asked herself. "I've despised my parents for depriving me of things I thought would make me happy and for giving me all the things they knew would. How can they ever forgive me? Will I ever get the chance to see them again and tell them how sorry I am?"

An unexpected voice startled Riley, snapping her back into position over the kitchen sink. She reined in her emotions and immediately began tackling the dirty pot again.

"Are you okay?" Deidra said.

"Yes, I'm fine. Why does everyone keep asking me that?"

Riley's irritation was provoked also by the way Deidra had of sneaking up on Riley. It was unnerving to her, especially now when she wanted desperately to be alone with her thoughts.

"You don't look okay."

"Yeah, well no one looks so great after they've been scrubbing toilets or when they're up to their elbows in dishwater, do they? And who do you know that looks hot in hand-me-down grab rags?"

Deidra arched her eyebrows and backed up a few steps.

"Somebody's really touchy today," she said while leaning back against the counter to the right of the sink basin. "I won't name names or anything."

Riley did not comment. She continued going through the motions of washing the grimy pot.

"You want to talk about why you're biting my head off?"

Riley wanted to talk to somebody – anybody – about her misery and how to reverse the downturn her life had taken, but she couldn't. There was no one with whom she could confide and share all the details of her life.

Riley shook her head "no." She sighed and looked over at Deidra, who returned a smile and playfully arched her eyebrows as if coaxing her for details.

"I'm sorry, Dee, for snapping at you. I'm just trying to work through some things and, unfortunately, you got caught in the crossfire of the argument in my head. Thank you, though, for your concern. I'll be alright."

Deidra picked up a drying towel and a dripping wet plate and began wiping the moisture from it.

"Eve?"

The tone of Deidra's voice changed and took on a child-like quality.

Riley half-heartedly answered, "Huh?" But she grew suspicious of what would come next.

"I've been curious about something. When you arrived here, you looked like the rest of us. I mean … you looked like you'd been in a street fight with the world and lost. But you were also very different. You were dressed in really nice clothes with fancy labels. You had a really great haircut, even though it was a bit of a mess when you got here, and it was pretty obvious that someone else did your nails. You also talk differently … real smart … using big words and stuff. I mean … you talk like you were somebody."

Riley listened, bracing for an inevitable dreaded question. Until now, no one at Faith House had actually quizzed her about her past – probably because of an unofficial code of secrecy that prevailed among those residents who did not want in turn to be cross-examined by other residents. But Nadine and Deidra had voluntarily broken that code of silence and had been more than candid with her. They were the only ones who had shared their stories with her. So Deidra had earned the right to ask Riley about her life. All the same, Riley grew anxious. She methodically washed a cookie sheet as she anticipated where Deidra was leading her in the conversation.

"I'm just curious," Deidra repeated. "What was it like?"

Riley, who had been staring blankly at the greasy pan, scrunched her face in confusion. "Did I miss something?" she thought, mentally backtracking to where her mind had wandered away from the conversation.

"What was what like, Deidra?"

"You know, having nice clothes, being able to afford nice hair and nails? Having money … enough money that Vivi could rob you and leave you stranded here with people like me?"

At first Riley was stunned. Deidra's question caught her by surprise. She said nothing. She was perplexed over the nature of the question. But as it sank in, she couldn't help but find the humor in both the timing and the irony of it.

Riley began laughing aloud at the question that had tortured her throughout the day as painfully as the nightmare she'd had that morning. Deidra's harmless, but serious query had thrown Riley into delirious laughter.

Meanwhile, Deidra watched Riley's reaction with great curiosity.

In the midst of her hilarity, Riley knew she was cornered; she was facing her demons, and was being tested with that one question. Instead of answering Deidra, Riley stalled with her laughter at the irony of being so transparent despite her many attempts to appear mysterious, secretive, and to blend in with the rest of the residents. The clothes didn't matter. Even wearing secondhand garments, she couldn't disguise who she was. Her present situation was no different than her previous circumstances. When dressed in expensive clothes, she didn't fit into New York's society either. The elite had also seen through her. They had recognized that she had come from a section of the world that was different from their own. Like the shelter residents, they had looked long and hard at her from a distance. They had watched her while they cast her under suspicion.

"What are you laughing at?" Deidra said. "I don't know what's so funny."

Deidra tossed the dish towel, opened a cabinet door, and slammed the dish down on top of a stack of other chipped plates.

When Riley saw Deidra pouting, she realized that Deidra thought she was laughing at her. She stopped scrubbing the pan and said, "Deidra, I'm sorry. Please forgive me for being insensitive." Riley paused, waiting for Deidra's countenance to change. When it didn't, Riley felt compelled to elaborate.

"I merely found the timing of your question humorous, but only because I've been wrestling with that very thing all day. I really was not laughing at you or your question. Please believe me."

"So?"

Riley sighed, then nodded in understanding. "You're still waiting for an answer, aren't you?"

Deidra raised her eyebrows, pursed her lips and nodded affirmatively.

Riley drew a deep breath - partly to think of how to respond without tipping her hand and partly to draw courage from within.

"First, you should know, I left home to get away from this kind of life. I didn't want to pinch pennies or live hand-to-mouth every day for the rest of my life. That was not my idea of success. But as you can see, I didn't get very far."

Riley had picked up the task of cleaning food stains from another pan, tightening her jaw as she did.

"You're very perceptive, Deidra."

"What do you mean?"

"I mean I did discover my fairy-tale-come-true, but like all fairy tales, it had its share of wicked stepmothers, villains, thorns, poison apples, and frogs with warts. The grass is not always greener on the other side of the fence," she said as she rinsed the pan. When she finished, she handed it to Deidra. While looking directly at her, she continued, "The truth is: I didn't have to run very far to come full circle. I learned the hard way that contentment and success are not tied to what you wear, what you drive, who you know, the size of your house, or the societal stature to which you marry. None of it guarantees your happiness."

Riley returned to her task. She swirled the dishwater with her dishrag to clean the surface of another pan. With each circular motion, she got lost in her own thoughts, secretly releasing the anger and frustration that had built up inside her over the course of the day. While looking at the whirlpool of water, she chuckled at the observation she, herself, had just made.

"It's taken time to realize it, but I'm happier now than I've ever been," she added. "Who would have thought?"

She looked over at the young woman who had stopped drying dishes and had propped her chin on her hand to give Riley her full attention.

"But don't you miss it?" Deidra said.

"Yes … but less and less every day. Gradually, that place in me that had devoted so much room for the cares of the world is being filled up with more satisfying things … for instance, special friendships like ours. Occasionally, I look back, only to see so many things that were temporary and lacking in true value. What I'm investing in now is mine forever."

Deidra furrowed her brow, apparently still dissatisfied with Riley's answer. After a few minutes of reflection, she spoke up again.

"Don't you think that there's room for both – for money and for relationships? I mean, do you think this is the end of the line for you … or for us?"

Deidra's sharp tone alerted Riley to stored bitterness. Riley sensed that she was searching for something outside the walls of Faith House, some ray of hope, some grain of encouragement that would one day lead her out of her present circumstances. But she was looking in the wrong direction. She was holding out for a lottery ticket or the pot of gold at the end of the rainbow. Riley recognized the symptoms – the look of longing, the frustration, the desperation. She had not so long ago suffered from the same delusions.

"Deidra, I don't know what tomorrow will bring. I only know I plan never again to live by my own agenda as I have in the past … driven by my own worthless ambitions. I threw that out after I threw away the designer clothes I was wearing the day I arrived here. Little did I know then that I would eventually trade it all for one valuable lesson. What I've discovered at Faith House, as I hope you have, is that if I will give the Lord my foremost attention and love, and treat others the way I want to be loved and treated, then the Lord will take care of the rest of the details. And he promises that, in the end, the grass is greener on His side of the fence."

A glimmer of light in Deidra's demure smile gave approval to Riley's explanation. She picked up the drying towel and began humming an unfamiliar tune as she returned to her work. Riley thought Deidra's reaction gratifying, so much that Riley found it contagious. Only Riley's glowing smile came about as the result of yet another reason as she recalled how differently her day was ending from the way it had begun.

Chapter 16

Residents of Faith House scurried about the shelter preparing for visitors. A group of philanthropists and board members would be touring the facility. Nadine had alerted Riley and all of the residents that about a dozen visitors would be there that morning and that some might stay for lunch, depending upon their schedules.

So everyone chipped in to help with final details to spruce up Faith House and make it presentable to their guests.

But some residents did so while voicing their contempt. Whining and complaining came from those who objected to being put on display for the rich, who they said were slumming in their neighborhood. Nadine tolerated some of the comments up to a point. But when it began to interfere with their goal of preparing for their guests, she silenced the grumbling with one comment, "Do you want to be back out on the street?"

The answer was always a resounding, "No!"

Under the sagging roof of Faith House, a diverse group of women from varying pasts and bizarre histories gathered to create a multi-cultural and sometimes dysfunctional family. The common thread that ran through the uncommon unit was that each of them had hit rock bottom before finding their first step up the ladder of life at Faith House. They each had known at one time what it was like to be cold, hungry, destitute, or deathly ill. Some had resorted to drugs to numb the pain. Some had sold their bodies for their next fix, their next meal, or their child's milk. Some had experienced abuse at the hand of the ones they trusted, whether it was a father, mother, brother, husband, or lover. Some had been betrayed by that trusted someone at a very young age, but the wounds were as fresh as if it had happened yesterday. Some had been violated by someone whose face they had seen only once, but whose face they'd never forget. Others could recall having their lives destroyed by the silhouette of a stranger, who came and slipped away quickly in the middle of the night. Every day after, they looked over their shoulder and feared being overtaken again by the shadow that followed them.

The memories of life on the street were also still fresh - fresher for some than for others. Each woman's recollection of her time lived in alleys, eating out of trash cans, or rummaging through garbage bins for clothes would never fade. They did not want to go back - even if it meant putting on a show for people who could afford to go anywhere in the world for their entertainment. After all, they had done worse things for money.

Riley was nervous about the visitors to Faith House, especially after her nightmare the day before. During the past couple of months at the shelter, she had been amazed at how quickly she had fallen into step with the other residents. They had embraced her as Nadine's assistant since it was not a job any of them had wanted. They were all aware of how tough Nadine could be to live with, let alone work for. But Riley, whose goal had always leaned toward perfection, had found Nadine's expectations slightly less demanding or unreasonable than did other residents. Their management styles complemented one another's and they were turning out to be a good team.

Riley, who had also found acceptance as an equal with the other women, had been successful at hiding her identity at Faith House. She had altered her appearance slightly to avoid recognition. She continued to dye her hair auburn, and by cutting a few inches off the length, she instantly achieved a new appearance. Slowly, she was adapting to her new look, her new home, her new family, and her new name. Regardless, she was keenly aware that the threat of being exposed as a fraud still existed despite the camouflage.

But she had become less guarded among her peers. At Faith House, slates were wiped clean. Each woman found confidence in being given a fresh start. That was the premise of most of their conversations - that and talk of the future, what they would do when they left Faith House. Each woman was in search of her big break.

This group of strangers who would be coming to Faith House with the specific purpose of prying into the operations of the shelter, however, made her uneasy. She felt defensive walls inside her going back up to prevent outsiders from intruding. She would fight against being compromised. Her life over the past few months had been peaceful and without fear of danger, retaliation, or brutality. Also, she had been more herself than she had been in years - no longer striving, stressing, or competing. Perfection had become less about the right clothes or the next headline story, but more about reading the Bible with Nadine, being a shoulder to cry on, and offering an encouraging word to a fellow resident.

Riley shared the sentiments of the other residents. She did not want to go back.

"Okay, I think we're ready," said Nadine, who had been buzzing from one room to the next all morning and spouting instructions for the residents to follow.

She stood, her hands on her hips, scoping out her surroundings for any missed details. Then her bright eyes settled on Riley, whose nod indicated agreement, but whose expression clearly showed that she was worried about something.

"What?" said Nadine, panicked that she might not have been as thorough as she thought. "Did I forget something?"

"No, no," Riley said, followed by nervous laughter at Nadine's conscientiousness. "It's perfect. You've done a remarkable job at pulling everything together. No surprise there."

Nadine was not convinced. Her assistant's words did not match the look of concern on her face.

"Eve, what are you not telling me?"

Riley, who became instantly uneasy, glanced around to see who was standing nearby to overhear their conversation. Upon seeing that they were alone, she debated what to say without divulging too much information.

"I'm just nervous," Riley said. "I don't want to let you down."

Nadine swatted at Riley with one hand and walked a few steps away from her before turning back to say, "Are you kidding me? You'll do just fine, Darlin'. I have no concerns about you."

Nadine cackled, causing Riley to blush.

"I thought it was something serious," Nadine said, followed by another cackle.

Riley knew full well the seriousness of the situation. She wanted to tell Nadine everything. She wanted to have an ally who could assist her with an alternate plan if one of the visitors recognized her. But she lacked the courage to trust anybody just yet - even Nadine.

"Why don't you go now and get cleaned up. We've got less than an hour before they arrive," Nadine said. She pointed her finger at Riley and, with a penetrating look, said, "Stop worrying."

"Okay," Riley said without conviction.

She pivoted around and darted toward her room. As assistant manager, Riley had been given her own room near the residents' sleeping quarters. It was a small room, furnished sparsely with a twin bed, a set of drawers, and a night stand. She had her own small closet and she and Nadine shared an adjoining restroom. Riley had fought the urge to decorate the room. What earnings she'd not spent on clothes found on bargain racks, she had stashed in a locker at the bus station around the corner along with her wedding ring and photo IDs. It had been difficult to resist the urge to shop. She was learning how to be frugal. It was a painful lesson, but her goal was to recoup the money Vivi had taken from her.

Riley had also been careful not to stray too far or too often from the shelter. When she did go out, it was generally on weekends when there were fewer people in the city. She had taken so many precautions and now her worlds were colliding.

Riley went through the motions of getting ready for the tour group. Despite her desire to ask Nadine about who would be in the group, she didn't. Riley had grown cautious around Nadine, who had an acute gift of perception. She was especially skilled at reading Riley's expressions and, sometimes, her mind. She feared that if Nadine said a familiar name, her face would betray her. So their intended guests remained a mystery to Riley.

The comfort and familial connection she experienced at Faith House often made her forget about the outside world. Memories of Paine, his cruelty and the life they had shared were fading. Aside from occasional nightmares, her thoughts also turned less and less to her co-workers and the explosion that killed them. Inside the shelter, she had indeed found refuge and safety. It didn't seem necessary to reveal to Nadine or the residents anything of her past life.

But today, the buzzing of women cleaning and straightening and talking of guests had stirred dormant thoughts and memories and fears. Their preparations to welcome outsiders into the place where Riley had found asylum were disrupting her newfound peace. To take her mind off her troubling thoughts, Riley threw herself into her work. But even though her hands were busy, her mind was over-actively negotiating all the ways this one event could turn her new world upside down. Riley had known about the scheduled visit for a week, so her anxieties about this day had been building. Staying busy did not stay the fears growing in her. It only brought her closer to the hour she had been dreading since the day Nadine told her of the scheduled tour.

From that point on, Riley had gone through the motions of her duties as Nadine's assistant, but her plans of moving forward in her job and restructured life unraveled. She was undecided about whether to stay at the shelter, or pack her few possessions, write off her losses and leave. In large part because of her growing attachment to Nadine, Deidra, and several other young women who had come to lean on her for help, Riley was torn. She also did not want to start over again - certainly not so soon. She knew the time would come when she would leave, presumably when she had earned the amount of wages equal to her losses. But right now, she wasn't ready to leave. Faith House and its inhabitants, in their own unobtrusive way, had made a home in her heart. Faced with the choice of whether to leave, Riley realized that, surprisingly, she was at home at the dilapidated shelter full of misfits.

After coming to terms with her feelings about her new residence, Riley decided to stay and ride out the storm. Meanwhile, the storm inside her continued to brew and gain strength.

Riley finished dressing for the special occasion. Clad in her khakis and a starched white button-down shirt, she took one last look in the mirror before departing to the common room, where they would meet the center's benefactors. She took a deep breath, opened the door, and marched down the hall. Walking toward the common area, she heard the front door slam and the sound of unrecognizable voices - an indication that guests were apparently arriving. The closer she got to the room, the more she became aware of one voice in particular. With each step, a knot formed tighter in the pit of Riley's stomach. She slowed her pace before reaching the room. Something in the intonation of that one voice stopped Riley dead in her tracks. Panic-stricken, she felt heat rise in her face. Riley immediately looked around. Fortunately, she had come down the hall unnoticed. She quietly backtracked a few steps, then slowly turned around and dashed back to her room, and grabbed her handbag, a scarf, wool cap, and coat.

Riley cracked her door and peeked through the narrow opening. The hallway was still empty and void of activity. She looked across the hall to the kitchen door that led to a back door of the shelter. Riley's breathing quickened and her pulse raced as she stood watching and waiting to make her move. A few seconds later, she heard the chatter of Rosemary, Lindsey, and Fatiqua as they exited the kitchen area and walked toward the common room. Riley grew more anxious as she continued to peek through the thin door opening. She waited a few more seconds, but no one else left the kitchen. She could hear snippets of conversation coming from the end of the hall, but all else was quiet. Riley held her breath as she opened the door, darted across the hall, where she gently opened the kitchen door. She stuck her head inside and much to her relief saw no one there. Riley ducked inside. She cut through the kitchen and went out the back door without being seen.

Once outside, Riley ran down the alley and onto the Twenty-ninth Street sidewalk, where she slowed her pace to a steady walk. She slid on her coat, pulled her cap on her head and wrapped the scarf around her neck. She frequently glanced back to see if she was being followed or watched. No one.

As she aimlessly wandered farther away from the shelter, Riley pondered what to do next. At that moment, she had a sinking feeling inside from the guilt of having let Nadine and the women down. Riley stopped at the intersection of Twenty-ninth Street and Broadway to catch her breath from running. She was only a few blocks from Madison Square Park, so she turned right at Broadway and headed to the park. But Riley felt like she was running away from home. Each step that moved her farther away from Faith House widened the gap between her and her surrogate family.

"I did the right thing," Riley repeated silently to herself like a mantra. "I did," she resolved.

But the self-talk did little to quiet the condemning voices in her head that sounded identical to her own.

Walking away from Faith House felt all too familiar. Her thoughts carried her back to that day, September 11, when she walked away from her office building, putting distance between her and her co-workers. In flashbacks of looking over her shoulder to see the building in flames, she felt as though she was reliving that moment all over again.

Riley arrived at the park and found a secluded bench. It was close to lunchtime and the park would soon fill up with folks eating lunch.

It was a clear day with a chilly breeze. On any other day, Riley would have enjoyed the beautiful outdoors and the peacefulness of the park. She was overtaken, however, by the miserable feeling that she had abandoned ship once the waters showed signs of unrest.

But the sound of Margaret Tarrington's voice resounded in her thoughts.

"No, it was definitely her," Riley reasoned.

In the last conversation they'd had, Mrs. Tarrington had relished hinting to her that Paine and Sarah Blackstone were having an affair. How could she possibly face her now - the friend of her enemy, who in this case, was her husband? By now, she had been declared dead and Paine and Sarah were probably making wedding plans. This woman's presence at Faith House threatened Riley's future. Despite that, a voice deep inside her told Riley to go back. The gnawing feeling that her place was at Faith House, not hiding out in the park, only grew in intensity.

Riley sat glued to the park bench in silent debate. "What if she recognizes me? Mrs. Tarrington could make it hard for Nadine to secure future funding," Riley silently argued.

"Not to mention, it will be a matter of minutes before Paine knows I'm alive. Then he'll do everything in his power to make me wish I was dead. I can't," she whispered. "I just can't."

Go back. The voice inside her grew stronger. She had difficulty ignoring it.

Go back, the voice urged.

The more she felt compelled to return to Faith House, the more turmoil she experienced.

But suddenly, going back became more about the ones she had left behind and less about her own needs and fears. She thought of letting Nadine down and the desire to return became overwhelming. Nadine had not turned her back out on the streets, destitute and a phony, even when she suspected that the name "Eve" was a pseudonym. Instead, she had nursed her, fed her, and exalted her to the Number Two position at Faith House.

"How could I desert her now when she needs me?"

Go back.

Her thoughts drifted to family - her father and mother, her substitute family she'd adopted at the TV station, and now Faith House. It suddenly occurred to her that she had a pattern of abandoning those she loved. She naturally left her parents when she became grown. But in her case, because of their beliefs and restrictive lifestyles, Riley also abandoned them and cut off most contact with them. She paid them the usual obligatory phone calls at Christmas, birthdays and holidays honoring parents, but only to keep in touch and ease her conscience. In truth, she was by definition a prodigal daughter, who through recent events, would never return to her parents' house again.

Memories of 9/11 continued to haunt Riley, particularly when her former co-workers' faces randomly popped to mind. While technically she did not abandon them in mind and spirit, she could not stop feeling like she had abandoned them physically.

Seated on the park bench, Riley became increasingly restless. It occurred to her that she was replaying similar events of her life. When she walked out the back door of Faith House, those whom she had come to hold dear had no clue that she had walked out on them. Could she have helped her co-workers on 9/11? Probably not, she concluded to herself. But the women at Faith House were depending on her. It was not too late to help them.

Go back, the voice continued to say.

Riley leapt from the park bench and dashed up Broadway back toward Faith House.

She did not know what she would do or how she would deal with the situation once she got there. But she decided to trust the voice that drew her back to Faith House.

The return trip was a short one. She paused at the back door of the shelter, again to catch her breath and this time to find courage, before opening to enter.

"God, I hope you know what you're doing," she whispered.

Feeling as though she was about to face a firing squad, Riley reasoned, "It's not a burning building." She exhaled and braced for the worst as she opened the door and went in.

Chapter 17

"Where have you been?" Nadine frantically asked when Riley joined her in the kitchen.

Riley had successfully slipped through the kitchen and back to her bedroom, where she dropped off her handbag, coat, cap, and scarf without being seen.

"I couldn't decide what to wear," Riley said. "I have so many choices." How quickly Riley had picked up Nadine's sense of humor.

Nadine narrowed her eyes in disapproval. At that moment, Nadine was not amused by Riley's comment.

"I'm sorry," Riley said. She scanned the kitchen to see who was in the room. Rosemary, Lindsey, and Fatiqua had returned and were busy preparing the meal.

"Listen, everyone showed up for the tour, which you missed, by the way, but only about six people are staying for lunch, Nadine said. "Can you supervise things here in the kitchen while I wine and dine our guests over tea and baked chicken?"

"Sure, I'd love to," said Riley, relieved that she would be tucked out of sight.

Nadine noticed a sudden change of expression on Riley's face.

"Unless you'd like to join me?" No sooner had she gotten the words out, Nadine realized that she had misread Riley, when her panicked expression betrayed her. Riley quickly recovered and said, "Oh, no. You go ahead, Nadine. You've done this so often I bet you could do this in your sleep. Besides, you know these people. I wouldn't want to do anything that might jeopardize the shelter's funding. Who knows? I might say the wrong thing or use the wrong fork."

Nadine narrowed her eyes again at Riley. She felt like Riley was mocking her. Nadine also suspected that there was more going on with Riley, but she didn't have time to pursue the matter. She had guests waiting.

"Okay, well, if you've got everything under control here, I'll be in the dining room," said Nadine, who carefully pulled her apron off over her braided hair and handed it to Riley.

"We'll be fine," said Riley. She donned the apron while Nadine checked her face and hair in the reflection of the stainless steel commercial refrigerator. Then she disappeared through the swinging door.

Before jumping into her responsibilities, Riley tiptoed over to the swinging door and cracked it open to peek at the half dozen people who had stayed behind to brave the shelter's meager, bland cuisine. Riley scanned the guests looking for Mrs. Tarrington's wrinkled face. Riley was elated to discover that the older woman was not among those who stayed behind to lunch with the shelter residents.

Riley shook her head. "Why am I surprised?" she thought.

Nor did the other guests look familiar to Riley, who breathed a deep sigh of relief.

Riley allowed the door to quietly shut. For a moment, she was overcome with indescribable peace. "I was right to come back," she thought. "The voice knew what it was talking about."

She had heard Nadine offer thanks to God on occasions when things had gone exceptionally well or when she said he had answered her prayer. This must be what those moments felt like to her, Riley thought. She smiled to herself. "Mm," she said, enjoying the moment. "Thank you," she whispered. "Thank you."

"Eve, what do you want us to do with this?" said Lindsey, pointing to broccoli steaming in a pot. "And what about this?" said Fatiqua, holding up a vat of pudding.

Riley spun around to see the bewildered faces of three women who were waiting for her direction.

Riley, who had been lost in the moment, forgot that others were depending on her. It was an odd feeling since for so many years she had primarily been responsible for herself. Even in her marriage to Paine, he had been so much in control that she had only her essential needs to worry about. Paine showed no desire for children and Riley was too busy with work to think about starting a family. In her job, it was every person for himself when it came to work responsibilities. She had not managed anyone but herself.

Suddenly, all eyes were on her. Had they looked to her for leadership a couple of months ago, Riley would have either fallen apart under the pressure or bolted from the responsibility, depending on the task.

Nadine, however, had refused to let Riley run from any job assignments, no matter how difficult or unfamiliar. She had either walked Riley through the steps of an assigned task or had given her instructions before leaving her alone with it. Even if the outcome had not measured up to Nadine's expectations, Riley had received nothing short of Nadine's praise and encouragement. "How well you're catching on, Darlin'," or "Splendid job, Darlin', just splendid," or "Well, it's not Picasso, but even he had to start somewhere. Your next attempt will be an absolute masterpiece. I'm confident."

Nadine had a way of making Riley and all of the women, no matter in what stage of their life, feel as though they could accomplish anything. Riley had found Nadine's perspective refreshing and her encouragement uplifting.

Much to her amazement, Riley was discovering emotional healing and inner strength in an unlikely place. Whether through the responsibility or through the trust of Nadine and her fellow residents, Riley was regaining her confidence. The absence of criticism and retribution was allowing Riley time to heal. Receiving encouragement instead of constant scrutiny was restoring Riley's faith in herself.

Riley spouted out instructions to her kitchen helpers with the ease of a *sous chef.* The four pairs of hands finished preparing the various components of the meal that were handed off to a couple of residents who agreed to serve the guests. When dessert was served, Riley instructed the kitchen crew to commence cleanup. About a half hour later, the glasses, dishes, and silverware used by the dignitaries began trickling back into the kitchen to be cleaned.

As several women washed and dried the dishes, Riley scraped food scraps into the trash can and rounded up the garbage to be discarded at the back door. Riley grabbed a heavy sweater hanging on a hook near the back door and put it on. She tugged at the heavy bundle and lifted it from the trash can. She strained to carry it outside, pushing the handle of the door with her elbow.

The door flew open and Riley stumbled down the back door steps into the alley with the overstuffed bag of trash. The door slammed behind her. Riley struggled to carry the heavy trash bag away from her clothing while trying not to lose her balance. She walked over to the trash bin about ten feet away and slung it in.

Riley turned around to head back, but stopped immediately when she realized that she wasn't alone.

Their eyes locked. Riley's jaw dropped at the sight of him. She froze, debating whether to turn and run or begin screaming for Nadine. The door had closed shut behind her. She had left the women bustling around the kitchen, chatting as they worked, so it was unlikely that they would hear her if she yelled.

"I see you're well," the man said.

Riley wrinkled her brow at the comment. She thought back to their last encounter.

"Yeah, I mean, yes, I am."

Riley wondered at that moment if she started walking toward the door if he would block her from going inside.

As if he had read her mind, the man dug his hands into his pockets and stood, hanging his head and lowering his eyes to focus on the ground.

Despite his sudden non-threatening appearance, Riley stood motionless, taking in every detail of the man. His graying, unwashed hair was straight and hung in disarray, like the strings of a mop head. Some strands of his oily hair clung to his forehead and covered one of his brown eyes. His clothes, dingy and stained and mismatched, were draped over his bony structure. He still hunched forward slightly as though he carried an invisible burden upon his shoulders. She noticed his multiple layers of clothes - shirts, a sweater, and a coat. Riley couldn't help but think how uncomfortable he must be.

The man timidly looked at Riley, then looked away. Riley caught his glance and realized that he was as afraid of her as she was of him. She questioned her own fear of the vagabond, who had months ago led her to safety. Thinking back on that night in the alley, where she was robbed, Riley realized that she should be grateful to this man. He had prevented her from being left stranded on the streets of New York without money. He had also preserved her identity by recovering her backpack, which contained her wallet. Riley realized at that moment that she had never thanked him for his heroic deed. The last time she saw him was before he slipped through the front door of Faith House, leaving her on the doorstep like an abandoned baby or package for whoever would find her and claim her.

"He knew Nadine would take me in," Riley thought to herself.

Riley opened her mouth to thank him, but her words and thoughts were clipped by the sudden opening of the back door. It was Nadine. Riley started to warn Nadine that the stranger was lurking behind the back door. Before she could say a word, Nadine swung around the door carrying a plate, covered with foil, and called out, "Ruben! Where have you been, Darlin'? I was just before canvasing the city for you."

Nadine noticed Riley standing nearby. She looked oddly at her when she realized that Riley was at a standstill in the middle of the alley.

"Eve, you remember Ruben, don't you?"

Riley slowly exhaled.

"Uh, yes ... yes, I do, vaguely. I'm afraid we were never formally introduced."

Riley moved closer to the giant, who in broad daylight, did not look so big or intimidating.

"Eve Campbell, meet Ruben Weintraub - man about town."

Ruben nodded at Riley while glancing at her, then quickly looked away. He refrained from making eye contact with her. At close range, Riley could see deep lines in the man's leathery face. She could also see his gentle eyes and humble manner. Riley stepped forward and held out her hand to the man. Her gesture took him by surprise. He could not remember the last time that someone had treated him like a gentleman, offering him a handshake for any reason. Most people took a wide berth when they saw him approaching. Few people showed him the respect he had once received as a Wall Street trader.

Ruben looked down at the slender pale hand. He thought of his own hands, which had earlier rummaged though trash bins in search of castoffs that could be sold or traded on the street or food scraps that could be eaten. He could not recall the last time he had washed them. Today was like any other. Time had no meaning to him. He stared at the clean, soft, fragile hand, wanting to reach out to it, to touch it. It was a thing of beauty to him, as was the woman reaching out to him. But he paused. He could not bring himself to soil the hand of this woman. It was the closest he had come in contact with an angel since his wife. Even though the days were all a blur to him, Ruben could vividly remember the night he first saw the young woman, who stood before him. She had almost run him down with her BMW as he crossed the street. He remembered his rage when the car screeched to a halt within less than a foot from him. He reacted by pounding his fist into the hood of her car. Living on the street and dealing with people who treated the homeless like they were invisible had made Ruben intolerant of their insensitivity and rudeness. Then he saw her. He saw her tears. He saw the pain in her apologetic face. He wondered then who or what had caused her tears. That vision remained clear in his mind. Her image was burned into his memory. He would never forget her sorrowful expression when she looked apologetically through the car windshield. His heart melted for her.

Then the morning Ruben discovered her slipping out of an alley disturbed him to the point that he began following her from a distance and watching her. He recognized her despite her changed hair color. He would not forget that face. One of the benefits of being invisible to the world was that he had been able to shadow her without being detected. After a short time, it became evident to him that she was a novice at street life. He tried to understand how she had gone so quickly from driving a luxury car to sleeping in an alley. Then he saw her bruised eye. She didn't know he saw it. He stayed nearby at night while she slept. One night he got close enough to look at her when she wasn't wearing sunglasses. As he looked at the angelic face, he found it hard to conceive how someone could tarnish or harm something so beautiful.

Ruben decided then to become her self-appointed guardian, determining that no one would harm her again. He took the job seriously, something the young man who took her backpack quickly discovered. He would have killed that punk kid, not so much for robbing her, but for striking her, if he had not stopped himself. He raised the plywood over the kid's head and intended to pummel him with it. When he realized that it was just a teenager, Ruben regained control of his temper. But he came face to face with the realization that as much as he wanted to be able to look at her every day and take care of her, she was not safe on the street. He had to get her to a place where she would be out of harm's way. He knew she would be in good hands at Faith House.

Ruben looked longingly at Riley's delicate hand. He was drawn to it, he couldn't bring himself to shake her hand.

He rubbed the palm of his right hand on his chest.

"I'm sorry, Miss, my hands are dirty," said Ruben, looking directly at Riley for the first time. "But I'm much obliged."

A puzzled look crossed Riley's face. Something about this man intrigued her. His appearance and his lifestyle did not match his speech and mannerisms. He was an enigma, she thought. In that one moment, she went from fearing him to wanting to know his story.

"I hope they're treating you well at Faith House," he said cordially.

Riley noticed the change in his tone from the night he had guided her to the shelter.

"Why, yes. Nadine has taken me under her wing. I've become her protégée, I suppose."

Her comment put a gleam in Ruben's eye and a faint smile on his bearded face - neither of which escaped Riley. It melted the chill in her heart toward the odd, coarse man.

"Yeah, well, I don't know who's teaching whom," said Nadine. Her sparkling eyes rested upon her assistant. She smiled fondly at the young woman, who was fast becoming her friend. "Folks, I'd love to stand around and chit-chat, but I've got some paperwork to catch up on. All this hobnobbing with rich folks has put me behind schedule." Before leaving, Nadine stopped and pointed her finger at the man. "Ruben, don't scare me like that again," she said, followed by a friendly slap on the man's arm. "You are the only man in my life, you know. If you come up missing, I'm going to have to go in search of somebody else. You know I'm too old and too out of practice for the dating game. So I expect you to hold up your end of this relationship."

Ruben smiled and nodded, then said, "Sure, Nadine." Adding, "Thanks," as he lifted the covered plate which had been prepared for him.

"You don't need to thank me. Just be careful," she said, smiling back at the vagabond.

Riley watched the tender exchange between them.

"By the way, Eve, thank you for your help today. I think it was a success." With that said, Nadine immediately spun around and was through the door without waiting for Riley to comment.

Riley and Ruben both shook their heads in amazement at Nadine's energy.

"She doesn't waste time, does she?"

"No, she doesn't," he said.

Silence fell between them. The older man, alone again with Riley, suddenly grew uncomfortable and avoided her direct gaze. Ruben wondered how he must appear to the beautiful woman. He supposed that he must look dirty and disgusting to her. He knew she would be right in her estimation. This was one occasion when he wished he was invisible. If only she had met him years ago, when he was a trader on Wall Street, when he wore five hundred dollar suits to work every day, he thought. She might have had a different opinion of him then.

Riley cleared her throat, breaking the silence and tearing Ruben from his thoughts. He immediately looked up at her.

"I feel terrible that I never thanked you for what you did," she said after getting his attention.

Ruben dropped his head again, this time in humility.

"I mean, bringing me here," she said. "You were truly a godsend. I didn't realize that then, so I'm sure I didn't properly show you the appreciation you deserved. As a matter of fact, I was probably quite rude, at least, what I remember of that night. I apologize. You were only being kind." Riley paused.

Despite the cold New York climate, Ruben could feel the temperature rising and sweat beads popping out on his forehead. He began to shuffle from side to side.

When Ruben did not say anything, she said, "I'm truly sorry."

Her tender apology brought Ruben's shuffling to an end. He found himself looking directly into the blue eyes of the woman and seeing almost the same apologetic expression she had the first time he saw her. He found his heart melting all over again. How could anyone get angry enough to hurt this woman, he pondered.

"Certainly not me," he thought.

When he didn't respond, Riley wondered if he comprehended what she had just said. So many homeless men and women were mentally incapacitated. Was he among those who suffered from some form of mental illness or dementia, she wondered, as she squinted to pick up any trace of acknowledgment. She saw no hint of psychological problems, but the prospect of mental instability suddenly made her uncomfortable and anxious to go back inside. Just as she was preparing to bid him farewell, he opened his mouth to speak.

"A protégée, huh? From what Nadine tells me, you're a fast learner. She says you have a future at Faith House. Is that what you want?"

Riley's own jaw dropped at the transformation, as well as at the news that he and Nadine had been exchanging progress reports about her. When she realized that he was now waiting for a response from her, she tried to recover from the sudden shock.

"Uh, well, I really haven't given it a lot of thought. I mean, a future at Faith House, I don't know. I guess I've just thought of the shelter as temporary, a place to hang out while I get back on my feet," Riley said.

Visions of working again as a journalist, living in a stylish apartment, eating Saturday breakfasts at the corner café, and making frequent stops at her favorite coffee shops and bookstores surfaced when she thought of the future.

"You could do worse," said the bearded man, who was sounding more like a grandfather.

Riley noticed the plate of food in the man's soiled hand. She knew she was keeping him from eating. "Are you going to eat that before it gets cold? You're welcome to come inside and sit at the table," she said.

Ruben shrugged his shoulders in reply.

"No, thank you."

Riley looked around, then motioned for him to sit on the back step of the shelter.

"If you won't come in, at least sit here and eat it while it's warm. Rice is not good when it's cold."

Another faint smile appeared and quickly disappeared from the man's face.

He slowly lowered himself to sit on the stoop. He began to unwrap the silver foil. Without warning, Riley plopped down on the space beside him. The woman's proximity to him caused him to fumble awkwardly with the foil. In his nervousness, he dropped the paper sack containing plastic eating utensils and condiments Nadine had packed for him. Riley leaned over, picked up the sack, and handed it to him.

Ruben suddenly longed for a shower, a shave, clean clothes, and cologne. He had not desired such things in the past seven years since he quit his job. He walked off the trading floor just days after burying his wife and son and never looked back. He had lost all interest in success, prosperity, and running the rat race of life.

But sitting next to this beautiful creature made him want what he had left behind.

"How long have you known Nadine?" she inquired.

When Ruben didn't answer right away, she noticed he was chewing a bite he had managed to take when she had looked away. She thought about how hungry he must be.

Riley detected a stench that had grown stronger. She casually put her fingertips to her nose to see if some of the garbage had rubbed onto her fingers when she took out the trash. When she didn't smell anything out of the ordinary, she tried to determine its source. She looked toward the trash bins and wondered if a breeze was carrying the smell in their direction. But then she turned back toward Ruben and noticed that the smell was emanating from him. She had not noticed it the night he had led her to Faith House. She wondered if or where he bathed. Then she remembered her own experiences of washing from public restroom sinks. It wasn't the same. She also wondered how strong her scent was by the time she arrived at the shelter. It made her admire and appreciate Nadine all the more.

"Nearly seven years," Ruben said between swallows. "She caught me digging around in the dumpster over there," he said, pointing across the alley. "She scolded me and told me to show up at mealtime and she'd make sure I got fed. I haven't always shown up, but when I have, she's always fed me. She's a good woman."

"Is that why you brought me here? You knew she wouldn't turn me away?"

Ruben nodded affirmatively while chewing another bite.

Riley watched the man, whose manners indicated that he had not grown up on the street. She wanted very much to inquire, to learn more about his history, but that meant, in all fairness, that she should be willing to answer questions about herself, too. That was a game she was not prepared to play, no matter how fair.

"You know? You saved my life that night - in more ways than one," Riley said. "I would probably be dead right now if you had not come along that night."

The man blushed at the woman's compliments as he continued to chomp down on the warm, baked chicken. He occasionally cast a sideways glance at her. He felt his face turn red when she caught him discreetly looking her way.

"I wish there was something I could do to repay you," Riley said.

Secretly, she held her breath wondering whether he would jump at her offer or what his repayment might entail. When he didn't answer, Riley began biting her lower lip.

Ruben swallowed another morsel. Without looking her way, he leaned his head back against the door of Faith House, as though he were in deep thought, contemplating how to respond. But he said nothing. He sat quietly and looked off into space.

A wrinkle formed on Riley's forehead. She watched him mentally travel to somewhere other than the New York back alley. She saw his eyes become glassy as he stared at a mental picture only he could see. Riley sat still, waiting and wondering what had drawn him away at a moment's notice. She was curious. She wanted to ask. But something in her last question had transported him to some exclusive location in his mind. As much as she wanted to join him, she didn't want to crowd him and chance never being invited into his world. She would wait.

As she waited, car horns, the acceleration of impatient motorists, as well as the screech of braking vehicles, resonated through the alley. The song of New York was made up of pushing and moving to get ahead. Riley had forgotten what it was like to just sit and listen and take in her surroundings.

She remembered as a little girl, climbing into the cradle of a mature live oak in the back yard of her parents' home to read, scribble in her diary, or to just sit and listen. There she could hear her own inner voice telling her the secrets of her heart. Here, seated with a front row view of the alley, she could hear her inner voice even above the traffic and other ambient noises. She was amazed at how at peace it was - an uncommon peace.

After a few more seconds, her waiting paid off.

Ruben began to shift his weight on the cement step. He turned slightly toward her.

"I was married. Did Nadine tell you?"

"No. She hasn't told me anything."

"I was. I had a son, too."

Riley braced for Ruben's story. She heard the angst in his voice.

"Where are they now?"

Ruben slowly covered the plate of uneaten food with the crinkled foil. He had lost his appetite. He gently lowered the plate to the pavement in front of him. Then he leaned forward and intertwined his fingers as he bent his head low and focused again on the ground before him.

From where she sat, Riley could not see Ruben's eyes. She could not see the emotional agony he was experiencing at that moment of reliving his greatest nightmare. She could not see the pain that sharing his broken heart with her was inflicting. That was his intention.

"I've come a long way from the man I once was," said Ruben.

Riley thought how much his story was starting out like a confession. She became more intrigued. She wondered what deep, dark secrets this man was hiding underneath all his many layers of clothes.

"My daily routine was comprised of long hours as a trader on the floor of the New York Stock Exchange. I was driven by my ambition to succeed."

Riley, understanding that kind of drive and desire, smiled at his comments. She nodded in approval. Unconsciously, her eyes roamed, taking in an inventory of Ruben's attire of mismatched, soiled clothes. She detected dirt under his fingernails and cracks in the skin of his leathery hands. She tried to visualize him clean-shaven, decked out in a navy, pin-striped suit, silk tie, and leather shoes.

"My son was seven - just the age when a boy wants his dad to teach him how to throw a baseball or to take him to a Yankees game. I know because he pleaded with me to do those things and more. But I was always too busy. I had my career to consider," he said, not once looking in her direction. "I didn't have time to play ball. I was too busy making a successful living and providing for my family."

Riley's approval rating of the man suddenly dropped. She didn't have children, but she felt certain that, if she did, they would not be neglected for her job. She would put as much energy into their lives as she did her career, she said to herself. Before long, however, her thoughts drifted to the things, the relationships she had neglected and that had suffered because of her own ambition. Her relationship with her parents was a perfect example. Riley shrank inside. Who was she to cast the first stone? she thought. She had been guilty of committing the same selfish act of putting her job ahead of others. Months went by without picking up the phone to call her aging parents. The few old friends she had went months without a word from her. She was no better than this executive-turned-bum. She cringed at the person she had become. The only difference between herself and this vagrant was that she was wearing better castoffs; otherwise, they were cut from the same cloth.

"I was at work when New York P.D.'s finest showed up to tell me that my wife and son were dead."

Riley gasped. "I'm so sorry," she said.

Ruben continued without stopping to acknowledge her sympathy.

"I had stayed late at the office. A couple of hours earlier, my wife had called and asked me to stop by the store and pick up some milk and a few other things on the way home. Our maid had taken the week off to visit her family in California, so my wife was juggling domestic chores with her own usual responsibilities. She worked out of our house as a freelance graphic artist, so leaving the house to get milk interrupted her creativity. But, I'm ashamed to say I didn't see her work as important as mine. As a matter of fact, I thought of it more as a hobby. When she called, I got angry with her. I had a profession. I didn't have time to run errands for my wife."

In a tear that ran down his cheek, Riley saw the first real sign of emotion coming from him.

"I refused to leave work on time and stop by the store. I was a busy man - too busy to deal with menial tasks. She tired of waiting for me, so I forced her to leave the safety of our home and go to the store at night. She was at the wrong place at the wrong time because I put her there. She needed milk for our meal that night," he said, laughing through his tears. "Can you believe it?" Ruben wiped the tears away with his dirty sleeve.

Picking up his story where he left off, Ruben said, "My son was too young to leave alone, so, of course, she took him with her. They walked into the corner market while it was being robbed. They startled the robbers, who reacted by opening gunfire on them. They killed my wife and son and immediately fled."

Riley covered her face with her hands to hide the look of horror on her face. Tears welled in her eyes at the image of his family being gunned down. Her co-workers' faces also flashed into her mind.

"Every night, I live with the thought that the bullets that killed my wife and my son were intended for me. I should have taken the bullets for them. But I was too self-centered, too attentive to my own needs and wants to give them what they really wanted and needed - and that was me. I was too busy with my own life to protect theirs."

The burly man drew his hands to his face and wept uncontrollably, no longer caring that this radiant woman, whom he had placed on a pedestal, saw him at his lowest, saw his weaknesses and vulnerability. It had been years since he had told anyone about his family. The attacks in New York had stirred up old, dormant feelings he thought he had managed to forget. He could not understand why he had just spilled out his history to this beautiful woman, whom he'd just met. It was so uncharacteristic of him to trust details of his life with anyone.

Ruben, even through his tears, found it hard not to look at the woman. He was drawn to her and had been for some mysterious reason since the first night he had laid eyes on her. When he glanced over at her, he saw her wiping back tears from her own cheeks.

Those rosy cheeks, those deep blue eyes, her red hair. He shuddered as he looked at her. Suddenly, an overwhelming familiarity, a *deja vu* of sorts came over him. With the odd feeling came the basis for attraction. In Riley, Ruben saw a resemblance to his bride of fifteen years ago. He had been unable to explain it until now. Riley bore a keen likeness to the woman he had sworn to love, honor and protect.

Ruben's pain intensified with the realization and the reminder of just how much he missed her. He began wailing for the loss of his wife.

The volume of his cries both alarmed Riley and touched a place deep inside her. She didn't know whether to run and get Nadine or wrap her arms around him and comfort him as she would any friend. His mournful cries echoed in the alley, sending a chill down Riley. She had heard similar eerie cries months ago from strangers mourning the lives lost at the World Trade

Center. She, herself, had cried aloud for those she knew who were killed. Remembering the pain she felt, Riley knew that it did not compare with losing a beloved wife and son.

Ruben wailed again and hugged his knees.

Riley grimaced. The giant who had intimidated her, who had overcome her thief and attacker, and whose gruff demeanor had frightened her, appeared real, not larger than life. She saw Ruben, the man with fears, vulnerabilities and tenderness, not Ruben the giant with brawn and gruffness.

Riley also wondered how much his pain was amplified by his aloneness. Carrying the weight of the world on your shoulders by yourself can be a daunting task. She knew because until she came to Faith House, the weight of the world had rested on her shoulders. While she had not confided in anyone about her personal demons and nightmares, she did have any number of shoulders at the shelter on which to cry and temporarily shift some of the emotional burden she carried.

Riley watched Ruben's body shake with each sob. Her own heart was breaking to watch this strapping man battle unseen demons by himself. She slowly and cautiously reached out to him. She debated whether to touch him, fearing that it might set him off and send him into a tantrum. Her left hand hovered over his back. She remembered being alone on the street and longing for human touch. As she recalled that desire, a magnetic pull drew Riley's hand closer to Ruben until it was firmly planted on his back. She held her breath, waiting for reaction. When there was none, she lightly caressed his back, like a mother soothing a fussy baby. With each stroke, Ruben's cries subsided, his shaking ceased, and his tense body relaxed.

"Shh," Riley said, trying to calm him.

After a while, a peace fell over the alley, over Ruben and over Riley. Time passed quietly in the stillness of the cold afternoon. When it appeared that Ruben was completely calm, Riley dug with her other hand into an apron pocket, where she had stuffed a paper towel after drying her hands on it in the kitchen. She pulled it out and dangled it in front of Ruben to see.

He took the towel from her and inconspicuously wiped his face and blew his nose before lifting his head and sitting back up. He exhaled deeply as though worn out from the emotional battle he'd just fought.

After mustering his courage, he looked over at Riley, who greeted him with a Mona Lisa smile.

"You certainly bring out the worst in me," said Ruben, trying to bring levity to the situation. "Don't I feel silly. A blubbering hobo - what a sight for sore eyes," he said, mocking himself.

"Yeah, maybe we should enter you in a circus sideshow. Millions will line up for a ticket. I can see it now - in bright, neon lights on the marquis," she said, her fingers forming the ends of a rectangular sign. "Homeless and blubbering. Get your tickets now!" Riley said, joining in the mockery.

Ruben turned, his brown eyes piercing hers as he tried to perceive if she was being vicious or just making light of the conversation.

She returned a sardonic smile while simultaneously shaking her head, indicating that she did not agree with his assessment of himself. He knew then that was her way of trying to cheer him up. He laughed - the first laugh he could remember sharing with anyone other than Nadine in a long time. She laughed, too.

Their light moment came to a halt when they felt the back door of Faith House opening and pushing them off their comfortable perch on the doorstep.

They turned simultaneously to see Nadine's head peeking around the door.

"Are you two still out here? Eve, are you making time with my man? Just so you know, that is a firing offense."

Riley and Ruben stood looking at each other. They burst into laughter again.

"Look, I hate to break up the party, but, Eve, you're needed in here. Ruben, if you want to join us, I'm sure I can find work for you to do, too!"

"I'm sorry, Nadine. I didn't mean to go AWOL on you." Riley took a few steps forward, but then remembered. Ruben was caught off guard when in one fell swoop she pivoted around and threw her arms around his neck in a heartfelt hug. Before he could wrap his arms around her to return the embrace, she had shot out of sight behind the door. Ruben, aghast at how quickly she had disappeared, stood alone in the alley looking up at Nadine's glowing face.

"I see you've made a friend," Nadine said.

Ruben's face reddened. He was speechless.

Nadine pushed the door open wider. "Ruben, you know you can come in."

He looked longingly at the open door. "I know I can."

He turned and trudged down the dim, dull alley toward the light of day and the busy street.

Chapter 18

Riley had no idea before accepting the job at Faith House how much was involved. Any management skills she possessed had previously been applied to her daily assignments at the TV station where she worked.

She and Paine had a housekeeper, who managed their home. She had her personal bank accounts, but Paine had managed their joint accounts. They had financial advisers, accountants, and attorneys who managed their investments and business affairs.

Until she married Paine, her world was small and simple and needed little management, thereby requiring her to have little expertise in that area. So being second in command at Faith House opened her eyes to just how inexperienced she was. Fortunately, no one seemed to mind, least of all Nadine. In her unflappable manner, Nadine would gently coach Riley toward the end goal whenever she detected that Riley was perplexed about how to do her job. She would immediately come to her new assistant's rescue without being asked. And Riley exhaled every time Nadine read her mind that she was in trouble.

One part of her job was juggling the many non-residents who were in and out of the shelter - vendors and inspectors and county and city code enforcement officials and the fire marshal and supporting nonprofit agency representatives. This part of her job created varying levels of stress, depending upon the person or the organization they represented. She couldn't help but fret over the prospect of being pegged a fraud by someone who recognized her. Dealing with outsiders posed a daily threat to her security at Faith House.

And never more so than the day Cal Gordon arrived at the shelter to make the usual delivery from the Bread of Life city food bank. It was Thursday. Thursday was Cal's favorite day of the week, so he was in an extraordinarily good mood when he rang the bell to the back door of the shelter. He looked up and down the alley for anyone approaching - something he had worried less about before moving to New York. The city had a way of transforming normally trusting individuals into cautious, guarded people, who were suspicious of everyone.

He never suspected on that particular Thursday, however, that he would be caught off guard by Nadine's assistant, who swung open the back door to greet him. The bright-eyed, redhead smiled at him and his legs instantly became as limp as cooked spaghetti noodles. He grabbed the door handle to keep from dropping to the cement floor.

"May I help you?" Riley inquired of the delivery man, whose truck was backed up to the door.

Cal wondered for a split second whether his sudden weakness was that obvious. But then he realized that she had no idea who he was or what business he had with the shelter and needed to introduce himself before she slammed the door in his face.

"I'm Cal Gordon. I'm the director of the city food bank. Nadine called and said the shelter was running low on food supplies."

"Oh, great! Yes, we are. Do come in."

"If you don't mind, I'll start unloading this food before it goes bad."

"Of course. Do you need a hand?"

"No, thanks. I've got it. You stay inside where it's warm."

"Wow, you certainly give personal service, don't you?"

A puzzled expression let her know that he didn't understand her meaning.

"It's unusual for a director to double as a delivery man, isn't it?"

"Oh, that? When you're in nonprofit, you do everything, even clean toilets."

"So I'm finding out."

"Besides, we're short-handed today. My driver's wife is in the hospital having a baby."

"I see."

Riley smiled, then ducked back inside when Cal realized he still didn't know who she was. Whoever she was, she didn't look like she belonged at Faith House.

"I'm sorry, I didn't get your name," he yelled as she disappeared into the shadows of the shelter. Seconds later, Riley reappeared at the door, hesitant to respond. She dreaded the question, knowing her answer would be a lie.

"I'm Eve, Nadine's assistant manager." She stuck out her hand for a handshake.

Cal looked at her long, slender fingers. He became weak all over again at the invitation to touch her. He removed his glove from his right hand before reaching out and clutching her hand while he sheepishly peered into her blue eyes.

"Hi, Eve. Nice to meet you."

Cal began perspiring from the nervousness he felt from holding her hand for those few seconds.

Riley ducked out of sight again.

Cal slipped his hand back inside the glove and feverishly stacked food crates on a pair of hand trucks. He was afraid that she was gone and he would not see her again before he left. Occasionally, he glanced over, looking for her to poke her head out or to reappear in the doorway. When she didn't, he cut the first load short to hasten the process and step over the threshold of the door that had swallowed this beautiful woman and snatched her from his view. He didn't want to lose any time in seeing her at least once more before he completed his delivery. He threw the portable ramp down over the steps, then dragged the loaded hand trucks backwards up the ramp. As he did, he glanced back and sideways, watching both for obstacles in his path and for the redhead, who had captured his interest.

After entering the kitchen, he heard Riley ask, "Do you know where everything goes? Or do you need direction?"

"I'm good," he said, as he began lifting a crate and walking toward the pantry. As much as he would have loved for her to help as a way of keeping her active in conversation and close in proximity, he didn't want to appear unknowledgeable or incompetent or weak.

"How long have you been at Faith House?"

"That's two questions in only a few minutes," Riley calculated to herself. She immediately became uncomfortable with this stranger's curiosity. She didn't want to offend him, but nor did she intend to hang around and play twenty questions with him.

"Not long," she said before steering the conversation back to the business at hand. "Do you have a bill of receipt or packing slip you need me to sign?"

"Yeah. It's in the truck. I'll get it as soon as I finish unloading everything, unless you're in a hurry."

Riley was disappointed, but said, "No. I'll finish my kitchen duty while you unload the food."

She returned to the kitchen sink and plunged her hands into dishwater. There she fished out a plate and began washing it. From that point on, she kept her back to Cal, who became more and more frustrated at feeling like he had been robbed of the opportunity to talk to her.

In the meantime, he made the best use of time. Every chance he got, he summed up the shape of her with his eyes. He admired her shoulder-length, beautiful red hair and watched and tried to memorize her movements. His eyes took in as much as they could each time he passed her on the way to the freezer and the pantry and the back door for another load. He got an occasional glimpse of her profile, but he wished she would turn around so he could lose himself again in those blue eyes and her lovely face. He also wished for another opening to say another word or ask another question so he could hear her voice.

After unloading the last crate and loading the portable ramp back onto the truck, Cal slammed the accordion backdoor of the truck shut and locked it into place. He opened the driver's side door and reached across the front seat for a clipboard holding the billing receipt and inventory of the foods he had just hauled into the shelter. He paused briefly to catch his breath. In that brief moment, he grabbed the rearview mirror and twisted it around to check out his hair. He pulled a comb from his back jean pocket and slid it through his hair to tame the strands that had fallen across his forehead and over his ears. When it met his approval, he re-deposited the comb to his pocket and turned the mirror back toward its original position.

With the clipboard tucked under his right arm, he slammed the truck door and raced up the steps in hope of getting his foot in the door with this blue-eyed beauty. He poked his head through the door and saw immediately that she continued to wash dishes with her back toward him. When she didn't look back, he cleared his throat to get her attention. He saw her glance over at him. He shifted his weight to one side with his arms dangling beside him. His right hand clutched the clipboard with paperwork on it. She didn't know how long he had been standing there, but she suddenly felt uncomfortable with him there.

"I'm sorry. I didn't realize you were finished." She withdrew her hands from the soap suds and quickly rinsed them. "I hope I haven't gotten you off schedule. We appreciate you giving us such personal attention today."

Riley's praise made Cal's face blister from embarrassment. He looked down at the floor as he mumbled, "Ah, it's no problem."

"Clearly, you didn't have to do that since you were down a man, but we thank you for making the sacrifice." She dried her hands on a green checked hand towel.

"No problem ... really. Actually, it's been my pleasure," Cal said while trying hard not to stare at her. "If I had not been the driver today, I would not have met you. That would have been my loss."

Riley blushed as she cut her eyes at Cal, then quickly looked away. She said nothing in reply, leaving Cal to wonder if she had heard him.

"Where do I need to sign?"

Riley determined that keeping this man on task was becoming no easy task for her. The sooner she sealed their business transaction and sent him on his way, the sooner she could exhale.

Cal handed her his ink pen and pointed to the blank line where he required her signature. He held the clipboard firmly in mid-air so that she could sign it, thereby putting her in closer proximity to him. He inhaled her sweet, subtle perfume that, even blended with the clean smell of dish detergent, caused his head to swim.

As she signed her name, she consciously kept as much space between them as she could, avoiding any accidental touch or brush against him. Riley scribbled her pseudonym, caring little about her penmanship. When the last curl of the "l" in "Campbell" was drawn, she thought she was off the hook and he would be on his merry way. She was wrong.

"Do you suppose I could get something to drink? Maybe some water?"

Riley hesitated, wanting desperately to deny his request. But she thought how cold and insensitive that would sound. Besides, he had just hauled a sizable load of crates into the shelter - a job she was spared from doing.

"Certainly," she said less than enthusiastically.

"I appreciate it. A guy can work up a thirst, especially if he's not accustomed to manual labor."

Riley grabbed a glass from the cabinet. She walked over to the ice machine and scooped crushed ice into a giant metal scoop and turned it upside down over the glass.

"How do you like working with Nadine?"

"More questions," Riley thought, cringing inside and trying to hide her growing irritation. She felt him closing in on her with every question.

"I enjoy it. She cares about Faith House and the women here. So how long have you known her?" She decided to beat him to the next question to get the focus off her.

"About five or six years ... ever since I took this job." He raised his eyebrows. "How time flies."

Riley finished filling the glass with tap water. She dried dripping water from the outside of the glass with a towel before handing it to him.

"Thank you," he said.

As he turned up the glass, Riley noticed that his straight thin brown hair, damp from perspiration, curled up slightly on the ends around his neck and ears. He had a five o'clock shadow and his small, thin mustache had gray highlights in it. Sweat beads glistened on his forehead. He was wearing a heavy jacket, but she could see he had a thin, lean build and long arms offset by broad shoulders and a thick neck. He was about Paine's height, but was much less meticulous about his appearance. He had a certain ruggedness that was accentuated by his apparel: jeans and a button-down twill shirt. His nails needed a manicure and his work boots a polish.

But despite his rugged appearance, his brown eyes and dimples, which appeared only when he flashed an occasional smile and exposed his straight, white teeth, the temptation to cast another peek at him was too great.

Riley propped her hands on her hips as she waited for him to drink the refreshment. She hoped that by waiting, he would pick up on her sense of urgency and not dawdle. Again, she was wrong. He took a few swallows, then persisted in continuing a conversation with her.

"If you don't mind me saying, you certainly are a breath of fresh air in this place," he said coyly.

Riley dropped her head, trying to hide her own embarrassment.

"Thank you," she said. She stared at the cracks in the tile floor to keep from facing him as she said, "But, actually, I do mind."

"I'm sorry. I didn't mean to offend you."

Riley glanced upward at his left hand, looking for signs of a wedding ring. No ring and no shadow of a ring. She cocked her head sideways to look at him.

"You didn't. I just prefer to keep things professional, if you don't mind."

Cal took another swig of water. He handed the glass of melted ice chips back to Riley, but maintained a tight grip on it as she attempted to take it from him.

"Actually, I do mind. You see, that's going to be a little difficult. If I had never seen you or spoken to you or learned your name, it would be no problem. But I have … now there's no turning back." He mocked Riley with his devilish grin.

Meanwhile, her shock could be read all over her face.

"So, Eve Campbell, you have a good day. And I'll be seeing you again soon."

When he finally released his hold on the glass, he caught Riley off guard. Little did he know, she nearly lost her own grip on it. He then grabbed the clipboard from off the kitchen counter and headed for the back door. He looked back once more in her direction. With a broad smile that emphasized his dimples, visible even from across the room, and a nod of his head, he was out the door.

Riley, frozen in her tracks, felt a lump in her throat and a sinking feeling in the pit of her stomach.

Thrill and terror. Excitement and dread. Flattery and fear. All came together to make her queasy and dizzy. Riley plopped the glass down on the table and planted her palms on top of the table to balance herself and still her shakiness. She leaned over the table, her head hanging low. Despite her every precaution and attempts at discouragement of this type of situation, her efforts backfired.

"Oh, dear," she muttered.

"Eve! What's wrong?"

Nadine's voice alarmed her. She had not heard the stout woman enter the kitchen.

Riley clung to the table with her head drooping over it.

"Are you sick? What is it?" Nadine marched over to her and pulled her red hair away from her face so she could get a better look at her.

"Cal Gordon. That's what's wrong."

"Oh, dear … Yeah, he's quite a heart throb, isn't he?"

"In a rugged, persistent kind of way," said Riley, glancing up at Nadine, who still had Riley's red hair pulled back.

"Yeah, that's Cal," she said, nodding her head for emphasis. "Did I also mention what a charmer he is?" Nadine released Riley's hair, allowing it to cascade around her face and hide it again from view. She shuffled toward the door to exit the kitchen, leaving Riley leaning heavily against the table.

"Oh, dear," Riley muttered again.

"You can say that again," she heard Nadine say, her voice trailing off as she disappeared through the door.

Chapter 19

Cal Gordon was true to his word.

The next day he called her to wish her a good day. Later that day, a basket of freshly-cut flowers arrived at the door for her. The card said, "I hope you don't mind ... ."

He waited until the following day to phone her again to ask if she'd have lunch with him. She refused, so he asked if she'd have dinner with him. When she said "No," he suggested breakfast the next morning. She declined.

"At least have coffee with me."

"Cal, as much as I would love a large caramel macchiato, my answer is still, 'No.'"

An hour later, the doorbell to the front door of the shelter rang. Seconds later, Deidra's voice could be heard throughout the home.

"Eve! Eve! It's for you!" Other women chimed in, repeating Deidra's message, sending an echo through the hall to Riley's room, where she was sitting Indian-style in the middle of her bed reading. Riley snarled at the interruption. "I'm coming!" she yelled back as she rolled off the bed. She opened her bedroom door and padded down the hall to the front door. She gathered a parade of followers, who were equally as curious about the surprise visitor.

Riley didn't know what to expect after the flowers arrived, but part of her was growing weary from the unwanted attention Cal was lavishing on her. She didn't want to have to explain why he was doting on her, not to mention that his flirtations were putting her job and residence at Faith House at risk. Another part of her, however, leaped inside when she heard his voice or thought of him. She peered cautiously around the corner, but the front door was cracked slightly and the visitor stood outside, so she couldn't see who it was.

Deidra was nowhere in sight. Riley rolled her eyes at the inconvenience of responding to the caller without first knowing who was calling. She pulled the door open to see Cal standing at attention like a sentry with his hands tucked behind his back. He smiled widely, showing off his dimples, when she came to the door. Riley tried to hide her annoyance. She couldn't help but notice how polished he was in comparison to when she first met him. He appeared less disheveled in his khakis and country blue oxford shirt and wool blazer. Before she could open her mouth to scold him for showing up without calling first, Cal pulled a coffee cup from behind his back and presented it to her.

"Special delivery ... large caramel macchiato ... for your enjoyment, Eve Campbell. I hope you don't mind."

Riley's jaw dropped at the gesture.

He grinned mischievously, then shot out of view before she could say anything. Riley was stunned. She stared at the large cup of coffee and then poked her head out the door, but Cal had completely vanished by the time she looked for him. She pulled her head back in and closed the door. The strong smell of coffee, blended with the candy sweet caramel, wafted up to her nostrils. It was a reminder of days gone by.

"Mm," she moaned to herself.

The temptation not to turn down this unexpected gift was too great. "One sip. What could it hurt?" she reasoned, as the familiar scent stirred longings that she had managed to repress since going underground. Riley padded back to her room. She crawled into the middle of her bed, where she sat cross-legged, still holding the large coffee like a trophy.

No longer able to resist, she took a sip of the hot, sweet coffee drink.

"Mm," she sighed. "Charming." That was the word Nadine had used to describe him. Frighteningly, however, his charm bore some resemblance to that once possessed by the man to whom she was still married, Riley reflected. Cal was similar to Paine in the way he was smothering her with gifts and pressuring her with his gift of persistence.

"Charming" had been Paine's most endearing quality in the beginning of their courtship. But it wasn't long before his charming nature grew at odds with a contemptible side he had masterfully hidden from her. Riley became caught in the crossfire of those two opposing halves of his personality more and more. As time went on, his contemptible side won out so often over his charming side that, in the end, there was no recognizable charm left in him.

She never quite understood at what point Paine completely crossed over from the man, who started out lavishing her with gifts and attention, to the monster, who took away her self-esteem and confidence and robbed her of emotional and mental well-being. It had been a slow process, but a long, anxious, and terrible ordeal - one to which she wanted never to return.

Riley had no warning when she married Paine that he would flip-flop between Dr. Jekyll and Mr. Hyde episodes. Even if someone had warned her, she would not have believed it because he was so adoring and kind and generous at the onset of their courtship. In hindsight, however, she could also look back and see how he used his charm to control her even from the beginning. He would ignore her wishes, but would sweep her off her feet with surprise trips and plans that made her forget her own agenda.

Now she could see clearly the many times and ways Paine had manipulated her toward his way of thinking. All of his manipulation was preceded by his charm. Riley shuddered to think as she took another sip that she was looking down the road to a similar situation with Cal Gordon. It was a mistake Riley could not afford to repeat. The stakes were too high to be swayed by someone else's school of thought - and that included Cal Gordon, regardless of how innocent his gestures. She had learned the hard way that outward appearances said nothing about a person's intentions or hidden nature.

Riley knew also that allowing Cal any more room in her life marked the beginning of more questions. She could not risk opening her world to him or falling prey to his charm. Doing so would only expose her to potential dangers. Yes, she minded deeply his attempts to get too close to her. At the shelter, she was among other women who closely guarded their secrets and their histories from prying outsiders. She was not subjected to the kinds of interrogations that accompanied new relationships with outsiders, particularly men in search of more than a platonic relationship. That brought her to another problem altogether.

Because she was still legally married, Riley was not free to pursue anything but a platonic relationship with another man. The problem was that no one knew she was married. Nor could she tell anyone she had a husband living in Manhattan. No one would understand why she chose to live in a rundown women's shelter when she could go home to luxury and comfort. Moreover, she didn't want anyone digging around for information about her husband. In this neighborhood, it could pose a threat to her and him if someone learned she had a wealthy spouse. They might decide to bankroll their future by holding her for ransom or use her as bait for blackmail.

Most of all, Riley needed to protect herself from Paine. Every day, she lived in fear that he might discover that she was alive, as well as her new location. She feared he would keep his word and kill her for leaving him and pretending to be dead. He would not tolerate the idea that she would rather be assumed dead than return to their picturesque marriage and posh home.

Although Cal was charming and although he appeared to mean well with his flirtations and surprise gifts, she did indeed mind. He posed a valid threat to her safety and to her anonymity.

Riley admitted to herself within the privacy of her bedroom that this man's attentions thrilled her. It excited her that she had captured the interest of a man who persisted in capturing hers. It had been a long time since she had been courted and pursued. His phone calls and surprise gifts had put a smile on her face and had secretly given her something to look forward to each morning and while she moved through her daily routine.

After putting everything into perspective, Riley realized that she was no stranger to the allure associated with romancing the wrong man. Riley wanted to give Cal the benefit of the doubt. But, in this case, it was also the wrong time.

Yes, Riley did mind. Getting involved with Cal Gordon was not an option for her - platonically or romantically. She didn't know how she would get her point across without raising red flags. She held the large coffee cup up and read the green and ivory label. It dawned on her that accepting any more gifts from him would not convince him of her disinterest. She frowned at the thought of giving up this one small luxury as she took one last sip.

Riley raised the cup in the air as she rolled off the bed and crossed her room. She opened the door and meandered through the hallway to the kitchen, dragging her feet every step of the way. She stopped in front of the sink. She popped the lid off the cup.

"Who was that at the door?" asked Rosie, a newcomer to the shelter.

Riley tilted the cup, which was almost full of coffee, minus three sips, and poured its contents down the drain.

"Nobody," Riley said, followed by a deep sigh. "Nobody I know."

She turned and plunked the empty cup and lid into a nearby trash can, then padded back down the hallway to her bedroom, slamming the door shut behind her.

Chapter 20

Riley had stopped tallying the number of phone calls she had avoided, the gifts she had refused, and the flower arrangements she had sent back to the florist - all attempts by Cal to move their relationship beyond the introduction phase.

It was growing more and more difficult for Riley to say "No" to his generosity. Each gift was more extravagant than the last and his pressure on her to accept them was increasing. Chocolates, trinkets, silk scarves, and leather gloves were Christmas presents followed by theater tickets for two and a hint that he was available to join her. Then a book of poetry - romantic poems, nonetheless - were sent to her by messenger. In between those deliveries were different floral arrangements showcasing assorted aster and lilies, Dahlia, wax begonias, chrysanthemums, poinsettias, and even an orchid, which withered days after delivery. They streamed in like a floral audition. Obviously, Cal didn't know Riley's favorite flower, so he appeared to be parading an assortment of flowers before her on the off-chance that he might guess the right one and win bonus points with her. Even though she turned down every floral delivery, Riley was impressed with the line-up. But she wondered why he thought a woman living in a homeless shelter needed silk scarves, except to make her feel pretty and luxurious. Months prior to living at Faith House, she probably would have found anything made of silk a desirable gift. But things had changed for her. Salvation and daily sustenance now replaced silk at the top of her list of preferred gifts.

Riley was impressed with the selections Cal had made in his attempts to win her heart. She also wondered how the director of a food bank could afford such extravagance. Paine's source of wealth was evident. And when Paine, drawing from his quiver of romantic arrows, wielded his wealth, he often flaunted it, carefully choosing gifts of great expense and rarity. But he could afford it. Precious gems. Out-of-print classics and autographed, star-studded novelty items and books. Airfare to exotic locations anywhere on the globe.

Celebrity auction tickets. Broadway Theater tickets for box seats on opening night. Paine knew no limits, at least not in the beginning.

Regardless, Cal's bank balance or purchasing power were not her concern. She needed to figure out how to put a stop to Cal's persistence.

He had thus far ignored her hints, her blatant rejections, and her refusal to take his calls or accept his invitations and gifts, as well as his requests to visit her at the shelter. It didn't seem to matter to him that she had repeatedly rejected him. Each rejection only fueled his persistence more.

"What am I going to do?" Riley finally broke down and asked Nadine.

"About what, Darlin'?"

"About charming Cal Gordon."

"Oh, that."

"What do you want to do?"

"I want to go back to business as usual without all of this uninvited attention."

"So tell him to stop."

"I have."

"Face-to-face?"

"Maybe not in so many words ... but I would think that as many times as I've turned him down over the phone and returned his gifts that he would get the point that I'm not interested. I mean, how thick-headed can one man be?"

"Thick-headed? Or smitten?"

"Huh!"

Nadine, seated behind her tiny desk in her nearly closet-size office, sifted through a stack of papers piled in the center of her desk. Her stout figure looked out of proportion behind the secondhand student desk in the small room. But Nadine took it all in stride, never complaining or pining for a better work environment. Riley, on the other hand, suffered claustrophobia whenever she went into Nadine's office.

"How can you get any work done in this compartment?"

"The same way I would in a penthouse office overlooking Central Park ... one step at a time. Besides, there's less room to mess up with a smaller space. Now, don't go changing the subject midstream."

"I wasn't ... ."

"Why aren't you interested?"

"What?"

"You heard me. Why aren't you interested in Mr. Gordon?"

Riley felt nervous knots immediately grip her stomach. Heat rose in her face and a lump formed in her throat. She grabbed a paper clip from off Nadine's desk and began untwisting it.

Nadine, out of the corner of her eye, saw Riley bending the clip. "Now you know we can't afford toilet paper, much less office supplies. Why do you want to go and ruin that gem clip so I can't use it?"

Riley blushed a deeper shade of red.

"I'm sorry."

She bent the clip back, trying to restore it to its original shape, but without success. She returned it to her desk top in its new contortion.

"So, are you going to answer my question or bit by bit tear up my cubicle?"

Riley grimaced. Nadine's questions were taking her where she didn't want to go. Her mind raced for a way out.

Nadine continued to wade through the paperwork, filing some in a two-drawer file cabinet that abutted the left end of Nadine's desk and that gave the appearance that her desktop was longer than it actually was. Other sheets of paper didn't make the cut, but found their way floating to the bottom of the cylindrical trash can tucked in the corner. When she realized that Riley had not answered the question, Nadine's hands, which clutched a thin stack of papers, dropped with a thud on the desktop and she peered over her rectangular-shaped, tortoise reading glasses and looked pleadingly at Riley.

"I'm just not, okay?"

"How do you know? You haven't given him a chance," said Nadine, who had picked back up on her office work.

"I just know," Riley said crisply.

Nadine tacitly thumbed through a fresh stack of papers, then dumped them into the wastebasket.

"Have you considered just going to have coffee or lunch with him as friends? After all, he's single; you're single," Nadine said while glancing up over her papers to read Riley's reaction. "There's no harm in that, is there?" Nadine had looked up just in time to see Riley's face turn crimson. She observed her start to wiggle in her chair and cross and uncross her legs. Riley's jaw tightened.

Her agitation came through her voice as she asked, "Nadine, are you my boss or my dating counselor?"

"You're right. It's none of my business. Besides, dating is off limits while you live here and we certainly don't want to give the other residents the impression that you're not abiding by the rules. It might send the wrong message to them. I don't need that problem on my hands," said Nadine.

"I just worry that you don't get out enough or have any friends." Nadine stopped filing and pulled off her glasses. She peered across the desk at Riley. "I can't help but wonder why that is."

Riley felt the heat turning up in that small, cramped closet of an office. If only Nadine had some art or plaques or something on the walls to look at so she could avoid Nadine's interrogating eyes. She felt herself shriveling under her glare. Maybe it was the heat, but she felt like she was melting like the Wicked Witch of the West in "The Wizard of Oz." Even the musty smell of the office was making her head swim.

"I'm fine, Nadine."

The women locked eyes with one another. Riley thought the stare would last forever. She wanted to clear the lump in her throat, but she was certain it would give her away as the deceiver she was.

"I see," Nadine said, then returned to her filing.

Riley, stunned at Nadine's comment, didn't know whether to pursue the conversation to learn more about what Nadine meant, or to bolt while she had the opening. One part of her was pleased that Nadine hinted that she was satisfied and the conversation was over. The reporter in her, however, wanted to know more. But the woman on the run from her husband and hiding out in a women's shelter knew better. This was definitely a time to keep silent and protect the mystery behind her current situation.

"I'm glad you agree with me," Riley said before sliding off her chair and disappearing through the doorway.

"Anytime," said Nadine, whose mind had returned to her elbow-deep filing project.

When Riley was out of sight, Nadine paused from her work again, removed her glasses, closed her eyes, and pinched the bridge of her nose as she drifted into deep thought. She knew there were probably many things Riley wasn't telling her. There was not a woman who had come through the doors of Faith House who didn't have her share of secrets. Still Riley was different from the rest. She had not come to her with tattoos and body piercings, scars from slit wrists, cigarette burns, or knife slashes. A bruised eye told Nadine only part of Riley's story. Most of the mystery remained unsolved. Her mannerisms and etiquette had not been formed on the streets or in a broken home. Her speech was not peppered with slang and profanity, but indicated that somewhere along the way, she had been exposed to education, knowledge, and values. Nothing in Riley's actions or speech indicated to Nadine that Riley had any sort of criminal involvement. On the contrary, she was refined. She was educated. She was well-bred. Circumstances that brought her to Faith House had to be extreme to drive her away from the kind of environment to which Nadine imagined her to be accustomed. She was convinced that Riley was hiding out. But from whom? From where?

In spite of all of these burning questions, it wasn't her place to pry, she reminded herself. Somehow, it didn't stop her from being concerned, especially for Riley.

The redheaded, blue-eyed young woman had immediately attached herself to Nadine's heart on her third day at the shelter. That was the day she awoke to her new reality and wet Nadine's bosom with her tears. They had bonded in an extraordinary way and working side by side had strengthened that tie. Riley had a way of bringing out Nadine's maternal instincts more than most of the residents. After hearing Riley's plea for help and watching her struggle alone in the dilemma Cal Gordon was creating for her, Nadine was finding it extremely difficult to resist the urge to get involved in Riley's personal affairs.

The question now was how to get unnoticeably involved. Nadine had made it a point not to meddle in the affairs of the residents, only to mentor them toward success, and monitor their activities while at the shelter. It was important not to veer from that philosophy in this particular case. She pondered the ordeal, prayed for wisdom, and pondered some more. After a while, Nadine picked up the telephone receiver, punched in a phone number, and waited. When a voice came through the receiver, Nadine said pleasantly, "Cal, how are you today, son?"

"Oh, that's good. Listen, I've got someone here who'd like to see you this afternoon. Do you suppose you could be here around two o'clock? ... Yeah? Lovely ... I'll see you then."

Nadine gently placed the phone down on the receiver and sighed a breath of relief.

"Who says I can't have a few secrets of my own," she muttered to herself. She picked up another stack of papers and read the top sheet to determine its value. She put it aside to be saved. She scanned the next document and frowned, showing her instant dissatisfaction with it.

"You are out of here," she muttered to the piece of paper. "Just taking up unnecessary space. There's only one place for you. In with the rest ... ."

With one hand, she wadded it into a firm paper ball and tossed it into the wastebasket.

Diedra, who had been walking past Nadine's office about that time, leaned her head in. "Who are you talking to?"

Nadine, still focused on her routine filing like nothing was out of the ordinary, shook her head in denial. "Do you see anybody here?" Nadine casually asked without lifting her head from her work.

"No, that's why I asked." A confused look crossed Deidra's face. "Talking to yourself again, huh? If you're not careful, Nadine, someone might get the wrong idea about you ... like maybe you're delirious."

Nadine stopped and looked up from her filing. "You know, I just might be. You might want to be careful. You just never know when I'll snap. If I were you, I'd be moving on and leaving me to the voices in my head."

Deidra giggled and then shot out of view.

"Mm ... I guess I can't have any secrets around here," Nadine said with disdain. "Mm."

Chapter 21

Nadine's desktop sparkled from the fresh coat of furniture polish she had applied to it. She was moving the dust cloth across the top of the filing cabinet when a knock on the door of her office rattled her concentration.

"Oh, Cal, you startled me. Won't you come in?"

"I'm sorry, your phone call was a little mysterious and I wasn't sure what to do when I got here, whether to clear my visit with you or what ... ."

"No problem ... You just caught me cleaning house ... you know, getting rid of unwanted clutter that piles up until you can't stand it any longer."

Cal was handsomely dressed in crisp khakis, a black turtleneck and a long, black wool coat and a charcoal gray scarf around his neck. His hair was neatly combed except for the spray of bangs that fell loosely across his forehead.

"Yeah, I know what you mean. I should probably take the time to do an overhaul in my own office, but there never seems to be much time."

Nadine tossed the disposable dust cloth into the wastebasket and moved a filing tray onto the top of the cabinet before taking her seat behind the desk. Cal's cologne was so strong that it competed with the fumes from the furniture polish she'd been using to dust her office. She was both secretly amused and filled with pity for Cal. He wanted what most people long for - companionship - and she was about to dash his hopes of Eve becoming his companion.

"Uh, Nadine, I'm a little confused. Is Eve here? I asked several of the women before I got to your office, but no one seems to know where she is."

"No, she's running some errands for the shelter."

Nadine had deliberately sent Riley out with a list of errands that would keep her away for a while.

"Oh, ... I thought," he stuttered. He scowled at her response.

"What? I'm sorry. Did you misunderstand?"

Cal withered as he looked blankly at Nadine from the doorway.

"Come in, Cal, and close the door. I'm the one who wanted to see you."

"Oh, ... I see," he said as he pushed the door shut and slumped down in disappointment in the chair facing Nadine.

"No, Cal, I'm not sure you do. That's why I invited you here today, to help you see things more clearly."

Cal sat up straight and braced for the ensuing confrontation.

Nadine peeled her reading glasses off her face to keep from looking over them and propped them on top of a stack of books that remained on her desk. She sighed a heavy sigh as she folded her arms and leaned forward, resting her elbows and her weight on the desk.

"Cal, you and I have worked together for a long time. You know I don't mince words, and I'm not going to start now."

"Is something wrong, Nadine?"

"Yes. You have put me in an awkward position."

"How's that?"

"From the looks of things, you have set your affections on my assistant resident manager, who also happens to be a resident of Faith House. As a resident, she is required to follow a set of rules. If she fails to follow those strict house rules, she will be asked to leave."

Cal sat stone-faced and as still as a monument, prepared for the worst.

"From all indications, Eve has been trying to adhere to those rules ... with no outside encouragement from you, however. In case you've forgotten, this is a safe haven for women who have had negative encounters in the outside world. It's a place where they come to heal, to start over on more successful footing, and to re-establish themselves into society. It's not, nor has it ever been, nor will it ever be as long as I'm here, a place to pick up women. Do I make myself perfectly clear?"

"I'm not picking up women," he said, defensively.

Nadine lifted her forefinger in front of him, signaling him to bring his side of the debate to an end. Cal's red face bobbed up and down as he repeatedly answered, "Yes ... Yes ... I understand - perfectly. I'm sorry, Nadine. I never meant to ... I just ... She's so different ... I didn't realize."

Nadine leaned back in her chair and laced her fingers together over her stomach.

"Cal, I don't care what they look like on the outside. They're all the same on the inside. They're hurting; they're scared; they're suffering pain you'll never comprehend; and they're broken. And it's not your job to fix them. It's not your job to fix her."

"Can't I just take her out for coffee occasionally. I'd like to be her friend," he pleaded.

"Not unless she's ready to find a new address and a new job, and I don't think she is," Nadine said, her tone becoming sharper. "Besides, how would it look to your Board of Directors if they knew you were on this side of town slumming for a date?"

"That's rather cruel, don't you think, Nadine?"

"I don't believe it to be true. But it's reality, Cal. Face up to it," she said. She sighed again, then rested her chin in the nook of her right hand between her thumb and forefinger. "You think I'm cruel? Think about it, Cal. Imagine the kinds of looks you'll receive, the rumors that'll be started, and the things that'll be said about Eve. None of this would be good for your career or for her recovery and we both know it."

"I suppose you're right." He slumped forward and hung his head, contemplating the matter.

"Well, can I at least tell her good-bye?"

Nadine pursed her lips and narrowed her eyes as she heaved another deep sigh. "Correct me if I'm wrong, but hasn't Eve already said more than a dozen good-byes with all the rejections of gifts and flowers and invitations you've sent? Swallow your pride, Cal. Take the hint and save face."

Cal, still slumped forward, avoided Nadine's piercing glare. "I guess it's over," he said without looking up.

"It can't be over what was never started," said Nadine.

Cal's head bobbed up and down again in agreement. He stood up and hovered in front of Nadine's desk.

"I'm sorry, Nadine. I didn't mean to create any tension between our organizations. And I certainly didn't mean to create any problems for Eve. I just thought ... ."

"I know."

Cal turned, twisted the door knob and started out the door when Nadine blurted out, "Cal!"

He looked back at her, hopeful that she was having a change of heart.

"Yeah?"

"I don't blame you. If it's any consolation, you have good taste in women. And under different circumstances, I'd be more than happy to give the two of you my blessings. And maybe when she leaves here and puts the pieces of her life back together ... but as long as she lives here, it's out of the question."

Cal hung his head and paused in brief thought.

"By the way," she added, "Eve doesn't know that we've had this conversation. I'm the one who sent her on errands."

He nodded. "I understand." He exhaled.

"Well, I'll let you get back to your cleaning and purging."

Nadine watched him leave. He walked into the hallway, where he lingered. His head turned left, then right, then left again. He didn't say anything, but Nadine sensed that he was hoping to either get one last glimpse of Eve or to cram in a last word before he exited her life. She heard him breathe a sigh of disappointment. Even after he dropped out of sight, cologne as fresh as when he had arrived at her office lingered behind. She realized, however, that he was not the same man who had bounced into her office with eagerness and confidence. She was responsible for that transformation. She had dashed his hopes of having a relationship with Eve. It was a hard decision - one that left Nadine with a twinge of guilt and sadness, but not doubt. Cal may have left without the confidence he had when he arrived, but Nadine gained more confidence that she had done the right thing.

She could clearly see that Cal Gordon had been threatening Eve's peace of mind. She would have intervened on behalf of any of the residents in similar situations.

The reason the majority of the women became residents at Faith House was because their lives had taken a turn for the worse, generally because of decisions resulting in clouded foresight or judgment. But while at Faith House, the goal for each of them was to find clarity, so they could achieve clear direction and make sound decisions that would enable them to put their bad decisions and broken lives behind them. Anything that hindered or challenged their healing or maturity process needed to be weeded out and purged, just like the growing mounds of paperwork on her desk. When not dealt with immediately or regularly, paperwork covers the usable spaces on a clear desk surface. It eventually becomes so overwhelming that it robs productivity and efficiency from the person staring at the paper mountains every day.

Nadine believed that daily life must be gleaned regularly for positives, purity, wholesomeness, and usefulness; otherwise, negativity, impurity, degradation, and laziness prevail. Eventually, if gone unchecked, the latter is all that's visible in a life.

Nadine opened a file cabinet drawer, tucked the can of furniture polish out of sight, then slammed the drawer shut and locked the cabinet.

Life is messy, she thought. But for the present, Nadine found self-satisfaction in the stillness and cleanliness of her tiny office, where the scent of furniture polish blended favorably with a man's cologne to create a fragrance all its own. Her meddling would pay off for a woman she believed was destined for greater things. Nadine had no idea what. She only knew that Cal was right. Eve Campbell was different. While she couldn't quite identify what made her unique, Nadine was certain that she above all her other residents didn't need to be hamstrung in her efforts to rise above her circumstances. Nadine couldn't help but wonder if she might be training her own replacement. More often, she had a strong feeling that Eve would surpass even her and do great things.

A demure smile of contentment crossed her face as she sat in solitude. In the middle of assessing her work, Nadine jumped slightly when another voice startled her.

"What are you smiling about?"

Nadine grabbed her chest to slow her racing heartbeat.

"People are trying hard today to hasten my death," she said.

"I'm sorry. I didn't mean to frighten you. I finished those errands you requested," Riley said while peeking around the doorjamb.

"Thank you."

"What are you doing?"

"I was admiring my clean office. It won't look like this tomorrow, so I was enjoying it for as long as it lasted."

"It does look nice ... less like a closet," Riley said with a smirk. "Smells good in here, too."

Nadine realized at that moment that she would not be able to hide the truth from her.

"You just missed Cal."

"Did I? I suppose he was looking for me."

"Yes, he was."

Nadine saw the strain on Riley's face as she breathed a sigh of weariness.

"He was looking for you to tell you good-bye."

"Really!"

"Yeah. He realized that the timing of your relationship was awkward, not to mention inappropriate. He also admitted that he was wrong for ignoring your subtle hints that you're not interested in him," Nadine said.

A crease that instantly flashed across Riley's forehead did not escape Nadine's notice.

"What's wrong?"

"Oh, nothing. It's kind of bittersweet," she said as she suddenly felt the loss of being noticed and wooed by this handsome stranger.

"I suppose it is. But now instead of being hounded, you're free to choose ... and to choose what you want and what is best ... not what is being forced upon you. You'll no longer feel like you're under duress."

A faint smile replaced the contemplation.

"You're right ... Mm," Riley said. "Your office looks really nice. Enjoy it."

Riley disappeared from the doorway.

Nadine was alone again with her clean office. She breathed a sigh of relief. "It's nice to have things neat and tidy again," she thought to herself. "At least until tomorrow." She quietly chuckled to herself. "Such is life," she said aloud. "Such is life."

Chapter 22

After several months of helping manage Faith House, Riley had dealt with ex-husbands and boyfriends showing up and demanding to see their significant other. She had survived the lengthy persistence of Cal Gordon, who would not be satisfied with a professional relationship with her. She had encountered problems with the state fire marshal issuing citations for potential fire hazards and city code officials citing the shelter for ordinance safety violations. In most cases, Nadine met with the local officials and law enforcement since Riley had purposely avoided them. She didn't know who might recognize her, so she stayed clear of them all. She traded off with Nadine by meeting with the state officials with whom she'd had less face contact. Generally, all the state officials required was a tour of the facility and for someone to sign off on paperwork verifying they had done their job and, unfortunately, to accept any citations written. Riley saw no deception or risk in that.

But none of those encounters compared with the tension Riley had felt since Vivi's return to the shelter.

Riley had dreaded her return for a week. Nadine had warned her that Vivi was completing rehab and would soon be returning to Faith House. She told her as much to warn her to guard her prized possessions and money, as to allow her time to prepare her attitude for Vivi's arrival at the residence.

Riley saw her when she arrived, but Vivi would not look at her. She hung her head and avoided eye contact before scurrying off to the sleeping quarters to unpack.

"She blames me," Riley surmised. She sighed at the probability of dancing around Vivi in days to come.

Life at the shelter had been good. It had its ups and downs, but overall, Riley felt at home there. Aside from the first altercation involving Vivi, it had also been peaceful at the shelter. Riley had not feared a fist or a backhand bearing down on her. She had not encountered a harsh word. At most, she had heard complaints about the food or about being out of soap or paper towels. Riley's life had settled into a calm she'd not experienced in all the years she was married to Paine.

Vivi's arrival, however, resurrected fears of reprisal and exposure. She became concerned for her own security all over again. Riley's stomach knotted the day Vivi walked through the front door, and every time their paths crossed or she saw her even briefly across a room, the knot grew. Vivi compounded the problem by keeping her distance from Riley and by completely ignoring Riley whenever she was around. Several times, Vivi appeared to run from Riley. "She blames me," Riley continued to tell herself. But Vivi gave her no opportunity to try and clear the air or make the situation right. The tension building in Riley began evolving into resentment. Even though no words or greetings or looks of acknowledgment had been exchanged between the two women, Riley could not seem to emotionally untie the knot growing in her stomach. She stayed in a perpetual state of anxiety.

Another month passed with no change. Riley could no longer take the tension between them. She had grown tired of tiptoeing around Vivi, especially since she had done nothing to create the problem between them.

One morning at breakfast, Riley found herself at one end of a table where Vivi was seated near the other end. Conversation was lively among all of the women, but Vivi.

The Hispanic woman reserved most of her comments for the woman seated next to her, but shied away from contributing to the general banter at the table. Neither did she look in Riley's direction.

Vivi was the first woman to clear her plate. Riley, who watched her rise from the table, began picking at her scrambled eggs and hash browns. The tension had destroyed her appetite. She finally pushed her plate back and watched Vivi slip out of the room without a word.

Anger swelled in Riley.

"Maybe I should be grateful for the silence," Riley thought. "At least we're staying in our neutral corners and not coming out fighting."

As chatter went on around her, Riley could concentrate on nothing but the deafening silence between her and Vivi.

"No, we're fighting, just not with words," she concluded.

Her mind wandered to the memory of painful silent treatments Paine had given her when she had committed some simple offense such as wearing the wrong shade of lipstick. She remembered how guilty she felt during each episode. When he would not readily explain his silence, her overactive imagination would come up with a long list of possible reasons, good reasons why he might be angry with her. The process sent her on a lengthy and exhausting guilt trip that kept her in turmoil. The longest period stemming from Paine's silent treatments was two weeks. She lost sleep, weight, and self-confidence. After he eventually confessed his reason for abstaining from conversation with her, she vowed to never let his petty issues and silent protests cause her so much distress.

But each time, Paine got the last word with his silence.

The silence between her and Vivi had long surpassed any gaps in conversation that she had experienced with Paine. Riley had turned the situation inside out and looked at it from every angle. Without talking to Vivi, she could come to no immediate resolution. After about three weeks of dancing around the problem, Riley asked Nadine for advice. Nadine told her that she needed to take the first step and talk to Vivi. But memories of confronting Paine were too fresh. She did not know Vivi well enough to ascertain how she would react. Riley decided to bide her time and give Vivi an opportunity to set things straight. "After all, she stole from me," Riley responded. "She should make the first move." In truth, however, Riley just wanted to go back to the way things were before Vivi's return. She wanted to be able to relax around Vivi and to stop tensing up when she saw her. Also, she didn't want to keep feeling guilty for unknown reasons.

Riley stabbed another clump of scrambled egg and stuffed it into her mouth. When she discovered that the bite was cold, she wrinkled her nose in disapproval. She slammed down her fork, pushed away from the table and picked up her tray. She carried it to the kitchen, deposited it in the service window and then headed down the hall to find Vivi. She poked her head in the door of the dormitory where she saw Vivi's bed made and a pair of shabby sneakers and her suitcase neatly tucked underneath.

Shauntay Jefferson, a new resident, was making her bed when Riley peeked inside.

"What's up?" the young black woman said.

"Have you seen Vivi?"

"Yeah, but she's gone. She got outta here in a hurry."

"Did she say where she was going?"

"She hasn't said much of anything since I've been here," Shauntay said. "And she don't be talkin' to me when she do talk."

"Thanks, Shauntay." Riley ducked out of the room, then turned back. "Hey, by the way ... you're doing a good job here. Keep up the good work."

Shauntay's eyes and face lit up from the compliment.

"Thanks," Shauntay said.

Riley shot her a thumbs up, then marched toward her own room. She decided that it was time to get out and get some fresh air. She wanted to get away and forget. "Where is that place of forgetfulness?" she asked herself.

It had been a long time between coffee breaks. She had been working hard and had saved quite a bit of money. She decided that she deserved to spring for a latte or cappuccino. The way she was feeling, she would even order whipped cream on top - anything to improve her disposition and make her feel better about life.

"I miss those little things," Riley thought as she grabbed her handbag, the secondhand brown corduroy coat and cap, scarf and gloves Nadine had given her, and her sunglasses, and went to find Nadine.

In her previous life, trips to coffee houses had been daily and sometimes twice a day. Coffee and fresh bagels and cream cheese had been her comfort food. Lately, however, she had found her comfort in other things - in prayer, scripture, helping the residents, and maintaining peace of mind. Riley felt compelled to go in search of a coffee shop - because her peace of mind at Faith House was being threatened. She was subconsciously rebounding to what was familiar and had once given her peace, however temporary. Regardless of where she went, Riley decided she couldn't stick around the shelter all day, wondering how to deal with Vivi.

Riley stuck her head in Nadine's office and told her that she was taking the day off.

"I think that's a good idea," Nadine said without looking up from her paperwork. "Thanks," Riley said.

"All work and no play, you know what they say," Nadine said. "I've been considering doing the same real soon."

Riley shut the door behind her, almost clipping Nadine's sentence before she finished it. Riley didn't want to give her time to change her mind. She scurried down the hallway, not stopping to speak to anyone. She donned her coat, cap and scarf as she walked toward the front exit. She pushed her hands into the gloves. Riley opened the door and stepped out into the cold, crisp, February air. Once outside, she exhaled deeply as if she had escaped to freedom. Then she remembered to put on her sunglasses to shield her identity.

Riley bounded down the snowy sidewalk toward Broadway. "That's always a good place to start," she thought.

Riley walked for a long stretch without seeing anyone. She had grown accustomed to few people traveling in their neighborhood. But also it was Saturday and fewer people trickled into the city.

The closer into town, the more congested the streets and sidewalks became. Riley merged with the thin stream of people winding through downtown Manhattan. It wasn't long before she sighted a coffee shop. She fell in line, ordered a hot coffee instead, then rejoined the flow of folks who paraded down the sidewalk before splintering off in different directions.

"How decadent," Riley thought. Seldom had she walked through Manhattan aimlessly with no destination or agenda. "The last time I did this ... ."

Riley's breathing suddenly felt constricted. Weeks had passed since she had thought about that day. Things around her began spinning. She grabbed her chest as she became short of breath. Slowly, she stepped toward an alcove of a bank building. She pressed herself against the wall of the building, trying to bring her spiraling surroundings to a halt. She leaned her head back firmly against the building and closed her eyes.

Flashbacks of that day - the falling debris, the falling bodies, the falling buildings - filled her mind like the dust and ash that had clouded the streets and air. The covering of snow on the ground and parked vehicles reminded her of the layer of ash that covered everything that dreadful day. Riley consciously slowed her breathing as perspiration broke out on her upper lip. She diverted her thoughts to Nadine, Ruben, Deidra and even Vivi. After a few more minutes, Riley regained control of her breathing. When it finally slowed to a regular pace, she gradually opened her eyes. Everything around her was in place, no longer spinning.

Riley, still glued to the building, watched people amble by. Hanging onto the building created a feeling of *deja vu*. She had been here or in such a place before. It was that Tuesday when she had hidden from the devastation and tried to avoid being caught up in its path of ruin.

She realized that she had pushed all of it to the back of her mind and had not truly revisited that day since she had found security at Faith House. She had stayed close to Faith House, not venturing too far to prevent disclosure of her identity. In truth, she stayed close because she felt safe. Now her security at the shelter was being threatened. Her safety factor was dropping incrementally with every day she was at odds with Vivi.

Riley could not understand how Vivi Garcia held the key to her safekeeping.

Do not fear.

Those words tapped into Riley's thoughts.

But Riley knew their origin. She had learned to recognize the voice. She also recognized the words. How often had she read them in scripture? Almost daily, her eyes had come across those very words sprinkled strategically throughout the Bible. They were God's words of encouragement to individuals in situations much like hers - situations where they felt weak, confused, frustrated, or backed into a corner.

Now they were words coming to her when she needed them most.

Suddenly, Riley knew where she was headed. She removed herself from the wall. She raced across the sidewalk, almost colliding with another pedestrian in her haste.

"Taxi!" she yelled while holding up her right hand to flag a yellow cab. She didn't have to wait long since there was less demand for taxicabs on Saturdays.

Inside the cab, Riley did not hesitate to share her destination with the taxi driver, whose head was turned in her direction.

"Ground Zero," Riley spouted.

It was the first time she had called the sight of her former workplace by its new name. She sat amazed at how naturally it had rolled off her tongue - much like her own new name. Her new name, however, was intended to mask the truth. She felt like she was still holding onto elements of her former life.

Riley wondered what it would take to transform her own life into one she no longer had to hide from the world - one no longer lived in fear. She dreamed about what that re-invented life would look like.

Surprisingly, it was a life that would not take place in a Manhattan high-rise. It wouldn't be lived out at posh parties and society fund-raisers. It wouldn't be a daily race dictated by day-timers and someone else's watch. She didn't know exactly what it would look like. She only knew the kind of life it would not resemble: her past life, the one she'd fled and had been trying to forget.

Furthermore, the new life she envisioned would not include Paine. It would be a life in which she no longer tolerated abuse in any form from a man who professed to love her. She would not find it necessary to hide her painful, troubled private life behind a false smile. Her re-invented life would not be a ruse, or one lived in fear of public scrutiny. She longed for a life that would not bring her shame or humiliation. In her mind's eye, she saw a future that allowed for transparency and peace of mind.

Riley leaned her head back as the cab zigzagged through traffic toward Lower Manhattan. Occasionally, the taxicab bounced slightly, causing her head to spring forward from where it was resting on the back of the seat.

Transparency and peace of mind - these were uncommon goals for Riley, who less than a year before, was concerned more about achieving professional goals, including producing award-winning stories, increasing the bottom line in her bank account, and adding to her wardrobe. She chuckled to herself at how much the past five months had changed her perspective.

Riley's thoughts ceased when the taxi drew to a sudden halt alongside the curb near the subway station at Vesey Street. She looked out of her window toward the spot where the towers had stood. Her chin dropped as her eyes looked up at the gaping hole in the sky left by the fall of the towers. Riley paid the cab driver, but hesitated to get out. The impact of the overwhelming void had already taken her breath away.

"Do you want me to wait?" the Arab cab driver said in broken English.

"No," said Riley. She opened the door and stepped out onto the snow-covered sidewalk. She crept nearer to the edge of devastation.

There on the fringes, Riley heard the roar and screech of heavy equipment and the hum of truck engines from where she stood transfixed on the sidewalk. She saw giant white and orange cranes with their spider arms raised over the site. What was left of the aftermath evoked deep sorrow and immediate tears. A mountain of debris, twisted steel and waffle-like metal structures that were once functional buildings filled the corner where Towers One and Two had just months earlier stood tall and strong.

Backhoes and dump trucks moved through, also cleaning up the remains of the other five buildings that had comprised the World Trade Center. Riley looked up and saw, as if for the first time, other buildings that had stood in the shadow of the World Trade Center. Now their exteriors, charred by the explosion, had found the light. She had taken for granted how much the presence of that majestic center had overshadowed everything around it and took up so much space in Lower Manhattan.

As Riley inspected the rubble from the Church Street sidewalk, the faces of her former co-workers were resurrected in her mind. She thought of their ashes mingled with the ashes of thousands of other victims, as well as with the molten steel, confetti, shards of glass, and bits and particles left by the explosion. She pinched her nose to keep from smelling a putrid odor that hung in the air. A dry cough followed - the persistent cough that had lingered with her days and nights on the street.

Tears trickled down Riley's cheeks, but inside, she felt numb. She pondered the trash heap - all that was left of the center that had previously held a position of prominence in the world. The World Trade Center was the height of financial success and the epitome of wealth, fame and fortune - icons of New York City. Everything she had dreamed of was here, Riley thought. In a matter of minutes, the center had been reduced to a rubbish heap. Riley zeroed in on the remains of the compacted towers. She realized that a split-second decision had prevented her from being among the rubble. The heaviness of that revelation weakened her to the point that she could no longer stand. Her legs folded underneath her and she dropped to the sidewalk. She sat cross-legged on the concrete overlooking the cleanup site and wept.

She mourned the loss of lives - known and unknown. She struggled with the guilt that she bore from choosing not to go to work that day.

Both she and the World Trade Towers were at Ground Zero, she thought. They were both recovering from devastation. They were both struggling to pick up the pieces and to put the past behind them. They were both in a state of disrepair. They were both in shambles. And they would both have to rebuild from the ground up.

Riley brushed away the last of her tears and sat listening to the heavy machinery clearing away the remains of any evidence of death and destruction. Soon, there would be nothing left to show the world that Thomas, Barbara, Brigette, Takashi, Salvatore, Catherine, Sean, and Peter had been part of the professional world. Unless their families recounted stories about them and shared photographs of them in years to come, would anyone remember them? What mark on this world indicating that they had been here would be found by future generations?

Riley pondered those same questions about her own life. "What difference has my life made? If I had died, would I have been forgotten?"

It occurred to her at the moment that no one truly knew her well enough to posthumously remember her. She had lived a life detached and disconnected from others. There would be little to recall about her other than what her TV audience saw of her on the television screen. She wondered if a funeral or memorial service had been held for her. She was suddenly curious about what had been said about her during the service. Who had felt comfortable enough in their relationship with her to eulogize her? When she mulled likely candidates for the responsibility, no one sprang to mind, except Paine. But the thought of Paine as the grieving widower, wallowing publicly in his grief, and sharing his feelings about her and about details of her life made her cringe. She also wondered if her parents had flown to New York for the service, or if they had conducted their own memorial service among friends and family at their own small church in Georgia. "Did Paine even notify them?" she ruminated.

The scraping motion of an orange backhoe scooping up sections of debris mesmerized Riley, whose thoughts returned to the messy details she had left behind. She thought of Paine, her parents, and an unfinished career.

"I wish it was that simple," she said, looking at the backhoe. "I wish I could just scoop everything up and haul it off to the city dump and be done with it."

She pinched her nose again to block the smell from reaching her nostrils. It occurred to her that while it would be easier, until the unfinished business of her past is cleared up, she would only be rebuilding on a trash heap. "What kind of new life will that be?" she asked herself. She turned her nose up at the stench. "And no matter how much perfume I splash on it, it will always be nothing more than an offensive odor that will eventually give me away," she said to herself.

Riley returned to her feet and brushed snow from her slacks. Before turning to flag a taxi, her eyes caught sight of a crudely welded replica of a cross that stood near the wreckage. Riley remembered seeing on TV news that the crossbeams had miraculously been welded together in the shape of a cross at some point during the disaster. It had been discovered by rescue workers and cleanup crews while sifting through the debris. The cross was hoisted to a place of prominence for all to see.

Riley stood in awe, realizing that the television cameras had not captured the full essence of the work of art. Or was it that it meant more to her now, seeing it up close and personal and at this point in her life.

The sight of the cross gave Riley encouragement that her broken life, too, would one day rise from the wreckage and be miraculously transformed. She found comfort as she gazed at the rustic metal cross that there was hope for brighter days ahead.

Seeing the cross also reminded her of the church across the street - the place where she had offered up a prayer for solutions and for the start of a new life.

"I think I'll visit an old friend," Riley said aloud.

She crossed the street and meandered up the winding walk to the nearby chapel. She reminisced about the last time she had climbed the incline to the charming little church. She had been in distress then, looking for a way out.

The closer she drew to the open door of the church, the more she noticed the effects of the explosion at the World Trade Center on the graveyard and the exterior of the building. Her brow crinkled as she scanned the charred headstones that peppered the lawn. Her eye caught a quick glance of the thin dark coating on the exterior wall. Nothing went untouched by the ripple effect of 9/11, she thought.

Seeing the sanctuary - its aqua blue and ivory tones - calmed her, however. She peeled off her cap and coat after entering the church. With each step toward the altar, Riley felt like she was returning to a place of peace and security. This time, Riley walked all the way to the front of the church. She removed her sunglasses, and drew closer to the familiar gold figure of Jesus Christ, close enough to see the details of his face and the miniature, refined cross in a way she had not seen it before. She felt drawn to the sculpted face, so much that she wanted to reach out and touch it.

Instead, she ducked behind the first pew and knelt on the prayer bench in front of her. Riley, in the past two months, had learned to connect the dots of her life through prayer. Her fragmented, disjointed life seemed less chaotic and stressful when she sought divine interaction. Nadine had helped her realize that God did not raise his children to stand on their own feet, but to sit at his feet. She explained that only in that position do we learn God's ways and stay humble to hear his voice. "Otherwise, his children get too big for their britches," Nadine had said to her.

Riley thought of how often throughout her life she had been too big for her britches. She wanted her way. She had turned a deaf ear to God and to her parents most of her entire life. She listened instead to the world calling her to a life that promised fame, fortune, and success. Now that she had claimed all the world's promises, she found herself alone, stranded by the world, and left with hollow promises.

Kneeling at the altar, her mind was filled with those echoing words, *Do not fear.* Images of her parents' faces also floated to the surface - her father working in the garden, tending his azaleas and roses, and her mother up to her elbows in flour while baking biscuits in their warm, cozy kitchen. Her heart ached for them.

Do not fear, the voice said.

The memory of Paine's fist driving toward her face replayed the pain inflicted by matrimony that had once fit her ideal union. In hindsight, she could identify red flags that had been raised to get her attention - flags she had deliberately ignored. Paine had been her ticket to power, position, and wealth. Being his wife had helped further her career. When she supposed that she was entering a marriage of convenience, she had actually said "I do" to being abused, belittled, robbed of her self-esteem and peace of mind. Now she could never go back or undo the "I do."

Do not fear.

Riley looked at the gold crucifix, wondering if it could talk to her, what would the statuette of Jesus say.

"What about Vivi?" Riley found herself praying.

Do not fear, she heard the voice inside her growing louder.

After a few more minutes, Riley arose and started toward the door. Then she saw cots lined up along the outer walls of the church. She did not remember them being there five months ago.

"How odd," she thought to herself. She walked over to get a closer look. She had never before seen or heard of cots stretched out in a church sanctuary.

"They were the beds used by firefighters and paramedics and volunteers on 9/11," a man's voice said, breaking the silence from the corner of the church.

Riley gasped and grabbed her chest in surprise.

"I'm sorry. I didn't mean to startle you," the man said.

"I didn't know anyone was here." After catching her breath, she said, "I couldn't help but notice the cots. They're quite unusual."

"Yes. Unusual cots for unusual people who've displayed unusual acts of courage. We left them out in their honor and to show that unselfish people with everyday lives and jobs have the potential for heroism," he said, poignantly.

"Mm," Riley said, feeling as though the man with the kind face had just eavesdropped on her silent prayers and delivered a personal message to her. She suddenly got lost in her thoughts, forgetting that the man was standing nearby.

"Is something wrong?" he said, calling her back from her mental retreat.

"What? Oh, no, just something you said."

"It's, uh, it's good to see you again. I mean, it's good to see you doing well."

Riley felt the blood drain out of her face. She furrowed her brow. Panic coursed through her insides. Should she play along or hurriedly squeeze out of this situation?

"How does he know me?" she thought, her mind racing to process his face, his voice, his identity. She could not recollect knowing him. Was her secret about to be revealed? She swallowed the lump that had immediately formed in her throat, then stood silent, not knowing what her next word should be.

"I'm sorry, but I couldn't help noticing your bruises the last time you were here, uh, I mean, when you removed your sunglasses. I don't usually pry when parishioners come here, but I overheard you crying. It troubled me deeply."

Riley dropped her head, wondering how much more he knew about her. Would he report her or alert authorities that she was alive?

"Don't be embarrassed," he said with compassion and sensitivity. "I prayed for you that day ... for your safety and deliverance from whatever or whoever had caused you pain."

Riley looked into the bright, blue eyes of the man, clad in a light blue oxford with rolled-up sleeves and khakis. His thick, wavy brown hair was neatly cut, but uncombed and dipped down on his forehead. Tears blurred her vision as she tried to take in the rest of his features.

"I didn't mean to make you sad. I'm just glad God heard my prayer that day. I have often wondered about you since then."

Riley bobbed her head and brushed away unexpected tears as quickly as they fell.

"Yes, yes he did. Thank you."

"I'm Father Patrick, Father Michael Patrick," he said, holding his hand out to shake hers.

Riley, still fighting back unexpected tears, shook his firm hand, but did not offer her name. She could not bring herself to deceive him.

Thinking back to the first day in the chapel, Riley could not remember seeing a minister.

"I hope I haven't upset you too much," he said. "I'll let you return to your meditation. But I hope you'll let me know from time to time how you're doing." Before leaving her alone, he turned back to her and said, "By the way, I like the change."

"Excuse me?"

The pastor pointed to his hair, then to hers. "Red. It's nice."

Her mouth formed the word "Oh."

"Don't fear. Your secret's safe with me." He smiled teasingly at her, then departed. She regarded him curiously.

Riley narrowed her eyes in wonder not only at whether there was hidden meaning in his statement, but also why he would care about her welfare.

She nodded, half-heartedly.

She quickly headed toward the exit. She pulled her cap and coat back on, then put on her sunglasses. Before walking out the front door, she glanced back to see that the minister had grabbed a mop and was pushing it back and forth. He smiled and waved at her just before dropping the mop and creating a loud "Thud!" The echo sent throughout the sanctuary jarred her memory.

"Ah! Not just a cleaning man," she thought, "… an everyday hero."

Chapter 23

Riley strolled down the last block toward Faith House. She was in no hurry to return if it meant returning to an air of tension and discord.

She was bringing to an end a day that had been a splendid blend of enjoyment, relaxation, soul-searching, and reflection. She didn't care to wrap it up with the stress of avoiding Vivi and exerting her energies trying to make the best of an uncomfortable situation. She wanted to know how to smooth out the wrinkles of their awkward relationship, to stop trying so hard to connect with her.

Riley sipped the remainder of a fresh hot cup of cappuccino - a last splash before returning to her responsibilities at Faith House. Riley sighed as she rounded the corner down from Faith House.

She slowed her walk and took in the sights around her. How different this neighborhood was from Lower Downtown, and even from the Upper East and West Sides, where on either side of the city was wealth, fortune and prosperity. Yet the place where she stood divided the two worlds. She read the graffiti spray-painted on the walls and saw signs of people wanting out, wanting more, simply wanting. They wanted to cross the invisible, dividing line and experience how the other half lives. She knew what that was about. All of her life she had wanted more and wanted out. How she wished she could tell them, the artists of the streets, that more is not always better. She wished she could encourage them to make the best of where they were instead of focusing all their time and energy on trying to get out. Her parents had tried to teach her to be content, to stop striving, but she had tuned out their lessons. She had interpreted their advice to mean that she should settle for what she had and not reach for anything higher.

Now, strolling down the sidewalk of one of the less desirable areas of town, she understood. She was finally at peace with herself, the direction her life had taken, and the work she was doing in spite of her environment. She did not desire more. She had no need to get out. She was content where she was until it came time to move on. The difference was she would not push or pull to make things happen. The time and the opportunity would present themselves and flow naturally in the scheme of things.

Do not fear.

Riley understood those words. She understood their meaning in a way that brought peace and harmony to what had until that afternoon been a restless spirit. She thought back over her life at how ridiculous she had been, chasing lofty dreams that she thought would bring her joy and contentment. All the while, the things she had been seeking were within her grasp.

Riley laughed out loud. She looked around to see if anyone had overheard her. When she saw that no one was around, she laughed louder and continued until she was laughing and coughing through tears.

She mopped up the tears with her sleeve, then began laughing again.

"Get a grip," she told herself. She scanned the streets again to see if she was still alone. She was pleased to have found a silly moment to herself.

Riley took a few more steps and came to the alley into which the back door of Faith House led. She had a habit of glancing down the alley to look for Ruben, who might be waiting for a meal. Riley was disappointed when she didn't see his bulky silhouette standing near the back door. Riley started to cross the alley and head toward the front entrance when she was distracted by an unusual sound - a cry of some sort.

Riley froze, straining to hear the sound again.

"Oh!"

Riley recognized the faint cry of a woman moaning. She eased down the alley, looking for the source of the weak cry. Riley cautiously approached the dumpster. On the other side, she saw the arms and legs of a woman sprawled across bundles of trash bags next to the trash bin.

Riley's face registered shock at the sight resembling something she'd seen from a distance only at New York crime scenes or on TV crime shows. She moved in closer to see more.

"Oh, Lord, help me!" Riley said.

Riley jumped up on the trash pile and carefully maneuvered the battered woman's head and torso into her arms and lap.

"Vivi! Oh, no, Vivi! What happened?"

Vivi continued to moan.

"Help! Somebody help!" Riley yelled until the back door sprang open and Fatiqua appeared.

"What is it?"

"Get help! Get Nadine! Hurry, it's Vivi!"

Fatiqua disappeared and in her place, Rosemary, Deidra and several other women filed out of the building to see what all the yelling was about.

"Help me get her inside," Riley ordered. "Deidra, go pull a folding cot into the kitchen so we can transport her on a flat surface. I don't know yet if she has any broken bones."

Deidra ran back inside without a word. She almost collided with Nadine, who was exiting through the back door. When she saw Vivi, Nadine raised her hands to her mouth to muffle a shriek. When she felt it was safe to uncover her mouth, she lifted up a quick prayer, "Oh, Jesus, please help this child."

Riley, in the meantime, inspected Vivi's body for any serious, visible injuries. After she discovered none, she said, "Fatiqua, go see if Deidra's got the cot into the kitchen. The two of you bring it out into the alley."

Some of the women stood around in shock and at a loss as to what to do. Some cried - the only thing they knew to do. Nadine stood back, praying and giving Riley room to work. Riley sat calmly holding Vivi close to her and waiting for the cot. She peered down into the bloody, bruised face of the Hispanic woman. Her beautiful, olive skin had already turned varying shades of black and blue. Patches of dried blood were on her face and matted in her shimmering, straight brunette hair. The sight tendered Riley's heart toward her. "You're going to be okay, Vivi. We're here for you," she said.

A few minutes later, Fatiqua and Deidra came through the back door hauling the portable bed. They planted it firmly next to the trash heap, then walked around to help Riley shift Vivi onto it. Riley calmly, but firmly, spouted out orders on how to move Vivi.

Vivi groaned slightly as she was being moved. Once on the cot, four women picked up the corners of the cot and transported it back inside, not stopping until they got to the dormitory.

"Let's put her over in the corner," Riley said. "Then help me move an empty cot beside her so I can keep a close watch over her tonight."

Nadine had followed the caravan inside and stood in the background watching Riley take command of the emergency situation. She wanted to chime in, to take control, but she deliberately held back, wanting to see how Riley would handle the crisis. While Riley worked, she watched and prayed.

"Rosemary, get some warm water, soap, wash cloths, a towel, and the hydrogen peroxide and cotton balls," Riley said. "Also, bring some blankets."

Riley looked up and saw the circle of women gathered around, observing. "Ladies, how's supper coming? I smell something and it smells really good. I'd hate for it to be burned. Besides, Vivi's going to be hungry when she wakes up, so we don't want to disappoint her."

The circle slowly disbanded, except for Deidra and Fatiqua, who helped Riley remove Vivi's torn, blood-stained shirt and pants. Rosemary set a pail of warm water and a bar of soap in a nearby chair. She pulled wash cloths and a towel from over her shoulder and handed them to Riley. As the four women treated Vivi, they moved quietly in contrast to their patient's random cries that stemmed from discomfort or pain.

Riley and Deidra each grabbed a wash cloth and cleaned the blood and soil from Vivi's face, arms, hands, and hair. A few minutes later, Rosemary returned with hydrogen peroxide and cotton balls on a tray.

As the blood disappeared from Vivi's face and arms, Nadine could see that Vivi's injuries were not as extensive as they originally appeared. Relief came in such a wave that it threw her off balance. She stumbled, then caught herself before landing on another cot.

Riley noticed Nadine's unsteadiness.

"Are you alright?"

Nadine, choking back tears, said, "Yes, now that I see that this child is going to be alright."

Riley could read on Nadine's face the deep concern, resembling that of a mother for her children.

"She's going to be fine," said Riley, who reached out and pressed Nadine's hand. "We're all going to be just fine. Do not fear," she said, repeating the divine words of comfort that had fallen like rain upon her all day.

Nadine's smile of confidence returned.

"You're right, Darlin'. You are so right."

After they finished bathing Vivi, Riley applied antiseptic to her open wounds, causing Vivi to occasionally groan louder. They redressed Vivi with a bathrobe before covering her with a blanket. Seeing that Vivi was still semi-conscious after moving and treating her wounds, Riley said, "Fatiqua, would you bring some hot tea and crackers?"

Fatiqua, eager to help, shot out of the room toward the kitchen and quickly returned with a tray laden with a stainless steel pitcher of hot water, sealed tea bags, and saltines. She set the tray on a folding table. Fatiqua picked up the pail of dull, soapy water turned pink from Vivi's blood and left the room to dispose of it.

Deidra and Rosemary plopped down on a cot opposite Nadine to wait for more instructions and for Vivi to awaken to fill them in on what had happened. They were anxious to know. They had questions: Who did this to her? How and why did it happen? Deidra bit her fingernails while she waited. They waited while Vivi moaned and whimpered.

Riley looked at the battered face left with cuts, scrapes, and bruises. These marks were not new to Riley. They were the marks of someone forcing their way upon another. They were the marks of a coward who hid behind a fist. They were the signature of someone who lived in fear and desperation and insecurity. They were the marks left by someone who fought the loss of control over another being.

Riley recognized these marks. She had received similar marks. Her own face had been marred by such a person. She surveyed Vivi's beautiful complexion and thought how tragic that it would be for it to be permanently scarred. Riley, aware of how invisible scars can also be left on another person's life, scrutinized the abrasions and cuts that most likely would change the complexion of this woman's life. She became angrier at the sight of each one.

Riley's jaw tightened as she studied the swollen face of the woman whose groans signaled pain - physical or emotional. They would not fully know which until Vivi opened her eyes.

Riley looked over at Nadine, whose face was pinched with worry in a way she'd not seen in the months they'd worked together. Their eyes locked. Nadine stopped reading Riley's thoughts long enough to send Rosemary, Deidra, and Fatiqua, who had only been back in the room a few minutes, to the kitchen to assist the others.

After they had departed, Riley asked, "Should we call the paramedics?"

Nadine did not answer right away. Her eyes shifted to Vivi, who had not moved since Riley finished treating her wounds.

"If what happened is in some way the result of a crime Vivi has committed, then this will be just the start of her pain," Nadine said in a low voice. "What do you think?"

Riley sat up straight, took a deep breath, held it, then exhaled slowly. She gnawed the inside of her left cheek as she contemplated their situation. She took one long look at Vivi's young, beaten face. Riley turned to Nadine and said, "I think I'll take the night shift. You'd better get some rest."

"Darlin', I won't be getting any rest. I'll be praying to the Great Physician."

Riley sighed deeply as she further surveyed Vivi's cuts and scrapes and said, "It looks like we're in this for the long haul."

Chapter 24

Riley sat straight up on the cot.

A woman's scream roused her, but it took a few seconds to determine its origin. Had she herself screamed? Had her own nightmares returned to haunt her?

When the fog lifted in her head, she realized that noises were coming from the next cot - from Vivi.

Riley jumped up, switched on a nearby lamp and saw that Vivi was thrashing about on the cot, fighting some unseen enemy.

"Vivi. Vivi, wake up," Riley said, trying to keep her voice low to avoid waking the other residents. But Vivi continued to wrestle an invisible foe.

"Vivi!" Riley yelled.

Vivi's eyelids fluttered.

"Vivi, come on, wake up. It's me, Eve. It's okay. You're safe now."

Vivi stopped flailing on the cot. She opened her eyes wide with terror and slowly drank in her surroundings and Eve's face.

Riley could see that Vivi was shaking from whatever had terrified her. She grabbed a blanket from her bed and spread it over Vivi.

"Do you know where you are?"

Vivi nodded. But Riley noticed her hesitance to respond.

"Do you know who I am?"

Vivi examined her half-lit face. Again, she nodded. As she looked up into Riley's face, she suddenly went into hysterics, crying and ranting in a way that Riley could not understand.

Riley reached for a bottled water and aspirin that had been set out for Vivi in the event that she awoke in pain. Riley could not determine from Vivi's emotional fit whether she was in physical pain or still experiencing a nightmare.

"Drink this ... slowly," said Riley, holding and tilting the bottle of water for her.

Vivi took one swig, then another. She dried tears from her face and water from her mouth with the back of her hand.

"Do you want another?"

Vivi shook her head.

"Can I help?" Riley heard someone from the other side of the room say. She recognized the sweet, young voice as Deidra's.

"No, Deidra, go back to sleep."

"Is she okay?" said Deidra.

"Yeah. She's going to be."

Riley looked at her watch still strapped on her arm to read the time: 1:47 a.m.

"Are you hungry?" Riley whispered to Vivi.

Vivi, after pondering the question, nodded.

"Do you feel like walking to the kitchen? I'll help you."

Vivi nodded again.

Riley was relieved that she consented to move to another room. She was concerned about waking the other residents.

Riley also noticed that Vivi grimaced when she stood. She offered support to Vivi, whose walk was stilted.

"Are you in a lot of pain or experiencing any unusual problems?"

"What are you? A doctor?" Vivi retorted.

Riley overlooked the sarcasm. She recognized it as part of Vivi's nature. It was her sarcasm that had created additional tension between Riley and Vivi on Riley's first day at Faith House. But after hours of worrying about Vivi's condition, Riley now interpreted her biting comments as a good sign that Vivi's injuries were not serious.

"Vivi, I'm trying to find out if we need to call a doctor."

Vivi dropped her head as she struggled to take each step. Finally, she said, "No, I don't think so."

Riley detected a change in Vivi's attitude. After helping her down the hall, Riley steered Vivi toward a wing chair near the kitchen. Riley retrieved the blanket she had grabbed off Vivi's bed and placed it over Vivi's legs, tucking it tightly around them, forming a cocoon.

From her crouched position in front of Vivi, Riley could see the marbled bruising and swollen contours of Vivi's face more clearly. One of Vivi's eyelids was nearly swollen shut. She tried to maintain a straight face. She did not want to horrify her or make Vivi self-conscious of her appearance.

"Want some scrambled eggs? It's my specialty."

Vivi looked at her with an odd expression. "Sure, that would be great," she said.

Before rising to the task, Riley cocked her head to one side and said, "What's wrong?"

Vivi sat silent for a moment, then shook her head.

"Okay, well, I'll be right back. Call me if you need me."

Riley disappeared into the kitchen, leaving Vivi alone with her thoughts. In the low light, Vivi tried to revisit the past twenty-four hours, but her memory failed her. There were blocks of time for which she could not account. The minutes she did remember seemed more like hours - painful, horrifying hours.

Suddenly, the thought of being alone became terrifying in itself. Vivi fought to release herself from the quilted cocoon. She crept into the kitchen, where the smell of eggs cooking had already begun to cause her gnawing stomach to ache. She quietly slipped into the room; however, she was uncertain of whether her presence there would be welcomed.

Riley had not heard her enter and jumped when she turned to see her standing there.

"Oh! You startled me!"

"I'm sorry. Would you rather I wait out there?" said Vivi, pointing to the sitting area.

"No, of course not! It's not your fault I'm skittish," said Riley. "Actually, I'm glad you're here. How do you like your eggs?"

"I don't like 'em runny."

"Now you're talkin' my language."

Vivi shot Riley another strange look. Once again, her expression did not escape Riley's notice.

"What is it, Vivi? What's on your mind?"

Vivi pulled a chair out from the table.

"I just don't understand why you're being so nice to me. I mean, I stole from you. In my neighborhood, that's grounds for revenge. I don't get it."

Riley stirred the eggs in the skillet. Her back was turned toward Vivi.

"Is that why you've been avoiding me since you got back?" she said while continuing to cook. "You thought I was going to retaliate?"

"Well, yeah."

Riley turned off the stove, picked up the frying pan and scooped a portion of the eggs into a plate. She twisted around toward Vivi. "Do you mind if I eat with you?"

Vivi looked at her with probing eyes. She didn't understand Riley's sudden evasion of the topic.

Vivi shook her head no.

"Good, because I'm starved. I guess, in all of the confusion, I forgot to eat supper."

Riley scraped the remaining scrambled eggs into another plate, put the frying pan in the sink, then moved both plates to the table.

"What would you like to drink? Milk? Orange juice? Coffee?"

"Juice."

Riley poured two glasses of juice while Vivi sat in suspense, wondering what direction their conversation was going to take. Riley served the juice, then plopped down in a chair opposite Vivi.

"Would you like for me to bless the food?"

Vivi's face reddened. She felt guilty that she had not even thought of it - after all this time at Faith House. She was relieved that Riley had offered to say the blessing. She had never been much for the religious habits instituted at the shelter by Nadine. Vivi had been raised Catholic, but she had not stepped into a church in years, much less been to confession or prayed. The thought of praying aloud terrified her. She consented to Riley's question with a nod. The words of Riley's prayer began to pour out in a steady stream.

"Father, you know we've all been worried about Vivi and you've heard our prayers for her healing, so I thank you that she's sitting across from me now, waiting to eat these scrambled eggs you've provided. Please continue to heal her. And please bless this food. Amen."

Vivi lifted her head and shot Riley an appraising glance. She could not recall ever being the subject of anyone's prayer.

Riley, meanwhile, grabbed her fork and began stabbing the eggs. "I don't know how good they are, but they sure smell good."

Timidly, Vivi picked up her fork and, almost in a whisper, said, "Thank you for cooking. I'm sorry if I put you to any trouble."

"No trouble at all. I was famished and didn't realize it. Now that I think of it, I don't think I've eaten since breakfast," Riley said. Her thoughts turned to breakfast and she remembered how little she had eaten then. She had been unable to eat because she was distracted by the tension between her and Vivi. "Huh!" She was disconcerted that she had skipped so many meals without noticing it.

As Vivi swallowed a few small bites, she was mustering the courage to tackle a much bigger issue. She washed the food down with the juice, but her inner turmoil had caused her to lose her appetite.

Riley had nearly cleaned her plate when she realized that Vivi had put down her fork. Riley gave her a puzzled look.

"You don't like 'em? I can fix you something else."

"No, the eggs are fine."

Riley's expression went from confusion to concern.

"Are you in pain? Can I get you something?"

"No, Eve, I'm not ... No!"

Vivi's outburst and agitation would typically have unnerved Riley, but she perceived that Vivi had something weighing heavily on her mind. In hopes that she was about to open up to her about the details of her accident, Riley withdrew from asking questions and waited silently.

The room grew uncomfortably quiet as Vivi's eyes panned the room, deliberately avoiding Riley's probing eyes.

After a while, Vivi cleared her throat. Then she faced Riley.

"That's not the only reason I've been avoiding you," Vivi said.

Riley looked across the table at the young woman, whose voice had begun to quaver. Riley wanted to help her, to make it easier for her, but she knew Vivi's pride was at stake. So Riley bit her tongue and allowed Vivi to wade through whatever dilemma was troubling her.

Vivi continued.

"As part of my drug rehab, I'm supposed to apologize to everyone I've offended." Vivi cleared her throat again before proceeding. "I was supposed to apologize to you. You were one of the last people on my list." Vivi's eyes locked with Riley's. She waited for some kind of reaction from Riley. But her expression remained unchanged. When it appeared safe to proceed, she said, "But I just couldn't face you ... because you were the hardest person for me to face."

While Riley was surprised to see tears pooling in Vivi's eyes, she tried not to show it. Clearly, this woman was hurting and not just from scrapes and bruises.

"Why was I the hardest?"

Vivi swallowed to clear the lump in her throat. When that didn't work, she turned up her juice glass and emptied it. She plopped the glass back down on the table.

"Need a refill?" Riley asked.

"Why are you being so nice to me? I don't deserve this royal treatment you're giving me," Vivi blurted. "Because of me, you're stuck here. With the money I took, you could be anywhere - anywhere but here. What's worse, I didn't even put your money to good use. I owed some guy a lot of money ... money I'd borrowed to buy drugs ... then I blew the rest on one fix," Vivi said, mockingly. With her forefinger pointing straight up for emphasis, Vivi yelled, "One fix!"

The young woman broke out into nervous laughter. Her face turned crimson when she realized that Riley did not share her humor. "How pathetic is that?" Vivi said. "I didn't even have enough sense to use it to buy my way out of here. Now we're both stuck here."

Riley listened to Vivi pour out her heart. For the first time, she understood Vivi's anger. She recognized in her a woman who had probably felt trapped her entire life. She became trapped by an addiction that created for her a financial prison, as well. Now she felt trapped in a place where she didn't fit in and she had wasted her single opportunity to get out.

Vivi had been fighting back tears, not wanting to appear weak to Riley. But her regrets far outweighed her pride at that moment, not to mention that the events of the day had made her entirely vulnerable to a host of emotions.

"I'm sorry. I'm so sorry," she said between sobs.

Riley debated whether to put her arm around her. She decided against it. Vivi had built a wall around her heart and her life and Riley knew it would have to come down brick by brick. A hug from a perceived enemy would feel too much like an arsenal ramming the wall from all sides and directions. Riley felt certain that Vivi would retaliate, then retreat if she poured on too much affection. She decided on another approach, one that softened her own defenses her first day at Faith House.

Riley shifted to the chair closest to Vivi. She faced the tearful woman and leaned over slowly and carefully took one of Vivi's hands in hers.

"Vivi, I want you to look at me."

Vivi hid her face behind her other hand. Riley reached up, gently removed it from her face and held it, too.

"Vivi. Look at me," she coaxed.

Vivi raised her head, but her angry eyes darted back and forth, occasionally meeting Riley's.

"Vivi. Look at me, please. I need you to hear me."

Vivi threw back her shoulders and gave Riley a guarded look. She wanted to withdraw her hands and retreat back into the dark and to her cot. Riley's tender touch felt like sandpaper. She was not accustomed to such closeness from other people and everything in her cried out to her to flee from it. But when she finally surrendered to Riley's request, she saw something she had seen only one other time in her life and in one other person's eyes – Nadine's.

She remembered the first time she had deeply disappointed Nadine, who had given her a second chance to kick her drug habit. Vivi couldn't bear to look into the face of disappointment again. She had seen that face her entire life. She never felt like she measured up in anyone's eyes.

But when Nadine cornered her and forced her to deal with her one-on-one, Vivi was mystified when disappointment did not show on her face that day.

Instead she saw a similar countenance - much like the one she was seeing on Riley's face. It was the face of mercy.

"How could that be?" Vivi wondered. "After the way I destroyed her life, how can she possibly forgive me?"

Once Riley had her attention, she paused to quickly organize her thoughts.

"Vivi, believe it or not, you did me a favor. I know you don't understand, but you did not know me before I came here. Frankly, I'm not sure I really knew myself before I came here. Just to fill you in, I'm the only child of simple parents with simple Christian values. I didn't want that. I didn't want anything to do with who they were or what they represented. So I turned my back on them at a very young age and I didn't look back.

"You see, I thought that what they modeled wasn't good enough for me. I wanted more. In hindsight, I see that my priorities were upside down," Riley shared.

Vivi listened intently as Riley confided in her. She tried to understand what any of what Riley was saying had to do with her.

"The day I came to Faith House, I was no different from you. I felt trapped. I was desperate. I was afraid and I was an emotional train wreck. But my priorities were the same. Secretly, I thought I was too good to stay in a women's shelter and to wear second-hand clothes and to hear the religious propaganda Nadine was pitching. It all felt too small to me ... too confining. I had immediately started plotting how I would leave.

"I admit that when you took all the money I had, I was livid. I'm not going to lie to you. I was so angry with you."

Vivi dropped her head in shame.

"But not anymore. Vivi, I want to thank you."

Vivi's head shot back up. She sat bewildered at Riley's comment.

"For the first time in my life, what I wanted was no longer an option. You forced me to look at what I needed. I realized that what I needed resided in the principles my parents had been trying for years to teach me. Coincidentally, they were the same principles that Nadine teaches and models. Maybe my parents' teachings had planted the seed, but they did not actually begin to sprout until I began helping other women. By serving them, I stopped focusing on myself and saw that there were other women who had bigger problems than I had. Eventually, I realized that life does not revolve around me. And my life is now larger than it's ever been. Partly because of you, I've reached greater heights than I ever attained when what I wanted was the primary goal in my life." Riley's face was aglow as she said, "I've wanted to tell you that since the day you returned, but you kept running from me. I'm indebted to you, Vivi. More importantly, I'd like to be your friend."

The request pierced Vivi's heart. A torrent of emotion swept over her. She began weeping uncontrollably.

Riley released Vivi's hands and wrapped her arms around Vivi, who fell into her embrace. Riley held her and stroked her hair, like her own mother did with her when she was a child.

Suddenly out of the corner of her eye, she saw a figure standing in the doorway. She turned her head to see Nadine, clad in her flannel robe and bedroom slippers, watching from a distance. Riley wondered how long she had been standing there and whether she had overheard their conversation.

Nadine smiled approvingly at Riley, then turned and tiptoed back toward her room.

Riley continued to comfort Vivi, slightly rocking her to help calm her. After a while, Vivi sat back in her chair and wiped her face with her hands.

"I didn't expect this from you," Vivi said. "I've never expected any more from other people than I've ever gotten. I guess I've never given any more than I've gotten."

"I can say this now, Vivi. At some point, you've got to let go of what's not working in your life and replace it with what is. That's no guarantee that people won't disappoint you. But it is a commitment to put an end to them dictating your actions and reactions," said Riley. "That's how we rise above our circumstances. That's how we break free from our cage. We become people who are affected, but not destroyed by others. In turn, we affect others by loving them, caring for them and, as difficult as it sounds, praying for them. Instead of desperate women clinging to our mistakes and our rotten pasts, we become women deserving of a new start."

Vivi hung on every word that came from Riley's lips. Someone was finally saying what Vivi had longed to hear - that she didn't have to keep repeating the endless cycle of failure in her life. But she had been trying to break loose from the drug scene since she got out of rehab. Her old life always seemed to trail her and find her. It would lure her back in, then pull her under like a drowning woman. Then someone would throw her a life preserver and she would start the cycle all over again by jumping in the murky, deep end where she would lose her way.

"I don't know how," Vivi said, almost in a whisper.

"What?" Riley said, straining to hear her.

"I don't know how to start fresh. I know how to start over, to begin the vicious cycle over again. I've been doing that for years," Vivi confided. "That's what happened yesterday. I was trying to stay clean, but other people don't want me to change. They don't take me seriously. Some guys I used to party with wanted me to join them at their place. I knew they also wanted to share more than just drugs. I refused," Vivi said.

She hung her head as she elaborated on the details of her encounter.

"I've never refused them before. They got angry and began forcing themselves on me. When I fought them off and started screaming, they knocked me around. I don't remember everything, but they loaded me in a vehicle and dumped me in the alley. I didn't want anyone to find me like that. I wanted to die."

A stream of tears flowed down her cheek.

"I want things to be different, Eve," she said. "But I don't know how to start clean, with a fresh slate. I only know how to keep repeating the same mistakes over and over and over again. I'm so tired."

Riley held out her hands, motioning to Vivi to take her hands again. Vivi's eyes narrowed. She didn't know what linking hands together had to do with her situation. She hesitated, growing irritated again.

When Riley saw her reluctance, she said, "Do you trust me?"

Vivi peered into the face of acceptance and compassion belonging to a woman who could have retaliated against her for her grievous crime. Vivi still had trouble believing that after she had burned this woman that she did not want revenge. "What do I have to lose," she reasoned. She set aside her frustration and suspicions and planted her hands into Riley's open hands.

Riley smiled. "I know how to help you start fresh."

Riley bowed her head and started praying, not waiting for Vivi's participation.

But Vivi did participate. While Riley said aloud a prayer for her, Vivi silently spoke her own prayer, starting with an apology to God - the last name on her list.

When Vivi opened her eyes, she was amazed at the indescribable peace that fell over her. In that solitary moment, Vivi knew that she had looked into God's face and seen divine mercy. The guilt of disappointment and disapproval was gone. She experienced a lightness of being unlike anything she had ever known.

Riley opened her eyes to see a transformation in Vivi's face. It was radiant.

Vivi, meanwhile, thought, "That wasn't so hard after all."

Riley tilted her head to the left and affectionately inquired, "Feel better?"

Vivi responded affirmatively, then smiled broadly.

The two women embraced again, then Riley looked down at her watch. "Wow! It's almost three o'clock in the morning. We need to get some sleep."

Vivi thought to herself, "Who can sleep? It's a new day."

Chapter 25

The winter months were drawing to a close. Riley had seen more new faces at the shelter - women seeking refuge from the harsh weather conditions, as well as harsh human conditions - than in the fall. Since fewer women had left than were coming in, residents were tripping all over each other.

Riley's one bright spot during confinement to the shelter were Ruben's frequent visits. During the snowy months, he would enter the shelter and remain in the kitchen, where he ate his meals after everyone else had eaten.

Ruben showed up about the same time every two or three days. Riley looked forward to those days and had made it a point to join him while he ate.

Ruben had begun to open up to her, telling her humorous stories about his experiences on the street or from when he was younger. Occasionally, when he appeared depressed, he would slip up and talk about his wife and son. But those were fleeting moments and they often ended with Ruben quickly ending his visit and leaving in a sadder state than when he arrived. Riley understood how he must miss them. Talking about his family only deepened her longing to see her parents.

Riley had come to enjoy Ruben's visits so much that not only was she disappointed when he didn't show up, but worried when didn't arrive at his usual time. She was concerned that at his age, he might not survive the severe cold. So she occasionally supplied him with extra blankets and men's clothing that had inadvertently been thrown into the donation boxes of women's clothing given to the shelter by charitable organizations.

On this particular day, Ruben was on time and Riley noticed that he was in an especially jovial mood when he stepped into the toasty kitchen. The smell of homemade soup hung in the room.

"Ruben, you're all smiles. Did you win the lottery?"

Riley tugged at his coat sleeve as she helped him remove his coat.

"Hah!" His throaty laugh filled the room. "No, but when I do, I'm taking all of you to the Rainbow Room and show you what truly fine dining is."

Riley cocked one eyebrow at Ruben's references to the shelter cuisine.

"Well, what then? I've never seen you this happy."

"It's my birthday," he said. "I'm always happy to wrap up another year of life. Plus, I'm hopeful that the coming year will be better than the last, so I try to help get it off to a good start."

"Oh, Ruben, I wish you had told me. We would have baked a cake and celebrated in style with you," Riley said.

"Ah!" he growled and swatted his hand at her. "I don't want you making a big fuss over it."

"Well, have a seat and let me serve you some of the best homemade soup in New York. I bet the Rainbow Room can't touch this," she said.

"You're probably right," he said.

Riley scooped piping hot soup into a bowl and set it in front of Ruben. When he wasn't looking, she found a candle, drove it into the center of a cornbread square and lit the candle with a match.

Ruben looked up from eating his soup when he heard a woman's voice singing, "Happy Birthday to you ... ."

Ruben threw back his head in glee as Riley approached him with the makeshift birthday cake.

She placed the cornbread at his place. "Happy Birthday to you," she finished singing. "Now make a wish and blow out your candle."

Ruben thought for a moment. A twinkle came to his eye and he said, "I wish I was about 10 years younger. I'd steal you away from all of this."

"Ruben, you're not supposed to tell your wish. It won't come true."

"What did I have to lose? It's not going to come true, anyway," he said with a wink, followed by a hearty laugh.

He puckered his lips and gave a small puff at the flame, instantly extinguishing it. He then pulled the smoking candle from the square in front of him. He picked up the block of bread and examined it from multiple sides. He raised one eyebrow at Riley, who had slid into a chair opposite him.

"What is this?"

Riley giggled, then said, "It's cornbread ... good, ole-fashioned, Southern cornbread like my Mama baked," she said. "That, I know you won't find on the menu at the Rainbow Room."

"I know you're right," he said, chuckling. "I have lived fifty-six years for this day, to taste cornbread baked by you. My life is certain to never be the same after today. What a befitting birthday treat."

Ruben bit into the cornbread, which had a sweet, grainy texture, dropping crumbs in his beard and lap. As he chewed the bread, Riley watched, anticipating his reaction.

He smacked his lips to show his approval. "Not bad, not bad at all," he said. "May I ask? Do you have something to wash it down with?"

Ruben began coughing to clear his throat of dry, bread particles.

"Oh, yes! I'm so sorry, Ruben. How about some milk?"

Ruben became amused over the dilemma while nodding and trying to cough up the lodged bread crumbs.

Riley rushed to pour milk into a glass before Ruben choked on her cornbread. Everyone at Faith House who had already teased her about introducing her cornbread recipe to them would never let her live it down if someone actually died from eating it.

She had no sooner put the glass down in front of Ruben than he picked it up and drank it dry. He returned the empty glass to the table and coughed one last time to clear the tickle in his throat.

He peered up at Riley, who stood ready to perform the Heimlich maneuver, if necessary.

With a smirk, he said, "Unforgettable."

Riley gave him an eye roll as she grabbed his glass for a refill.

"You know, I never told you this story," Ruben said before lifting another spoonful of hot broth to his lips.

"Yeah? What story?"

"The story about the night that I met this incredibly, beautiful, but sad woman."

Riley returned with his refilled glass. Her interest piqued, she slid down into the chair and propped her elbow on the table and rested her chin in her hand as she listened for more details.

"I was just walking along one night, making my usual rounds at night ... you know, stopping at some of the finest restaurants." He interrupted his story with a wink. "Yeah, I was walking along just minding my own business, lost in my own thoughts, when out of nowhere, this car almost comes crashing into me."

Riley, appalled at what she was hearing, lifted her head from her hand and straightened her back to sit at attention.

"I couldn't believe it," he continued. In all my years of walking the streets, that had never happened to me. And me in the pedestrian lane at that! Can you believe it?"

"Ruben, were you hurt? What did you do?"

"Nah, I wasn't hurt. But I was furious, as you can imagine," he said. "I threw up my hands and slammed them down on the hood of the teal BMW."

Riley's face went ashen as Ruben's tale instantly struck a deep chord with her. It was more than a story. It was a memory that caused tears to rush forth.

"But then I saw her, this angel sitting behind the wheel. She was the most beautiful, young woman I'd ever seen. She was also the saddest creature I could ever remember seeing."

Riley brushed the stream of tears away, her eyes avoiding Ruben's.

"I wondered then what or who could have brought her such pain and misery," he said. "Clearly, she had everything she wanted, everything the world could buy her, but it was evident to me that it could not buy her happiness."

Riley hung her head in shame. She vividly remembered that night - the night her husband's betrayal became obvious to her. She remembered almost hitting the homeless man with her car. She remembered her remorse and his anger. She remembered - and so did Ruben. He was that homeless man she had almost collided with that night. She slowly raised her head and looked up into Ruben's soft, brown eyes. In his eyes, she found security and assurance, not judgment or blame.

"I'm sorry that happened to you, Ruben," she said, before pausing to ask, "So, what happened to the woman?"

"Oh, you know ... like most beautiful, young women, she drove off into the sunset," he said, followed by a grin. "My hope is that she ran into some handsome old devil like myself, who took her hand and led her to somewhere safe and secure, where she'll live happily-ever-after. That's my hope."

He stared back at Riley and said, pointedly, "What do you think? Do you think she will?"

Riley blushed at the question. She began to wiggle in her chair under Ruben's directness.

"Live happily ever after? Come on, Ruben, does anybody?"

"I can still hope, can't I?" He slurped some more of the hot soup. "She was beautiful," he said after swallowing the spoonful. Then Ruben, his face aglow, looked across the table at Riley and said, "And she still is."

Riley could feel the sting of tears again. She jumped up from the chair and began putting away some of the uneaten soup and cornbread.

Ruben returned to eating his soup, basking in the satisfaction he derived from both the warmth of the food and from the way his story ended. Then, casually changing the subject, he inquired, "Where's Nadine?"

"She had a doctor's appointment," Riley answered between sniffles. "She should be back soon."

"Is she okay?"

"Yeah, I think so."

Riley was not aware of how much Ruben or anyone knew about Nadine's condition. But she had been sworn to secrecy, so she said little when asked. Nadine had been in remission, and showed little sign of having complications from the cancer, so it did not seem necessary to Riley to talk about it.

"Where is everyone? It seems unusually quiet here today."

"Most of the women now have jobs. Those who don't are either in school or out looking for a job."

"Buzz."

"Did you hear that?" Riley said to Ruben. Riley scrunched her face in wonder at who could be at their front door. The shelter was near capacity, so she didn't know how many more residents they could comfortably accommodate.

Seconds later, the echo of the shelter's buzzer sounded again. "Buzzz."

"I'll be right back, Ruben. Don't eat all the cornbread while I'm gone."

They exchanged grins as she was departing the room.

Riley headed toward the front door. She passed Deidra in the hall.

"Are we expecting guests?" Deidra asked.

"Not to my knowledge," Riley said in passing.

Riley reached the front door and peeked through the peep hole of the door. She saw stacks of boxes, but she could not see who was holding them.

"Who is it?" Riley yelled through the door. Part of the man's face appeared to one side of the stack he carried.

"Office Warehouse delivery for Nadine Franklin," the man responded.

"She's not here," Riley called out.

"Then you can sign for them. Otherwise, you'll have to pick them up at the warehouse. I can't return without charging you additional delivery charges," he said.

Finances were already dipping into the red. Riley sighed.

"What's it going to be, lady? I have other deliveries to make."

"Okay!"

Riley unbolted the security locks and cracked the door. Before she could fully open it to receive the packages, the man had emptied his arms of the load he was carrying and was pushing his way in and holding a gun to Riley's face. He slammed the door behind him, then grabbed Riley's arm and spun her around. In one swift movement, he had placed Riley in a choke hold with one arm wrapped around her neck and was pressing the gun to her head with his other.

"How many people are here?" he said low in her ear.

"Four, five ... I'm not sure. And Nadine is expected back at any moment."

With the nozzle of the pistol cutting into her temple, the man maneuvered Riley into the common room. "If you scream or make a noise without my instructions, I will blow your brains out," he said close to Riley's ear. "Do you understand me?"

Riley tried to nod, but the man's arm was propped tightly under her chin.

"Yes," she said softly where only he could hear.

"Good. Now I want you to take me to the money you've got stashed in this place."

Riley began to panic. Nadine was gone and with her the combination to the safe. Riley did not have access to either - the combination or the safe. Her mind churned to think of a way to both satisfy the man and keep everyone out of danger.

"Lord, please save us," she silently pleaded.

"Where is it?" the man asked, impatiently. He tightened his grip around her neck, reminding her that he was in control.

"It's in the office," she said, nervously.

"Where is that and where is everybody else?"

"Down the hall."

"Is the office on this end of the hall from everybody or the other end?"

"This end."

"Good. You're going to help me get to that safe and then out of here without drawing any attention. Got it?" he said.

Riley could hear anger in the familiar voice. She would be as compliant as possible to prevent bloodshed. But she did not know what to do about giving him what he wanted - money from the safe.

Riley nodded again, agreeing to his terms.

The man pushed Riley away from him and shoved the gun into the center of her back.

"Walk slowly and don't create any problems. If anyone asks, I'm here to deliver a package."

Riley turned toward him to get a glimpse of his face and to let him know that she would cooperate, but when she did, he shoved the gun deeper into her back.

"Look straight ahead and keep moving until we get to the office," he said, sharply. "No tricks! You got it?"

"Yes," she said, her voice quavering.

Riley exited the common room and walked toward the office, the gunman close on her heels.

But before they reached the office, Deidra bounded around the corner unexpectedly. She saw Riley, then she saw the gun pointed at her back. Deidra started screaming and continued until the surprised gunman pointed the gun at her and yelled, "Shut up!"

Riley grabbed Deidra and pulled her behind her to shield her from the gunman. "Don't hurt her, please? I'm going to try to give you what you want, but please, don't hurt anyone," Riley pleaded.

Meanwhile, two other residents, who were new to Faith House, poked their heads out of the dormitory to check out the commotion. When the man saw them, he yelled, "Get out here, all of you. Now!"

The two women, both clinging to each other in fear, slowly stepped into the hallway. "If you cooperate, nobody'll get hurt. Understand?" The women nodded in unison.

"Is there anyone else here?" he said, waving the gun back and forth. Riley shook her head "No." The gunman scanned the faces of the women to detect if her answer was true. When he was satisfied with their reactions, he yelled, "You," he said, directing his comments to Riley, "where's the office?"

Riley pointed around the corner.

"Alright, ladies, line up and follow her. Just remember that you've got a gun at your back. If you get out of line, I'll shoot her first and the rest of you can clean up the mess later."

Deidra, who was crying uncontrollably, became frantic.

"He's going to kill us," she started murmuring repeatedly.

Riley immediately turned to her, grabbed her wrists and drew her face nose-to-nose with Deidra's.

"Deidra, get a grip now or you are going to get us all killed. I mean it," said Riley in a commanding tone.

Deidra nodded over and again. "Okay, okay, I will."

Riley took her by the hand like a child and led her down the hall with the other women following and the gunman in the rear.

Riley's mind was racing to figure a way out. Without the combination, they were all in trouble. She remembered the petty cash box was often left out when Nadine was out of the building in case someone needed change or to make a quick grocery purchase.

After they rounded the corner and Riley was in the office out of the gunman's sights, she shoved Deidra and the two women, whose names Riley couldn't remember, into the office and slammed the door behind her. When she did, Deidra immediately locked the door to keep the gunman out, trusting that Riley had a plan.

"What are you doing?" the gunman said as he pointed the gun in Riley's face. "What are you doing?"

Riley, filled with unusual boldness, said, "Look, I don't have the combination to the safe. I can waste your time and mine by stalling and making you think I can give you something I don't have the ability to give you. The petty cash box may or may not be sitting outside the safe in the office, but at most, it has fifty dollars in it," she said with the gun staring back at her.

"If you want the fifty dollars, it's yours," she said. "But I am not going to stand by and let you hurt these women, certainly not over fifty dollars. Do you hear *me?*"

The gunman looked into the face of the redhead. Suddenly, he lost his focus. He had seen this face before. But she had vanished. He had looked everywhere for her. D. Roy thought he had killed her. Here she was, standing before him and he had a gun on her. The last time he saw her, he had been forced to hit her to get her to turn loose of her backpack. D. Roy was confounded about what to do. He felt confident that she meant what she said.

Riley, in the meantime, detected a glint of change in his expression. He just stood there looking at her. She had no idea what he was thinking, but she tried to mentally prepare for what he might do to her.

"So do you want the fifty dollars?"

"Grrr!"

D. Roy swung around at the sound of Ruben, who had suddenly, out of nowhere, come rushing around the corner, growling and yelling like a madman as he charged toward him.

"You!" Ruben yelled. Without warning, he tackled the young man as he yelled at him, "I should have killed you the last time you tried to hurt her!"

Riley watched the two men rolling around on the floor, taking turns throwing punches when possible and latching on to one another to prevent blows from being exchanged.

Ruben grabbed the young man and began to pummel his face. Riley gasped as she saw blood splattering from the young man with each blow Ruben landed. Just when Riley thought it was all over, she heard a gunshot followed by startled female screams.

Riley froze, stunned and uncertain of what had just happened. Everything appeared surreal to her as she saw the young man push Ruben to one side, climb to his feet and dart out of the shelter. Realizing that Ruben was not going after him, Riley yelled, "No!"

Not giving it a second thought, she darted after the young man. He had scurried out the front door and was running down the street, not once looking back. When it was apparent that he would not be returning, Riley slammed the door and bolted it before running to the office. She knocked on the door and yelled to Deidra to call 911, giving her instructions to have them send an ambulance and the police. Riley dropped to Ruben's side, rolling him over slightly to examine him.

"Ruben! Please, Ruben," she said, holding her breath until he answered. He moaned as she turned him over on his back. Blood pooled at his abdominal area.

"Oh, God!" Riley said.

"Ruben, stay with me. Help is on the way. Don't you dare leave!"

"I left you some cornbread," he said in a breathy voice.

"Good, because we've got some more celebrating to do," said Riley, attempting to be humorous in spite of her breaking heart.

Ruben chuckled to himself, then he began coughing.

"What is it, Ruben? What's so funny?"

"I finally got my wish," he said, his voice fading in volume and strength.

"What? What was your wish?" Riley asked.

"I got a second chance. I was there to take the bullet."

"Oh, Ruben, yes, you did. Your wife would be proud of you," said Riley, smiling despite the tears that ran down her face.

Ruben's eyelids began to droop.

"I think I'll tell her all about it," he said in a whisper. "Did I ever tell you that you remind me of her?"

He began choking, then coughing up blood until he coughed one last breath.

"No! Ruben, no!"

Riley fell across his still chest and wailed for her friend.

Deidra and the other women stood over them, leaning on one another and shedding tears of their own. About that time, they heard someone at the front door. They became paralyzed, afraid that Ruben's assailant had returned to finish what he had started. The sight of Nadine was a welcome relief to them, but Nadine's shocked expression when she saw Ruben's body on the floor spoke for everyone.

"What happened?" said Nadine, who clutched her chest. She stood traumatized at the sight of Ruben lying motionless on the floor.

Riley lifted her head from off Ruben's chest. She turned her tear-stained face toward Nadine, who read the sorrow in Riley's eyes. Nadine braced for the devastating details.

"It was his birthday, Nadine. Did you know that?"

Chapter 26

Paine awoke from a drunken stupor. He lifted his head from his desk and immediately wiped saliva from his face from where it had pooled on his desk top. He had forgotten where he was. He panned his surroundings with glazed pupils. He tried to focus on the numbers on his watch. It appeared to be after 4:00 a.m.

Paine sat up and massaged his numb face with his hands to try to revive himself from his drowsy condition.

But after uncovering his sleepy eyes with his hands, he was reminded of what had led him to start drinking.

Staring him in the face, although slightly fuzzy in nature, was the indictment that had been delivered to his office the afternoon before. It was amazing to Paine how the simple document had dropped the hammer on his life.

Westin's Board of Directors had already called an emergency meeting and voted to remove him as an officer of the company. The news media had picked up the scent and was trailing him for comments about the multiple felony charges of money laundering, fraud and securities violations facing Paine and Westin's chief financial officer. His parents, while they had pledged their legal support for Paine, had withdrawn their emotional support. Paine could hear the disappointment in their voices when he broke the news to them over the phone soon after the indictments were delivered to his office. But the hardest to accept was Sarah's reaction. She had disassociated herself from Paine months earlier upon learning of the pending FBI investigation. He had tried to convince her that the whole ordeal would blow over and that the accusations were without merit. Regardless, Sarah wanted nothing to do with the scandal. She also questioned why Paine was shuffling money. She thought she was courting wealth, but she sensed that she had been wrong about Paine's personal finances.

When he glimpsed failure and disapproval in her suspecting eyes, Paine died inside. He didn't care what the law did to him. He had lost Sarah's trust and respect, and nothing else mattered.

He began drinking to deaden the pain of losing her, but he was finding that there wasn't enough liquor to anesthetize the degree of pain he was experiencing. His painkiller of choice: Tennessee bourbon. No matter how much he drank to forget the intense pain caused by his broken heart, he always awakened to pick up where he left off in his suffering.

Paine got up from his chair and grabbed his crystal high ball to fill it again, but tripped over a box filled with some of his personal belongings. He staggered to regain his balance. Paine had been given the opportunity to gather his things. After a few hours in his office, his secretary found him passed out on his desk. She felt sorry for him. She locked his office door and made excuses for him to Westin executives, who inquired about his unwanted presence in the building. They had threatened to have security remove him, but decided against it when they realized it would only draw more negative public attention to the company. So they gave him twenty-four hours to pack his personal items. After all, they said, he was still family and should be treated with courtesy. However, he would be required to pass through a security check.

"Huh!" Paine said aloud as he poured another drink. "Who do they think they are, kicking me out? I'm a Westin. That name ought to be good for something!" he said, his speech slurred.

Paine slunk down in a nearby wing chair and guzzled the bourbon that felt warm as it went down. He thought about the mess he was in, but when he closed his eyes, the image of Sarah's face floated to the surface of his thoughts. She was all he longed for. He wanted and missed her so much.

After a few minutes, he could feel her breath on his ear. "Paine," he heard her whisper. She touched his shoulder before running her hand down his arm. Her touch, her voice brought peace to the storm raging inside him. She had that power over him. No one had ever had that kind of power over him.

His main goal, especially over the past year, had been to gain her approval. Without her in his life, he had lost his focus, his sense of direction, and his purpose. He had begun trying to find hope in the bottom of a glass. Every time, he came up empty. Tonight was no exception.

To feel her touch again brought a smile to Paine and warmed him in places the alcohol could not touch.

Then he heard her say it again just like he had every night when the world stood still and he was alone with his thoughts.

"Good-bye, Paine."

His eyes opened to the reality that Sarah was gone. Those chilling words once again robbed him of the effects of the alcohol. He took another swallow to try to numb the pain caused by her last words before she departed from his life.

She had agreed to marry him once Riley's estate had been settled and it was legally proper for him to remarry. But when his assets were frozen by the FBI, she ended their relationship. Sitting alone in the deafening quietness of his plush office, Paine seethed over her abandonment.

After all, he had risked everything for her - his marriage, his career, his wealth, his position, his reputation, and his family. When everything he had built for her began to crumble, he expected her to stand by him, not to turn her back on him like he no longer existed. How could she leave him? He had asked himself that question over and again. He had even attempted numerous times to ask her, but she refused his phone calls and had not responded to his emails.

After a while, Paine just gave up. He lost all hope of getting her back.

To add insult to injury, being asked to remove himself from the family business and from his office dashed all his hopes of being restored to his executive post at Westin. How could he possibly return to the company? He had been humiliated by the board, which had lost faith in him. They had evidently seen or heard the evidence against him. As much as he would never admit it, he secretly felt that it was probably compelling evidence. They would not permit him to return to this office, Paine thought as he scanned the room, admiring what had become his own private sanctuary seated on top of the world.

The rich, dark gold-tones, aubergine, black and forest green combined to create the decor in the office suite and often fit his dark moods. Westin had paid dearly for the exquisite European antique furnishings encapsulated in the oak-paneled office suite, complete with drink bar, sitting area and floor-to-ceiling bookshelves. His office had a museum quality created partly by Paine's collection of antique artifacts, including an oak gong with carved flowers and a lion's head on the crown; an American Gothic cast bronze eagle lectern with claw feet; an American officer's sword with engraved blue steel, ivory grips with eagle's head handle and the original leather scabbard; an antique phonograph with rare oak horn; and leatherbound books covering a vast array of subjects.

Paine had hand-picked his desk at auction - an impressive partners desk in carved walnut with a parquet top and doors finely carved with urns. The antique desk was originally from a judge's office. It rested on a palace size Kerman rug with blue field with rose and ivory border and medallion center.

The wall of glass overlooking New York, however, was still Paine's focal point. The glass window on the world had been the selling point that drew Paine to this particular office suite. The view was spectacular - day and night. Through his vintage brass telescope, he could peer down at life below. From the start, it had a calming effect on Paine, settling him at the end of a chaotic day or helping him regain a calm perspective whenever turmoil was at its height - professionally or personally. But on this particular night, it would take more than a penthouse view on the world through the eye of a telescope to bring calm to his world.

Paine arose from his slouched position to pour himself another drink from his personal bar - a Renaissance counter in oak detailed with marble accents, bronze capped columns, and intricate intarsia. Paine spilled alcohol all over the counter as he refreshed his drink. He turned up the glass, drank it dry, then filled the glass again.

Paine staggered over to the floor-to-ceiling window to gaze out at the city's skyline. This would be his last view of the city from where he stood. He pressed his hand against the glass wall to balance himself. Standing in front of the panoramic view had an opposite effect on him this evening. The longer his eyes feasted on the city lights, high-rises and all the other highlights of his spectacular view from the top, the deeper Paine sank into an emotional abyss. Paine was at the bottom of his professional game and social standing. He was without emotional support from his family, and his girlfriend had checked out of the relationship. All that he viewed from where he stood was no longer accessible to him. The world was no longer at his fingertips.

Paine had no idea how to start from the bottom. He had always been on top. He had snubbed those on the bottom rung of the social ladder and quashed those on the professional ladder who threatened his position at the top. As a Westin, he had been afforded many advantages that those on the bottom and middle rungs had never been given.

In hindsight, he saw how his infractions had sent his life spiraling out of control. At that moment, he wished he could turn back the clock. Going backwards in time would bring Sarah back to him. He snickered to himself, then gulped another sip. Reversing time, however, would not change the way he had lavished everything on her. If he had it to do over, he would have done the same - possibly even more if it meant she might be convinced to stay with him longer.

As Paine stood in front of the window, loneliness enveloped him on the outside and gnawed at him on the inside. He grew angry at the thought of living without her. He threw back another swallow before realizing that he was not alone. He looked at the glass wall, and saw the reflection of a man staring back at him.

Paine squinted at the crumpled, disheveled image of a man, whose life was washed up. The appearance of the man, whose shoulders slumped forward and who leaned far to one side, sickened Paine. He was staring into the murky face of one guilty of robbing him of everything. As he assessed the reflection, Paine understood for the first time why Sarah had left. He realized that he was looking at the remains of the man he was.

The mirror image embodied his failures, diminished self-esteem, weaknesses, and professional demise.

Paine detested the man before him. His hatred for him grew into a sudden rage. He took a few steps back, then slammed his high ball against the glass wall, sending the drink glass shattering everywhere with a loud crash. When Paine saw that he had hit his target, but that it did not so much as cripple the man staring back at him, he became further enraged.

"I know how to destroy you," Paine ranted at the blurry outline.

He stormed over to his desk, tripping again on the box of personal items - the few remnants of his successful life and career. He snatched open the center drawer of his desk. There, tucked out of sight, was a brushed, stainless steel, snub-nose revolver - perfect for short-range duty.

Paine had made a few enemies over his twenty-year career. He stood ready for any one of them should they burst into his office unannounced to register their complaints. But at that moment, he faced the biggest enemy of his life.

"What else do I have to lose?" he thought to himself. "I may have lost everything, but I won't lose this battle," he mumbled.

Paine marched back toward the window. His head reeled as he faced his blurry opponent. The view of the man fell into and out of focus as Paine's own head was weaving back and forth. Paine squinted to regain focus. When he could see him more clearly, Paine pointed the gun at the image that was off-balance in front of him. Paine shuddered when he saw in the glass the gun barrel pointing back at him. He became frightened and alarmed at the sight, immediately dropping the pistol on the marble floor. Seeing that the man was still standing revived his anger. He evaluated the situation.

"Ah-hah! I've got you now!" Paine said to his glassy likeness.

Paine scrambled for the gun and returned to his nemesis in the window.

Paine pressed the end of the gun barrel to his own right temple. He smiled, proud that he had outsmarted the man who stood for everything he hated in himself. When Paine saw a smirk spring to the face of disappointment that glared back at him, he decided he would not be outdone. He pulled the trigger while feeling the euphoria once again that he was back on top of his game.

Chapter 27

Over two months had passed since Ruben's death.

Riley slipped into a deep depression and Nadine had been unable to pull her out of it. Riley went through the motions of doing her job, but she withdrew from mingling with the residents and limited her conversations to work-related issues. Nothing lifted her spirits - not words of encouragement, not new projects, or even surprise gifts.

Nadine had not realized how attached to Ruben that Riley had become. She wondered if Riley was experiencing more than just grief and if his death had somehow resurrected buried emotions from her past.

Nadine sought the opportunity to counsel her, but the volume of residents at Faith House created far more pressing demands than there were people to meet them. She and Riley were spread too thin to stop and take care of their own needs.

In the meantime, Riley seemed to drift from one day to the next, doing only what was expected of her. The slightest word or deed triggered fresh tears and sent her fleeing from the room in search of solitude. The other residents had begun to treat Riley with kid gloves. Nadine noticed that she was spending an inordinate amount of her spare time scribbling in a journal or sleeping, and less and less time interacting with other people. Nadine feared that she was becoming the recluse that Ruben had been. He appeared to have opened up to Riley more than he had to anyone before his death. But Nadine often wondered if Ruben's feelings for Riley had been more than platonic. She could understand if they had been. He was a lonely man. As for Riley, Nadine couldn't explain the uncommon relationship. Nadine knew so little about Riley's family background or her past.

"Why was Ruben's death causing her to want to give up?" Nadine wondered. She allowed things to rock on until one May afternoon. The temperatures were rising and spring was in full bloom. Many residents had jobs and were moving out of the shelter, and others were more motivated by sunnier skies to venture out in search of jobs. The warmer weather drew still others to the parks and common areas of the city. Everyone seemed to be eager to get outdoors, except Riley. Nadine could no longer attribute her sadness to grief compounded by winter doldrums.

Nadine decided that she could not stand by and continue to watch her outgoing, vivacious assistant wither and fade like the grass under the winter snow. She would confront her the next morning, timing her confrontation when most of the residents had cleared out after breakfast.

The following day started out like most days, with some of the residents complaining about others who monopolized the bathroom. Mornings were typically noisy, chaotic and stressful. Nadine looked forward to that moment when she could plop down in her favorite wing chair and read her Bible, the newspaper, and a few pages of her newest paperback book before beginning her official workday.

Nadine watched the back of the last woman exit the shelter. When she heard the sound of the door latch behind them, Nadine sighed a heavy sigh of relief.

"Whew!" Nadine said, her voice traveling throughout the building. "I thought they'd never leave."

Nadine trudged to the kitchen to pour her second cup of coffee for the day. In silence, Riley was wiping away the breakfast crumbs from kitchen counters and tables. As much as Nadine wanted to strike up a conversation at that moment, she needed time to pray, to gather her thoughts, and to unwind from the morning's chaos before attacking someone else's problems.

Nadine lived by the adage, "Timing is everything."

She said to Riley, "I'm going to be in my chair if you need me."

Riley simply nodded.

Nadine sighed as she pushed against the swinging kitchen door. With her coffee in hand, Nadine headed out of the kitchen. "By the way, there's today's newspaper," she called back to Riley as she pointed to the folded *New York Times* lying on a table near the kitchen door. "I know how much you enjoy being the first one to crack it open."

Riley perked up slightly. She tossed the dish cloth into the sink, then poured herself a cup of coffee. She picked up the daily newspaper and tossed it on the table. She took a sip of the hot brew and spread open the newspaper. She was drawn to headlines about the war in Afghanistan that was heating up and to news of plans to redevelop Ground Zero.

A project was conceived in the spring and had reached out to the public for input on proposed designs for the new buildings to be built at the World Trade Center site. The first round of designs was scheduled to be released in July, the article said. The concepts would be designed based on the new mayor's three principles to satisfy his "Vision for Lower Manhattan." The article listed the principles: Connect Lower Manhattan to the world around it, create new neighborhoods, and create new public spaces.

Riley recalled the piles of ash and debris that were once towers, which had stretched to the sky. She thought of the amount of rebuilding that would be required to resurrect the site to its former glory. She wondered just how high the new buildings would have to reach for New Yorkers to forget about Towers One and Two. But as she thought about the prospects of renewal of the site, images of flames bursting forth from the top of both towers and bodies falling to their death struck an emotional chord. She quickly shook off the mental images and moved on in her reading to the next news story.

A few pages over, there beneath the fold, amidst the local news, was a headline that immediately captured Riley's attention and stirred her more than stories about the war or stories about revival of the World Trade Center site. She rose up when she read in Times-Roman bold letters the words: Westin's Chief Executive Officer Commits Suicide.

Riley's heart raced as she read the news story notifying her of her husband's suicide. According to the newspaper account, indictments against Paine and Westin Company's CFO had been made two days ago. They were both going to be arrested the day before, but Paine shot himself in the head around 4:00 a.m. in his penthouse office.

The newspaper story reported that "Paine's family members said he had been suffering depression over the September 11 death of his wife, the late Riley Davenport-Westin, a newswoman with WTNY, Channel 6. The TV station had been located in one of the World Trade Towers."

They explained that, "more recently, the breakup of Paine and his betrothed, Sarah Blackstone, had exacerbated his depression."

According to *The Times*, "Paine had been funneling money through a dummy off-shore corporation, P.W. Developments, giving a strong appearance of money-laundering. One of the company's private capitalists, retired banker Joe Weitzmann, had become suspicious when questions about interim accounting reports went unanswered and when, after two years, P.W. Developments had not broken ground on any proposed construction projects.

"Following a Federal Bureau of Investigation report, Paine was indicted on multiple charges of embezzlement, fraud, and a number of federal securities violations. Paine had been using the funds siphoned from the company to buy a private plane for his personal use, to take elaborate vacations with his fiancé, gambling in Las Vegas, and buying expensive jewelry for Blackstone, the indictment said."

Riley read the article over again, still in disbelief.

She had known he was abusive and had been cheating on her. She had no idea that he had also been cheating his company, his business partners, and his family. She realized that had she stayed in the marriage, he would have destroyed more than her confidence and self-esteem. He would have dragged her name and her professional career down with him. He would have ruined her credibility along with his. Not to mention, his affair would have been made public as a result of crimes he was accused of committing. But Riley realized that his suicide was most likely Paine's admission of guilt.

"He was never proficient in apologizing," she thought. "Running from the scene of his crimes was his mode of operation. Some things never change."

In hindsight, Riley saw that her decision to leave when she did was the right decision. But reading the story struck a chord of sympathy for the man she had loved. She thought of how he had died alone and without hope - and without salvation. Then she thought of how desperate this man, who had exuded an enormous amount of confidence, charisma, and self-assurance, had been to convince himself to end it all with the pull of a trigger. She could not imagine Paine in that state of mind.

"Just how bad did he get after I left?" she wondered.

Riley had just finished reading the article a second time when Nadine walked into the kitchen.

Nadine took one look at Riley's pallid face and asked, "Eve, what's wrong?"

Riley looked up from the newspaper and, without stopping to organize her thoughts, said, "My husband's dead."

Nadine's eyes got wide as saucers.

Saying the words aloud made it real. Those words represented the end of a long, exhausting journey rapt in fear, uncertainty, shame, and disappointment. It meant she no longer had to look over her shoulder in fear. Saying the words out loud brought a tidal wave of emotion that far exceeded the mourning Riley had experienced when Ruben was killed.

Nadine saw it erupting in Riley - months of pent-up feelings. She quickly put down her empty coffee cup and wrapped her arms around the woman like a warm, snug blanket. She held Riley tight as she shook and wailed and screamed. It was a while before Riley finally calmed down, but Nadine continued to hold her and hum a tune unfamiliar to Riley.

About a half hour later, Riley pulled away from Nadine and reached for a couple of napkins from a stack on the table.

Nadine wanted to break the silence, but waited instead for Riley to explain her comment when she was ready.

Riley stopped drying her eyes long enough to push the newspaper in front of Nadine. She pointed to the article and broke the silence between them.

"There, it's my husband's obituary."

Nadine read the article in horror. When she came to the end, she looked at Riley with a furrowed brow. She had at least a dozen burning questions on her mind. But Riley's swollen, sad eyes met hers. Nadine looked into the sorrowful eyes of someone who had dealt with more than her share of trauma. As much as she wanted to start pumping her for answers, Nadine knew that Riley needed time, space, much love, and prayer. She needed someone to listen to her - even to her silence. Riley needed to go at her own pace, not to be rushed toward healing.

Riley looked across the table at her boss and friend, and she appreciated her all the more for sticking by her during her emotional meltdown. At that moment, Riley felt numb. There was so much she wanted to say, but she didn't know where to start. Her eyes were drawn to a bread crumb on the table that she had overlooked when she was cleaning the counter tops. She was bothered by it, but not enough to wipe it away. Riley felt burdened by intense fatigue. She propped her left elbow on the table and rested her chin in the palm of her hand. She closed her eyes with Nadine looking on. Images floated in and out of her mind's eye - images of peoples' faces.

She thought of the people, who had directly and indirectly impacted her life. She thought of the people she knew well and those she barely knew. She thought of those who had told her with lying lips that they loved her and those who never said it with words, but sincerely showed their love for her with their actions. She never knew how others who were gone felt about her, and they died not knowing how she felt about them. She thought of the people she never had the opportunity to say good-bye to - some of those missed opportunities she deeply regretted.

It suddenly became apparent to her that she had no idea why her life had been spared. On three different occasions, she had escaped death. Three times, she should have been listed as a fatality. The revelation caused her to open her eyes.

Nadine saw Riley's startled look. She could no longer sit by and wait for Riley to wade through her situation alone.

"What is it, Darlin'?"

"I should be dead, Nadine. By all accounts, I should be dead, too."

"What makes you say that?"

Riley took Nadine to the beginning, sharing with her about Paine's abuse, his threats, his affair, and the last night she saw him.

Riley told her about how her decision not to go to work on September 11 had been the end of Paine's abuse, of a very comfortable lifestyle and of a career she had spent years building. She also recounted the horror of watching her co-workers and thousands of people she passed daily en route to her office die in the unspeakable, terroristic act.

She told Nadine how a prayer on bended knees after years and years of spiritual drought had closed one door and opened another.

She told her about days of living on the street, about the man who had assaulted her and attempted to rob her, and how Ruben had recovered her possessions and led her to Faith House. Then she shared with her about how the man returned to take more than he had during his first robbery attempt. She explained that Ruben's bullet was intended for her.

"You see? I should be dead. And some days, I wish I was!" Riley said, tears stinging her eyes.

"But you're not," Nadine said. "You are very much alive."

Nadine leaned in and said in her firm tone that had a way of commanding her attention, "Look at me." Riley looked into the steely eyes of a woman bent on being heard. "God has spared you for a definite reason - one only he knows. I can assure you that you are not still alive by chance because you drew the long straw. It's deliberate that you are still breathing God's beautiful gift of life," said Nadine, smiling her comforting smile.

"Now the question is, how do you plan to use that beautiful gift? Do you plan to spend the rest of your days in pajamas, wallowing in self-pity because you survived?" said Nadine, arching one eyebrow.

"Or do you have the courage to live a life that glorifies the one who gives you life? Do you have the courage to live without those who no longer live - those who left a huge imprint on your life and heart? Wouldn't you want them to be proud of the way you carried on in their absence?"

Riley's eyes rested again on the single bread crumb left behind on the table. She listened intently as Nadine pricked her heart with her questions.

"I didn't know your other friends or co-workers or even your husband. But I knew Ruben. He would not have led you here if he thought your life was not worth saving. He saw something valuable and precious in your life. He led you here so that you would have every available opportunity to a safe existence and to go forward, living a full life, not a fraction of a life or a life immersed in guilt.

Riley hung on every word Nadine said.

"He must have recognized your potential to make your mark on this world. Do you think he would have been willing to sacrifice his own life for yours if he had not thought you were worth it?"

Nadine's last question caused Riley to lift her head and lock her tear-filled eyes with Nadine's.

Riley realized that Paine's decision to take a bullet at his own hand had been an act of cowardice and a clear indication that he had lost all hope. While the thought saddened her more, it also put things into perspective. Suddenly, she saw Ruben's extreme sacrifice for what it truly was - an act of love for her.

She realized that he had done so because he had hopes for her. It was clear to her that his act of heroism had set the example for her and others to follow, to sacrifice their lives in at least small ways. She knew that she could not let him down. As her eyes met Nadine's consoling eyes, she secretly vowed to use all of her life - her resources, her strength, her courage - to instill hope in others. She had been given the miraculous gift of hope. She knew it was time to stop being selfish with it and wasting it on herself. She would begin spending it on others - a debt she would pay with her life. She would repay it the way Ruben had - unselfishly, willingly, and humbly. She vowed in her heart that his example of love would live on through her.

Riley sat up straight in her chair, wiped the dampness from her face with the napkin and looked directly at Nadine with conviction.

"You're right, Nadine," Riley said. "I didn't die with Ruben. I'm alive because of Ruben. Taking that bullet was his final moment of glory. By not living, I'm depriving him of that shining moment. How disappointed he would be."

Nadine nodded, a demure smile showing her satisfaction with Riley's revelation.

"It's time to stop wallowing in the past and start living for the future. So now to figure out how and where to begin," said Riley, as she peeled another napkin off the stack and wiped up the annoying bread crumb from off the table. She turned and discarded the napkin in a trash can behind her.

"Well, before you go making huge plans, we need to get one thing straight," Nadine said.

A crease formed on Riley's forehead as she prepared for the worst.

"Does this mean we can no longer call you Eve?"

Riley gave Nadine a confused look since the thought had not even occurred to her that her true identity was now out in the open. Then Riley saw the glimmer of amusement on Nadine's face and realized the humor she intended by her question.

"Oh!" Riley said.

The two women burst into laughter, stopping only to embrace one another.

Nadine reflected on how the morning had started, with sadness and gloom clouding her assistant's vision. She had watched Riley push through the wilderness of desperation and despair. Across the table sat a woman in whose eyes she saw restored joy and a spark of light shining. Nadine smiled with pleasure, knowing that in Riley's eyes, she was also seeing the future of Faith House.

Chapter 28

"What do you think?"

Riley bristled with excitement as she anticipated Nadine's response.

"I think it's outside of our budget."

While it was not what Riley was hoping to hear, it did not dampen her enthusiasm.

"Aside from that, what do you think?"

The vastness of the rooms, the newness of the appliances in the commercial kitchen, the proximity to downtown - it was all overwhelming to Nadine.

"I think it's grand, absolutely grand!" Nadine said. "Now tell me what this is all about."

"You're looking at the new home of Faith House!" said Riley, whose eyes were bright with excitement. "But only if you approve."

"What?" Nadine said.

Her face was contorted with a mix of amazement and confusion.

"How?" she said before Riley could answer her first question.

Riley giggled with glee to be able to surprise Nadine with the news. She had kept the secret for a couple of weeks while Westin executives worked through negotiations to acquire the abandoned hotel near downtown. Acquiring the hotel that had been foreclosed for over a year meant that residents could move into a safer neighborhood. The property would more comfortably accommodate the residents, allowing them to get out of the dormitory and into more private rooms. There were a few suites for women with children so they could bring their children to visit and have more one-on-one time with them. The structure of the building was sound and most likely would not earn the number of code violations that their current building had. Also, plumbing and furnishings were up-to-date.

When Joe Weitzmann first approached Riley about purchasing the hotel, she had thought it was too good to be true. It had been difficult for her to keep the news to herself.

Details of the acquisition now came spilling from Riley's lips in a steady stream of information. She became breathless from talking so fast.

She was thrilled that in her new role as executive director of the Westin Foundation she could help Faith House. The company established the Foundation at Weitzmann's insistence.

Hearing Riley's testimony to the Westin Board of Directors about her whereabouts during the nine months leading up to Paine's suicide and why she had dropped out of sight had tugged at Weitzmann's heartstrings. He had seen Paine's dark side on several occasions. Nadine's testimony to Riley's condition when she arrived at the shelter reinforced Riley's claims of physical abuse and mental cruelty. Weitzmann had no reason to doubt either of them.

But when Riley segued her explanation into a testimony to the lives being restored at Faith House, followed by a plea to the board for financial support for the shelter, Weitzmann was hooked. Weitzmann was even more impressed when Riley convinced the board to help fund the shelter in Paine's memory. Weitzmann imagined the strength and courage it must have taken to display her forgiveness for all Paine had done to hurt her. It was an example of the kind of mercy Weitzmann and other board members needed to have for the deceased executive, he thought. Weitzmann and the board decided to follow her example and get behind her in helping Faith House. It wasn't difficult since other company officials viewed it as a good public relations move in light of the bad press that Paine's indictment and suicide had created for the company.

"Slow down, slow down!" Nadine said, her head swimming from the news.

"What is this going to cost us? What do we have to do?" Nadine said.

Riley began twirling around the room with her arms outstretched. "Nothing!" she said. "Absolutely nothing!" Riley giggled as she twirled some more. "That's the beauty of it, Nadine. It's a gift - a gift to you and to all the women at Faith House."

Nadine wrinkled her brow in disbelief and bewilderment.

"But, how, Eve? I mean, Riley?"

"Westin Company set up a foundation in Paine's memory and they made me executive director over it," Riley explained. "It is for the benefit of New York's abused and homeless women and children."

Nadine's excitement immediately dissipated. Disappointment sank in when Riley shared the news of her new job.

Riley read the changed expression on Nadine's face. She stopped mid-step, nearly losing her balance.

"What's wrong? You don't like it?"

"No, I love it. It's more than I could ever hope for," Nadine said, her voice lacking enthusiasm.

206 | V<small>ALERIE</small> D<small>AVIS</small> B<small>ENTON</small>

"Then what?" said Riley, whose mind raced ahead to all the potential disadvantages of moving into the new location.

"I just, uh, I thought we made a great team," Nadine said.

"We do!"

Nadine paused. She tried to choose her words carefully because she didn't want to discourage Riley or hold her back. "I want you and all my residents to be happy and successful above all. It was just nice to share the leadership at Faith House with someone as capable and as energetic and as devoted as you. I guess I thought you would be around longer," she said. "I guess our agreement ran out when you recovered your losses."

Riley narrowed her eyelids at Nadine, who wondered if she had said the wrong thing after all. Nadine cocked her head, waiting for the fallout.

"Are you firing me?" Riley said.

A look of complete confusion fell upon Nadine's face.

"No! Absolutely not! But I don't understand. I thought Westin offered you a better job, and that you accepted. I can't say that I blame you, but I just assumed that you would be leaving Faith House," Nadine said.

Riley began laughing heartily.

"What's so funny?" Nadine said indignantly. She stood with her hands propped on her hips waiting for an answer.

Riley's laughter finally subsided when she saw that Nadine was on the brink of being pushed beyond her limits by her sense of humor. Much to Nadine's surprise, Riley walked over to Nadine, wrapped her arms around her and squeezed her until Nadine returned the embrace. Riley pulled away and her warm, bright eyes met Nadine's inquisitive stare.

"Don't you understand? I still need a place to live," said Riley, smiling sweetly. "And Faith House is my home. So, unless you're firing me, you're stuck with me."

Nadine breathed a sigh of relief.

"The only difference now is, you don't have to pay me. Consider me a glorified volunteer. Or, we could take my salary and hire an assistant," she teased.

Nadine's eyes filled with tears. When Riley saw that Nadine was starting to cry, she said, "Look, if you're going to be sad about me staying, I can always find another place to live."

"That's not funny," said Nadine, who playfully pushed Riley away.

Nadine walked to a nearby mirror, which was covered in a thin layer of dust. She dug a tissue out of her purse and, with it, formed a circle in the dust large enough to see her round face looking back.

"I hope you're happy. You've made me cry and now I'm a mess," Nadine said. She looked down at her watch. "And we don't have time to go by the shelter for me to repair my makeup before the ceremony."

Mention of the ceremony instantly dampened Riley's spirits. A sadness fell over Riley that quickly put an end to the celebration that had started her day. Riley was facing the memorial for the first anniversary of the 9/11 attacks with mixed emotions. The thought of attending the ceremony made Riley want to retreat again from the world. While becoming lost in her thoughts, Riley began wandering around the empty hotel alone.

For most of the past year, she had fought a silent battle, not being able to talk about specific details of her association with the World Trade Center or her personal losses from that tragic day. Nor had she been able to comfortably join others in sharing their grief over that day that impacted New Yorkers, Americans, and countries around the globe.

Today's ceremony would be her first real opportunity to openly and publicly grieve the loss of her co-workers and all the people whose lives were lost on September 11, 2001. It would also mark her debut to the world as a survivor of the terrorist attacks. She would stand alongside other survivors and mourn the unfortunate deaths of friends, family, and co-workers.

Riley mustered courage, knowing she would probably hear many accounts of that day's events - stories that would excavate her own buried memories and stir dormant emotions.

After applying a fresh coat of lipstick in front of the dull mirror, Nadine realized that she was alone and that the laughter and conversation had ceased. She looked around the lobby of the hotel in search of Riley. When she couldn't find her, she called out to her.

"Eve! Eve ... I mean, Riley!" Nadine shook her head in frustration. "Am I ever going to get used to her new name?" she mumbled to herself. "Where are you?"

She rounded a corner and found Riley standing alone in the center of a ballroom with her arms folded. She was staring off into space. Nadine could see that Riley was deep in thought, so she tried not to disturb her. As she waited, Nadine noted the changes that had occurred in the woman - now a tower of strength - standing before her. She recalled the battered, emotionally troubled, and insecure woman who had been led to her doorstep by Ruben. Over the past year, she had watched Riley transform into a strong, courageous woman, whose chief concern was no longer herself or the name brand on her clothing tags. Nadine had seen Riley's faith blossom and her concern for others grow inwardly and outwardly.

Nadine also thought of how Riley's leadership qualities had complemented her own. Riley's light, charming nature served as positive sandpaper sometimes smoothing out Nadine's blunt, serious style. Together, they had been able to address more of the residents' needs. Nadine was relieved that she would not be leaving Faith House behind in her pursuit of new ventures. Of all the women who had passed through Faith House, Nadine thought she would miss Riley most. Feeling herself getting choked up again, she cleared her throat, which startled Riley. Nadine heard her gasp and saw her grab her chest as she quickly spun around to see Nadine standing at the door.

"Oh! I didn't know you were standing there. I thought for a split second that we were buying a haunted building."

"I'm sorry," Nadine said. "I was trying to give you some solitude, but it's about time to leave."

Riley nodded slightly in agreement. Nadine sensed, however, that she was far from ready for the ceremony.

"Don't you want to go to the memorial service?"

Riley gave her another half-hearted nod.

"Why do I get the sense that you're telling a half-truth?" said Nadine, tilting her head to one side.

Riley sighed before responding, "Probably because I am."

"So what's the whole truth?"

"I'm scared; I'm sad; and I don't understand why any of this had to happen to these innocent people," Riley said. She turned back around and walked over to a round table, where she pulled out a chair and sat down. "That just about sums it up," she said. She waited for a response from Nadine, but when she didn't get one and silence hung like a thick cloud in the air, Riley felt compelled to elaborate.

"I feel like a Johnny-come-lately. People who are going to be there today have been in the trenches from the moment that the first plane hit the North Tower. Me? I ran. I hid. I kept silent. I changed my name. I was a coward," said Riley, running her fingers through her mane, which she had restored to blonde soon after the news of Paine's death.

"How can I possibly face these people and claim to be in the same league with them in terms of mourning 9/11 victims? The truth is, I barely even knew the people I worked with," she said, confessing her regrets.

"You didn't know me, but before I came to Faith House, I was self-absorbed, self-centered, and detached from people. I put very little effort or time into relationships. As a result, I got very little out of them," she said. "I was extremely focused on what I wanted in life, where I was going, and how I could get there. That probably explains why I ended up with someone like Paine. I didn't take the time to find out what he was really like. All I could see was what the relationship held for me - a means to an end," said Riley, shaking her head in disgust at her own confession. "Looking back, I realize that I deserved Paine. In some ways, maybe I deserved his abuse. It certainly served as a wake-up call."

Nadine, from the door of the ballroom, could see Riley's clenched jaw and flared nostrils. Riley sat with her arms folded. Nadine walked over and took the seat next to her. She said nothing as she waited for Riley to finish airing her feelings.

A few minutes passed and Riley dropped her hands in her lap, turned to Nadine, and continued.

"I'm sad, too, because I miss some of my co-workers - the ones I actually called by name. I miss parts of my former life. I wish I could have a second chance at getting to know them. I'm sad that I blew my first opportunity," she said. "Most of all, I miss Ruben. He was the first person I really took time to get to know, someone with whom there were no strings attached. I probably learned more about him in the short time I knew him than I ever learned about my own parents. There were no hidden agendas with him," she said, her voice quavering. "In hindsight, losing my job ... losing everything has made me see the true value of life and to understand what's important. Even getting punched in the face by Paine opened my eyes to what my priorities should be. Thanks to you, to Faith House, to God, I see that now. It's remarkable that it took a whole year and going through so much to reach a higher understanding of the kind of person I was to realize the kind of person I want to be - someone more like you."

Nadine responded with a puzzled expression.

"Don't look surprised!" Riley said. "But now that I have the opportunity to go back to the life I knew, to the wealth, prestige, position, and everything I once aspired to, I'm apprehensive. I'm afraid I'll be tempted to return to the person I was," she said. "I'm afraid that those things will begin to rule my life again - not all at once or at the start, but gradually, you know, like any other addiction. How do you guard against that, Nadine?"

Nadine squirmed in her chair. She had never told anyone at the shelter that there were days when she wanted to throw up her hands, quit her job, and lease a Manhattan townhouse with state-of-the-art conveniences and luxurious furnishings. Every pay day, she fought the urge to take her earnings and spend it all on herself, to shop at Saks Fifth Avenue for a designer suit or stop at Prada for a new handbag and matching shoes. She missed leisurely lunches and exquisite dining at the finest restaurants New York had to offer, and occasional Broadway shows. Instead, some or all of her paychecks often went right back into the shelter for food, tuition for residents, or whatever was needed.

"Oh, Darlin', selflessness doesn't come easy. Putting others first takes an enormous amount of love and humility, which, for most people, doesn't come naturally. That's why 'Love others as thyself' is a commandment. It requires effort and willpower on our part," Nadine said. "Even Christ, who was God come down to earth, sweat blood drops in the Garden of Gethsemane as he mustered courage to give his life for the world. Sacrificing our lives for others comes at a great price, but it's the highest calling and the purest gift of love," she said.

"Nadine, I know you're right. But that kind of sacrifice also comes with great pain and heartbreak and struggle when you get close to people and they die unnecessarily or they reject you," said Riley, whose thoughts immediately turned to Ruben, to Vivi, to the victims of 9/11 and, lastly, to Paine. "It makes you stop and wonder if it's worth the costs."

Nadine sighed. She had experienced the same doubts, the same struggles, and the same heartbreak when the results of her sacrifices didn't turn out the way she wanted. It was on those days that she fought the urge to quit and return to putting her energies into herself and her life, leaving everyone else to fend for themselves.

"It's worth it, Riley," Nadine said. "You may not see immediate results and you may not even see visible results, but our sacrifices are not in vain." Nadine smiled demurely at her protégé.

Riley wrinkled her brow, sensing Nadine had more to say. "What?"

"You were worth it."

Tears welled in Riley's eyes.

Nadine chuckled to herself.

"What's so funny?" said Riley, who dabbed her tears with her fingertips.

"When you doubt the costs, use my Litmus test. Imagine standing before God one day and having to justify the way you spent your time, your energy, and your money. On one arm," she said while holding up her left hand to make her point, "you've got a five hundred dollar handbag and on your feet, new crocodile-trimmed leather shoes. You're dressed to the nines in the latest style; you're trimmed in gold and diamonds; and your nails and makeup are immaculate." She held up her right hand as she continued. "Standing next to you is a woman whose next meal came from you. The first new clothes she received in months, maybe years, were bargain basement castoffs from your closet and were all you had to give her. She had shelter because you took her in, and she had a bed to sleep in that you provided. More importantly, she had a shoulder to cry on and a listening ear to turn to because you showed you care. But best of all, you gave her hope and showed her the way to a new start in life."

Nadine paused, giving Riley time to digest what she had said.

"Now, which would you want to boast about to God?" she asked as she alternately lifted her left and right hand for emphasis. "That you spent all you had on looking your best? Or that you spent your best on the least of his children?"

Tears flowed down Riley's face as she thought of how she had spent most of her life making more of things that were unimportant and less of things that were more important. She felt at that moment that she had squandered everything for nothing.

"Don't cry, Darlin'. I can't tell you how many times I have failed that Litmus test. But because of God's mercy, I received forgiveness and a second chance," said Nadine.

Riley felt peace at that moment. She knew that God had given her a do-over, an opportunity to see life from a new perspective. She hoped that when the day came, she would pass the test. She breathed deeply, throwing off the sadness she felt.

"You know, Nadine, I can't help but look at my wasted life and wonder why he spared me. I know there were people in the Towers on 9/11 that were kinder, more thoughtful, less selfish, and more compassionate than me. I don't understand the senseless waste of their lives," she said.

"9/11 was an eye opener, a wake-up call for us all, Riley - New Yorkers, especially. It made us appreciate the fragility of life - that life is but a vapor and can go up in the smoke of an exploding building. It made us stop and look at our neighbors and notice the commonalities of going through a tragic event like 9/11 together and to focus less on our differences," she said. "It made us look up in the midst of a catastrophic event, to look up to the one who controls all things, to seek God's divine help and healing. It made us look far above the towers to greater heights, to a place where there is no pain, no sorrow, no darkness, no night," said Nadine, whose gentle, calm voice spoke words that were quieting the storm inside Riley. "9/11 reminded New Yorkers and the people of this nation and this globe that evil exists in this world that we call home," she said.

"We fight an unseen enemy that seeks to kill, steal, and destroy. Terrorists were successful in their goal to kill Americans, rob the United States of life and property, and to destroy those buildings, destroy lives, create loss for families, and break the hearts of survivors," Nadine said. "Terrorists will continue in their attempts to bring pain and suffering. That's what hate does. It drives evil."

Riley scowled at Nadine's explanation. "But why these people? Why the Towers? Why that Tuesday?"

"Evil doesn't discriminate, child. It doesn't care who is hurt, what is destroyed, or when it strikes, as long as the results are the same," said Nadine, whose own thoughts drifted to her husband. "But regardless of whether evil or death befalls us, Darlin', we were not intended to become attached to this life on earth. It's just part of the journey. Our sights need to remain on the one who is greater than he who is in the world."

Riley listened intently, hanging on every word.

"You see, Riley, evil will not have the final word. Why do you think architects and builders are raising their sights and planning to rebuild the towers higher and taller and more majestic than those that were destroyed?"

Riley shrugged her shoulders, indicating that she didn't have an answer.

"It's because hope and faith will not allow us to be defeated. We are designed to be overcomers. We have planted inside us the desire to reach higher and want more and achieve greater," Nadine said, "because God has set eternity in our hearts."

Even as the words spilled from her lips, Nadine could feel her own spirit being lifted and the momentary sadness over her husband being lifted.

"It's because the one who is in us inspires us to have hope and faith that a new day is coming," she said.

A slight smile sprang across her face as she realized that Riley's countenance had been transformed as well. Tears had been replaced by sparkling eyes. The corners of her mouth were no longer downturned, but turned up in delight. And her shoulders were not drooping, but thrown back in confidence.

Nadine wondered what lay ahead for Riley, what new doors she would kick open, and what positive changes she would make. She had been on a roller coaster for the past year, but she had survived. Nadine was convinced that Faith House would be in good hands, no matter what direction her own health took. Riley had paid close attention and would pass on the lessons she had taught her. Under her tutelage and mentoring, other women would learn how to survive. Better yet, they would begin to live again.

"It's a special day for you, Riley. Today is the anniversary of when your new life started and your old one ended. It's time to begin celebrating life and stop dwelling on what's behind you. There's no need for you to fear the future. There are brighter days ahead," Nadine said.

Nadine looked down at her watch. "Are you ready to go? The ceremony will be beginning soon."

"Just one more thing, Nadine … if I haven't told you lately, 'Thank you,'" Riley said.

"Oh, it's nothing, Darlin'."

"No, really! Thank you. Thank you for getting me through this past year … for trying to steer me even when I fought hard to keep steering my own course. Thank you for taking me in, giving me a job when I was so desperate, and for being my friend when I needed a friend most."

Nadine dropped her head in modesty.

"And thank you for being with me today. I would not get through this day without you."

Nadine reached over and patted Riley's arm.

"Yes, you would," Nadine said with a gleam in her eye. "You're a survivor. You can get through anything."

Nadine stood up and started toward the door with Riley following.

"When do we move in?" Nadine said, indicating her approval of the new location for Faith House.

Riley's excitement returned.

"In a couple of weeks. Westin closes on the property at the end of this month," she said. "In the meantime, I was wondering if you could spare me for a couple of weeks. I haven't had a vacation since I started working at Faith House. That is included in the perks of the job, isn't it?" Riley said, raising her eyebrows inquisitively at Nadine.

"Perks? Who said anything about perks? The rewards are in the job," Nadine said, teasingly. She chuckled at how often that seemed to be the case since there was little time for anything more. "Two weeks, huh? That's a long time to be without an assistant."

"I know you'll manage. You managed before I stumbled onto your doorstep."

Nadine stopped in her tracks and turned and faced Riley.

"Well, I'm spoiled now and I don't prefer to find myself without your assistance again ... not for long-term periods, anyway," said Nadine, smiling with satisfaction over their arrangement. "Take two weeks, or longer, if you need it. Just promise me you'll be back."

Turning back and trudging toward the door, Nadine said, "So what are your plans? Or should I expect more surprises in the near future?"

"No surprises," Riley said, followed by a chuckle. "No surprises ... none for you, anyway."

"What do you mean?"

"I mean, it's been a long time and I hope they forgive me for being gone and not staying in touch, but I'm planning on going to see my parents."

Nadine spun around to see Riley's face lit up. Riley had briefly shared with her about the gap between her and her parents, how she had not appreciated their simple lifestyles, their sacrifices, or their spiritual priorities. Nadine could hear elation in Riley's voice as she shared her plans to make the trip back to Georgia. Nadine smiled broadly, knowing that Riley was about to close the gap and bring healing to her relationship with her family.

"I'm going home," Riley said. "I'm going home." She took a deep breath and exhaled. "Do you think they'll forgive me? Better yet, do you think they'll recognize me? I'm not the same person who left home, you know."

Nadine, still glowing from Riley's announcement, said, "No, you're not the same. You're a better person. But no matter how much you've changed, how long you've been gone, or what you've done during your absence, you can always go home, Darlin'. You were a stranger and I took you in. But you're their daughter."

Nadine and Riley locked arms and walked side-by-side as they moved toward the exit.

Riley pulled away and stopped to turn off one last light.

"You know, it just occurred to me. We'll each have our own bathrooms now," Nadine said.

"Yeah. Isn't it grand?"

"Now that's what I call moving up in the world."

The women exchanged looks and burst into laughter as they exited and locked the door behind them.

Chapter 29

As Riley looked at the imperfect circle of people created at the 16-acre concrete pit that formed the floor of Ground Zero, she couldn't help but think of the irony of how she had come full circle.

She stood with others around the memorial circle, just yards away from where she had stood last year when she made the split-second decision that completely changed her life. In the solemnity of the one-year anniversary ceremony, Riley's thoughts got lost in flashbacks to that day. While mourners placed flowers, American flags, and pictures inside the memorial ring - the focal point of hallowed ground - she fought the guilt associated with choosing to walk away. As a result of that choice, she was left standing outside the burning Twin Towers, watching while her co-workers were transformed into a memory. A year later, the recollection of the details of that day was no less painful to her.

The first moment of silence at 8:46 a.m., to observe the moment when the first plane struck the North Tower sent chills through Riley. She vividly recalled the thundering crash that inevitably brought her co-workers' lives to an end. The deafening silence at Ground Zero was emotionally overwhelming. She could not hold back the tears for the lives lost that day. Comfort came to her, however, when she felt Nadine's arm pulling her to her side, holding her, and giving her strength to keep standing. Even then, just as she did that day, she wanted to flee, to escape the misery and the pain. But this time, she didn't. She stood firm. She stood tall. She stood still.

"The world will little note, nor long remember what we say here," said New York's governor, reciting The Gettysburg Address. "It is for us the living, rather, to be dedicated here to the unfinished work ...," he said, his voice echoing through the sound system. "It is rather for us to be here dedicated to the great task remaining before us ..."

Riley's thoughts drifted briefly to the mission unfolding before her to care for the widows, single mothers, orphans and homeless women, who would show up at the doorstep of Faith House and knock on the door, wanting entrance. She could relate to their fears, anxieties and uncertainties. She had walked in their shoes not so long ago. Calming their fears, giving them shelter, food and provision; helping them get a new start; and giving them hope represented the unfinished work before her.

"That we here highly resolve that these dead shall not have died in vain - that this nation, under God, shall have a new birth of freedom," the governor said, bringing the recitation to a close.

"New birth of freedom."

Those words resounded in Riley's ears and stuck in her thoughts. She reflected on where she had been over a year ago - trapped in an unhappy marriage and in a life driven by ambition, success, and wealth. The accumulation of money and material gains had dictated many of her decisions. It wasn't the kind of wealth Riley had come to appreciate over the past year. She had learned to desire the kind of wealth that lasts and is not perishable in an explosion or lost in death. Her former brand of wealth had been replaced by a treasure that sustains and satisfies - that treasure being her faith in Jesus Christ. Riley had found its dividends over the past year to be peace and joy and sacrificial love for others.

Riley had found "new birth of freedom" at Faith House - an eternal freedom from death. She had been freed from the trappings of a life motivated by worldly ambitions.

As she listened to the names of the victims being called out alphabetically, Riley raised her bowed head and looked up at the sky. She looked at the gaping hole in the skyline once filled by the two grand skyscrapers and their man-made majesty.

For the first time, however, as she stared upward, she could see past all of that toward the heavens, where the existence of true majesty resided - a lesson she had come to learn over the past year. At Faith House, she had gained a fuller understanding of the riches of glory and of a place where skyscrapers and structures created by men would one day pale greatly in comparison.

"...Wilhelm B. Weinstein, Michael Willson, Mary Catherine Winslow, Alison Marie Woodall, ..."

A city official continued to call out the names of lives reported missing following that day of destruction.

Riley wished at that moment, as she took in the details of the sky and clouds overhead, that she had known whether her co-workers had possessed that kind of faith before they perished. She wondered if she would one day see them again, and if she would walk with them on the streets of gold, as referred to in Revelation of the Bible.

After all 2,801 names were read aloud, Riley was relieved that her name had been removed from the missing persons list compiled by law enforcement. She suffered a certain amount of guilt that it was ever on the list.

A trumpeter's rendition of "Taps" reverberated through the silence that hung like a blanket over Ground Zero. Seconds later, a chorus of bells could be heard, echoing throughout the city. The church bells, rung by houses of worship, sang in memory of the actual time that the second tower collapsed.

10:29 a.m.

That was the moment that changed everything for Riley. That was the moment when Riley ran for her life while simultaneously fleeing from all that was comfortable and familiar to her including the unpleasantness that had become part of the fabric of her marriage.

When that monument to wealth and power and ambition came crumbling down, Riley's own ideas and aspirations plunged to their death, too. At that moment, her existence became more about survival, living day to day, and less about reaching - always reaching for more, for better, for what was out of reach. It was the beginning of her lesson in finding contentment. It was the start of finding satisfaction in the life God had given her and the end of wasting it in search of what she presumed was best for her, what she didn't already possess. That moment was her "new birth of freedom."

It also was a pivotal moment in the life of the nation. The demise of those seven buildings set the nation back financially. It put the nation on a continuous state of alert unlike it had been in decades - since Pearl Harbor was attacked. Riley silently questioned whether it had awakened the nation to a new birth of freedom. It had certainly set the nation on a course of fighting for its freedom from terrorism. Riley likened the nation's striving for new birth more to prolonged labor pains of a woman longing to give birth to new life.

A second, designated moment of silence gave Riley and others more time to remember - even though Riley had fought hard over the past year to forget the tragedy that haunted her less with each passing day. But she appreciated the opportunity to stand in recognition of those who died in those final moments.

The silence was broken by someone reciting words from the Declaration of Independence.

"We hold these truths to be self-evident, that all men are created equal, that they are endowed by their Creator with certain unalienable Rights, that among these are Life, Liberty, and the pursuit of Happiness," said the state official, whose voice trailed off over the memorial site.

Riley thought of the unfairness of how her co-workers' God-given rights had been violated. Their lives had been snuffed out and deprived of "Life,

Liberty, and the pursuit of Happiness." A familiar wave of guilt washed over her as she stood with her rights intact. She was free to keep living, enjoying each day as though nothing had happened. She was free, in general, to enjoy all the liberties associated with being an American. And she was free to pursue happiness.

She was free to start a new life again.

She was free to work again and free to love again.

The latter revelation caused her to shudder. Had she ever really loved before? When she thought of Paine, her memory of him compounded her feelings of sadness. She could muster neither sorrow nor intense grief for her late husband. Instead, she wondered at that moment what true love must feel like.

What would it be like to have a man encourage her, support her, even sincerely praise her for qualities beyond her beauty? What would it be like to tingle somewhere deep inside when gazing into the eyes of a man who longingly gazed back at her? She had temporarily experienced those emotions when Cal Gordon doted on her. But she couldn't call that love. Even in Paine's case, she had confused love for something else. She could see that now. It made her wonder: What would loving a man for anything other than his resume and bank account be like?

As she curiously pondered the benefits of being truly in love, she became keenly aware of someone's eyes burrowing into her. She shifted her weight from one foot to the other as the sensation of being watched made her increasingly uncomfortable. She fought the temptation to turn around and face her observer. Instead, she tried to concentrate on the ceremony. It had come to the point in the ceremony when victims' families were descending on a ramp to the lowest level of the World Trade Center site, each carrying a rose for their loved one.

Riley struggled to remain attentive to the special tribute, but the desire to look around and see whose eyes were focused on her grew with each passing second. Riley debated on the appropriateness of turning around during the ceremony and facing the onlooker - friend or foe.

Riley bided her time until there was a lull in the ceremony. She took advantage of the pause in the ceremony and turned her head slightly. Trying not to be too obvious, she nonchalantly rubbed her chin against her shoulder.

Riley could not hide both her astonishment and her delight when her eyes met for a split second with Father Patrick's. After realizing that he had been watching her, she felt both compelled and thrilled to turn back again and acknowledge him.

She smiled warmly as she gave him a nod. She couldn't help but notice that his broad smile lit up his face. His reaction caused heat to rise in Riley's own face. She touched her right cheek and found her skin warm to her fingertips. Her discovery made her blush even more.

It had been a long time since Riley had responded like a school girl to a man's gaze. The attention made her self-conscious of every move she made; of the way she stood; of whether her hair was in place or had been picked up by a gentle September breeze and left in disarray. She became uneasy about what she was wearing. She looked down at her dress and shoes and wondered if she should not have worn something more feminine, or if her apparel tastefully flattered her figure as much as it could.

More families filed down the ramp. Riley's attention drifted to the sight of a little girl, about six years old, carrying a long-stemmed rose, the end of which nearly touched her toes. The child, with blonde ringlets hanging down past her shoulders, looked lost amidst the row of adults lined single file on the ramp. The youngster's other hand was gripped by the hand of a blonde woman, who was an older version of the girl. The sight stirred a pang of remorse in Riley.

"Here I am, once again thinking about myself," she silently admonished herself, "and at a time like this."

Riley lowered her head out of respect for the parade of families and the victims the families represented. She reined in her thoughts and refocused on her purpose for being there: paying her respects for the victims, specifically her former co-workers. She wasn't there to pick up men, she secretly scolded herself.

About that time, the wind whipped up and created a dust devil in the circle. Riley could taste again the mix of ash. She covered her mouth, but her eyes stung from the faint particles of dust picked up and carried by the wind. The wind took her back to that day when everywhere she looked, everything and everyone was coated by ash from the explosion. She looked around at the many faces encircled around the memorial pit. A veil of dust that hung in the air prevented her from seeing anyone or anything clearly. What was evident to her was that, once again, particles from Ground Zero were forming a thin blanket over everyone and everything within the vicinity. Nothing had gone untouched by this catastrophic event.

She closed her eyes and said a prayer for the family members, who were mourning the death of their loved ones; for the rebuilding of lives and of the World Trade Center site; and for the future of Faith House. She prayed for Nadine and her health. She prayed for direction in her new role, as well as for healing from the inside out. Not long after ending her prayer, the ceremony drew to a close.

The circle of people disbanded, breaking off into micro-circles of people hugging, shaking hands, and generally comforting one another. Riley glanced at Nadine, who pulled her toward her in an embrace. Looking over Nadine's shoulder, she could see Father Patrick weaving through the crowd to where they were. She felt an unexpected pang of anticipation rise within her. Riley tried to ignore the bells and alarms going off inside of her.

Withdrawing from the warmth of Nadine's comforting arms, Riley said, "It has meant so much to me having you here by my side through all of this."

Nadine smiled at her young friend.

"You are so welcome, Darlin'. I would not have dreamed of being anywhere else in the world today."

By then, Father Patrick had made his way to where they stood and hovered close by, waiting for an opportunity to speak. His sudden appearance caught Nadine off guard. She gave the man a puzzled look, but quickly realized that he did not have business with her. From the way this man gazed at Riley, it was apparent to Nadine that he had eyes only for Riley and that he had more than just business to discuss with her. Nadine turned toward Riley, whose eyes possessed their own sparkle at the sight of this man. It became clear to Nadine that she was suddenly invisible to them both. She took that as her cue to dismiss herself from the happy reunion.

"Darlin', I'll be waiting over there when you're ready," she said, pointing to the Fulton Street gate.

"No, don't go, Nadine," said Riley, grabbing her plump arm to stop her. She immediately broke into introductions. Gesturing with her hand toward the man, Riley said, "This is Father Michael Patrick. He is from the chapel across the street." Riley pointed toward the small church for emphasis. While lacing her arm around Nadine's to demonstrate her affection for the woman at her side, Riley said, "And this is my boss, my mentor, and my friend, Nadine Franklin. She is the director of Faith House ... where I've been for the past year," she said, sheepishly explaining her whereabouts to the minister.

Riley wondered at that moment what he must think of her. "It can't be any worse than the thoughts I have about myself," she reasoned. With that conclusion, she gained the confidence to face Father Patrick rather than avoid eye contact.

"Father Patrick," said Nadine, offering her hand for a handshake, "so very nice to meet you. It's always a pleasure to meet a man of God," she said, followed by a demure smile. "Now, if you'll pardon me, I see someone I'd like to catch before they get away." Speaking directly to Riley, she excused herself by saying, "I will be waiting for you near the gate. Take all the time you need, Darlin'," said Nadine as she unlocked her arm from Riley's. As she did, a glimmer in Nadine's eyes left Riley with an odd feeling and wondering what her wise friend was thinking.

"Okay ... sure," said Riley, releasing Nadine's arm.

Riley and Father Patrick watched Nadine disappear into the crowd before speaking. Then, nervously, their next words overlapped so that neither heard or understood what the other was saying. After several attempts to be heard by the other while trying to speak at the same time, they both stopped and then burst into spontaneous laughter. When the laughter ceased, Father Patrick said, "It's good to see you smile and hear you laugh. The last two times I've seen you, you've been sad. I can see that God has continued to answer my prayers for you."

Riley smiled at the man whose concern for her had quietly gone unnoticed.

"After reading the headlines and listening to the news on TV, I regret, however, that I didn't do more for you ... maybe listen more ... or even ask more questions ... something," he said. "I'm sorry for your pain, for what you had to go through."

Riley's eyes began swimming with tears at the man's comments that were warm with sincerity and concern. She brushed away a stray tear that rolled down her cheek before clearing her throat to speak.

"You couldn't have known," she said. "That was my intention, to live quietly and in the background. I thank you for your prayers and concern, though. They may very well have saved my life in more ways than you know. Over these past months, I've come to be a huge proponent of prayer.

"You know, I've only been to your chapel twice in my life. But each of those visits were significant turning points for me for which I'll be eternally grateful," she said. "I was at a very low point both times I stepped through the door of your church. I can't tell you what it meant to also find an ally in you, especially when I felt like there were few people I could trust."

Father Patrick hung his head and shuffled his feet under the uncomfortable shower of praise Riley was pouring on him.

Continuing, she said, "I think it's because you didn't pry that I felt comfortable returning to your sanctuary. I will always be indebted to you and to your church for being a safe haven for me."

Father Patrick suddenly raised his head, planted his feet firmly and threw back his shoulders. Riley noticed the immediate change in his posture and realized that she had not noticed before how tall he was or what broad shoulders he had. Nor had she noticed before the confidence and strength he exuded. Riley looked past the wavy mass of hair that fell across his forehead into the bright, blue eyes that had fast become familiar to her. She was enchanted by his steady gaze.

A wave of unique feelings rippled through Riley and gripped her, throwing her psyche completely off balance. All at once, she was seeing this man in a different way - not as a man of the cloth, but as a mere mortal to whom she was suddenly attracted. Her face turned a deeper shade of red at the idea.

"Well, I know how you can begin to repay that debt ... to the church, I mean," he said, his own face reddening at the near slip of the tongue.

Riley arched her eyebrows with piqued interest.

"How do you propose I do that?"

"By allowing us to partner with Faith House."

Her eyes widened at the suggestion. "In what way?"

"Well, it just so happens that members of our congregation have been wanting to get involved in a local mission, but in a way that goes beyond simply throwing money at community problems. They want to participate in a project that provides for more interaction between the parishioners and those benefiting from their gifts ... sort of a hands-on, up-close-and-personal missions project. They feel like they have for too long been too far removed from the needs in the community."

After ending his proposal, he narrowed his eyes and pursed his lips and said apprehensively, "So ... what do you think?"

Riley's eyes glistened as they filled again with tears. But she said nothing.

Not knowing her well enough, Father Patrick creased his forehead. He didn't quite know how to interpret Riley's silence. He waited for some indication of what it meant. Soon, his waiting paid off.

Through the tears, a smile pushed forth and flashed across her face. Riley's voice quavered as she finally managed to speak. "I think it's the most wonderful proposal I've ever heard. But, of course, I would need to discuss it with Nadine. She is the director."

"Well, uh, there is one catch," he said.

Riley was now the one left hanging, waiting for an explanation. She wrinkled her brow in wonderment over what hurdle she was going to have to jump. But when he did not quickly elaborate, she became somewhat impatient.

"So what's the catch?"

"Whew! I thought you'd never ask," he said before shooting her a boyish grin - the sight of which chased away her angst.

"Well, since our organizations would be working closely together on this missions project, that means that you and I would be working closely together to coordinate the level of participation."

Riley nodded in agreement as Father Patrick stalled.

"... And, since we would be working closely together, I thought it only proper that we get to know one another ... and I thought maybe we could start tonight over dinner. I mean, it seems appropriate that we would begin this partnership, for lack of a better term, on the anniversary of the day we first met."

Riley, wide-eyed and stunned by the latter clause in his proposal, found herself speechless as she mentally processed what she'd just heard.

Had he seen her as more than a parishioner? Had his concern become at some point not merely concern for one of his flock, but the kind of concern a man has for a woman? Even though she had only just realized a spark of attraction for Father Patrick, she had not expected him to share the attraction.

Again, Father Patrick waited silently, holding his breath, and anticipating Riley's response. While he waited, he found himself getting lost in her sparkling blue eyes and her beauty.

The image of her, broken-hearted and physically bruised as she cried to God a year ago had immediately endeared her to him. He was so mesmerized by the sight of this beautiful, yet hurting woman on her knees that day that he could barely focus on his chores. He remembered how he repeatedly dropped his mop during her visit. He had looked for her return every day after she left that morning. When days and months passed and there was no sign of her, he feared that she had been among the victims of 9/11. He never knew her name, but he'd never forget her face. He was surprised the day she reappeared in the chapel as a redhead. He remembered the relief he felt that she was alive. He didn't care what color her hair was. He had vowed that, given a second chance, he would introduce himself to her. On that second visit, he kept his vow. But when she had declined to give her name, he decided then to be content to respect her privacy and to continue admiring her from a distance. In the meantime, he bombarded God with prayers for her.

Everything became clear to Father Patrick when he picked up *The New York Times* and saw her photo next to the story about her philanthropic efforts, launched on the heels of her husband's suicide. He read about the account of her husband's illegal activities and incidents of domestic abuse. It also elaborated on how the former TV journalist had gone into hiding to escape his abuse. He understood why she had shown up that day in his chapel, why she had a bruised face, and why she was in such agony. He also understood her need for anonymity.

But God had answered all of his prayers. He had brought her back into his presence a third time. He had cleared the way for him to get to know her better. Father Patrick had waited for months. Now, it was all up to her. Waiting for her answer, however, he thought he could wait no longer. He felt like he would implode from anticipation.

"So, is it a deal? Or do you need time to consider it?"

Riley peered into the gentle eyes of the man before her. She did not wonder if she could trust him. He had already proven that. What was foremost on her mind was whether she had the time to invest in a relationship outside of those at Faith House. The women needed her now. She would be giving them high priority. It would take a special man to understand the importance they held for her.

More to the point, did she have the courage? Lost relationships had taken their emotional toll on her over the past year. Did she have the courage to gamble on a new relationship?

He cocked his head to one side and raised his eyebrows, as if inviting a response from her. He wished at that moment that he could read her mind.

Riley looked deep into his kind, comforting eyes and found her answer.

"No," she said.

His countenance immediately fell. "Okay, if you're sure," he said, trying to disguise his voice to hide his disappointment.

Riley nodded affirmatively. "Yes, I'm sure. I'm certain that, no, I don't need time to consider your offer." Coyly, she beamed at him and watched him instantly perk up again. "I accept your proposal to benefit Faith House ... and I accept your invitation to dinner. But, I must ask, Father Patrick, should I wear my business suit?"

Amused by her question, he said, "I can assure you that I won't be discussing business ... unless you want to. And, you can call me Michael; all my friends do."

"In that case, I'm looking forward to it," she said.

After exchanging phone numbers with him, Riley turned to search for Nadine. She glanced back one last time to see him standing where she had left him in the crowd. He was watching her walk away. She felt heat rise again to her face.

Riley waded through the lingering crowd until she found Nadine on the sidewalk near the exit.

Nadine took one look at Riley's flushed face. "Darlin', what's wrong? Are you okay?"

Riley, who didn't understand the sudden interrogation, replied, "I'm fine. Why do you ask?"

"Your face ... It's red. Have you been crying?"

The questions made Riley's face turn a deeper shade of crimson at being discovered. She laughed a nervous laugh.

"No," Riley said sheepishly. "Not crying."

"What then?"

"You might say I've just been swept off my feet."

"Ah ... the tall, handsome man of God," Nadine said.

"According to Father Patrick, his church wants to take Faith House under its wing and provide personal assistance to the residents," Riley explained.

Nadine stopped dead in her tracks. Her eyes probed Riley's face for more information. Riley's face had taken on a certain glow since she had left her with Father Patrick.

But Riley clammed up and offered no additional details. She began squirming under Nadine's stare and her interrogation.

"So what are you not telling me about Father Patrick?" inquired Nadine, who was no longer willing to wait for Riley to volunteer new information.

"Oh, just one small detail … ."

Nadine, giving her a hard stare, pressed Riley to share what she knew. "Well? What is it?"

"Only that we're going out tonight to celebrate our first anniversary." After saying it aloud, she slowly exhaled. She realized at that moment the magnitude of what she had committed to and how nervous she was to be dating again. In that same instant, she began second-guessing her decision to have dinner with him until Nadine's approving smile calmed her anxieties and gave her renewed confidence in her decision.

"First anniversary, huh?"

"Yeah," Riley replied, followed by an explanation of the events leading up to the one-year reunion.

"It's the first of many anniversaries, I suspect," Nadine said.

The comment left Riley puzzled. "What makes you say that?"

"Like I said earlier, Darlin', brighter days ahead … brighter days."

Nadine looked down at her watch. "We better get going," she said. "We haven't much time."

Riley scrunched her face - again puzzled over Nadine's last comment. "Much time for what?" she said, as she tried to mentally trace back to whether she had forgotten an appointment. "What are you talking about?"

"We've got to go shopping," said Nadine, her voice, bristling with excitement. "We've got to find you something to wear for dinner. A second-hand dress won't do for this occasion."

Riley grinned at Nadine's suggestion, but then said, sarcastically, "He's already seen me at my worst. What makes you think that me dressed in hand-me-downs will matter?"

Nadine stopped again, turned and faced the younger woman. Her tone took on a serious note as she answered, "Because you are a different woman today than you were then.

"You may have been wounded and physically and emotionally at your worst then, but you are healed now," Nadine continued. "You may have lost your way then, but today you have new direction. Your life may have been shattered, but God has put the pieces back together. Today you are whole."

Riley listened intently. Each word uttered from her friend's lips seemed to breathe strength and confidence into her.

"Today is a new day. You are a new woman. And a new woman deserves a new dress," said Nadine.

Just as quickly as she had turned toward Riley, Nadine pivoted and turned away, then ambled toward the street and began hailing a cab. Nadine had left Riley little time to digest her comments, much less argue with them. Riley, noticing that Nadine was leaving her, ran after her. The two women climbed into the back seat of a yellow taxi that sped away from the curb once their door shut.

Riley twisted in her seat to look back at Ground Zero one more time. The farther the taxi moved away from the site, the smaller it became in appearance. It slowly disappeared from Riley's view. When she could no longer see any traces of Ground Zero, she turned and faced forward in her seat.

"Good morning, ladies. Where to?" a gray-haired taxi driver with thick Bronx dialect said as he peered at them through the rear view mirror.

Nadine gave the driver directions to the nearest downtown shopping district.

But secretly, Riley was muttering different directions under her breath as she looked ahead through the front window of the vehicle. "To brighter days," she said to herself. "To brighter days ahead."

Future prospects were already looking much brighter, she thought. As they whizzed past the many storefronts, Riley's eyes flickered at the thought of all that lay ahead. But then suddenly, it occurred to her that something was missing from the celebration.

Then, on a whim, Riley shouted above the traffic noises to the taxi driver, "Oh, driver, let's stop at the nearest coffee shop on the way!"

Why I Wrote This Book

I remember where I was on September 11, 2001. I was a bureau chief with The Albany Herald in Albany, Ga., and was covering court at the Lee County Courthouse in neighboring Leesburg, Ga. I had wandered into the Sheriff's Office, where law enforcement officers were uncharacteristically encircled around a television. At first, I was not certain what I was watching. But by the end of the day, I was heavily embroiled in this story and what it meant for our nation and for our community.

I didn't lose anyone close to me that day in the World Trade Center attack. And as far as I knew, I didn't lose anyone I know.

No, I was among millions of Americans who felt helpless and somewhat guilty as a survivor as we watched the horrific details aired on hour after hour of news coverage.

Even though it did not impact me personally, it impacted me as an American and as a reporter. It happened close to home - in my homeland. I became as curious and as hungry for information as the families of the victims. I wanted to know how this could happen on our watch and what led up to outsiders successfully masterminding a plot that was tantamount to an act of war on American soil. And I wanted to do something – something that would help tell the story and that would also help me express how I felt as a survivor.

In my research, I read a few accounts of people who were reported among the missing, but who actually were never at the World Trade Center that day. Instead, they used this event as an opportunity to go underground, change their identities and start new lives. I wondered what circumstances might cause a person to manipulate such a devastating event for their own, personal benefit. What would prompt them to take such drastic measures and take advantage of an event that had created so much pain for others? The answers led me to my characters that began in 2003 to come alive in my imagination.

In 2004, my sister and I traveled to New York, where I interviewed taxi drivers and hotel cleaning ladies and anyone willing to talk about where they were that day. I wanted to know all I could about the details of that day to make this story as real as possible. You see, I wasn't there in New York on Sept. 11 or the days that followed. I was sitting on the sidelines with a broken heart, crying for the losses, the pain, the terror, the grief, the suffering, and the confusion I saw in the faces picked up by video cameras.

Writing, editing and praying over this book has been an eight-year process that included pitching the manuscript to agents, who told me that no one wants to read about 9/11. I don't believe that. After all, we as Americans waved American flags and posted banners across the nation, promising: We'll never forget.

I know I won't.

In this 10th Anniversary Year marking the World Trade Center attack, I hope people across this nation will remember those who went to work on September 11, 2001, with plans to go through their normal routine and conduct business as usual. That day changed us. In a world where evil exists, it reminds us that it's no longer business as usual.

In Ephesians 6:12-13 (KJV), we're told that "We wrestle not against flesh and blood, but against principalities, against powers, against the rulers of the darkness of this world, against spiritual wickedness in high places. Wherefore take unto you the whole armour of God, that ye may be able to withstand in the evil day, and having done all, to stand."

That armour includes faith – faith that we are destined for greater heights, where "God shall wipe away all tears from their eyes; and there shall be no more death, neither sorrow, nor crying, neither shall there be any more pain: for the former things are passed away." (KJV, Revelations 21:4)

September 11, 2001, was our wake-up call. It's a day that caused us as a nation to look to God. And it's a day we promised: We'll never forget.

Acknowledgments

I am so grateful to the dear people in my life who poured into this project, whether tangibly or intangibly. To my sister, Shirley Davis - without her dedication to her gym membership, she would not have won the airline tickets that got us to New York so I could do research to launch this book project. Thank you, Sis, for bearing with me while I took pictures of everything and interviewed every taxi driver we met – and for holding me accountable every so often to finish what I started.

To my husband Harold Benton, thank you for being my sounding board, my editor, my kind critic, my support, and my best friend through this long journey. We celebrate 15 years of marriage this year.

Thank you, Bill Sadler, CPA, for your financial savvy and securities knowledge and for helping fine-tune those tricky parts of the book that fell outside my areas of expertise.

Todd Stone with Todd Stone Photography, you've been a friend and colleague for years. Thank you for volunteering photos of Ground Zero that were taken days after the devastation and that assisted my research.

To Claire Leavy, director of the Lee County Library in Leesburg, Ga., thank you for your years of friendship and support of my writing, as well as for lending me library materials for indefinite lengths of time so I could complete my research for this project.

To my youngest sister Sandra Hart, thank you for being a third pair of eyes and helping edit the manuscript.

Thank you, Kim James Russell with K&R Photography for capturing the best image of me for this project.

To my many prayer partners, including Robert and Kim Chambless, Gloria Harper, Reggie and Patty Mobley, Pam Johnson, Lesha Cawley, Susan Sanders, and members of my women's Bible study classes – past and present.

And to my best friend Rhonda Coleman, thank you for including me in your prayers and for being my cheerleader since middle school. You've known me all these years and loved me anyway. You've been no less supportive when it came to holding my feet to the fire to write – this project and many others.

Above all, to "Him who is able to do exceeding, abundantly above what we ask or think, according to the power that worketh in us," may God be praised!

Bibliography

"BBC ON THIS DAY/26/1993: World Trade Center bomb terrorizes New York." <u>BBC News</u>. 25 February 2005 http://news.bbc.co.uk/onthisday/hi/dates/stories/february/26/newsid_2516000/2516469.stm.

Bull, Chris, and Sam Erman. <u>Ground Zero: 25 Stories From Young Reporters Who Were There</u>. New York: Thunder's Mouth Press. 2002.

Chilson-Rose, Lisa. <u>As The Towers Fell: Stories of Unshakable Faith on 9-11</u>. Birmingham, Ala.: New Hope Publishers. 2003.

"CNS – February 1992 Bombing of the World Trade Center in New York City." <u>CNS – Monterey Institute of International Studies</u>. 25 July 2005 http://cns.miis.edu/pubs/reports/wtc93.htm.

Darton, Eric. <u>Divided We Stand</u>. New York: Basic Books. 1999.

Giunta, Ray, and Lynda Rutledge Stephenson. <u>God @ Ground Zero</u>. Brentwood, TN: Integrity Publishers. 2002.

Glanz, James, and Eric Lipton. <u>City in the Sky: The Rise and Fall of the World Trade Center</u>. New York: Times Books. 2003.

"Governor George E. Pataki's Remarks to the Joint Session of the Legislature September 13, 2001." <u>U.S. Government Website</u>. 28 April 2003 www.state.NY.US/September11,2001/JointSessionoftheLegislature.

Halberstam, David, and Magnum photographers. <u>New York: September 11 – Seen by Magnum Photographers</u>. New York: powerHouse Books. 2001.

Haskin, Leslie. <u>Between Heaven and Ground Zero</u>. Bloomington, MN: Bethany House Publishers. 2006.

"ImagineNewYork: Track the Planning Process." ImagineNY. 22 October 2003. http://www.imaginenyideas.org/Projects/Imagine/planform.asp.

Inside 9/11. Prod. Bernard Dudek, Rachel Milton, Lance Hori and Alex Flaster. National Geographic Channel. National Geographic Society. 2005.

Kugler, Sara. "Complex of angular buildings with spire chosen to replace World Trade Center." The Associated Press. [The Seattle Times]. 26 February 2003.

Labriola, John. Walking Forward Looking Back – Lessons From the World Trade Center: A Survivor's Story. New York: Hyper Publishing. 2003.

McNally, Joe. Faces of Ground Zero – Portraits of the Heroes of September 11, 2001. Boston, New York, London: Little, Brown and Company. 2002.

Metal of Honor – The Ironworkers of 9/11. Prod./Dir. Rachel Maguire. Naja Productions, LLC. 2006.

"Missing Persons List." NYC.gov – 9/11 NYC Services Center. 28 April 2003. http://home.nyc.gov/html/911/html/dnapr_a-d.html.

"New York City Department of Health – DOH pr86-New York City Health Department, Office o … ." New York City Website – nyc.gov. 16 February 2004 http://www.nyc.gov/html/doh/html/public/press01/pr86-925.html.

"NYCDHS – How To Access Services: Drop-In Centers Directions." NYC.gov – NYC Department of Homeless Services. 28 April 2003 http://home.nyc.gov/html/dhs/html/di-directions.html.

On Native Soil. Prod./Dir. Linda Ellman. Court TV. Jeff Hays Films/Ellman Entertainment. 2005.

One Nation – America Remembers September 11, 2001. Boston, New York, London: Little, Brown and Company. 2001.

Pecker, David, American Media, Inc., et. al. The Official 9/11 Report: What You Need To Know!. Boca Raton, FL: AMI Specials, Inc. 2004.

Pressley, Sue Ann. "Bomb Kills Dozens in Oklahoma Federal Building." WashingtonPost.com: Oklahoma City Bombing Trial Report. 25 July

2005. http://www.washingtonpost.com/wp-srv/national/longterm/oklahoma/stories/firststory.html.

Raines, Howell, *et. al.* The New York Times – A Nation Challenged: A Visual History of 9/11 And Its Aftermath. New York: Callaway. 2002.

"Real Estate Fraud Investigations Increase." Internal Revenue Service. 12 June 2006. http://www.irs.gov/newsroom/article/O,,id=118224,00.html.

The 9/11 Commission Report. Ex. Prod. Brett Alexander and Tom Seligson. History Channel. 2005.

"The Joint Terrorism Task Force: The World Trade Center Bombing." Anti-Defamation League. 25 July 2005. http://www.adl.org/learn/jttf/wtcb_jttf.asp.

The World Trade Center Memorial. The WTC Memorial.org. 16 February 2004. http://thewtcmemorial.com/history/.

"The WTC Memorial." The World Trade Center Memorial – Tenant Listings. 16 February 2004. http://wwwthewtcmemorial.com/history/tenants.php.

Wallace, Mike, and Peter Skinner. World Trade Center: The Giants That Defied The Sky. Vercelli, Italy: White Star Publishers. 2002.

"Welcome to Imagine New York: Giving Voice to the People's Visions." ImagineNY. 28 April 2003. http://www.imagineny.org/index.html.

"World Trade Center History." FactMonster. 9 December 2003 http://print.factmonster.com/ipka/A0903568.html.

World Trade Center History. 16 February 2004 http://www.werismyki.com/articles/wtc_history.html.

World Trade Center – Rise and Fall of An American Icon. Ex. Prod. Don Cambou. Actuality Productions, Inc., for The History Channel. A&E Television Networks. 2002.

"World Trade Center Vicinity Tenants Information and Hotlines." The New York Times. 22 October 2003. http://www.nytimes.com/2001/09/12/national/WTC-Tenants.html?ei=5070&en=7bbfda7.,,.

CPSIA information can be obtained at www.ICGtesting.com
Printed in the USA
240797LV00001B/45/P

9 781449 718930